# ICEHENGE

By Kim Stanley Robinson

KIM STANLEY ROBINSON

# ICEHENGE

A TOM DOHERTY ASSOCIATES BOOK
NEW YORK

ICEHENGE

Copyright © 1984 by Kim Stanley Robinson

"Tea at the Palaz of Hoon" copyright © 1923 and renewed 1951 by
Wallace Stevens. Reprinted from *The Collected Poems of Wallace Stevens*
by permission of Alfred A. Knopf, Inc.

Parts of this novel have appeared in substantially different form under
the titles:

"To Leave a Mark," copyright © 1982 by The Mercury Press. Published in the November 1982 issue of *The Magazine of Fantasy and Science Fiction*.

"On the North Pole of Pluto," copyright © 1980 by Damon Knight.
Published in *Orbit 21*.

An Orb Edition
Published by Tom Doherty Associates, Inc.
175 Fifth Avenue
New York, NY 10010

Tor Books on the World Wide Web : http://www.tor.com

Library of Congress Cataloging-in-Publication Data

Robinson, Kim Stanley.
    Icehenge / Kim Stanley Robinson. — 1st Orb ed.
        p.    cm.
    "A Tom Doherty Associates book."
    ISBN 0-312-86609-7   ISBN 978-0-312-86609-9
    I. Title.
PS3568.02893134   1998
813'.54—dc21                                          98-23487
                                                          CIP

Printed in the United States of America

P1

for
Damon Knight
and
Kate Wilhelm

# I

◆

# EMMA WEIL

## 2248 A.D.

"A ship is floating in the harbor now,
 A wind is hovering o'er the mountain's brow;
 There is a path on the sea's azure floor,
 No keel has ever plowed that path before;
 The halcyons brood around the foamless isles;
 The treacherous Ocean has forsworn its wiles;
 The merry mariners are bold and free:
 Say, my heart's sister, wilt thou sail with me?"

—*Shelley*, "Epipsychidion"

**The first indication** I had of the mutiny came as we approached the inner limit of the first asteroid belt. Of course I didn't know what it meant at the time; it was no more than a locked door.

The first belt we call the dud belt, because the asteroids in it are basaltic achondrite, and no use to miners. But we would be among the carbonaceous chondrites soon enough, and one day I went down to the farm to get ready. I fed a bit more light to the algae, for in the following weeks when the boats went out to break up rocks there would be a significant oxygen depletion, and we would need more *chlorella* around to help balance the gas exchange. I activated a few more bulbs in the lamps and started fooling around with the suspension medium. Biologic life-support systems are my work and play (I am one of the best at it), and since I was making room for more *chlorella*, I once again became interested in the excess biomass problem. Thinking to cut down on surplus algae by suspending it less densely, I walked between long rows of spinach and cabbage to the door of one of the storage rooms at the back of the farm, to get a few more tanks. I turned the handle of the door. It was locked.

"Emma!" called a voice. I looked up. It was Al Nordhoff, one of my assistants.

"Do you know why this door is locked?" I asked.

He shook his head. "I was wondering myself yesterday. I guess there's classified cargo in there. I was told to leave it alone."

"It's our storage room," I said, irritated.

Al shrugged. "Ask Captain Swann about it."

"I will."

Now Eric Swann and I were old friends, and I was upset that something was going on in my area that he had failed to tell me about. So when I found him on the bridge, I came straight to the point.

"Eric, how come I'm locked out of one of my own storage rooms? What have you got in there?"

Immediately he blushed as red as his hair, and hung his head. The two rocketry and guidance officers on the bridge looked down at their consoles.

"I can't tell you what's in there, Emma. It's classified. I can't tell anyone until later."

I stared at him. I know I can intimidate people if I look at them hard enough. His blush got deeper, his freckles disappeared in the general redness, his blue eyes gave me a watery stare. But he wasn't going to tell me. I curled my lip at him and left the bridge.

That was the first sign: a locked door, a secret reason for it. I thought to myself, We're taking something for the Committee out to Ceres, perhaps. Weapons, no doubt. It was typical of the Mars Development Committee to keep secrets. But I didn't jump to any conclusions; merely stayed alert.

The second sign was one I probably would have missed, had I not been alerted by the first. I was walking down the corridor to the dining commons, past the tapestry lounges between the commons and the bedrooms, when I heard voices from a lounge and stopped. Just the voices sounded funny, all whispery and rapid. I recognized John Dancer's voice:

"We can't do anything of the sort until after the rendezvous, and you know it."

"No one will notice," said a woman, perhaps Ilene Breton.

"You hope no one would notice," Dancer replied. "But you can't be sure that Duggins or Nordhoff wouldn't stumble across it. We have to wait on everything until after the rendezvous, you know that."

Then I heard steps across the velcro carpet behind me, and with a start I began to walk again, past the door of the lounge. I looked in; John and Ilene, sure enough, among several others. They all looked up as I appeared in the doorway, and their conversation abruptly died. I stared at them and they stared back, at a loss for speech. I walked on to the dining commons.

A rendezvous in the belt. A group of people, not the superior officers of the ship, in on this event and keeping it a secret from the others. A locked storage hold. . . . Things were not falling together for me.

After that I began to see things everywhere. People stopped talking when I walked by. There were meetings late at night, in bedrooms. I walked by the radio room once, and someone was sending out a long message through the coding machine. Quite a few of the storage room doors were locked, back behind the farm; and some of the ore holds were locked as well.

After a few days of this I shook my head and wondered if I were making it all up. There were explanations for everything I had noticed. Shipboard life tends to become cliquish on the best of runs; even though there were only forty of us, divisions would spring up over the year of an expedition. And these were troubled times, back on Mars. The consolidation of the various sectors under the central coordination of the Committee was causing a lot of dissatisfaction. Sectionalism was rife, subversive groups were everywhere, supposedly. These facts were enough to explain all the little factions I now noticed on the *Rust Eagle*. And paranoia is one of the most common shipboard disorders . . . seeing patterns is easy in such a heavily patterned environment.

So I began to discount it all. Perhaps we were carrying something to Ceres for the Committee, but that was nothing.

Still, there was something about the atmosphere of the ship in those days. More people than usual were jumpy and strained. There were mysterious glances exchanged . . . in an atmosphere of mystery. But here hindsight may be influencing me. The facts are what I want here. This record will help me to remember these events many years, perhaps centuries, from now, and so I must set down the facts, the sharpest spur to the memory.

In any case, the third sign was unmistakable. By this time the sun was nearly between us and Mars, and I went to the radio room to get a last letter off to my fool of a father, in jail temporarily for his loud mouth. Afterwards, I went to the jump tube, and was about to fall down to the living quarters when I heard voices floating down the tube from the bridge. Had that been my name? I pulled myself up the rail to the steps that led to the bridge, and stayed there, eavesdropping again. A habit of mine. Once more, John Dancer was speaking.

"Emma Weil is pro-Committee all the way," he said as if arguing the point.

"Even so," said another man, and a couple of voices cut over so that I didn't hear what he said.

"No," Dancer said, interrupting the other voices quickly. "Weil is probably the most important person aboard this ship. We can't talk to her about any of this until Swann says so, and that won't be until after the rendezvous. So you can forget it."

That did it. When it was clear the conversation was over I hopped back to the jump tube and fell down it, aiding the faint acceleration-gravity with some pulls on the rail. I ticked off in my mind the places Swann would most likely be at that hour, intent on finding him and having a long talk. It is not healthy to believe yourself the focus of a ship-wide conspiracy.

I had known Eric Swann for a long time.

Before the turn of the century, every sector ran its own mining expeditions. Royal Dutch looked for carbonaceous chondrite; Mobil was after the basaltic chondrites in the dud belt; Texas mined the silicate types. Chevron had the project of pulling one of the Amors into a Martian orbit, to make another moon. (This became the moon Amor, which was turned into a detention center. My father lived there.) So each sector had its own asteroid crew, and I got to know the Royal Dutch miners pretty well. Swann was one of the rocketry and guidance officers, and a good friend of my husband Charlie, who was also in R and G. Over the course of many runs in the belt I talked with Swann often, and even after Charlie and I divorced we remained close.

But when the Committee took over the mining operations in 2213, all the teams, even the Soviets, were thrown into a common pool, and I saw all of my friends from Royal Dutch a lot less often. My infrequent assignments with Swann had been cause for celebration, and this present assignment, with him as captain, I had thought would be a real pleasure.

Now, pulling around the ship I was the most important person on, I was not so sure. But I thought, Swann will tell me what's going on. And if he doesn't know anything about all this, then he'd better be told that something funny is happening.

I found him in one of the little window rooms, seated before the thick plasteel separating him from the vacuum. His long legs were crossed in the yoga position, and he hummed softly: meditating, his mind a floating mirror of the changing square of stars.

"Hey Eric," I said, none too softly.

"Emma," he said dreamily, and stretched his arms like a cat. "Sit down." He showed me a chunk of rock he had had in his lap. "Look at this Chantonnay." That's a chondrite that has been shocked into harder rock. "Pretty, isn't it?"

I sat. "Yes," I said. "So what's happening on this trip?"

He blushed. Swann was faster at that than anyone I ever saw. "Not much. Beyond that I can't say."

"I know that's the official position. But you can tell me here."

He shook his head. "I'm going to tell you, but it has to wait a while longer." He looked at me directly. "Don't get angry, Emma."

"But other people know what's going on! A lot of them. And they're talking about *me*." I told him about the things I had noticed and overheard. "Now why should I be the most important person on this ship? That's absurd! And why should they know about whatever it is we're doing, and not me?"

Swann looked worried, annoyed. "They don't all know. . . . You see, your help will be important, essential perhaps—" He stopped, as if he had already said too much. His freckled face twisted as his mouth moved about. Finally he shook his head violently. "You'll just have to wait a few more days, Emma. Trust me, all right? Just trust me and wait."

That was hardly satisfactory, but what could I do? He knew something, but he wasn't going to tell it to me. Tight-lipped, I nodded my good-bye and left.

The mutiny occurred, ironically enough, on my eightieth birthday, a few days after my talk with Swann. August 5, 2248.

I woke up thinking, now you are an octogenarian. I got out of bed (deceleration-gee entirely gone, weightless now as we coasted), sponged my face, looked in the mirror. It is a strange experience to look inside your own retinas; down there inside is the one thinking, in that other face . . . it seems as if, if you could get the light right, you could see yourself.

I grasped the handholds of my exerciser and worked out for a while, thinking about birthdays. All the birthdays in this new age. One of my earliest memories, now, was my tenth birthday. My mother took me to the medical station, where I had to drink foul-tasting stuff and submit to tests and some shots—just quick blasts of air on the skin, but they scared me. "You'll appreciate this later," my mom said, with a funny expression. "You won't get sick and weak when you're old. Your immune system will stay strong. You'll live for ever so long, Emma, don't cry."

Yes, yes. Apparently she was right, I thought, looking into the mirror again, where my image seemed to pulse with color under the artificial lights. Very long lives, young at eighty: the triumph of gerontology. As always, I wondered what I would do with all the extra years—the extra lives. Would I live to stand free on Martian soil, and breathe Martian air?

Thinking these thoughts I left my room, intent on breakfast. The lounges down the hall from the bedrooms were empty, an unusual thing. I walked into the last lounge before the corridor turned, to look out the small window in it, with its view over the bridge.

And there they were: two silver rectangles, like asteroids crushed into ingots of the metals they contained. Spaceships!

They were asteroid miners of the PR class, sister ships of our own. I stared at them motionlessly, my heart thudding like a drum, thinking *rendezvous*. The ships grew to the size of decks of cards, very slowly. They were the shape of a card deck as well, with the mining cranes and drills folded together at their fronts, bridge ceilings just barely bulging from their sides (tiny crescents of light), rocket exhausts large at their rear, like beads on their sides and front. Brilliant points of light shone from the windows, like the fluorescent spots on the deep-sea fish of Earth. They looked small beside an irregular blue-gray asteroid, against the dead black of space.

I left the lounge slowly. Turned and walked down the corridor—

In the dining commons it was bedlam.

I stopped and stared. Of the entire crew of forty-three, at least twenty-five must have been in the commons, shouting and laughing, six or seven singing the Ode to Joy, others setting up the drinks table (Ilene maneuvering the mass of the big coffee pot), John and Steven and Lanya in a mass hugging and laughing-sobbing, tears in their eyes. And on the video screen was a straight-on camera shot of the two ships, silver dots against a blue-gray asteroid, so that it looked like a die thrown through the vacuum.

They all had known. Every single one of them in the room. I found myself blinking rapidly, embarrassed and angry. Why hadn't I been told? I wiped my eyes and got out of the doorway before I was noticed by someone inside.

Andrew Duggins flew by, pulling himself along the hall rails. His big face was scowling. "Emma!" he said, "come on," and pulled away. I only looked at him, and he stopped. "This is a mutiny!" he said, jerking his head in the direction of the commons. "They're taking over the ship, and those others out there too. We've got to try and get a message off to Ceres—to defend ourselves!" With a hard yank he pulled himself away, in the direction of the radio room.

*Mutiny*. All of the mysterious events I had noticed fell together, into a pattern. A plan to take over the ship. Had Swann been too afraid of the possibility to discuss it?

But there was no time for a detailed analysis. I leaped off the floor, and with a strong pull on the rail was after Duggins.

Outside the radio room there was a full-fledged fight going on. I saw Al Nordhoff striking one of the ship police in the face, Amy Van Danke twisting furiously in the hold of two men, trying to bite one in the throat. Others struggled in the doorway. Shouts and Amy's shrieks filled the air. The fight had that awkward, dangerous quality that all brawls in weightlessness exhibit. A blow that connected (one of Al's vicious kicks to the head of a policeman, for instance) sent both parties spinning across the room. . . .

"Mutiny!" Duggins bellowed, and diving forward crashed into the group in the doorway. His momentum bowled several people into the radio room, and an opening was cleared. I shoved off from the wall and grazed my head on the doorjamb going in.

After that things were blurry, but I was angry—angry that I had been deceived, that Swann and the general order of things were being challenged, that friends of mine were being hit—and I swung blindly. I caught one of the policemen on the nose with my fist, and his head smacked the wall with a loud thump. The room was crowded, arms and legs were swinging. The radio console itself was crawling with bodies. Duggins was bellowing still, and hauling figures away from the mass on the radio controls. Someone got me in a choke hold from behind. I put heel to groin and discovered it was a woman—put elbow in diaphragm and twisted under her arm, nearly strangled. Duggins had cleared the radio and was desperately manipulating the dials. I put a haymaker on the ear of a man trying to pull him away. Screams and spherical droplets of blood filled the air—

Reinforcements arrived. Eric Swann slipped through the doorway, his red hair flying wild, a tranquilizer gun in his hand. Others followed him. Darts whizzed through the air, sounding like arrows. "Mutiny!" I shrieked. "Eric! Mutiny! Mutiny!"

He saw me, pointed his gun at me and shot. I looked at the dart hanging from my forearm.

. . . The next thing I knew, I was being guided down the jump tube. Leaving it at my floor. I saw Swann's face swimming above me. "Mutiny," I said.

"That's true," Eric replied. "We're going to have to put you under arrest for a few hours." His freckle-face was stretched into a fool's grin.

"Asshole," I muttered. I wanted to run. I could outrun all of them. "I thought you were m'friend."

"I am your friend, Emma. It was just too dangerous to explain. Davydov will tell you all about it when you see him."

Davydov. Davydov? "But he was lost," I muttered, fighting sleep and very confused. "He's dead."

Then I was in my bed, strapped securely. "Get some sleep," Swann said. "I'll be back in a few hours." I gave him a look planned to turn him to stone, but he just grinned and I fell asleep in the middle of it, thinking, Mutiny. . . .

When I woke up again, Swann was by my bed, tilted in the no-gee so that his head hung over me. "How are you feeling?" he asked.

"Bad." I waved him away and he pushed off into the air above the bed. I rubbed my eyes. "What happened, Swann?"

"A mutiny, you've been calling it." He smiled.

"And it's true?"

He nodded.

"But why? Who are you?"

"Did you ever hear of the Mars Starship Association?"

I thought. "A long time ago? One of those secret anti-Committee groups."

"We weren't anti-Committee," he said. "We were just a club. An advocacy group. We wanted the Committee to support research for an interstellar expedition."

"So?"

"So the Committee didn't want to do it. And they took us to be part of the anti-Committee movement, so they outlawed us. Jailed the leaders, transferred the members to different sectors. They made us anti-Committee."

"Didn't all that happen a long time ago?" I asked, still disoriented. "What has that got to do with this?"

"We regrouped," he said. "Secretly. We've existed underground for all these years. This is our coming out, you might say."

"But why? What good does it do you to take over a few asteroid miners? You aren't planning to use them as starships, are you?" I laughed shortly at the idea.

He stared at me without answering, and suddenly I knew that I had guessed it.

I sat up carefully, feeling cold and a touch dizzy. "You must be joking."

"Not at all. We're going to join the *Lermontov* and the *Hidalgo*, and complete their life-support systems' closure."

"Impossible," I breathed, still stunned at the very idea.

"Not impossible," he said patiently. "That's what the MSA has been working on these last forty years—"

"One of those ships is *Hidalgo?*" I interrupted. My processing was still impaired by the drugs he had shot me with.

"That's right."

"So Davydov is alive. . . ."

"He certainly is. You knew him, didn't you?"

"Yes." Davydov had been the captain of *Hidalgo* when it disappeared in the Achilles group three years before. I had thought him dead. . . .

"There's no way I'll go," I said after a pause. "You can't kidnap me and drag me along on some insane interstellar attempt—"

"No! No. We're sending *Rust Eagle* back with all the non-MSA people from the three ships."

I let out a long sigh of relief. Yet sudden anguish filled me at the thought of the mess I was suddenly in, of the fanatics who now had control of my life, and I cried out, "Eric, you knew this was going to happen out here. Why didn't you arrange to keep me off this flight?"

He looked away from me, pushed himself down to the floor. Red-faced, he said, "I did the opposite, Emma."

"You *what?*"

"There are MSA people in the expedition scheduling office, and"—still staring at the floor—"I told them to arrange for you to be aboard *Rust Eagle* this time."

"But, Swann!" I said, struggling for words. "Why? Why did you do that to me?"

"Well—because, Emma, you're one of the best life-support systems designers there is on Mars, or anywhere. Everyone knows that, you know that. And even though our systems designers have got a lot of improvements for the starship, they still have to be installed in those two ships, and made to work. And we have to do it before the Committee police find us. Your help could make the difference, Emma."

"Oh, Swann."

"It could! Look, I knew it was imposing on you, but I thought, if we got you out here ignorant of our plans, then you couldn't be held responsible. When you return to Mars you can tell them you didn't know anything about the MSA, that we made you help us. That was why I didn't tell you anything on the way out here, don't you see? And I know you aren't that strong a supporter of the Committee, are you? They're just a bunch of thugs. So that if your old friends asked you for help that only you can give, and you couldn't be held culpable, you might help? Even if it was illegal?" He looked up at me, his blue eyes grave.

"You're asking for the impossible," I told him. "Your MSA has lost touch with reality. You're talking about travel across *light-years*, for God's sake, and you've got five-year systems to do it with!"

"They can be modified," Swann insisted. "Davydov will explain the whole project when you see him. He wants to talk with you as soon as you'd like to."

"Davydov," I said darkly. "He's the one behind this madness."

"We're all behind it, Emma. And it isn't mad."

I waved an arm and held my head in my hands, as it was pulsing with all the bad news. "Just leave me alone for a while."

"Sure," he said. "I know it's a lot to take in. Just tell me when you want to see Davydov. He's over on *Hidalgo.*"

"I'll tell you," I said, and looked at the wall until he left the room.

I had better tell about Oleg Davydov here, for we were lovers once, and for me the memory of him was marked with pain and anger, and a sense of loss—loss that no matter how long I lived could not be recouped or forgotten.

I was just out of the University of Mars, working at the Hellas Basin, in the new settlement near the western edge of the Basin where underground reservoirs and aquifers had been discovered. It was a good supply of water, but the situation was delicate, and the use of the water caused ecologic problems. I was set to work with others to solve these problems, and I quickly proved that I was the best among the systems people there. I had a grasp of the whole Hellas set-up that seemed perfectly natural to me, but was (I could see) impressive to others. And I was a good middle-distance runner—so that all in all, I was a confident youth, perhaps even a bit arrogant.

During my second year there I met Oleg Davydov. He was staying in Burroughs, the big government center to the north, doing some work for the Soviet mining cartel. We met in a restaurant, introduced by a mutual acquaintance.

He was tall and bulky, a handsome man. One of the Soviet blacks, they call them. I guess some of their ancestors came from one of the USSR's client countries in Africa. The color had been pretty well watered down over the generations, and Davydov had coffee-and-cream-colored skin. His hair was black and wooly; he had thick lips under a thin, aquiline nose; a heavy beard, shaved so that his lower face was rough; and his eyes were ice blue. They seemed to jump out of his face. So he was a pretty good racial mix. But on Mars, where ninety-nine percent of the population is fish-belly white, as they say, any touch of skin color is highly valued. It made one look so . . . healthy, and vital. This Davydov was really extremely good-looking, a color delight to the eye. I watched him then, as we sat on adjacent stools in that Burroughs restaurant, talking, drinking, flirting a little . . . watched so closely that I can recall the potted palm and white wall that were behind him, although I don't remember a word we said. It was one of those charmed nights, when both parties are aware of the mutual attraction.

We spent that night together, and the next several nights as well. We visited the first colony in the area, The Can, and marvelled at the exhibits in the museum there. We scrambled around the base of the Fluted Cliffs in Hellespontus Montes, and spent a night out in a survival tent. I beat him easily in a footrace, and then won a 1500-meter race for him at a Burroughs track. Every hour available to us we spent together, and I fell in love. Oleg was young, witty, proud of his many abilities; he was exotically bilingual (a Russian!), affectionate, sensual. We spent a lot of time in bed. I remember that in the dark I could see little more than his teeth when he grinned, and his eyes, which seemed light grey. I loved making love with him . . . I remember late dinners together, in Burroughs or out at the station. And innumerable train rides, together or alone, across the sere rust deserts between Burroughs and Hellas—sitting by the window looking out at the curved red horizon, feeling happy and excited. . . . Well, those are the kind of times that you only live through once. I remember them well.

The arguments began quite soon after those first weeks. We were an arrogant pair and didn't know any better. For a long time I didn't even realize that our disagreements were particularly serious, for I couldn't imagine anyone arguing with *me* for very long. (Yes, I was that self-important.) But Oleg Davydov did. I can't remember much of what we argued about—that period of time, unlike the beginning, is a convenient blur in my memory. One time I do remember (of course the rest could be called up as well): I had come into Burroughs on the late train, and we were out eating in a Greek restaurant behind the train station. I was tired, and nervous about our relationship, and sick of Hellas. Hoping to compliment him, I made some comment about how much more fun it would be to be an asteroid miner like he was.

"We aren't doing anything out there," he said in response. "Just making money for the corporations—making a few people on Earth rich, while everything else down there falls apart."

"Well, at least you're out there exploring," I said.

He looked annoyed, an expression I was becoming familiar with. "But we aren't, that's what I'm saying. With our capabilities we could be exploring the whole solar system. We could have stations on the Jovian moons, around Saturn, all the way out to Pluto. We *need* a solar watch station on Pluto."

"I wasn't aware of that fact," I said sarcastically.

His pale blue eyes pierced me. "Of course you weren't. You

think it's perfectly all right to continue making money from those stupid asteroids, and nothing more, here at the end of the twenty-second century."

"Well?" I said, annoyed myself by this time. "We're all going to live for a thousand years, so what's your rush? There's time for all of your great projects. Right now we need those asteroids."

"The corporations need them. And the Committee."

"The Committee's just organizing all of our efforts for our own good," I said.

"They just make the trains run on time, eh?" he said, taking a deep swallow from his drink.

"Yes," I said, not understanding what he meant. "Yes, they do."

He shook his head with disgust. "You're an all-American girl, all right. Everything is *oh kay*. Leave the politics to the others."

"And you are a true Soviet," I retorted, struggling away from him in our dining booth. "Blaming your problems on the government. . . ."

And we went on from there, senselessly and for no reason but pride and hurt feelings. I remember him making a grim prediction: "They will make a happy American Kremlin up here, and you won't care, as long as your job is secure." But most of what we said was less logical than that.

And a long, miserable week later, a blur of bitter fights, one of those times when you have ruined a relationship though you don't know how, and wish desperately that time could be reversed and the unknown mistake undone, he left. The Soviet mining people wanted him in space again and he just left, without saying good-bye, though I called his dorm again and again in those last few days. And then I knew—I learned it, in the course of long black walks over the broad basin, standing alone on that rocky plain— that I could be spurned. It was a hard lesson.

In a few years I was out among the asteroids myself, working for Royal Dutch. I heard stories about Davydov getting in trouble with the Soviet mining command, but I didn't pay much attention. It was a matter of pride to ignore anything I heard about him. So I never got the full story of what had happened to him.

Then, many years later—just three years before this mutiny,

in fact—the *Hidalgo* disappeared out in the Trojans, breaking radio contact with the famous last words, "Now wait just a minute." No wreckage was ever found, the matter was hushed up by the Committee censors, and no explanation was ever offered. Looking over the list of crew members I saw his name at the top— *Oleg Davydov*—and the pain flooded through me again, worse than ever before. It was one of the worst moments of my life. We had parted in anger, he had left me without even saying good-bye, and now, no matter how many years the gerontologists gave me, I would never be able to change those facts, for he was dead. It was very sad.

. . . Thus, when Eric Swann came to take me across to the *Hidalgo*, to see Davydov again, I did not know exactly what I felt. My heart beat rapidly, I had to strain to make casual, terse conversation with Eric. What would he look like? What would I say to him, or him to me? I didn't have the slightest idea.

Well, he looked very much like he had sixty years before. Perhaps a little heavier, bearlike with his dark hair, his broad shoulders and chest and rump. His ice-blue eyes surveyed me without any visible sign of recognition.

We were on the empty bridge of the *Hidalgo*. At a nod from Davydov, Eric had slipped away down the jump tube. In the breathy vented silence I walked around the bridge slowly, my velcro slippers making little *rip rip rip* noises. My pulse was fast. I discovered that I was still angry with him. And I felt that he had personally deceived me with the news of his death. Or perhaps it was the mutiny. . . .

"You look much the same," he said. The sound of his voice triggered a hundred memories. I looked at him without replying. Finally he said, with a stiff, slight smile, "Has Eric apologized for our kidnapping of you?"

I shook my head.

"I am sorry we shocked you. I hear you fought hard against the takeover. Eric probably explained that we kept you ignorant for your own protection."

So smooth, he was. It just made me mad. He squinted at me, trying to gauge my mood. Hard without a voice.

"The truth of the matter is," he went on, "the success of all the MSA's years of effort depends on the creation of a fully closed life-support system in the starship. I believe our scientists will be able to do it, but Swann has always said your ability with BLS systems is extraordinary, and our scientists agree that you are the best. And they tell me we need your help."

Did he think I would still be vain? "You're not—" I cleared my throat. "You're not going to get it."

He stared at me, calm and bemused. "You still support the Committee? Even though they have jailed your father on Amor, isn't that true?"

"Yes," I said. "But the Committee doesn't have anything to do with this."

"That is the equivalent of saying you still support them. But enough of that. We need your help. Why won't you help us?"

After I didn't reply, he began to stride back and forth, *rip rip rip.* "You know," he said with a nervous glance, "what happened between us occurred a long time ago. We were both children then—"

"We were *not* children," I broke in. "We were free adults, on our own. We were just as responsible for our actions then as we are now."

"All right," he said, pushing a hand through his hair. "You're right. We were not children, admittedly." This was turning out to be more difficult than he had expected. "But it was a long time ago."

"This has nothing to do with that time, anyway."

He looked confused. "Then why won't you help?"

"Because what you are attempting is impossible," I cried. "This is all a monstrous fantasy of yours. You're ignoring the hard cold realities of deep space and leading people to a miserable death out there, all because of some boyish notion of adventure that you've been nursing all these years—for so long that you can't distinguish between fantasy and reality anymore!" I stopped, surprised by my vehemence. Davydov was wide-eyed.

"It's not my idea alone," he said weakly. "Every member of the MSA believes it is possible."

"There have been mass delusions larger than this," I said, "following a fanatic leader."

His eyes glittered angrily. (This effect is the result, I believe, of tensing the forehead muscles, thus shifting the layer of water over the eyes.) "I am no fanatic. We started as a group without a leader. I was made leader by the Committee when they tried to destroy us—they wanted to say it was a single person's doing. Like you do. When we reorganized, I was the one everyone knew about. But there are other leaders—"

"You started the reorganization, right?" Somehow I knew this was true. "Started up your little secret society, invented the handshake—"

"The fact that we had to work in secret," he said loudly, and then lowered his voice, "is incidental. A political reality, a fact of our time and place. A lot of work had to be done that the Committee didn't want done. They wouldn't support us, but that doesn't make the project bad! We're free of political motives, we are an act of cooperation between Soviets and Americans—we try to take humanity to permanent homes outside the solar system, while we still can."

He stopped for breath, staring at me with his swarthy jaws bunched. "Now you"—pointing at me—"completely ignorant of all this, call me a fanatic. Leading fools in a fantasy world." He looked away, out the wide bridge window. "I could have told Swann you would react like this."

My face burned. There we were, exactly as we had left off sixty years before. Furiously I said, "You kidnap me, put my future in great danger, and then call me a fool because I don't fall in with your fantastic schemes. Well you aren't going to get my help, Oleg Davydov, you and your secret club." I moved to the jump tube. "Just tell me when we can take *Rust Eagle* back to Mars. Until then I'll be in my room."

Crossing back over to our ship, Eric didn't dare say a word to me. Once on *Rust Eagle* I left him and went to my room, hit the desk and nearly cracked my skull on the ceiling. I hate no-gee. I went to the centrifuge and ran, ignoring my complaining knee. Then I went back to my little room to brood and imagine crushing rejoinders to Davydov. Why do all the best lines come to you when the argument is over? What I should have said was . . . I know, I know. Only serious brooding will hatch those real crushers.

But why had I fought with him at all, when he was asking for my help?

Later that day Andrew Duggins told me that the people who were not members of the MSA were getting together in the lounge down the hall. I went to see who they were. There were fourteen of us. Among them were Ethel Jurgenson, Amy Van Danke, Al Nordhoff, Sandra Starr, Yuri Kopanev, and Olga Dzindzhik. The others had faces I knew but couldn't put names to. We sat about exchanging our experiences during the rendezvous; everyone had been arrested, and most only released a few hours before. After these stories were exchanged we began to discuss possible courses of action, and the bickering began.

I told them what I knew, keeping to myself only the fact that I had been asked for help.

More discussion and arguing.

"We have to find out if there were any prisoners on *Lermontov.*"

"Or *Hidalgo.*" I thought about that—prisoners for three years.

"We have to act," Duggins said. "We could organize another attack on the radio room. Take it over and put out a call to Mars or Ceres."

"We could slip out of the ship," Al put in. "Patch a radio onto the high gain antenna. . . ."

"They're probably listening to us right now," Yuri said, and Olga nodded. In the Soviet sector they're used to such practices—or perhaps I should say they are more aware of them.

Anyway, the conversation was killed for a while. We stared at each other. It was a strange situation: prisoners of our shipmates, on what had been our ship. The talk resumed, quieter than before, until disagreements about what to do brought the volume back up. "I don't care if they steal the Committee blind," Yuri said, "and I certainly wouldn't risk myself to stop them."

"What do you think we should do, Weil?" asked Andrew, refusing to look at Yuri. He seemed annoyed at my lack of involvement.

"I think we should sit tight, take *Rust Eagle* back to Mars when they let us, and then tell the authorities what we know. To try to stop them here just puts us in danger."

Andrew didn't like that either. "We should fight! Sitting here passively would be helping them, and the Committee will know it." He squinted at me suspiciously. "You're close friends with Swann, aren't you? Didn't he ever tell you what was going on?"

"No," I said, feeling myself blush. They all watched me.

"You're telling us he just let you walk into this situation without any kind of warning or anything?" Duggins said.

"That's right," I snapped. "You saw me in the radio room, Duggins. I was as surprised as anyone by the mutiny."

But Duggins was unconvinced, and the rest of them looked skeptical as well. They all knew Swann was a considerate person, and it didn't make sense to them that he would have deceived a good friend so. There was a long, uncomfortable silence. Duggins stood up. "I'll talk to some of you another time," he said, and left the lounge. Suddenly angry, I left too. Looking back at the confused, suspicious people in the lounge, grouped in a disconsolate circle with their colored drink bulbs floating around them, I thought, They look scared.

When I got back to my room, two people were moving into it. A Nadezhda Malkiv, and a Marie-Anne Kotovskaya—both BLSS engineers, both members of the Soviet branch of the MSA. The other two ships were being emptied so that they could be worked on freely, they told me. Nadezhda was 124 years old, a specialist in the gas exchange; Marie-Anne was 108, a biologist whose study was the algae and bacteria in the waste recycling system. They were both from *Lermontov*, which they said, had been in the asteroid belt nearly four months before the MSA took over, broke radio contact with Mars, and circled around to the rendezvous behind the sun.

Shocked into a stiff silence by this new development, I went back into the halls, and then to the small lounge around the corner from my room. There I met the leader of the non-MSA people from *Lermontov*, a dour man named Ivan Valenski. He had been the Committee police leader aboard, until the mutiny. I did not like him—he was a sort of dully furious Soviet bureaucrat, a petty man used to giving orders and being obeyed. He seemed as little impressed by me as I by him. Duggins, I thought, would be more to his taste. They were men scarred by so many years of authority that they actively worked for its continuance—to justify their lives up to this point, perhaps. But how was I different from them?

I returned to my room. My new roommates left me the top bunk; the bottom, which I had used as a convenient counter, was occupied by Nadezhda. Marie-Anne planned to sleep in the corner where the walls met the ceiling. Their belongings were strapped all over the floor. I talked with them for a while in English, with some fumbling attempts on my part at Russian. They were nice women, and after the earlier meetings of the day I appreciated the company of calm, undemanding people.

That night Swann came by my room, and asked me if I wanted to eat dinner with him. After a moment's thought I agreed.

"I'm glad you aren't still angry with me," he babbled, ingenuous as ever. Although I had to remind myself that he had been high in the councils of the MSA for as long as I'd known him. So how well had I known him?

"Shut up about that and let's go eat," I said. Somewhat subdued, he led the way to the dining commons through the dark halls.

Once there I looked around at the place, imagining it as the dining commons of the starship. People in neutral-toned one-piece suits walked up to the food counter; there they pushed the buttons for the meal they desired, most of them never looking up at the menu. The foods grown on ship—salads, vegetable drinks, fish or scallops or chicken or rabbit, goat cheese, milk, yoghurt—were supplemented by non-renewable supplies: coffee, tea, bread, beef. . . . They would run out of those things pretty fast. Then it would be the ship-grown stuff, in enclosed plates, with drinks in bulbs. I watched all the precise forking going on around me. It had a Japanese tea ceremony atmosphere.

"You'll have to keep accelerating," I said. "You can't stay weightless for long, it would kill you."

He smiled. "We've got forty-two cesium tanks." I stared at him. "That's right. This is the biggest theft in history, Emma. At least that's one way to think of it."

"It sure is."

"So, we plan to keep a constant acceleration-deceleration pattern, and create half-Mars gravity most of the time." We walked up to the food counter and punched out our orders. Our trays slid out of their slot.

We sat down against the wall away from the mirror wall; I don't like to eat next to the mirror image of myself. The other three walls of the commons were bright tones of yellow, red, orange, yellow-green. It was autumn on *Rust Eagle.*

"We'll keep up the seasonal colors on board the starship," Swann said as we ate. "Shorten the daylight hours in winter, make it colder, colors all silver and white and black. . . . I like winter best. The solstice festival and all."

"But it'll just be a game."

He chewed thoughtfully. "I guess."

"Where will you go?"

"Not sure. No, seriously! There's a planetary system around Barnard's Star. That's nine light-years. We'll probably check that out, and at least resupply with water and deuterium, if nothing else."

We ate in silence for a time. At the next table a trio sat excavating their trays, arguing about the hydrogen-fixing capabilities of a certain *Hydrogenomonas eutropha.* Engineering the rebirth of breath. At the next table a young woman reached up to capture an escaping particle of chicken. The diminution of it all!

"How long?" I asked, eating steadily.

Swann's freckle-face took on a calculating look as he chewed. "We could go a hundred, maybe two hundred years. . . ."

"For God's sake, Eric."

"It's only a quarter of our predicted lifetimes. It's not like generations will live and die on the ship. We'll have a past on Mars, and a future on some world that could be more like Earth than

Mars is! You act like we're leaving such a natural way of life on Mars. Mars is just a big starship, Emma."

"It is not! It's a *planet*. You can go outside and stand on the ground. Run around."

Swann shoved his tray away, sucked on his drink bulb. "Your five-hundred-year project is the terraforming of Mars," he said. "Ours is the colonization of a planet in another system. What's the big difference?"

"About ten or twenty light-years."

We finished our drinks in silence. Swann took our trays to the counter and brought back bulbs of coffee.

"Was—is Charlie one of you?"

"Charlie?" He looked at me strangely. "No. He works for the Committee's secret police, didn't you know that? Internal security?"

I shook my head.

"That's why you don't see him on miners anymore."

"Ah." Who *did* I know, I thought unhappily.

He was looking beyond me. "I remember . . . about 2220 or 21 . . . Charlie dropped by one of our labs with one of his police friends. This was in Argyre. We had completely infiltrated the Soviet space research labs, and had requisitioned this particular one for some tests—reactor-mass conservation, I think it was. I was visiting to help with a supply problem. They couldn't get all the cesium they wanted. And then there was Charlie and this woman, him saying hello how are you Eric, just dropped by to see how you're doing. . . . And I could not tell whether the woman was his girlfriend and he really was just saying hello to me, or whether they were checking out the lab as part of their police work. I showed them all around the lab, told them that we were doing all the work for a Soviet-Arco-Mobil consortium, which of course the record would confirm. I remember walking around talking about old times with him, explaining some of the lab rooms, all the time wondering if both of us were acting, or just me. And I was scared, that somehow our security had broken, and this was the first sign of it. . . ." He shook his head, laughed shortly. "But computer government came through again. They scarcely knew enough to be aware of their losses. Computer bureaucracy—no wonder Earth is falling apart. I have no doubt all of those governments are being stolen blind."

"There's probably a Terran Starship Association that you've never heard of," I said absently, thinking of the past.

He laughed. "I wouldn't doubt it." He put his drink bulb down. "Although we have kept pretty good track of the other underground organizations on Mars. In fact, we chose this particular time for the construction of the starship because we think that the Committee police will be too busy back on Mars to make much of a search for us."

"Why is that?"

"A group called the Washington-Lenin Alliance is planning to start a revolt sometime in mid-August, when Mars is farthest from Earth. Some other groups are going to join them. We don't know how big it will get, but there should be enough turmoil to keep the police occupied."

"Great." Oh, no, I thought. Not Mars, too. Please. Not Mars. Swann moved his hands nervously. I sipped coffee.

"So you're not going to help us?" he said suddenly.

I shook my head, swallowed. "Nope."

The corners of his mouth tightened. He looked down at the table.

"Does that end your starship attempt?" I asked.

"No," he said. "They'll get very near full closure, I'm sure. It's just—well, on a voyage this long, the slightest difference in the ship's efficiency will mean a lot. Really a lot. You know that. And I know that if you were to help them the system would end up being more efficient."

"Listen, Eric," I said, and took a deep breath. "What I don't understand is this. You people have been working on this problem for years. You and I have been friends for years, and all during that time you've known that I'm good at life-support systems. So why didn't you ever tell me about it?"

He reddened, chewed his lower lip. "Oh—no reason—"

"*Why*, Eric? Why?"

"Well—at first it was Charlie, you know. Being your husband and all—"

"Come on, Eric. We were only married a few years. You and I have been friends a lot longer than that. Or was it like with Charlie in the lab that day—just acting?"

"No, no," he said emphatically. "Not at all. I wanted to tell you, believe me." He looked up from the table at me. "I just couldn't be sure about you, Emma. I couldn't be sure that you wouldn't tell the Committee about us. You always spoke in favor of the Committee and its policies, whenever the subject came up—"

"I did not!"

He stared at me. "You did. You'd complain about being given too much work and being shunted from place to place, but you'd always end up saying you were glad the sectors were being coordinated, pulled off each others' throats. And that you were pleased with the life the Committee arranged for you. That's what you *said*, Emma!" He pulled at his cheeks as I shook my head. "Then when they jailed your father I thought you would change—"

"My father broke the law," I said, thinking about things I had said through the years.

"So are we! See? What if I had told you about us back on Mars, and you had said, you're breaking the law. I couldn't take the chance. Davydov was against it, and I couldn't take the chance on my own, although believe me I wanted to—"

"Damn you," I said. "Damn Oleg Davydov—"

"How were we to know any better?" he asked, his blue eyes unflinching. "I'm sorry, but you asked me why. We thought you were Committee all the way. I was the only one who thought otherwise, and even with me it was just a hope. *We couldn't take the chance.* It was too important, we were trying to accomplish something great—"

"You were pursuing a crackpot scheme that is going to kill sixty people for no reason," I said harshly, standing up as I spoke. "A stupid plan that takes you off into space and leaves you there with no way to colonize a planet even if you found one—" I shoved my chair back and walked quickly away, my eyes filling with tears so that it was hard to balance. People were watching me; I had shouted.

I pulled myself furiously through the halls of the living quarters, cursing Swann and Davydov and the entire MSA. He should have known. How could they not have known? I crashed into my room, and happily it was empty. I banged from wall to wall for a time, crying and muttering angrily to myself. Why didn't he know? Why couldn't he tell, the idiot?

For a moment I caught sight of my reflection in my little washstand mirror, and I went over to look at it, floating in midair. I was so upset I had to squeeze my eyes shut as hard as I could, before I could look in the glass at myself: and when I did, I experienced a frightening thing. It seemed that the true three-dimensional world was on the other side of the glass, and that I was looking into it through a window. The person floating in there was looking out. She appeared distraught over something or other. . . .

And in this curious state I had the realization, at the moment of seeing that stranger there, that I was a person like everybody else. That I was known by my actions and words, that my internal universe was unavailable for inspection by others.

They didn't know.

They didn't know, because I never told them. I didn't tell them that I hated the Mars Development Committee—yes, admit it, I did hate them!—I hated those petty tyrants as much as I hated anything. I hated the way they had treated my foolish father. I hated their lies—that they were taking over power to make a better life on an alien planet, etc., etc. Everyone knew that was a lie. They just wanted power for themselves. But we kept our mouths shut; talk too much and you might get relocated to Texas. Or on Amor. The members of the MSA had compensated with a stupid plan, to escape to the stars in secret—but they resisted, they stole, they subverted, they disbelieved, they resisted! And me? I didn't even have the guts to tell my friends how I felt. I had thought that cowardice was the norm, and that made it okay. I had thought that resistance necessarily would be like the rash and drunken words of my father, pointless and dangerous. I had been scared of the idea of resistance, and the worst of it was, I had thought that everyone was like me.

I looked at the stranger in the other room through the glass. There was Emma Weil. You couldn't read her mind. She looked plain and grim, skinny, dedicated, unhumorous. What was she thinking? You would never know. She sounded pretty self-satisfied. People who sound self-satisfied usually are. But you would never know for sure. You could look in her eyes as hard as you wanted, for an hour and more: nothing there but empty, weightless black pools. . . .

For a couple of days I sat in my room and did nothing. Then one morning when Nadezhda and Marie-Anne were leaving to work on the starship, I said, "Take me with you."

They looked at each other. "If you like," Nadezhda said.

The two ships had been placed side by side. We took our boat into the bay of *Hidalgo*. I followed my roommates back to the farm, ignoring the occasional stare we received from other workers in the halls.

They had already added a few rows of vegetable tanks to the standard farm set-up. The glare of white light from the many lamps made me blink. I trailed behind the two women, listening as they talked to other technicians. Then we were off by ourselves, among the big suspension bottles, spotted green and brown, of the algae room. The glare of the lamps forced us to put on dark blue sunglasses.

"*Chlorella pyrenoidosa* with nitrate as its nitrogen source takes ten times less iron out of that nutrient medium than when urea is the nitrogen source, see?" Nadezhda was talking.

"But we have to use that urea somewhere," Marie-Anne said.

"Sure. But I'm worried that the biomass created will eventually become too much to handle."

"Feed it to the goats?"

"But what happens when the nutrient medium is exhausted? No source of iron in the vacuum, you know. . . ."

They had a problem there. There had to be a very close agreement between the photosynthetic coefficient for algae and the respiratory coefficient for the humans and animals; otherwise too much $CO_2$ or too much oxygen would build up, depending. One way to deal with this is to provide different sources of nitrogen to different sections of algae, as this will alter the photosynthetic co-efficient. But the algae use up their mineral supplies at different rates, depending on their type of nitrogen feed. And over long periods of time this could be significant; to keep up a balanced gas exchange might take more minerals than the rest of the biocenosis would be producing.

"Can't you use urea and ammonia exclusively," I asked them, "and shift amounts of *pyrenoidosa* and *vulgaris* to keep the exchange balanced? That way you'd be using more urea, and avoiding the problem of nitrates."

They looked at each other.

"Well, no," Nadezhda said. "See, look at this—the damn algae grow so fast with urea—too much biomass, we can't use it all."

"What about giving it less light?"

"But that makes for problems with the *vulgaris*," Marie-Anne explained. "Stupid stuff, it either dies or grows wild."

Clearly I was repeating the most obvious solutions. Problem-solving for a biologic life-support system is like a game. One of the very finest intellectual games ever devised, in fact. In many ways it is like chess. Now, Nadezhda and Marie-Anne were certainly grand masters at this game, and they had been working with this particular model for years. So they were a big step ahead of me at that moment, discussing modifications that I had never heard of. But I had never met anybody who had a flair for the game like I did—if it had been chess, I would have been Martian champion, I am sure. When I saw the patient look on Marie-Anne's face as she explained why my suggestion wouldn't work, something snapped in me, and my vague intentions for this visit crystallized.

"All right," I said in a mean tone of voice. "You'd better give me the whole story here, all the details of your model, your new improvements that Swann told me about, everything. If you want me to help."

The two women nodded politely, as if this request were the most ordinary thing in the world. And we got down to it.

So I helped them, yes, I did. And more than ever before, the I who thought and felt was distanced from the I who did the work on this particular example of the BLSS problem—more than ever the work seemed a game, a giant intricate puzzle that we would look at when we finished—we would stand back to look at it, and admire it, and then we would forget it and go home to dinner. In this frame of mind I was especially inventive, and I helped a lot.

It got to the point where I even began to return to the starship in the evenings after dinner, to wander the farm alone and type some figures into the model programs to check the results. Because they had a real problem on their hands—I'd never worked on a harder one. The two ships were Deimos PRs: about forty years old, shaped like decks of cards, just over a kilometer long; powered by cesium reactor-mass, deuterium-fueled, direct-explosion rockets. The crew of forty or forty-five lived in the forward or upper part of the ships, behind the bridges. Below them were the recreational facilities, the various chambers of the farms, and the recycling plants, and below those were the huge masses of the rocket systems, and the shield that protected the crews from them. The ships were biogeocenoses, that is, enclosed ecology systems, combining biologic and technologic methods to create closures. Total closure was not possible, of course; it approached eighty percent complete for a three-year period, tailing off rapidly after that. So they were good asteroid miners, they really were. But there were loss-points that had never been satisfactorily solved, and although these were the best closed biologic life-support systems ever built, they were no starships.

I walked in circles through the rooms of *Hidalgo*'s farm, following the course of the various processes as I tried to think my way through the system. Most of the rooms were darkened, but the algae rooms still required sunglasses. Here the whole thing began. Heat and light generated by the nuclear reactions in the rocketry provided energy for the photoautotropic plants, mostly the algae *chlorella pyrenoidosa* and *chlorella vulgaris*. These were suspended in large bottles under the lights, and I thought that, despite the nutrient problems, they could be manipulated genetically or environmentally to make the gas exchange as needed.

I took off the sunglasses and stumbled around the darkened aqua room until my sight returned. Here the excess algae was brought to feed the bottom of the food chain. Plankton and crustacea ate algae, little fish ate the plankton, big fish ate the little fish. It was the same in the barns farther along; under night lights I could make out the cages and pens for the rabbits, chickens, pigs and goats—and my nose confirmed their presence. These animals ate the plant wastes that humans didn't use, and provided food themselves. Beyond the animals' barn was the series of rooms planted with rows of vegetables—the farm proper—and here some lights were still on, providing a pleasant, mild illumination. I sat down against one wall and looked at a long row of cabbages. Beside me on the wall was drawn a simple schematic, left wordless like a religious token—a diagram of the system's circular processes. Light fed algae. Algae fed plants and fish. Plants fed animals and humans, and created oxygen and water. Animals fed humans, and humans and animals created wastes which sustained microorganisms that mineralized the wastes (to an extent), making it possible to plow them back into the plants' soil.

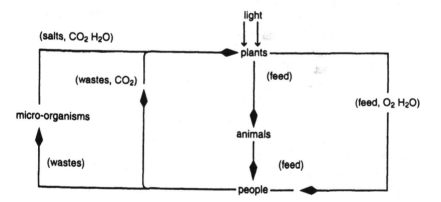

The cabbages glowed in the dim light like rows of brains, working on the problem with me. The circle made by the diagram, supplemented by physiochemical operations to aid the gas exchange and the use of wastes, was nearly closed: a neat, reliable, artificial biogeocenosis. But there were two major loss points that had me stumped; and I wasn't going to see the solution walking around the farm. One was the incomplete use of wastes. Direct use of human waste products as nutrients for plant life is limited by the build-up of chlorine ions not used by plants. Sodium chloride, for instance, is a compound used by human beings as a palatable substance, but it isn't required in equivalent amounts by the other components of the system. So the use of algae to mineralize wastes on *Hidalgo* had to be supplemented by physiochemical mineralization—thermal combustion in this case, which resulted in a small but significant amount of useless furnace ash. It would be difficult to find ways to return those poorly soluble metal oxides into the system.

The other major problem was the very minute disappearance of water. Though water could be filtered out of the air, and recaptured in a number of ways, a certain percentage would coat the interior of the ship, bond with various surfaces, pool in cracks and hidden spots on the floor, and even escape the ship if they ever had EVA.

And the more I thought of it, the more little problems appeared to augment these larger ones, and all of the problems impinged on each other, making a large and interconnected web of cause and effect, mostly measurable, but sometimes not . . . the game. The hardest game. And this time, by these people, played for keeps.

I got up nervously and paced between the long soil strips. They could create water using a fuel cell and electrolysis. With the power plant they had along, that might be all they would need. It would depend on their water recovery, their fuel supply, the amount of time they spent between stars. I turned and headed for the farm computers, intent on trying some figures. And as for those wastes, Marie-Anne had spoken of new mutant bacteria to mineralize them, bacteria that could chew up the metals they would slowly be piling up outside the system. . . .

The whoosh of the vents, the clicking of a counter, the soft snuffling of the animals in their sleep. Maybe they could do it, I thought. A very high degree of closure might be possible. But the question was, once accomplished, would they want to live inside it?

How long could humans live in a spaceship?
How long would they have to?

One morning after a night like that there was a knock at my door, and I opened it. It was Davydov.

"Yes?" I said.

He ducked his head. "I'm sorry about the way I behaved during our talk. It's been so long since I've gotten any criticism of the project, I'd forgotten how to react to it. I guess I lost my temper." Head raised, a shy little smile—Forgive me? Forgive me for kidnapping you and then yelling at you to boot?

"Umm," I said cautiously. "I see."

The smile disappeared, he pulled at his swarthy cheeks with one hand. "Could I perhaps, um, take you on a tour of the starship? Show you what we plan to do?"

I stood thoughtfully for as long as I could, knowing that I would accept the offer, curious to see what they had managed to steal from the Committee. "I suppose," I said.

I saw from the boat's dome, during our crossing, that they had finished connecting the two ships, with thin struts that held them side by side, and contained narrow passageways. It was one fat and ungainly-looking starship. Its windows gleamed like the luminous patches of ocean-floor fish. We were still in a tiny cluster of asteroids. The big one, I had learned, was Hilda, and around it were several daughter rocks.

It took Davydov several hours to show me what they had. They had: ore-holds full of minerals, medical supplies, food-stuffs, spices, clothing, equipment for planetfall, color panels and other material for the seasonal changes; a microfiche library of forty million volumes in three hundred languages; an equally vast collection of recorded music, with several each of almost every musical instrument; sports equipment; a lot of movies in English and Russian; a nursery full of toys and games; a room full of computers and computer parts; an observatory with several large telescopes.

During this ever more amazing tour we kept up a running debate, mostly joking. It was actually very enjoyable, although I think the sparring began to bother Davydov after a while. But I couldn't help it. Their efforts had been so thorough, but still, there was something adolescent about it all, something surreal: all the details logically worked out, from an initial proposition that was absurd.

We ended up in the farm, among the splotched algae bottles that made the light green, in the rich scent of manure from the barn next door. Davydov looked funny in sunglasses. Here I was the guide, and Davydov the tourist. I told him about Nadezhda's algae suspension tricks, Marie-Anne's mutant bacteria.

"I hear you have been helping them."

By now it could be said I was in charge of the project. "A little," I said sarcastically.

"I appreciate it."

"Oh, don't take it personally."

He laughed wryly. But I saw that I could wound him.

And then we came to the back wall of the farm, and it had all been seen. Behind the wall the shield silently vibrated, protecting us all from the nuclear reactions in the rear of the ship. There was another part of their project that must hold without fail, and the arcane studies that enabled the shield technicians to do it were nearly beyond explanation to those of us who had not committed our lives to the mysteries. To us it was simply a matter of faith.

"But this is what I want to know," I said at the wall. "Why do you have to do it this way? People will leave the solar system eventually, right? You don't *need* to do it this way."

He pulled at his face again. I remembered it was a gesture of Swann's, and I thought, this is where Swann got it. "I don't agree that it is inevitable that humans will leave the solar system," he said. "Nothing is inevitable, there is no such thing as historical determinism. It is people who act, not history, and people choose their acts. We could have built a really adequate starship at any time since the late twentieth century, for instance. But it hasn't been done. And it could be that those two hundred years are a sort of launch window, you know. A launch window that may close soon."

"What do you mean?"

"That the chance may pass. Our ability to do it might disap-

pear. There's a revolution going on on Mars this very minute—
Swann told you?"

"Yes."

"So who knows? We may be escaping the end of civilization!
Life on Mars could end, and that would damage Earth—they depend on that Mars colony for minerals, you know. And those Terran governments are just bigger versions of the Committee, doing
just as bad a job. They've taken Earth into another of its crisis periods."

"They've gotten through those before," I said, worrying about
Mars.

"That doesn't mean much. They never had a population of six
billion before. Even the trouble on Mars may be enough to push
them over the brink! It's a very delicate, artificial ecology, Emma.
Much like this little starship of ours. And if it falls apart, then the
chance to go to the stars is gone for a long time. Maybe forever. So
we're doing it ourselves, right here and now."

"You have a vision—"

"Not just me!"

"I meant all of you."

"Ah. Sorry. English should make that distinction."

"Does Russian?"

"Not really." We laughed.

The force of his ideas had impelled Davydov around the farm,
and velcro *rips* had accompanied his words as he walked between
the rows of vegetables. When he finished, I watched his dark face
through the distorting glass of a spare algae bottle—his ice-blue
eyes were the size of eggs, staring at me intently. I thought, He
wants to convince me of these things. It matters to him what I
think. This idea made me flush with pleasure, and it occurred to
me that this was how he had become the leader of this visionary
group. Not by any choice of the Mars Development Committee,
looking for a scapegoat. He was the leader because he could make
people feel this way.

The intercom system crackled. "Oleg?" It was John Dancer's
voice, sounding scared. "Oleg, are you hearing me? Respond
quickly please."

Davydov hurried to the wall with the intercom and flicked it on. "What is it, John?"

"Oleg! We need you on the bridge quick. Emergency."

"What is it?"

"We've spotted three ships approaching through two-belt central. Looks like police craft."

Davydov looked across at me. "I'll be there right away," he said. He ran between the vegetables to my side. "Looks like that trouble on Mars isn't occupying all of them." His voice was still light and joking, but his eyes were grim. "Come along."

So I went with him, across to the bridge of *Rust Eagle*. There were about a dozen people there, a few attending to the *Eagle*, the rest to Davydov and Ilene Breton.

"They're coming in an equilateral triangle pattern," Ilene said. "Simon spotted them by visual check—after he had seen the one, he ran through the police patterns and found the other two. If they don't make any adjustments, they'll come by with one on each side of us and one below."

"How long do we have?" Davydov asked.

"They're decelerating now. They'll pass this sub-group in about three hours."

I have never seen such a grim collection of people in my life. Only the clicks and breath of the ship's functions broke the silence that followed this announcement. I thought of it. Everything I had just seen, and the forty years of dangerous work it had taken to get it here, were now the prey of a diligent hunter. It could all end in four hours, in capture and imprisonment, return to Mars under guard, in the "starship." Or it could end in sudden death. Those Committee ships carry quite the arsenals.

"How fast are they moving?" Davydov asked.

Ilene said, "Two or three k's per second."

"They've got a lot of space to search," Swann said hopefully.

"They're bracketing us!" Ilene said. "They'll see us. By radar, heat scan, metal scan, visual, radio pick-up—somehow they'll see us."

"No more radio transmissions," Davydov said.

"We've already shut down," Ilene replied. Her white, pinched face looked impatient—she was waiting for everyone to catch up with her, and help.

They looked at each other.

"We could line up all of our lasers," said Olga Borg, captain of *Lermontov*. "Fire them up their exhaust vents"—she realized that would have no effect on the shields—"or hit them in the bridges, or the reactor shield generators."

"Those shields are too well protected," Swann said. But several others were nodding, their mouths pressed tight. They couldn't run—their backs were to the wall. They would fight and die. And, I thought, I would die too.

Ilene said, "If we give them any time they'll have a message off, and our position will be revealed. Other police ships would be here in a week."

"More than that—"

"Why don't you just hide?" I interjected.

They all stared at me. It reminded me of Nadezhda and Marie-Anne.

"We're being bracketed," Swann explained.

"I know that. But you aren't at the exact center of the triangle, are you? So if you were to bring these ships right onto the surface of Hilda, or near it, and moved around the top as the bottom ship moved under you, if you see what I mean, then you might stay out of sight the entire time."

"One of the side ships would see us," Ilene said.

"Maybe," I began, but Davydov interrupted: "We could shade to one side of Hilda, and keep Hilda itself between us and one side ship—then maneuver to keep one of the adjacent rocks between us and the other side ship. So Hilda would protect us from two of them, and one of her daughters from the third!"

"If that's possible," Ilene said.

"It won't work," Olga Borg declared.

"You tell me how they will detect you through an asteroid," I said.

Swann was smiling, crookedly. "We can hide, but we can't run."

"We can't use rockets to move around Hilda," Ilene said practically. "They'd see the exhaust."

It was like the games of hide-and-seek I had played as a child, on the broad boulder plains of Syrtis Major.

"You could pull the ships around with lines," I said. "Anchor winches here and there on the surface, and haul us around the rock as the ships go by. That'd give you better control anyway."

They liked that one. "But how will we see them?" Ilene asked. "What if they change directions while we're behind Hilda?"

"We'll put observers on the surface," Davydov said. "They can report with hand signals. Relay teams of observers." He thought about it. "Right. Let's go with that." He started pacing around the room, *rip rip rip.* "Let's go, we don't have much time! Ilene, get two boats onto the surface of Hilda. Make sure they take everything they'll need, because they won't be able to come back till it's over. Have them place a couple of deadmen as deep as they can in fifteen minutes."

The nice thing about the plan was that most of it was standard mining procedure: closing on a rock, preparing for drilling. . . . "Have John and the other mining people work out the lines. Oh— tell the boats to use their thrusters only in the boat bays and on the back side of Hilda." A thought struck Davydov, and he started to look in my direction. Thought better of it. "All of the non-MSA people are to be paired with their roommates, where possible, or with someone else if the roommates are busy. I want Duggins, Nordhoff, and Valenski under close surveillance. Keep them in the living quarters and don't tell them what's going on. Emma, you stay here."

I lifted an eyebrow. "I'll miss my nap."

With a nervous pattering of laughter the group scattered to their various tasks.

Davydov walked over to me. "Thank you, Emma. It's a good plan."

I waved a hand, wondering what I had done—or rather, why I had done it. "The only plan, I think."

"Maybe. But still, it saved us time." His smile and his eyes were bright in his dark face, but he wasn't really thinking about me anymore. His jaw bunched with tension. Ilene called him and he turned and walked over to her.

I sat and waited.

When the lines had been set—it took nearly an hour—I went with Davydov and Olga to the little window room opposite the bridge, which gave a view from the other side of the ship. The lines stretching from us to Hilda (the asteroid was about seven kilometers long, I judged, not an over-large object to hide three ships behind) were like silver thread, only visible by a sort of act of the imagination. The pulling began and the lines came straight. Off to one side the lines leading to the starship could just be seen. Davydov left to return to the bridge. A long time passed; Hilda came closer. At last the bare, rough blue-gray rock of the asteroid was no more than a hundred meters away. Now the *Eagle's* center rocket was expelling tiny puffs to keep the two objects from coming together—to keep us from falling (drifting, actually) onto the surface. I imagined I could feel the mysterious tug of gravity.

Swann came by and asked me to return to the bridge. As I walked up the tube (and now there was an up), I noticed an unusual silence. A lot of systems had been shut down. The three ships had become, to the outer world, inert objects.

Ilene had set up a computer display on the big viewscreen, which indicated our two ships, the outline of the asteroid as seen from our original location, and the three police ships. These were out of our radar view, and were being located by observers out on the asteroid's surface—people crawling around in EVA suits, hiding behind rocks like the scouts of old Earth. The bridge was crowded again.

We waited, watching the green screen with its shifting purple lines and points. The computer people and John Dancer were still programming our maneuvers. The rest of us sat and watched.

"I've got them on visual," came the report from one of the surface observers. "About ten degrees above my horizon, vertical ninety-five or a hundred."

"Tell him to point his suit exhaust at the ground," Davydov said into the mike.

The lines started to pull us around the asteroid, moving at a pretty snappy pace. On the green display screen we stayed near the center, two purple squares; the asteroid's outline shifted down, and the tiny red circles of the police ships rose slowly toward the edge of the outline. If they broached it, they would be in our sky. One of them certainly would. Ilene introduced the small shape of one of the rocks following Hilda onto the screen, the daughter rock that would be between us and that cruiser, for a while at least.

Looking out the bridge's wide plasteel window we could see Hilda curving away from us, the underside of the starship just above us, and behind it the vacuum sky, star-studded. The events on the computer screen could have been a movie, a war game, abstract art—for we could no more see the police than they could see us. Abstract art—and the esthetic was to keep all the dots within the irregular circle. . . .

The quiet voices kept reporting in for the observers, giving us positions, and Ilene tapped them out accordingly. The little red dots skipped up the screen.

With the police ship below us, it was simple. It would fly by, and we would move up and around the asteroid, keeping it between us and them, and it would never see us. With the ship on our right it was the same, only there wasn't such a big margin. We would remain just under the horizon to that one. This would put us just above the horizon for the third ship, for a few minutes. That was the bad part—but during that time a daughter rock, no more than two kilometers across, would be floating between us and the third ship. By the time this ship flew out from behind the daughter rock, we hoped to be over the horizon of Hilda again, and out of sight of all three of them.

We watched the screen. I looked over at Davydov. He stared impassively at the display, a quizzical, resigned look on his face.

The third ship came over Hilda's horizon, behind the daughter rock. Davydov leaned forward. "Station Three, draw us toward you," he said into the mike, overriding the program. He waved aside Ilene's protest. "We've got some room to spare on that side," he said. He concentrated on the screen. "Simon, tell us when you see them," he said into the mike. I thought of Simon, prone on the surface—

"He says he sees them," came his observer's voice.

"Pull to Station One, as fast as you can," Davydov said.

The little blip of the third ship crawled to the line demarcating the daughter rock, and there it sat, on the line—on our horizon, its detecting instruments just above or below it, who could say? "Pull," Davydov whispered to himself, "*pull.*" I thought, alarm bells could be going off. . . .

After no more than two minutes, the dot marking the third ship slipped back down under the rock's horizon, and then behind Hilda again. Now Hilda protected us from all three of them.

But we might have been visible, there, for those two minutes.

Simon kept sending us positions, and everyone on the bridge listened with consuming interest.

"They're not slowing," Swann ventured.

. . . And so they bombed on by, three police ships of my lawful government. I felt as happy as the others acted, and proud of myself. Although, really, they could have caught us in that minute on the horizon. So it hadn't been that great a plan. But it had worked.

It had been five hours since the first sighting of them—five very long hours, during which I had had little to do but contemplate my life and its potential ending . . . the kind of dense thinking that is shorthanded by, "my whole life passed before my eyes." A tornado of the mind. I was tired.

"We'll stay behind Hilda for a day or so," Davydov said. "Then back to work." He heaved out a breath, grinned at us. "Time to get out of here."

When the relieved celebration was over, and I had calmed down, I went into my room and fell into a deep sleep. Just before I woke up, I had a vivid dream:

I was a child, on Mars, and we were playing hide-and-seek, as we often did. We were at the station on Syrtis Major, on one of those broad desert plains that are strewn with boulders—boulders from the size of basketballs up to the size of a small room, all scattered across the plain in a regular pattern that used to baffle our elders. "There's no way such even distribution could be natural," my father would say, sitting on one of the rocks and staring out at the nearby horizon. "It looks like a stage set."

But to us children it was perfectly natural. And in the late afternoons, after dinner, we would play hide-and-seek. In my dream it was near sunset, one of the dust sunsets, when you could look straight at the little red sun, and the sky was ribbed with pink bands of dust, and the rust-colored plain was marked by long black shadows, one for each rock. I was hiding behind a spherical boulder about waist-high, crouched down, watching the other kids make their dashes for home base. Home base was a long way away. I could see the wind, picking up swirls of sand, but in my suit I couldn't feel it. There were giggles and quick breathing on the radio band, which was turned down so that the sounds were all very quiet. My mike was turned off. The person who was it gave up; there were too many boulders, too many shadows. "Olly olly oxen, free free free," she called; singing the phrase in a quavering voice. "Olly olly oxen, free free free."

But I couldn't come in. There was another it, something I didn't recognize, a tall dark thing like one of the long black shadows come alive. It was nearly sunset, the ruby sun was touching the old crater wall to the west. I was hiding in earnest. I could just dare to put one eye over the rock, to see the dark shape move around, looking behind one rock after the other. Where was home base? The radio transmitter hissed. No one called. The dark thing that was it was moving toward my hiding place, checking boulder after boulder. The shadow of the crater wall was stretching across the plain, blacking out everywhere. . . .

I shifted against the bed, half woke for a moment. Then my father had me by the hand. We were free of suits, under the dome. I was younger, about seven. We were walking across the baseball diamond. Dad had our gloves and the ball, one of the kids' softballs that wouldn't go very far when you hit it. "When I was your age and played baseball," Dad told me, "the field was about the same size as this one."

"This one's little."

"On Mars it is. But on Earth even the grown-up balls wouldn't go very far when you hit them."

"Because of gravity." Whatever that meant.

"Right. The Earth pulls harder." He gave me my glove and I stood behind home plate. He stood on the pitcher's mound and we threw the ball back and forth. "That pitcher really got you yesterday."

"Yeah. Right on my kneecap."

Dad grinned. "I saw how you hung in there the next time you got up. I like that." He caught and threw. "But why did you try to steal third when you had just been hit on the knee?"

"I don't know."

"You were out by a mile." He fielded a low one. "And Sandy had just bunted and got out to get you to second. And once you're on second you're in scoring position."

"I know," I said. "I just took off when I got a good lead."

"You sure did." Dad was grinning, he threw a hard one at me. "That's my Emma. You're awful fast. You could probably steal third, if you worked hard enough. Sure. We work hard at it, you could be a real speedster. . . ."

And then I was running, across the open desert, the hard-baked oxidized sand of south Syrtis. In my dream the broad plain was like the Lazuli Canyon, filled with breathable air. I ran barefoot, in my gym shorts and shirt. In Mars's gentle grasp I bounded forward, arms making a sort of swimming motion, as my father had taught me. No one had really worked on running in Martian gravity; I was working it out for myself, with Dad's help. I was in some sort of race, far ahead of the others, pushing off the warm gritty sand with great shoves of my thighs; feeling the thin chill air rush by. I could hear my father's voice: "Run, Emma, run!" And I ran across that red plain, free and powerful, faster and faster, feeling like I could run over the horizon before me and on forever, all the way around the planet.

Nadezhda and Marie-Anne woke me coming through the door, talking of excess biomass. My heart was thumping, my skin was damp. In my mind I still heard my father's voice. "Run!"

* * *

They began working incessantly to complete the starship. Nadezhda and Marie-Anne stayed up to all hours in our room, poring over programs and program results. It was laughable, really, for having missed them the Committee police weren't likely to pass that way again. Nevertheless they hurried, and my roommates grew more and more serious as days passed.

". . . Degree of closure of any substance is established by its rate of consumption in the system, $E$, and the rate of flow in incomplete closure, $e$," Nadezhda would mutter, as if praying, glancing balefully at me as I refused to work with them for more than several hours a day. The lights focused on the little desk, Marie-Anne hunched over the computer screen, copying down figures. . . . "The substance's closure coefficient $K$ is determined by $K$ equals I minus $e$ over $E$. . . ."

And closure for the whole system was a complex compilation of the degrees of closure for all the substances being recycled. But they could not get that master coefficient high enough, do what they might. I tried hard to figure out something myself. But perfect closure is not natural, it does not exist anywhere, except perhaps in the universe as a whole. Even there, no doubt each big bang is a little bit smaller. . . . In the starship, the leaks would be in waste recycling. They couldn't deal with the accumulation of chlorides, or the accumulation of humic matter in the algal reactors. And they wouldn't be able to completely recycle corpses, neither animal nor human. Certain minerals . . . if only they could be re-introduced into the system, made useful to something which would transform them into something back in the mainstream of the cycle. . . . So we worked, for hours and hours, mutating and testing bacteria, juggling the physiochemical processes, trying to make a tail-in-mouth snake that would roll across the galaxy.

One night when they were gone I typed out the full program and filled in estimated figures of my own, to find the point where the accumulations would imbalance the system enough to break it down. I got about seventy years.

It was an impressive achievement, given what they were given, but the universe is a big place, and they needed to do better.

One day while thinking about this problem of closure, a week or more after the fly-by, Andrew Duggins, Al Nordhoff, and Valenski stopped me in the hall. Duggins looked fat and unhealthy, as if the situation were taking its toll on him.

"We hear that you helped the mutineers evade a Committee police fleet that came near here," he accused.

"Who told you that?" I said.

"It's the talk of the ship," he said angrily.

"Among whom?" I asked.

"That doesn't matter," Valenski said in his clipped, accented English. "The question is, did Committee police pass us by while we three were incarcerated last Friday?"

"Yes, they did."

"And you were instrumental in making the plans to hide from them?"

I considered it. Well, I had done it. And I wanted to be known for what I was. I stared Valenski in the eye. "You could say that, yes." A strange feeling, to be in the open—

"You helped them escape capture!" Duggins burst out. "We could have been free by now!"

"I doubt it," I said. "These people would have resisted. The police would have blown us all to dust. I saved your lives, probably."

"The point is," said Valenski, "you aided the mutineers."

"You've been helping them all along," Duggins said. The animosity flowing from him was almost tangible, and I couldn't understand it. "Your part in the attack on the radio room was a sham, wasn't it? Designed to get you into our confidence. It was you who told them about our plans, and now you're *helping* them."

I refrained from pointing out the lack of logic in his indictment. As I said, paranoia on spaceships is common. "What do you think, Al?" I said flippantly.

"I think you're a traitor," quiet Al Nordhoff said, and I felt it.

"When we return to Mars," Valenski pronounced, "your behavior will have to be reported. And you will have no part in commanding the return flight. If you return."

"I'm going back to Mars," I said firmly, still shaken by Al's words.

"Are you?" Duggins sneered. "Are you sure you're going to be able to jump out of Oleg Davydov's bed when the time comes?"

"Andrew," I heard Al protest; by that time I was taking an alternative route to the dining commons, walking fast, *rip rip rip*.

"Damned treacherous *woman,*" Duggins shouted after me. His two companions were remonstrating with him as I turned a corner and hurried out of earshot.

Upset by this confrontation, aware of the pressures that were steadily mounting on me from all sides (when would I be compressed to a new substance, I wondered?), I wandered through the complex of lounges outside the dining area. The autumn colors were getting closer to winter: torpid browns, more silver and white. In the tapestry gallery, among the complicated wall hangings, there was a bulletin screen filled with messages and games and jokes. I stopped before it, and a sentence struck my eye. "Only under the stresses of total social emergencies do the effectively adequate alternative technical strategies synergetically emerge." Jeez, I thought, what prose artist penned that? I looked down—the ascription was to one Buckminster Fuller. The quote continued: "Here we witness mind over matter and humanity's escape from the limitations of his identity with some circumscribed geographical locality." That was for sure.

Part of the bulletin screen was reserved for suggestions for the name of the starship. Anyone could pick his color and typeface, and tap a name onto the space on the screen. It was getting crowded. Most of them were dull: *First, One, The Starship.* Others were better. There were classical allusions, of course: *The Ark, Santa Maria, Kon-Tiki III, Because It's There.* The names of the two halves of the ship had been joined—*Lerdalgo, Himontov*—I doubted they would be chosen. In the center of the screen was the suggestion rumored to be Davydov's: *Anicarus.* I liked that one. Also *Transplutonia,* which sounded like the Vampires of Outer Space. About a third of the names were in the Cyrillic alphabet, which I can barely transliterate. And the names would have been Russian, anyway. They all looked good, though.

Looking at the names I thought about all that had happened, about Davydov, Swann and Breton, Duggins and Valenski. I would be in trouble if I returned to Mars . . . if I returned? *When* I returned! Seized by undirected danger, I was suddenly inspired to add a name to the screen. In the biggest letters available, in orange, just below Davydov's suggestion, I typed out THE SHIP OF FOOLS. The ship of fools. How perfect. We would make an illustration for the allegory, with me large among the foreground characters. It made me laugh, and feeling better, though I knew that was illogical, I went to eat.

But the next day the feeling of pressure returned. I felt like a chunk of chondrite being transformed to Chantonnay. My life's course had been bent by this event, and there was no way to straighten it out; all my choices lay in a new direction, where eventual disaster seemed more and more likely. This sense of pressure became unbearable, and I went to the centrifuge to run. It felt good to get in the gravity and run like a hamster in a wheel, like a creature without choices.

So I was running. The floor of the centrifuge was made of curved wooden planking, the walls and ceiling were white, dotted by numbered red circles to tell runners where they were. There were unmarked, informal lanes—slow to the right, fast to the left. Usually I just went to the left wall and started running, looking at the planks as they passed under me.

This time I heard the thump of feet directly behind me, and I moved over, thinking, stupid sprinters. It was Davydov. He drew even with me.

"Mind if I run with you?"

I shook my head, although I don't like running with others. We ran side by side for a few revolutions.

"Do you always run this fast?" he said.

Now when I run, I am doing a middle-distance workout, and the point is to get up to about ninety percent maximum pulse rate and keep it there for up to twenty or thirty minutes. It is working to the limit. When Davydov asked me this question I had been going for almost half an hour, and I was about to collapse. Nevertheless, I said, "Or faster."

He grunted. We ran on. His breathing quickened.

"You about ready to take off?" I asked.

"Yeah. A few days. I think."

"Going to make closure?"

He glanced at me briefly; he knew that I knew that they weren't. Then he looked back at the floor, thinking about it.

"No," he said. A few strides. "Water loss. Waste build-up. Not enough fuel."

"How long can you go?"

"Eighty. Eighty years."

I smiled for a moment, pleased with the accuracy of my own calculations. They should have had me from the start, I thought. I said, "Doesn't that worry you?"

Again he watched the floor. We took quite a few strides, nearly circled the run.

"Yes," he expelled suddenly. A slight stumble to mark the admission. "Yes, I'm worried." Several strides. "I've got to. Stop now. Join me? In game room?"

"In a few minutes." He slowed abruptly and dropped back to the right. I waved a hand without turning and started to run freely again, thinking about the look on his face and the sense of release when he said yes, I'm worried.

After six thousand meters I climbed up to the hub and got out of the centrifuge, took a quick sponge bath. I walked down to the game room, feeling much better, tired and strong in the no-gee.

Davydov was over in an isolated corner of the game room, sitting at a table for two, staring out the tiny port in the wall beside him. It seemed that the seasons were accelerating aboard our ship, for the room was walled in somber tones, brown and thunderhead blue and silver. I sat down beside him and we stared at the little square of stars. He got me a bulb of milk. His big dark face was lined with concern, and he didn't meet my gaze.

"Eighty years isn't very long," I observed.

"No. It could be enough, if we're lucky."

"But it isn't as much as you had hoped for."

"No." His mouth was set. "Not at all."

"What will you do?"

He didn't answer. He took sips from his bulb, pulled at his

rough face. I had never seen such an expression of uncertainty on his face before. I thought of it. He had committed much of his long life to the idea of the starship and its voyage. Suddenly the idea was realized!—and it was not as perfect as the idea had been; thus more dangerous. And he was filled with doubts. He now saw that he could be leading people to death; I saw it in his expression. That transition, from idea to reality, had had its usual effect on him—it had clarified the possibility of failure, heightened his sense of danger, frightened him.

"You could just take it back," I said. "You could fly it into an Earth orbit and tell the Terrans what you've done and why. You could advocate a real starship. The Committee wouldn't dare attack you in Earth space."

He was shaking his head. "They wouldn't have to. The American and Soviet military would do it for them. Board us and take us down and ask the Committee what they'd like done with us."

"Not if the Committee's been overthrown by this revolt you've told me about."

"I doubt that will happen. The Committee controls too much, and they have the Earth powers behind them."

"Well, you've got eighty years—you could play hide-and-seek in the system, radio Earth and Mars and tell them about yourselves, avoid capture until you become a *cause célèbre* and no one will dare harm you—"

Again he was shaking his head. "They'd just hunt us down. That isn't what we did all this for."

"But eighty years isn't long enough for interstellar flight!"

"Yes, yes it is—"

"Oleg," I said. "You can't say it's enough just because it might be enough to get you to one of the nearest stars. You're going to have to search for a habitable planet, and eighty years isn't enough time for that."

He stared out the window, took several sips from his bulb. "But during that time," he said, "we'll improve the life-support system. And that will give us more time."

"I don't know how you can say that."

"We've got a lot of equipment and parts with us, and one of the finest system-design teams ever assembled. If they're good enough, then we'll have all the time we'll need."

I stared at him. "That's a big if."

He nodded, the worried expression still on his face. "I know it is. I just have to hope that the systems team is the best one it could possibly be."

We sat in silence for a while longer, and then Ilene's voice called Davydov back to some business or other, and I was left to brood over the meaning of that last statement of his. It wasn't all that obscure, and I gritted my teeth as I felt the pressure mount.

Later that day, still feeling the slow progress of compression and transformation, I ate dinner with Swann. He was in an excellent mood, and talked at length about improvements made in the R and G of the starship. They were going to have to switch from acceleration to deceleration quite a few times, and now they would be able to do it using less fuel.

"What's with you?" he asked, when he noticed how much of the conversation he was supplying.

"How are you going to get out of the solar system?" I replied. "Without the Committee police seeing your exhaust?"

"We're going to keep something between us and them the whole time our rockets are firing. At first we'll have the sun between us and Mars, then we'll shut down until we meet with Saturn. Orbit it for a while, then coast out to Pluto." He looked at me oddly. "That's only a few open bursts. But you'll keep this all a secret?"

"Unless they drag it out of me," I said morosely. "Or drug it out of me. You'd probably better not tell me any more."

"What's this?"

"Duggins and Valenski plan to tell the Committee that I collaborted with you. I may end up on Amor, for all I know."

"Oh my. Oh, Emma—you'll have to deny their accusations. Most of the people returning will support you."

"Maybe. It's going to be a mess."

"Here. I'm going to get a liter of wine." They made a good white wine on *Rust Eagle*, with only a few vines. While he got it I

tried to remember whether the starship would have any grape-
vines. No. Too much waste.

I proceeded to drink most of the wine, without responding
much to Swann's conversation. After dinner we went down to our
rooms. In front of my door Eric kissed me, and almost angrily I
kissed back, hard. Drunk.... "Let's go to my room," he said, and
I agreed, surprising myself. We went, and it never occurred to me,
then, to wonder if this was exactly the man I had in mind to go to
bed with.... In his room we turned off the lights and undressed
as we floated about kissing. Making love was the usual clumsy,
pleasant affair in the weightlessness—holding onto the bed, moving slowly at unfortunate moments, using the velcro straps. I lost
myself in the sensations, marveling once again at how open lovers
become to one another. I felt a surge of affection for this friend of
mine, this cheerful and gentle man, this crazy exile fleeing from
humanity. How to think of him? What was he fleeing, after all, but
the turmoil and repression on Mars, the absolute madness of
Earth, our home world, our home—fleeing all the hatred and war.
If only they all understood, that everyone is as human as your lover
is.... Maybe on the starship they would remember it, I thought
disconsolately.

"Emma," he said, as we floated quietly in our embrace.
"Emma?"

"Yes?"

"Please come with us."

"... Oh, Eric."

"Please, Emma. We need you. It'll be a good life, one of the
great human lives. And I want you along. It will make all the difference for me—"

"Eric," I said.

"Yes?"

"I want to live on Mars. That's my home."

"But—" He stopped, sighed.

We floated, and for once the weightlessness felt like gravity,
gravity pressing from every direction. Tears leaked out of my eyes.

This was my chance to join humanity's greatest voyage. I
wished I hadn't drunk so much. "I want to go back to my room,"

I whispered. I switched on the desk lamp, retrieved my clothes from the air, avoided Eric's sad gaze. I kissed him before I left.

"Think about it?" he said.

"Oh I will," I said. "I will. . . ."

In the last few days they gutted the *Rust Eagle*, leaving it just able to get home. Nadezhda and Marie-Anne looked haggard. One day I helped them get their belongings together, as they were moving to the starship. Marie-Anne dabbed at her eyes and embraced me and the three of us stood there, a triad of sane femininity in a crazy world . . . but they left.

The bare empty room was very oppressive. I left it and floated through the ship, disdaining the velcro-and-balance routine, making lazy fingertip-turns to negotiate the frequent bends. I flew as if in a dream, touring the ship, refusing to acknowledge the few people I passed. It was night-time, the halls were dimmed to nothing but guidance lights. Occasional clumps of people sat in the lounges, talking softly, drink bulbs hovering over them like *djinn*-jars. They didn't look up as I passed.

Through the quiet living quarters (in open doors people packed their goods to cross to the starship), up to the huge, dark bays at the top, amongst the mining equipment that was left, the waldoes like monsters or sad mangled robots, half seen in the shadows they cast. Down the long jump tube back to the power station, where it was bright, humming, empty. And then back up the tube to the bridge, where I stood before the broad window and looked across at the thing.

Well, I thought, there it is. I could go on the first flight to the stars. I felt that it somehow should have been more momentous, an invitation filled with ceremony: interviews by large committees, batteries of tests, acceptance by videogram, the attention of two worlds. Instead, two old miners fused by insubordinate friends— and me invited by these friends, including two men I had cared about for years. It didn't seem right. I recalled all the stories in literature about interstellar flight, all the deranged, degenerate, incestuous little societies. Yet this expedition, its members living through and beyond the voyage, would not turn out like that. Or would it? Maybe the dream of the savannah would drive them mad. Suddenly I was acutely conscious of the fact that I was in a little bulb of air like an extended spacesuit—I was in a submarine, millions of fathoms deep in a vacuum ocean.

No, I could not go with them. They might be able to do it—if I went, Nadezhda and I could keep that life-support system working, surely—but I could not go. I needed to be able to walk on ground, bare Mars ground.

The vision of the books struck me again, and I saw the double ship floating out there empty, light years away, the skeleton of a failed idea.

I could prevent them from leaving. The thought made me glance furtively at the silent figures sitting at the ship's controls. They ignored me.

I couldn't do anything to the starship. But if I disabled *Rust Eagle*, they would be forced to—to what? They wouldn't kill us, and so perhaps all would be saved. . . . There were key codes in Davydov's cabin, that would open the cocks in the deuterium holds.

Without really thinking about it I drifted out of the bridge, and, still floating about like a disembodied spirit, I came to Davydov's room off in a corner bend of the upper hall. The door was about a quarter open. It was light inside.

I tapped the door, holding the jamb beside it for support. No reply. I stuck my head in and looked around. Empty? A single desk lamp lit the room. I was about to put my feet to the velcro strip on the floor, but thought better of it—too noisy. I pushed the door open a little farther and slipped in.

He was asleep. He had put two chairs together, and was draped across them head and shoulders on one, knees on the other. His mouth hung open, and he breathed easily. Under the lamp I noticed that his hair had the same kinked texture as the velcro carpet below him.

For a long time I coasted through the air, watching his dark face, darker still in the shadows. He looked so ordinary.

On the desk, in the lamp's gleam under a clamp, were a few scattered papers. I was already intruding; I tiptoed off a wall and floated over to look at them.

They were diagrams, several versions of the same thing. Under one sheet lay a compass and straight-edge. The diagrams were all circular, or near it: constructions made with several arcs of the compass, that resulted in circles flattened slightly on one side. Around this faint circumference were little rectangles, set at different angles, blackened by pencil. I looked at a faint scrawl, written under a long series of numbers. *"Something to leave a mark on the world, something to show we were here at all—"* The penciling was smeared, as if by the back of a hand. The final dash trailed off across the page.

I stared at the little black rectangles for a long time, looking over at Davydov once or twice. Plans for a monument to themselves, to a group leaving all that humans knew and shared together. "Something to show we were here at all. . . ." Floating in the dark room, no sound but the airy *hooooooo* of the vents, the desolation began to fill me, the vacuum. We all will die. It was the first time in my life I had had that thought and truly believed it. The postponements we have devised make it easy not to think of, for it might be a millennium away. But it will come. The diagrams below me seemed like circles of gravestones. Designs for a tomb. That's how we show we were here; that's all we can do.

I floated over the sleeping man, stretched out horizontally above him. Even the exile wants to be remembered. This poor ragged group, with their stupid dream . . . I wished I were a succubus, and could possess him without his full awakening, without his becoming conscious and human. He breathed on. With a convulsive shudder I drifted away, touched off a wall to the door, slipped out and down the hall, my plan to disable the *Eagle* abandoned. It was not my part to interfere with anyone else's method of dying, or of leaving their mark before.

Soon they all would be gone.

Back in my room I drifted off into a troubled sleep. Once I half woke and found myself wedged in a corner, lying upright beside the bed. I groped about until my hand hit a velcro strap, stuck it against the stick-strips on either side of me, and fell asleep again. It was that sort of sleep in which you wake every hour and think to yourself that you have not been sleeping at all; you can remember dreams that are like reflections, daytime thinking slightly warped. I slept and slept, sleepfloated down to the toilet and back, slept yet again. I didn't want to wake up. I was tired.

Many hours later I was awakened by a knock on the door. I burst out of my velcro strapping, landed on the far wall. I collected myself and answered the door.

It was Davydov. I blinked, confusing this moment with the last time I had seen him. Still dreaming.

"We'd like everybody to come over to the starship for a final meeting. It'll be in a couple of hours."

"Is it time?"

He nodded. "Would you like to go over there with me? I'm crossing in a little while."

"Uh. Sure. Let me get myself together."

After I had cleaned up I joined him in the boat bay, and we crossed the space separating the two ships. The starship looked the same, a work in progress.

*Lermontov* was emptier than I remembered. Davydov took me through the rough tunnel of the lock-tube connecting the two ships, and showed me the living quarters of *Hidalgo*: walls had been knocked out, and all of the bedrooms were twice as big as before. The hospital had been extended, mostly for storage space. We passed stacks of plastic boxes, one nearly blocking a hallway. "Still moving in," Davydov said. He seemed full of quiet pride, the captain of a bright new spaceship, all of his doubts vanished in the night while mine had accumulated.

"I'm tired," I complained.

We returned to the bridge of *Lermontov*. There was still some time before the meeting. After that, those of us returning would cross to *Rust Eagle*. It was time for the parting.

They were going to leave *Rust Eagle* one boat, and just enough fuel to accelerate to about fifty km/sec and decelerate again—that meant a weightless coast around the sun, for most of the return, in fact. I cursed when Davydov told me that. So sick of no-gee!

"I'm sorry about what we've done to you," he said from the window. "All the impositions—the danger we've put you in."

"Eh," I said.

He stayed with his back to me. "Everything should be calm by the time you get back."

"Hope so." I didn't want to think of it. We deserved to return to calmness.

"I'm sorry you're not coming with us, Emma."

That woke me up. I looked at his back. "Why is that?"

"You . . . were the last outsider. And I hadn't talked with any outsiders for years—not really talked, I mean. If . . . if you had decided to join us, it would have meant a lot to me."

"You wouldn't have to feel guilty about sending me back to whatever's happening on Mars," I said cruelly.

"Yes, yes," he said. "I suppose that's true. And—and I wouldn't have to consider what happened between us so long ago finished. . . ." Finally he turned and faced me, rip-ripped over to me. "I would have enjoyed your company," he said slowly.

"And if I were going," I said, "I would have enjoyed your company too. But I'm not going." I clung to that.

"I know." He looked away, searching for words, it seemed. "Your approval has become important to me."

Wearily I said, "Not all that important." Which was true.

He winced. I watched his mouth tighten unhappily. Somewhere in me a tide turned, my mood began to lighten. After a long silence I stood up carefully (I had been leaning on the navigator's chair, I noticed), approached him, reached up on tiptoe (hand on his shoulder) and kissed him, lightly on the lips. A thousand phrases jammed on my tongue. "I like you, Oleg Davydov," I said inadequately. I stepped away as he reached for me. "Come on, let's go down to that soccer field. The meeting can't start without you." I led the way to the door, quite certain that I didn't want the conversation to continue any longer.

At the doorway he stopped me, and without a word pulled me into his arms, into one of those big Russian bear hugs that let you know that you are not the only consciousness in the world, because of the intensity of the flesh. I hugged back, remembering when we were young. Then we pulled our way down the jump tube to the enlarged recreation field. . . . And so we parted.

There was a final meeting in the big space they had cleared in the *Lermontov*, a meeting strange and tentative. To each group there the other was dying. I felt as if miles of plasteel separated me from everyone else. Then they were all milling about, saying good-bye. It all happened very quickly. I felt very tired. Nadezhda and Marie-Anne found me and hugged me. I moved with the others toward the corridor leading to the boat bay, saying "Good-bye . . . farewell . . . good-bye." Then Eric was standing before me, holding me. Davydov was at his side. They looked at each other. Davydov said, "She's what you leave behind, eh?" Then he took my arm, led me to the corridor. "Good-bye!" Eric called. "Yes," I mumbled. Then we were in the boat bay.

"Good-bye, Emma," Davydov said. "Thank you for your help."

"Don't run into anything," I said, my voice tight.

He shook his head.

"Good-bye, Oleg Davydov." I could hardly say it.

He turned and walked out of the bay. I got on the boat and we shot out into space, back to *Rust Eagle* where we began. Once there the new crew members looked at each other. Three MSA members who had decided to return; ten or a dozen people bitterly opposed to the starship effort, clustered around Valenski and Duggins; and another dozen people who had not cared, or who had helped the effort. We moved to the bridge by unspoken consent. I went to the window and looked at the starship again. The sun was behind us, and for a second our shadow crossed over the double ship.

I stood inside the window, watching. I couldn't think—every thought I had short-circuited and died.

The starship moved forward. Helplessly I moved along the window with it, watching with the others as it receded, angling away: first a bright belt, then a necklace, a bracelet, a ring, and lastly a silver jewel, that diminished and diminished and disappeared.

All that was left was to go home, home to the red planet. At the thought, over everything else, I felt immense relief.

Since then we have all taken on the various tasks we are capable of, and I, in the privacy of my empty room, have written this record—

an attempt to save, for the Emma of the following centuries, some account of these months.

Without a doubt this is the strangest crew *Rust Eagle* has ever carried. Ethel Jurgenson, Yuri Kopanev and I have taken over the work on the bridge, which is mostly monitoring at this point. Valenski in turn monitors us, walking about the bridge like a teacher during a test. Ginger Sims and Amy Van Danke and Nikos Micora, one of the MSA people who decided to return (very quiet he is), are taking care of the farm, with the help of three or four others, including Al Nordhoff. They report to me, but Valenski insists on being present all the time we are working.

Despite this suspicious atmosphere, the relations between the various factions aboard are better than they were at first. About four days into our return Yuri and Duggins started a fight in the dining commons; they had to be pulled apart by Sandra and several others. The two principals were pretty well bruised, Duggins from flying backwards over a table, a wonderful sight to my eyes. For a couple of days we were like two armed camps. Eventually I went to Valenski's room to talk. "You mind your own business and we'll mind ours. Everybody just do their job. When we get back to Mars they'll take the ship into custody and we can all say what we like."

"Fine with me," he said. "It's you who'll be in trouble then, not me."

True enough, perhaps. But since then things have been relatively calm. In our private meetings Yuri suggested taking over the ship and going to Earth, but the idea was rejected. First of all, no one wanted to risk a violent confrontation with the loyalists. But more importantly, I think, no one was willing to face the idea of going to Earth. With its wars, its hungry billions, its gravity—we all instinctively felt that nothing on Mars could be as bad. Besides, as Sandra pointed out, Earth is no more than the home of the Committee's bosses, and so not much of an asylum.

So we coast toward Mars and wait. I have spent these days like a somnambulist, my mind existing in the past months as I wrote this record, or wandering toward Saturn with the starship and its crew, my friends. At first I was helpless to control this behavior, and I floated through *Rust Eagle* without responding to my mates. Later I cultivated it as a sort of act, as I noticed that it tended to subdue everyone else aboard.

We have no transmitter, so we have listened mutely to what we can hear on the receiver. There isn't much. Clearly the trouble has continued on Mars, and that makes it hard—not knowing what we are returning to.

But it won't be much longer until we know. I have filled up the weeks with this record, inadequate though it certainly is, for who can translate the amazing bombardment of experience into words? Yet it has passed the time. Deceleration starts today, bringing the blessed attraction to the floor. And soon we will be back in Mars space. If I can I will continue penning away in this little notebook, to give it a sort of ending. But I fear they will throw us all in jail.

It was the rebels who met us.

I'll never forget the look on Andrew Duggins' face. Reality had betrayed him; the brave were springing up everywhere, even on his home ground where he might least expect it, and he couldn't escape them.

And yet I am sure that several of us collaborators were not much less dismayed to be received by anti-Committee forces.

Well, this is how it happened. They met us just outside the orbit of Amor, in one of those little police craft that are used to patrol the space around Phobos and Deimos, and to take prisoners up to Amor. As I stared out the bridge window at the red crescent of the planet, wondering if I would set foot on it again, they hurried out of the jump tube—about ten tense-looking men and women, dressed in working one-pieces. They pointed long-nosed weapons at us, hot light guns, and for a long adrenaline-filled moment I thought they were removing all the witnesses to the mutiny. . . .

"Is this *Rust Eagle?*" asked a blond-haired man, for we had been unable to respond to their angry questions by radio.

"Yes," two or three of us replied.

The man nodded. "We are the Texan cell of the Washington-Lenin Alliance. You have been liberated—" He smiled, at our expressions I suppose. "And we are taking you as quickly as we can to New Houston, a free city."

That was when Duggins looked as if the world had turned upside down. Ethel and I looked at each other open-mouthed—Yuri held us both in a hug, moving slowly in front of the guns. It was he who began to explain us to the blond man, but he hadn't got far before we were ushered to the boat bay, to transfer to the police craft. There we were separated into smaller groups and interviewed by a pair of the rebels. Soon I was led to a room containing the blond man and a woman about my age.

"You're Emma Weil?"

I told them I was. They asked me some questions about the MSA and their adventures, and I confirmed the story that Yuri and the others had told.

"So there has been a revolution?" I said. "And the Committee overthrown?"

They were both shaking their heads. "The battle is still on," said the woman, whose name was Susan Jones.

The blond man was her brother. "Actually," he said, "we aren't doing so well." He stood. "At first the uprising was planet-wide, but now—we still hold Texas—"

"Of course," I said, and they grinned.

"And the Soviet sector. There's still fighting in Mobil and the Atlantic, and in the tunnels on Phobos. But everywhere else, the Committee troops have regained control."

"Royal Dutch?" I asked, my windpipe suddenly constricted.

They shook their heads. "Committee."

"Has it been very violent?"

Susan Jones said firmly, "A lot of people have been killed."

Her brother said, "They broke the dome at Hellas. Killed a lot of people inside."

"They couldn't have!" I cried. Hellas . . .

"They did. They don't care how many people they kill. There's always more on Earth to take their places."

"They're careful of property, though," Susan said bitterly. "That's to our advantage. Otherwise I have no doubt they would have destroyed New Houston outright by now."

"It sounds like you're losing," I said.

They didn't contradict me.

Suddenly the gravity shifted up, and we became heavier. Heavier still.

"But I'm with you," I said, without planning to. "I'm with you if you'll have me."

They both nodded. "We'll have you," Andrew Jones said. "We're going to need life-support people, one way or another."

The gee diminished to the familiar pressure of Mars. A minute later there was a gentle bump-and-rock. I was home again.

So I joined the revolution.

When we had been settled in the apartment the revolutionaries were using for their command post—it's in the Dallas district, the industrial section of town near the air and water facilities, under the rim of New Houston's crater—I asked Susan Jones what they were doing with Duggins, Valenski, and their group.

She smiled. "We explained the situation to them, and gave them their choice—join us, or be detained. We told them the truth about the Committee, explained Amor to them. We told them that if any of them joined us and then did anything anti-revolutionary, we'd shoot them."

"And?"

"Not all of them have decided yet. Most who have decided have chosen to be detained."

"That Al Nordhoff is a good man—"

"He chose detention."

Of course. And all of us who helped build the starship have chosen to join the revolution. No surprise, although I still have the feeling some of us might have preferred to be met by the Committee. (Am I one of those?)

We were taken to a short meeting with the revolutionary command here—a different sort of committee, a smelly and disheveled group of about twenty-five. They looked like my farm crew used to look after a hard day's work. Or worse. Susan Jones told them what she knew of our adventure, and the story of our rescue—or whatever it was. We answered some questions. They looked pleased to see us; here was an anti-Committee project that had succeeded. I became very tired. It had been a long time since I had last slept. Finally they led us back to our rooms, and I fell asleep the moment I hit the bed.

Today they want us to rest. Andrew Jones says some of them want to talk to us again. I've taken the opportunity to get down the story of our arrival. Now, again, I'm going to sleep. The Martian gravity I love feels pretty heavy these days.

I talked to Andrew Jones this afternoon. He told me that the revolution began all at once, in every major city on the planet. The entire Soviet space fleet rebelled and pearl-harbored the rest of the Committee's spaceships, with devastating success. "That's why we were able to go up there and intercept you. We still have partial control of Marsspace." The railroad tracks connecting the cities were sabotaged, especially at bridges and other problem points. Air and water buildings in every city were stormed, as were some of the police barracks. These last attacks had uneven success. There were as many police as rebels, so it had been a pitched battle from the start. Fighting in the streets, in every city. . . . "The U.S. and U.S.S.R. have sent reinforcements to the Committee," Andrew finished. "They've arrived recently. A few big spaceships, really long-distance killers, and some advanced weapons. Personnel killers."

"They must not be too worried about you," I said, "if they're still trying to save the buildings and facilities."

"I know," Andrew said, discouraged and bitter. "They think they can just kill us and walk back into their property."

"And you've lost contact with a lot of rebel-held cities?"

"You bet." He became grimly cheerful. "They've retaken most of the sectors, like I told you. They drop in on the air and water buildings and blast the people there—if there's still resistance in the city, they take away the air. A lot of buildings are self-contained, but that's just mopping up. These cities"—he grimaced—"they're too centralized. Some of the rebel cells have set up underground retreats in the chaos. We hope they made it out to them."

"What about the general population?"

"Most of them fought for us. At first. That's why we did so well."

"A lot of people must be dead."

"Yes."

Thousands of people dead. Killed. People who would have lived a thousand years. My father—jail may have protected him, but on the other hand, he may be dead. And my turn may be coming.

They asked me to make a small speech for the rebels in New Houston, which they would then transmit to the other rebel outposts. "When the revolt began," Susan Jones told me, "the MSA members still here joined the fight, and they told everyone about the starship effort. It's been a big story, people are very interested and excited about it. To hear you announce that the starship has taken off would be good for morale."

They're in bad shape, I thought to myself. But I got the dozen of us who had helped Davydov's people to sit with me at another meeting in the lounge of the command building. The same group, slightly larger and slightly more exhausted, was gathered there. A couple of video cameras were trained on us, and I was given a mike. I said,

"The Mars Starship Association was part of the revolution. They worked isolated from the main effort, and have existed for the last forty years." I told them what I knew of the Association's history, aware as I spoke of the strangeness of the fact that it was *me* telling them this story. I described the starship and its capabilities, and events from the previous two months flashed in my mind, disturbing my concentration. "When I left Mars on *Rust Eagle* I didn't know there was an MSA. I didn't know there was an underground movement dedicated to the overthrow of the Committee. I did know that—I did know . . ."—suddenly it was hard to talk—"that I hated the Committee and its control over our lives. When I found out about the MSA, sort of by accident out there"—a sympathetic laugh—"I helped it. So did my friends sitting up here with me. Now that we're here, we want to help you, too. I'm glad—I'm glad that the Mars Development Committee wasn't here to greet us." I paused to catch my breath properly. "I hope they never rule Mars again."

And at that they stood up and cheered. Clapped and cheered. But I hadn't been finished! I had wanted to say, Listen, there is a starship leaving the solar system! I wanted to say that out of all our petty and stupid and destructive squabbles on this planet, a pure, feeble effort had struggled away—that the revolution had been responsible for it, partially, and that it was a historical event to stun the imagination. . . .

But I never got to say any of that. My friends from *Rust Eagle* crowded around me, familiar faces all, filled with affection, and my speech was over. We looked at each other with a new tenderness— now, and perhaps from now on, we were each other's only family. Noah's cousins, left behind.

Not much time left. The city has been broached by police troops, and we'll be evacuating soon.

I was up on the crater's rim with Andrew Jones when the missiles started falling on the spaceport to the north of the city crater. The explosions were bright enough to leave blue after-images in our eyes, and they lofted tall, lazy clouds of rusty dust above the larger chunks of spaceport.

Inside our daysuits the attack had been soundless, though I felt the thumps of the explosions even in Mars's thin air. "Our turn," Andrew said without emotion. "We'd better get back inside."

We went to the passage lock in the crater's dome, and hurried down the escalator on the rim wall. We were just outside the command building when the dome fell. I guess the police weren't worrying about property anymore; perhaps New Houston is the last rebel city left, and they are anxious to be done with us. We saw the starring appear around the perimeter, saw the huge sections of thin plasteel crack and tilt as they slowly dropped toward us. Then we were under the eaves of the building and in the protection of the door lock.

The plasteel rained down for over a minute. Police troops followed immediately, coming down on individual rocket backpacks.

Figures in suits began pouring into our lock from indoors, not worrying about air loss. Andrew and I were handed two of the long-nosed light rifles, and we slung the straps over our shoulders and stepped out of the lock.

There were a lot of them falling, in pale red suits. But it was a vulnerable way to come down. Beams of light laced the dark pink sky, and the police troops shot back as they descended. But they had to control their rocket packs, and they were falling. Their aim was bad. We shot them out of the sky. I pushed the trigger button on my gun and watched the beam intersect with a human form that was falling and shooting in my direction. Suddenly he tilted over and his rockets powered him down into buildings a few blocks away. I sat down, feeling sick, cursing the Committee for attacking in such a stupid and wasteful manner, cursing and cursing. The common band roared with voices. A beam hissed near me and I scrambled for cover under a building's eave, thinking, not rain drops but death beams, these eaves are for . . . stupid stuff like that. I looked up again. If a beam hit the rocket packs for more than an instant they exploded. Little pops like obscene firecrackers burst everywhere above me. I cursed and sobbed, hit the wall of the building with my gun, pointed it at the sky and shot again.

Over on the other side of the city the defense wasn't doing well. Hundreds of police descended in the residential district across the crater from us. Then they stopped falling.

A voice on the radio said, "Enemy is trapped in the residential quarter, northwest. Return to headquarters or to outposts five, six, seven or nine." This was the first sentence in half an hour I had understood. I found Andrew and followed him to the command building. It was just three hours after dawn, when we had ascended the crater wall.

In the command apartment everyone took off the head-pieces. Andrew looked fierce, desperate. Others were helping a man who was shaking uncontrollably.

After an hour to clear our senses and take accounts, there was a meeting in the central lounge. Susan Jones, still in her silver day-suit, sat down beside me. "We're going to evacuate the city."

"And go where?" I asked dully.

"We have a contingency plan for this situation."

"Good."

Ethel and Sandra and Yuri joined us, and Susan raised her voice to include them.

"There was always the chance this would happen, of course. We had to risk it." Her mouth pursed. "Anyway, we've got some retreats in the chaos to the north of here. Hidden colonies, underground or in caves. They're all small and well separated. Since we took over the cities we've been stocking them and supplying them with the equipment we'll need to make them self-contained systems."

"They'll spot us from satellite photos," I said.

She shook her head. "There's almost as much land surface on Mars as on Earth. And geographic features so impenetrable as to defy belief. I know, I've been up there. Even if they photograph it all, they'll never have the time or the people to examine all the photographs."

"Computer scan—"

"Can only catch regular shapes. Ours are disguised and hidden. They'd have to check all the photos by eye, and even then they wouldn't see us. Mars is too big, and the retreats too well hidden. So. We have a refuge, and it's ready.

"The other choice," she continued, looking at our faces, "is to fade away in the city, and pretend you were neutral and hiding the whole time. Could be tough. But we've programmed a lot of imaginary people into the city register, and you could become one of those."

Then the meeting was called to order by a tall thin man, and Susan joined him. "The police are contained for now," he said. "But our situation in New Houston is untenable, as you know. As soon as it's dark, we're going to disperse, and either evacuate or infiltrate the city. Field cars hidden in Spear Canyon will take off for the north. There we'll start the revolution over again." The man looked tired, disappointed. "You all knew this was a possibility. That the best we would do this time would be to establish the hidden outposts. Well, that's how it has turned out. I'm afraid we're losing space control. And that we're one of the last cities left holding out." He consulted with Susan. "Those of you who want to continue on in the city, we've got a list of apartments near here that still have air. And we've got the fake identities ready for your pictures and fingerprints and all."

He whispered with the people around him some more. Ginger Sims joined us. Conversations began among the forty or fifty people in the room. "Okay. Get some rest before sunset. That's all for now."

So there it is. Ethel and Yuri are in the next room, arguing about what to do. But I never even thought about it. I'm going into the chaos. In a curious way it is as though I had decided to go with the starship after all . . . enclosed in a little underground colony, where we will have to work hard to establish a life-support system, I have no doubt. And yet we are still on Mars, and still opposing the Committee. So I have what I want. I'm satisfied.

There is little time left. I am too nervous to rest, I have been writing for an hour or more. We will leave soon. All of my friends from *Rust Eagle* are coming along—Ethel and Yuri have just decided. I think of the starship, flying away from all this . . . of my father. My thoughts are dense and confused, it's hard to write one thing at a time.

The police will follow us into the chaotic terrain. The Committee will want to wipe out every vestige of resistance. But this desire is part of what insures that we will succeed. We didn't come to this red planet to repeat all the miserable mistakes of history, we didn't. Even if it looks like it so far. Martians want to be free; truly free.

I'm going to go in the car with Andrew, so he tells me. His sister and my companions will be along. That will be the most dangerous part, the escape tonight. It looks as though it will all happen as I dreamed it out there with the starship, in the asteroid belt—I will run over the surface of red Mars forever and ever, for the rest of my life. Except in the real world they'll be chasing me.

# II
◆

# HJALMAR
# NEDERLAND

## 2547 A.D.

"I was the world in which I walked, and what I saw
  Or heard or felt came not but from myself;
  And there I found myself more truly and more strange."

—*Wallace Stevens*, "Tea at the Palaz of Hoon"

**Memory is the** weak link. This year I will be three hundred and ten years old, but most of my life is lost to me, buried in the years. I might as well be a creature of incarnations, moving from life to life, ignorant of my own past. Oh, I "know" that once I climbed Olympus Mons, that once I visited the Earth, and so on; I can check the record like anyone else; but to recall none of the detail, to *feel* nothing for this knowledge, is not to have done it.

It isn't as simple as that, I admit. Certain events, moments scattered here and there in my life, exist in my memory like artifacts in the layers of an excavation: fragments of meaning in the debris of time, left in a pattern of deposition that I fail to understand. On occasion I will stumble on one of these artifacts—a trolley bell in the street, and I see an Alexandrian's smile—a whiff of ammonia, and suddenly I am reacquainted with my first daughter's birth—but the process of deposition, the process of recovery, both are mysteries to me. And each little epiphany reminds me that there are things I have forgotten forever—things that might explain me to myself, which explanation I sorely need—and I clutch at the fragment knowing I might never stumble across it again.

So I have decided to collect these artifacts, with the idea that I had better try to understand them now, while they are still within my reach—working as the archaeologists of old did so often, against rising waters in haste, while the chance yet exists: hurrying to invent a new archaeology of the self.

What we feel most, we remember best.

*The Tharsis Bulge—the bulge is five thousand kilometers across and seven kilometers high, and formed early in Mars's history. The stresses caused by this deformation in the crust were instrumental in the formation of the large volcanoes, the equatorial canyon system, and an extensive system of radial fractures.*

We came on the site in a hundred field cars, a caravan that lofted a plume of umber dust over the rocky plain. The site looked like any other youngish crater: a low rampart we could drive right up, and then a flat-topped symmetrical rim-hill, surrounded by the hummocky slope of the ejecta shield. Few craters look impressive from the outside, and this was not one of the exceptions. But my pulse quickened at the sight of it. It had been a long time coming.

I put on a thermal suit, and ordered those of my students in the car to do the same, as I needed companions for a hike to the rim. Gritting my teeth I walked up to the car containing Satarwal and Petrini, and knocked on their door window. The door popped open with a hiss and there they were, faces poking out like Tweedle-dum and Tweedle-dee: the codirectors of my dig. Blandly I told them I was going up to the rim with a few students to have a look around.

Satarwal, flexing his boss muscle: "Shouldn't we set camp first?"

"You've got more than enough people for that. And someone needs to go up there and confirm that we're at the right crater."

Giving excuses: a mistake. "We're at the right crater," said Satarwal.

Petrini grinned. "Don't you think we're at the right crater, Hjalmar?"

"I'm sure we are. Still it wouldn't hurt to see, would it. Before the whole camp is set."

They glanced at each other, paused to make me stew. "Okay," Satarwal said. "You can go."

"Thanks," I said, bland as ever. Petrini shot a look at Satarwal to see how the head of the Planetary Survey would take this sarcasm; but Satarwal hadn't noticed it. Stupid policeman.

With a jerk of the head I led half a dozen students, and staff toward the rim. It was midafternoon, and we hiked up the gentle slope with the sun over our shoulders and the quartet of dusk mirrors almost overhead. It felt good to walk off the exchange with Satarwal and Petrini, and I left my group behind. They knew better than to catch up with me when I walked that fast. Those two clowns: I blew frost plumes as solid as cotton balls into the chill highland air at the thought of them. This was *my* dig. I had worked for twenty years to get the site off the Committee's proscribed list; and I would have worked a hundred years more and never gotten their permission, too, if a friend hadn't been put on the Committee. But it pleased him to sanction the dig for the season directly following the end of my stint as chairman of the department. So that the new chairman, Petrini, was made the codirector of the dig along with the Committee watchdog Satarwal; while I, whose work the dig would support or refute, was nearly forbidden to accompany it. I had had to grovel for the better part of a year before they allowed me to join the expedition. And my friend only laughed. "You're lucky to be going at all, you fearsome radical!"

But here we were. I booted a rock uphill to remind me of the reality of our presence, to clear my mind of all the poison poured into it by the government. We were here. That meant that, no matter what else happened, I had won: a site had been taken off the proscribed list for the first time. And now it loomed before me—ah!—my heart leaped at the thought. I picked up my pace; the only thing that kept me from bounding up the slope was the presence of my students behind me. The ejecta shield became steeper and rougher as I approached the rim; above me blocks stuck into the dirty lavender sky, and they gave me an excuse to bound upward, to clear them. Below me the shouts of my companions sounded like the cheeps of snow finches. Between the broken blocks of compressed basalt were drifts of fine frost-crunchy sand—

And then the slope curved flat and I was on the rim. Topping it was an embankment of tan concrete; I ran to it. Concrete, with a steel coping laid in its top: a dome foundation of the early twenty-second century. So we were at the right crater. From my new vantage I could see around the circumference of the rim, and the embankment grew or shrank to level it off. Here and there struts stuck out of the embankment over the crater below, for two meters or five or ten, until they twisted down and broke off. The supports for the dome. In several places the embankment was blasted down into the rim; one such disruption was a short distance away from me, and I went to have a look. The concrete in the break had been reduced to something like black sandstone, which crumbled into my glove when rubbed. So they had blown down the dome. I shook my head. Nasty shock for the inhabitants, no doubt.

Hana Ingtal, the least stupid of my students, popped over the rim and interrupted my survey. "Professor Nederland!" she cried, holding out between two gloved fingers a chip of blue plastic.

"What."

"Look here—it's a taggart."

I took the chip from her and inspected it.

"Explosives companies put them in their products so they can determine whose explosives made any particular—"

"I know what taggarts are, Ingtal. Put this back where you found it. You know excavation procedures, don't you? Move nothing except as part of a methodical exploration, that can be confirmed by others and recorded as authentic data. Especially on this dig. You may have destroyed this piece's worth as data already!"

Crestfallen, she turned and walked back down the rim. But that is how students learn. "And make sure you put it where you can find it again!" I shouted after her. She was one of those students who progress in leaps, and miss things along the way—practical matters like methodology. No doubt she had developed a complete theory of the city's end from that single chip of plastic. But she was young. A century or two of defeat would teach her what it took to build a case in Martian history.

I hiked to the inner edge of the rim, and looked down a nearly sheer cliff onto the crater floor.

A lot of sand had been deposited in the last three hundred years, but some of the roofs were still exposed. From my vantage it looked like a village of dirt hummocks, at the bottom of a big dirt bowl. The hummocks stood in faint squares and oblongs, and together they formed a grid of sand-filled depressions, that once had been busy streets, and wide boulevards lined with trees. The pattern extended to the crater wall on all sides, although to the east the sand tended to bury everything.

Trembling slightly, I stepped as close to the cliff's edge as I dared. Those were the ruins of New Houston, down there. I had been born in that ruined city; my first years had been spent in the confines of this very crater.—This had impeded my efforts to get the dig approved, in fact, although I never understood why. My birthplace: so what? No one remembers their childhood. I knew I had been born there in the same way anybody else did—I looked it up. So the unspoken implication that my motives were in some way personal was entirely unfounded, as was tacitly admitted when the dig was approved and I was allowed to join it.

Nevertheless, as I looked down onto the hummock roofs and the solar-panel ridges and the sand-filled streets, I caught myself searching for something in the pattern, or in the etching of vertical ravines into the crater wall, that I might recognize from those first years. But it was just a site. An old city in ruins.

New Houston. During the Unrest of 2248 the city had been taken over by rioters, and held against the police of the Mars Development Committee. (I must have been there?) The police reports said the rebels had blown down the dome, destroyed the city, and killed all the noncombatants; but the samizdat said otherwise. In these ruins I intended to find the truth.

So as I surveyed the crater floor and its faint gridwork, now accentuated by the growing shadows of late afternoon, my pulse quickened, my spirits soared. For as long as I could remember I had wanted to excavate one of the lost Martian cities, and now I was here at last. Now I would be an archaeologist in deed, as well as in name. Visions of the digs I had taught in classes jumbled in my mind—all those cities that had been razed and abandoned by conquerors, Troy, Carthage, Palmyra, Tenochtitlán, all resurrected by scientists and their work; now New Houston would be added to those, to become part of history again. Oh, yes—it was that moment in a dig, before the work has begun, when the site lies undisturbed in its shadows and all things seem possible, when one can imagine the ruins to be those of a city as ancient and huge as Persepolis, with the strata of centuries under the rubble-crazed surface, containing the debris of countless lives that can be deciphered and understood, recouped from the dead past to be known and treasured and made part of us forever. Why, down in those ruins we might find almost *anything*.

Of course it is easy to feel that way above a site on a good prospect, in late afternoon light, alone. Everything looks burnished and charged with meaning, and somehow one's own.

Down in the tents it was different. That evening I entered the large commons tent where everyone was celebrating our arrival, and felt like an ant dropped in a terrarium of trapdoor spiders. Satarwal and his thugs from Planetary Survey stared at me, and Petrini and his faintly insolent students glanced at me as they stood in rings around tables, poking at maps and arguing like experts, and my students and McNeil's and Kalinin's blinked at me as stupidly as sheep. I went in search of the Kleserts and found them in the dining room, and joined them for a silent meal. I didn't know them well, but they were my age and knew how to leave one alone. It was too bad for me that their work on water stations would take them away, to Nirgal Vallis some kilometers to the southwest of us.

Then it was back to the main room, to the arguing and poking. Petrini's group was determined to be vehement, yet there was no point to their talk—except to show Satarwal how *reliable* they were, how fiercely they could go after "the facts" without endangering the official version of New Houston's history. They were good at that. And Satarwal soaked it up. He enjoyed the meaningless chatter about the Athenian and Parisian models of crater city planning, because it so obviously avoided the central question of the dig. His stubbly blue jowls bounced with pleasure at this spectacle of his power over us, and I could not stand it. I had to leave the room.

Only to run into Petrini in one of the smaller lounges. But Petrini was easier on the nerves than Satarwal. It was like going from the dentist to an ear specialist (I have poor hearing): someone still working on you, but without the drills.

"Well, Hjalmar, how was the view from the rim? The old city still there, eh?"

"Ah—yes. Yes it is."

"Did you find anything interesting on the rim?"

"Well—the dome foundation, of course. I won't know until we have studied it more closely."

"Of course."

"Nothing extraordinary, though."

"No. I guess we'd have heard if you had, from your students."

"Do you think so?"

"Oh, come now, Hjalmar. You know students."

"Do I?"

"Who better? You're the pillar of the university, Hjalmar, you've been there longer than the buildings."

"Not really. Besides, only the buildings stay. The students keep changing." Until you end up teaching members of a different civilization.

Petrini tilted his head back and laughed. "Well," he said, sobering rapidly and making sure I saw he was now serious: "I'll have a tough time filling your shoes, I really will."

"Nonsense. You'll be the best chairman yet."

Conversation on automatic pilot. Meanwhile I watched him work on me. Such charm. But Petrini's problem was his transparency. He was one of those people who made it their life's project to rise into the halls of power; everything he did was part of his campaign. I knew someone like that myself, so I recognized the type. But Petrini's purpose was always obvious, and this would impede his progress. The best politicans appear to fall upward accidentally, so that people are inclined to help them on their way.

He slapped me on the arm affectionately. "Thanks for the vote of confidence. Now—I hope you don't mind me saying this—I know what you will be trying to prove here on this dig. And believe me, I'm sympathetic to it. But the evidence, Hjalmar. The Aimes Report, you know, and Colonel Shay's account. Those things couldn't have been falsified."

"Certainly they could have." I tilted my head at him curiously. "Those aren't things, Petrini. The things are here, on the site. The only good evidence is here, because the city can't lie. We'll see what we find out."

"Just be prepared for a letdown." He put his hand to my arm again. "I tell you this for your own sake."

"Thanks."

I considered going back to my tent and reading. My supervisors were intolerable, my colleagues irritating, my students dull. But then Hana Ingtal appeared as if I had called her up by the thought, and asked me to join her for a drink with an enthusiasm that made it difficult for me to refuse. Reluctantly I nodded, and followed her into the dining room's bar. While she mixed us drinks she chattered about our afternoon on the rim. I watched her, perplexed. We had worked together for over five years, and she still seemed to like me. I didn't understand it. Most students so obviously work their professors for advancement, and how can they help it? It is that sort of master-slave situation. I doubt I would ever go near a university if I had it to do again. Twenty years of indenture to some old man or woman who "knows," all to get into a position where you too can be treated as master by people you barely know. Stupid (although it beat mining).

But Hana appeared to enjoy conversation with me for its own sake. She was undeferential, and watching her I could almost imagine what it would be like to learn the discipline anew. Fifty-two years old, chestnut hair, hazel eyes, nice bones, calm expression: my single graduate students were tripping over each other to be with her, and here she was at a corner table with me, a man who truly did not know how to speak with her. Once I knew what to say to the young (when I was young myself, perhaps) but I've lost the art. Life is the history of losses.

So she said, "Is this dig much like the ones you did on Earth?" and I tried to figure out what she meant by it.

"Well. I never actually participated in a dig on Earth—as I thought you knew?" I was almost certain she knew that. "But the site is much like an abandoned Norse settlement on the west coast of Greenland that I visited when I was there," and I described the terran site using what I could remember of my lecture notes on the place—for my trip to Earth was a blank to me—until I became too aware of the discrepancy between what I described and what we had actually seen that afternoon, and stumbled to a halt, and waited with some trepidation for her to bring up something else to discuss. You see, quiet people know they have a reputation for being close-mouthed. Sometimes the reputation is like a power, for they see their acquaintances think that when they are moved to speak it will be for something special. But that is also a sort of pressure, a pressure that grows as the years pass and the quiet person's reputation ages. What, after all, is really important enough to say? Not much. And quiet people become overly aware of that, and thus aware that most talk is a code masking vastly more complex meanings—meanings unfathomable to the very people most aware of their existence.

Abruptly I stood. "I'm off to bed now," I said, and went back to my tent.

"—When we were sure they would honor the truce we met seven of them at the spaceport depot. We told them they were the last city on Mars resisting legal authority, but they did not believe us. I told them their situation was hopeless no matter what was happening elsewhere, and offered them the terms we had offered all the rioters: due process; suspension of the death penalty; and a reasonable dialogue (to be defined later) to be established to air grievances concerning planetary policy. I added that all noncombatants in New Houston were to be released to us immediately. The leader of the group, a bearded man of seventy or eighty years, demanded complete amnesty as a condition of surrender. I said I was unau-

*thorized to grant amnesty, but that it would be considered by the Committee when violence ceased. The rioters discussed the matter in Russian among themselves, and my officers heard the word "Leningrad" repeated. The leader said they would return to the city and put the matter to a vote, and we agreed to meet again in two days. The next morning, however, more than twenty explosions from the crater rim indicated they had brought down the city dome. By the time our forces could enter the city the power plant was destroyed and fires had gone out for lack of oxygen, though the smoke was still thick. This smoke covered rebel snipers, and by the time we could subdue them nearly all the noncombatants in the city had died of asphyxiation. Rescue work continued for three days, and thirty-eight people were found in intact rooms, air locks, individual suits, and the like. All of them claimed noncombatant status; their interviews are appended. When the city was secured it was no longer habitable; damage caused by the rioters was such that it would have been easier to build in a new crater than to reconstruct the city."*

So said Police Colonel Ernest Shay, field commander for the Committee police during the Unrest, when he was questioned by the Aimes Commission in 2250. But I had found records of the Royal Dutch police division showing that Shay was in Enkhuisen in December 2248, supervising the war there. Why had he answered the Commission's questions, and not the officer actually in charge at New Houston? Why had he lied, and said he was there conducting negotiations himself?

I put the bulky printout of the 194th Volume of the Aimes Report down on my nightstand, on top of a thick folder of samizdat, an illegal collection of newsletters, pamphlets, xeroxes and broadsides I had made over many years. In slangy, sarcastic, bitter Russian (the underground language of Mars, the language of resistance, the counter-English) the samizdat, many of them handwritten to avoid police identification of printer or typewriter, told the real story of New Houston. Should I pull out the newsletter *carry on with it*, by "Yevgeny"? *"The Dragon descended, lightning bolted from its mouth, 'the sky is falling, the sky is falling!' and no air for the fire so that it fled down throats to combust in lungs, fire balloon people wafting up past the dragon chicks falling on stacks of fire. . . ."* Or the more prosaic account by "Medvedev"? *"24 December 2248—tenth politzei*

*blitzkrieg—New Houston, Texan sector—estimated two thousand attack
troops descended on rocket packs onto open city after dome knocked down
at dawn—resistance continued three days—captured rebels executed—"*
But I knew them all by heart. These ragged narratives told the
true story of the Unrest, I had become convinced. Few historians
agreed with me; they sided with the Committee's official view, that
the samizdat were written by malcontents, and were nothing but
lies, filled with contradictions and obvious inaccuracies. And it was
true that they were anonymous, and contained contradictions, they
were sourceless, and had no evidence to support them; and some
were full of tall tales, the Unrest made myth. But in some ways
writers like "Medvedev" made a more coherent account of the
Unrest than the Aimes Report did. And if they were nothing but
fictions, why had the Committee made it illegal to publish or own
them? Why had the Committee begun the process of installing
"watermarks" in every Xerox machine, to help them locate the
ones used to print samizdat? And why had excavation of over a
dozen abandoned cities been forbidden? No. There was something wrong; the Committee had lied, was lying. The true story of
the Unrest had yet to be told.

The excavation teams got to street level in the old city at different
speeds, depending on their method and what they found. McNeil
worked as if he had the rest of his life to finish the next centime-
ter of the dig, and he had his students record everything so thoroughly that they could have reconstructed their ruins just as they
found them. "You never know what questions you may want to ask
a hundred years from now," McNeil declared. The rest of us already had questions, and only used the string grids and tooth-
brushes when we were near what we were looking for. I set my
team to work in the area of the city's physical plant, under the
eastern wall of the crater. Under several meters of sand we found
the big buildings of the plant, partially buried under the
avalanched crater wall, so that the walls were broken and the interiors filled with rubble and shattered equipment. Moving away
from the plant we found control terminal housing, administrative
offices, and supply sheds; then outside a wrought iron fence were

service shops, restaurants, and bars, and beyond them were the dormitories and apartments of those who had worked in the plant. All of these structures, especially the physical plant itself, were scorched, melted, knocked over. Sifting through this evidence of destruction took weeks. We took holograms, and made models of what we found, and programmed computer explosions, and even set up little real explosions in the models, to see what form the assault had taken; and all the while I kept one group enlarging the excavation of the surrounding neighborhood, especially to the north of the plant where the damage was most extensive.

Street level against the crater's east wall was about nine meters below the top of the sand drift, and so we worked at the bottom of a craterling of our own making. Elsewhere teams had dug other holes, and as I walked about the sand surface in the evenings, stopping here or there to scuff an exposed solar panel's edge, or inspect a patch of lichen, it seemed that I strolled across an old battlefield, a no-man's land pocked with bomb craters and giant foxholes. Looking into the trenches gave me an odd feeling, as if I stared into graves—archaeology regressing to graverobbing—and might see the dead carrying on with their daily lives. Tall dredges stood insectlike over the rim of each craterling, and tubes extended from them across the crater floor, up and over the rim. It was an eerie place, this dead city. Frost crunched under my boots, my nose and lungs were cold. I hiked back to our own little graben (grave) and looked down at the sand-filled apartments we had recently exposed. They had built eaves on the roofs, here where no rain would ever have fallen. Where were we? What city of the mind?

Down on the shadowy streets figures emerged from a building, carrying the long vacuum tubes that led back to the dredge. Ghost firemen. Bill Strickland looked up and saw me; he shouted something I couldn't hear. He pointed back into the building, waved me down. My heart gave a skip and I hurried to the ramp, descended. Xhosa, the chief of my staff, ran by. "What have they found?" I said.

"I don't know, they just said hurry."

"It's not likely to run away," I said, but Xhosa was already down the street. I kept my pace steady to show them I was not excitable. I rounded a bluff in our new sand cliff and found five or six of them in the entrance of a newly exposed building; it appeared to be a hotel with a tavern in the ground floor. I walked past them and entered. Rooms free of sand gaped like caves, and it smelled of clay and paint. I heard voices in an inner room and continued in.

"Has anyone checked this building for its structural integrity?" I said loudly.

Strickland and a few others were in a large room. "Sort of," he said.

"Fine. The whole building could come down on us."

Strickland moved aside, so I could see through a door into an adjoining room.

Four bodies lay on the floor, dressed in old spacesuits. Two held light rifles in their gloved hands. One was curled around the leg of a big empty desk. The dead: how still they are, how *other.*

"Get out of here before the place falls down," I said harshly, shocked at the sight. "Xhosa, give this place a structural check and get holo crews in here. Holos of every room. Look at the tracks you've made. Who vacuumed this building?" Strickland and Heidi Mueller stepped forward. "How often did you check the filters?"

"After every room," Heidi said. Bill looked sullen.

"Find anything?"

"It's all in the boxes in the front room," Bill said.

I grimaced. Here McNeil's maddening slowness might have done some good. Hana Ingtal entered the room, stopped when she saw the bodies through the doorway. Frost plumed from her nostrils and drifted to the floor.

"Hana, go find Petrini and bring him here," I said. "Tell him I want his help."

She looked at me as if I had gone mad at last.

"I want him to see it," I said.

She nodded and left.

"Leave everything alone," I said. "When Petrini gets here we'll start work again." I herded them out of the building. I didn't want to stay in there with those bodies; they made me uneasy and disoriented, and something more I could not name. Out in the street my students walked down the excavated sand canyon to our little working tent: pale blue and brown figures in a residential street, at the bottom of two steep walls of red sand. I looked out of the shadows to the dark crater rim, and the plum-colored sky. No stars. But once they had been thick—and that pungent smell, of wet dust and street surface fixative—

My father had sewn a flag, stripes and a star, the lone star state, he had said, with a red star that made him laugh.

Dizzily I took a step in the street, looked up at a black second-story window in the apartment across the way—gasped—

My father came home late to find a group of us kids gathered before the big maps in the window of the Leaky Tap. The generals! he cried cheerily. He took my arm to lead me in and—and—

I was at the plant to get the day's water ration when the dome fell. *The dome fell.* Great crashing outside and the roar of air rushing up. I ran to struggle into a daysuit, clamped on helmet and turned on oxygen as I had been taught. Excited at my chance to fight I rushed into the street and couldn't see a thing in the smoke. The ground was vibrating, the smoke cleared and plates of the dome rained down, tumbling in the turbulence. Flashes on the crater rim made my sight swim with red spurts, and through the spurts dorm-sized boulders rolled down the wall onto us. Fear stunned me like a blow to the head, it smashed me into a different world. I ran for home thinking only to hide, tripped over big plates—pieces of the dome—got lost in smoke, looked up and saw red figures falling out of the sky on rocket backpacks. Hundreds of them fell, like drops of blood or meteorites or pieces of the dome come to life. Red beams lanced the smoke, I fell, got up and ran head down for home. A woman lay sprawled in the street. I ran up my steps relieved to see them, but when I pulled open the door I saw I had been fooled—the apartment front had been left whole, but it was like a stage prop now, because behind it an immense tan chunk of the crater wall had crushed the apartment and its contents into a meter-thick pancake of plastic paneling. Door in my hand. I could have pulled the facade down.

Sudden time in a world without time: I found myself sitting in the street. I had broken a sweat; my suit's thermostat had been overwhelmed. I stood carefully, finishing crossing the street, and climbed the front steps to the apartment door under the black second-story window. Hesitantly I pulled it back. Tan rock. I closed the door, sat on the step.

Vague impression of parents, sisters. They must have been killed. Perhaps not in the apartment itself, but somewhere. Otherwise they would have reunited me with them when the survivors were sorted out. Gingerly I probed my memory: what had happened after I opened the door? Nothing. The blank of the past, as empty as always. The images that had just welled up in me still lived, but they were fragments, bright in the surrounding darkness like mirror suns in a twilight sky—broken out of the past by the smell of a street, the sight of rock behind a door, or bodies in a hallway. Trembling uncontrollably I racked my mind to learn more, I rocked back and forth on the stoop under the force of *feeling* what it meant to raze a city and murder its inhabitants—my family—

"Professor Nederland?"

I looked up. Petrini; and behind him, among others, Satarwal. "What."

He looked confused. "Well, you had us brought over here."

"Oh. Yes. We've found something I need your help with. A resistance center, perhaps."

He smiled. "You want my help?"

"We need independent confirmation of what we find."

"Oh!" His smile disappeared. "I see. Well, let's have a look." He extended a hand. "Need some help? You look a bit shaken."

I declined the hand and stood. Gestured at the apartment behind us. "I used to live here."

"You did?" He was surprised. Behind him his staff members glanced at each other. "You looked it up?"

"I remembered." I walked through the group to the Leaky Tap.

Inside holos had been taken and the strength of the building checked, and we went to work. Xhosa and Hana and Bill directed the others, and I watched. They took seven bodies out and drove them over to the escalator we had set up to cross the rim. We would have to start a cemetery beyond the main camp when our studies were done. Lamps and heaters were turned on as night fell. I stood outside the door and watched the bodies carted away; my hands would not hold steady. Graverobbers, I thought as the last cart left.

A desk in the back room appeared to have been cleared hastily; all the drawers were empty, but under it was a scrap of paper with its curl frozen into it. On it was scrawled, *Susan—start the evacuation at dusk—A.* Hana brought the scrap out to show it to me; when I was done examining it I gave it back to her and walked away. Dark and cold in the empty street. The voices behind were like those of workers in a tavern. I sat on my old apartment stoop, turned up my suit's heat, felt the hot air waft out of my hood vents onto my face. I breathed the cold night air deep into me. So they had broken the dome of New Houston. And how many other cities had died like it?

The others left the tavern in a group, arguing. "Obviously there was a well organized resistance," Hana said angrily. "This is one of their headquarters! The reason we've never found more evidence of them is they were a secret organization, and the police didn't want to acknowledge their existence—"

"I know," Petrini said in a soothing voice. "Professor Nederland has argued that view very cogently for many years." They walked before a light spearing the length of the street and split it four ways. "But still—Hjalmar, you must admit this," he said to me on my stoop. "You are explaining an absence of data, not the presence of it. And you can't rely on those samizdat you prize so highly. After all, we have samizdat accounts of green Martian natives joining the riots from their hideaways"—this got a laugh or two from his staff—"and then leading the defeated rioters into their Pellucidarian refuge. But we can't believe in them just because there is a suspicious *lack* of other data proving their existence, now can we."

I suppose he thought he was being funny. "Here's your evidence," I said.

Satarwal spoke up. "This is just the nest of some of the rioters who destroyed this city. An isolated cell of killers."

"I notice they're the dead ones."

Satarwal waved a finger at me angrily. "There was no organized resistance! No Washington-Lenin Alliance, as some of your cohorts call it. It is nothing more than a malicious fiction, made up by dissidents to attempt to embarrass the government."

Wearily I explained to Petrini, "The size of the revolt is itself the largest and most obvious sort of evidence. There is no way a spontaneous revolt could have held off the police for five months. And taken over all these cities."

"That was due to the Soviet fleet's defection," Satarwal answered.

"That was the Lenin half of the Alliance. Here we stand in a Texan city that had to be destroyed, it was so well defended. This is the Washington half."

"The rioters themselves destroyed the city," Satarwal insisted. "I have proved this—"

"You work for the Committee," I said, and stood. My head spun, lights crawled in my vision. I spoke loudly so everyone there would hear me. "The rebels didn't destroy this city." Hana stared at me, consternation deforming her face. The rest of them stared as well. "The police troopers did it. I know because I was there." I waved around me. "I was right here when it happened!"

"You may have been in the city," Petrini said reassuringly, "but you can't possibly recall the incident—"

"It wasn't an *incident*. It was war—a massacre, do you understand? They blasted the dome and came down on rocket packs and—and *killed* everybody! When I stood in this street I had an epiphanic recollection—you've all had those, you know what they're like—and I remembered it all. I was young then, but I remember."

"Ridiculous!" Satarwal cried furiously. "Why should we believe somebody so biased—"

"Because *I was there!*"

At that moment a student bumped the light, and its beam fell on me. In an intact window across the street I could suddenly see my reflection: short, tubby, licks of electric hair tufting away from a large head, rubbery small-eyed face puffy with vehemence . . . an old man fizzing with indignation, over something only he cared about. And there were Hana and Bill and Xhosa and Heidi and all the rest, staring at me. What a ludicrous figure I must have cut, crying out my testament as though anyone there would believe it! In disgust I snarled and twisted away, as if when I could not see my reflection, they could not see me.

But I had been there, and I remembered.

Petrini, pleading in his let's-be-reasonable tone: "A three-hundred-year-old memory, Hjalmar? Again you must agree, it's not very *strong* evidence."

I shrugged, wishing to escape. "When human witness becomes weak evidence we're in bad trouble. I say it happened. I was here, I saw it. That's how we make history, by eyewitness accounts. That's what the samizdat are."

"Even the green Martian one?" Petrini said gently. "Besides, we are archaeologists."

I shook my head, stared around at the dark apartments, desperation filling me, flooding me. "We are *amnesiacs*," I cried. Helplessly I saw again the rock behind the door, the dome falling. My students watched me tensely, ready for an opportunity to extricate me from my folly; they didn't believe me any more than Petrini did.

*Graben—a depressed crustal block, bounded by faults on its long sides.*

Once I said nearly the same thing to the Shrike. We were up in his bedroom on the eightieth floor of the Barnard Tower, and he adjusted the wall-sized window so we could see out. He stood before the glass watching a big Arctic eagle gliding on the stiff wind coursing over Alexandria. From the bed I observed his supple back, the curve of his buttock against the bruised sky and the last flare of the dusk mirrors' sunset. Below the myriad city lights blinked on. "We're amnesiacs, Shrike," I said to him. I call him Shrike (he doesn't get it); his real name is Alexander Graham Selkirk (his father's best joke). So I watched him there at his island's window lighting a pipe, and I said, "We're amnesiacs, it doesn't matter what we do. It doesn't matter what you do, Shrike. You won't remember it in a century."

"By that time I doubt I'll care," he said, expelling the fruity smoke of his pipe. "Why should I? Besides, there's always the memory drugs."

"They don't work."

He shrugged. "It depends on how particular you are when you say *work*. Besides, what can you do? Would you rather be dead?" He puffed energetically. "It's just the way things are."

"Sometimes I get so tired of things as they are. Look down there at all those people in the street, Shrike. Can you see them?"

"They look like ants."

"Very original. And that's how you think of them, too. The workers, the poor, the miners who make this planet profitable to its owners on Earth—what do you care for them? You live up here like Syrtis grass in its sheath of ice, shielded from the grubby Martian world and all its ants."

"You're up here too, aren't you."

"Who wouldn't be if they could? But we're all bound in the same system. We struggle in our casings and then forget whatever efforts we make."

"The way you describe it, perhaps it's better that way."

"Bah. Have you ever been poor, I mean Martian poor?"

"Yes. I was born in a mine, actually. And grew up in a mining camp."

"And do you remember it?"

"Of course not. Can't say I'd care to."

"You'd rather stay sheathed in privilege."

He nodded. "And so would you. Please—don't protest. How often you've said all this. Get comfortable and you start feeling guilty. Is that why you like going off on those awful digs all the time? And now you're being kept from it? But don't be cross. You'll get your dig, I'll see to that."

"You haven't been on the Committee long enough to see to anything," I said. "You've got a century more of running errands first. And the Committee will let me go to New Houston as soon as I'm no longer department chair, and no sooner."

He smiled sardonically. "But they will let you go. And you'll know who to thank."

"Oh yes," I said, and threw myself back against the big pillows. "I'll know. But how will I thank you, Shrike? What can poor I, lowly professor at university, give you? You who have—" I waved out at the vast lit map of Alexandria.

He shrugged, a beautiful movement to watch—a movement I tried to imitate in my own affairs. "You do fine. I like your company."

"I don't see why."

"Sometimes I don't either!" He laughed. "Usually you aren't this cranky."

"Ach—" I looked away. "I'm your pet scientist, and we both know it. How many other pets do you keep."

The silence stretched on. Shrike stepped to the music console, pushed buttons, and the very slowest version of "Django" made its melancholy beginning. When he saw I was watching him again he pointed his pipe at me. "How many other governors do you keep?"

"None!"

He laughed at me, went back to the window. "Perhaps it's best we forget our pasts. How much could we be saddled with before we buckled under the stupidity of it all?"

"Perhaps we would learn to do better."

"Perhaps. But I doubt it. Meanwhile, we have no choice. Think of your dig, Hjalmar. When you get to New Houston you'll be in your element, out in nowhere land up to your elbows in mud and junk, putting together ancient history like a puzzle. What could be nicer?" He laughed again, and again he was laughing at me, but something in it—his pleasure at his own charm—and the sight of him, and the view over the city and Noctis Labyrinthus beyond, and the music, all filled me and forced a turn in my mood. Or something did. Often my moods shift on their own, for no reason I can tell. But frequently Shrike has something to do with it. "Come back to bed?"

*Densely Cratered Terrain—the central and southern uplands are as much as a hundred times more cratered than the plains of the north, and are over 3.9 billion years old.*

Excavation is slow work. Each dig becomes a little culture of its own, formed partly by the digger's culture, partly by what they find. McNeil estimated that there were 3,500 buildings on the crater floor, and Kalinin guessed 2,000 of them were still standing, and all of them were filled with the artifacts—and sometimes the occupants—of three hundred years before. We built quite a cemetery out on the ejecta shield. Kalinin's team came across a mass grave containing four hundred and twenty-eight bodies. Most had been shot or killed in explosions, or asphyxiated. Bodies frozen together like packed fish. Satarwal declared they were victims of the rioters. I only had to walk out on him to make my point, and even Petrini looked disbelieving, in the moment when he knew Satarwal wasn't watching, in the moment when he knew I was.

I hiked up to the crater rim as I had so often before, for the solitude and the view over the great Martian uplands. Those bodies. Where among them were my parents, my sisters?—But it was stupid to think of it. The real problem was to prove the police had destroyed the city. But what in New Houston would *prove* it?

I was halfway around the rim before I noticed someone trying to catch up to me. A surprise; since my outburst at the Leaky Tap, my reputation as a madman was enough to keep me undisturbed. When I saw it was Hana I slowed down. "What do you want?" I called out.

She joined me without speaking up, then said, "I've identified the taggarts in the explosives that brought down the dome." Her face glowed under the oxygen flowing from her hood's edge. She was upset. "They're American."

"I'm not surprised."

"But—" She made her mouth into a side-funnel to suck down more oxygen, and her eyes watered. She wanted praise, reassurance, I didn't know what. "The Americans?"

"Of course." I was irritated with her naiveté. "Who do you think owns this planet?"

"I know," she protested. "I mean, they back the Committee. But this—"

"This isn't anything new. That 1776 thing is just a story. America runs an empire, and we're part of it. The outermost colony."

"I'm not so sure it's that simple—"

"A colony, I say! The Committee works directly for the Americans and the Soviets."

She sat down on a squarish boulder.

"What's the matter?" I asked. "You've heard me say this before."

"I know, but . . ." She held up the taggart, stared at it.

"But now you know it's true."

She nodded, and I felt sorry for her. But I was angry at her too. She should have believed me before. Wasn't that why she studied with me, to learn what I had taken the trouble to abstract from this mess of a world? That is the trouble with teaching; students only really believe what they've discovered for themselves. You might as well give them a hammer and magnifying glass and throw them into the field.

She sat there like a train had run over her dog. I took a seat on an impact-tortured boulder next to her. Down on the crater floor they were ending the day's work. Through the sepia haze it looked like a town under construction: half the houses done, the other sites covered with building material.

I tried to explain to her how it had come about. "It's the worst of the American and Soviet systems that combined here, I'm afraid." I hefted a shard of compressed basalt. "They wanted the same things out of us, and by the time they were partners down there it was a long established fact up here. And the worst of both systems were the parts that meshed the easiest. So that's what rules us, and everything else too."

"I suppose so."

"Now it was the best of the American and Soviet ways that combined to fight the Committee in 2248, if you ask me. An attempt to enact ideals that never were realized on Earth. But—" I waved the rock at the scene below. "You see what happened to them. And after that they cracked down harder than ever."

Hana nodded. "But they're letting up now, don't you think? I mean, here we are at New Houston. And Publications Review lets through almost everything submitted."

"They know we'll censor ourselves before submitting."

"But not you, or Nakayama, or Lebedyan. And all of you have been published extensively. And people can move wherever they want, now. When the forms come through."

"Publications Review doesn't care about the past. Try an anti-Committee editorial and it would be a different story." I tossed the rock down at the city. "But they are letting up a bit, you're right."

"Maybe the Committee is getting more liberal. New members and all."

Did she mean Shrike? Her face was carefully averted, as she pretended to look down at the city. Perhaps this was a try at a personal comment.

"I think it's only that they don't need to keep the reins so tight anymore. They can afford to ease off, and in fact it makes sense. Keeping the happy consciousness, you know. Everybody's happy."

"You're not."

"Uhn." There, she was doing it again! What did she mean by it? "Maybe I remember too much," I said, to put her off; but then I laughed. "Which is funny, because I hardly remember anything."

She looked up at me curiously. "But you remember the fall of the city?"

"I did remember, that night down in the street. Now I remember that I remembered. Which isn't the same, but it's enough."

"So you want to prove the police did it, because you were there."

Time for some distance; this was making me uncomfortable. "There are other revisionists working with me. Or in the same direction. Nakayama and Lebedyan are both older than me—I wonder if they didn't see the truth too, in some other city. . . ."

But she was looking back toward the escalator. "That's Bill!" She hadn't heard me. "I wonder if he's up here after me."

"You're the only one, then," I said, and was immediately shocked at my rudeness. "He's after you all right," I heard myself go on, with an inane giggle.

"I like him," she said sharply.

"That's good. That makes it easier for him." I could scarcely believe what I heard; I was making it worse with every word! I stood. "I mean, sorry, I mean that makes it better for him. I—I think I'll finish my walk now."

She nodded, still looking back at Bill.

"Those American taggarts will help," I said. "Very useful part of our case."

"I'll write up the results with Bill and Xhosa," she said evenly, without looking up.

We fragment these ruins against our shore: items brushed and tagged and numbered, laid in neat rows on the floor of the museum tent, as we each play Sherlock Holmes with the junk of the past. Archaeology.

So we dug and we sifted, we cleaned and we squinted, and day followed day and week followed week, in a house-to-house search of the dead city. Loss of air pressure when the dome fell had caused some well sealed houses to explode like popped balloons. Messy. Occasionally we discovered the bodies of police troopers, hidden so well that their fellow soldiers had not found them; and what could we say of them? Satarwal proclaimed them victims of the riots, and had them buried. It was driving me mad. Perhaps we would never disprove the Aimes Report. Perhaps it would stand as part of Martian history forever. History is made by the winners, after all; and it is always the loser's fault. Eight hundred thousand people killed?—A very serious riot indeed, and a treacherous mutiny on the part of the Soviet fleet. Two hundred volumes will show you how it happened, and if you want to know more, perhaps we will send you to do research in the asteroids. Perhaps you do not want to know more? We understand.

And so history is made, because facts are not things. But things make facts or break them, or so the archaeologist believes. For every great lie of history—if we assume they were all caught, which would be wrong—for the Tudor's Richard III, for the first Soviet century, the Americans' Truman, the South African war, the Mercury disaster—for each of these lies there had been a revision based on things.

And I swore there would be a revision here too. Satarwal's sneer: "We can explain every thing you find." And his Ministry of

Truth stood massively behind him, confident because the real history never got written down. But archaeology is the art of reading what did not get written. And things don't lie.

"The dome fell and suddenly the rim defense is useless," I said to Hana and Bill and Heidi, one day as we stood in the ruins of the physical plant. "Thousands are dead and the rest are trapped in shelters, and police troops are falling out of the sky. So what do you do? Where do you go?"

"The physical plant here was their last hold-out, right?" said Bill. I regarded him with a skeptical eye; he was quick with the freewheeling theory, slow to back it. "Over the rim from here is what they called Spear Canyon—maybe they used it for cover, and tried to evacuate. Like that note we found seemed to indicate."

"They'd be seen going over the rim," I said. "We need something more likely than that."

Bill shrugged, turned away. And the more I thought of it, the more sense it made. But I said, "Any better ideas?"

"They could have mingled with the civilians and disappeared," Hana said. "When the police made their final assault they would find no one there."

"In which case they would roust the civilians and jail all of them. Although that beats getting killed, I admit. The police reported finding thirty-eight people alive"—including me, I thought—"but they might have lied about that too."

Heidi said, "Kalinin's team found a burn zone just south of here that they think marks a rocket's descent—police supply ship, they're guessing. But maybe the rebels had a ship ready to take off if necessary. Maybe they blasted right out of here."

"Awfully dangerous," Hana said.

"They would be shot right down," I said. "They wouldn't do something that stupid."

So they all stood around and looked cross, as if it were my fault they couldn't think of anything sensible. Though that Spear Canyon was an idea. "No doubt they were captured, executed and shipped out of here," I said.

\* \* \*

*Radial fracture—crustal stresses caused by the Tharsis bulge have re-sulted in an extensive system of fractures in the terrain around it.*

The time came for my visit to the gerontologist, and I got the necessary releases from Satarwal and Burroughs, and took a car to the train depot at Coprates Overlook. I took the train into Alexandria, and went to the clinic early one morning.

It was an all-day exam. I spent the usual hour in Dr. Laird's waiting room, looking at the same old photographs of the Jovian moons. When I walked into his examining room we greeted each other and he went to work in his businesslike way. He had me strip and put me before the gaze of his machines. I drank liquids and stood in front of a battery of mechanical eyes, then was injected and clamped to a slab to submit to more penetrations. Meanwhile pieces of me—blood, urine, feces, saliva, skin, muscle tissue, bone, etc.—were taken away for tests. Dr. Laird then thumped and prodded me with his fingers; primitive stuff, but he appeared to think it necessary. While the samples were being tested and the pictures developed, he pinched my skin in places and asked me questions.

"How's the tendinitis in the knee?"

"Bad. I've felt it more than ever this year."

"Hmm. Well, we could strip that tendon clean, you know. But I'm not sure you shouldn't wait a few years."

"I'll wait."

"How have your moods been?"

Naturally I refused to reply to such an impertinent question. But as he continued to prod and pinch, like a plant geneticist testing the roots and leaves of a new hybrid (will this little shrub live on Mars, Dr. Science?) I thought, why not. When they test the plant they need to know how the flower fares.

"My moods have been up and down." What was the technical terminology for all this? "Out of my control. I'm depressed. I worry about losing it and falling into a funk. Sometimes I feel one

coming so clearly . . . to counteract it I may work too hard, I don't
know. I'm frustrated—"

The nurse came in with the developed pictures, and interrupted my confession. Dr. Laird didn't seem to mind. He took the
pictures from her and pored over them. Still checking them he said
slowly, "Your physiological signs don't show any indication of reduced affectual function. I wouldn't worry about it."

It's worse than reduction, I wanted to say. It's absence. Total indifference. Thalamic shutdown, and so no new memories. Emotional death.

"Your heart is a little enlarged. How much time are you spending in a centrifuge?"

"None."

"That's not quite enough." A disapproving look. "Humans
weren't made for this gravity, you know. We can do the whole program for your immune system and your cell division accuracy, and
you can still ruin it with negligence. I notice also that your facial
skin is severely chapped, and your bone calcium deficient," and so
on—going into his usual litany of my ills. It lasted about ten minutes. Then he began writing out prescriptions and giving me "the
whole program" for curing these ills, talking as if to somebody
else about a plant with problems, a Hokkaido pine with sick nee-
dles, broken bark, twisted limbs, stunted roots. He used up almost
an entire prescription pad, and we spent half an hour going
through the explanation of the drugs and the instructions for their
use. Acetylcholine stimulants, new form of vasopressin-equivalent:
these drugs were new to me, so perhaps he had been listening to
my confession after all. Perhaps there were signs of a funk he
hadn't told me about. "And that tendinitis—I'm going to have you
try this," and he rattled off a new syllabic witches' brew for me.
"Remember—take care of yourself, and you've got an endlessly
replicating system, there. Think about that. If you don't take care,
nothing else is going to matter." A friendly shake of the hand.
Good little shrub. "See you next year."

I put my clothes on and walked into the waiting room. Mimas's
bull's-eye crater stared at me from its poster like the Cyclops. I

looked at the sheaf of prescriptions in my hand. Things as they are have been destroyed. . . .

I could not stand to be in fleshy hothouse Alexandria that night, and I walked to the station to take the very next train east, back to New Houston. In the station I stopped in the drug store and got my prescriptions filled.

> Once we were taut bowstrings, vibrant on the bow of mortality—now the bow has been unstrung, and we lie limp, and the arrow
>    has clattered to the ground.

### Graben

But then I left the station and went back into the city, to see Shrike. That night we had dinner in an Indian restaurant in the lower part of the city, where canals alternate with industrial plants and tenement dormitories, and the poor live everywhere, even under the bridges where the icy canals abrade their skin until the sores look like leprosy. Of course they could get a prescription for it, if they could afford it.

"It's like Soviet history," I said on one of the canal bridges.

Shrike stopped at the bridge's peak. Above us between the shabby dormitories the sky was marbled like a jar of marmalade. "What is?"

"We are. Right after the 1917 revolution the Bolsheviks set up the government, and it ruled the country. Then Lenin built up the party until it was his tool. To get into the government you had to be in the party first, so the party lay on top of the government and was the real power system. Then when Stalin took over, he built the security network as his personal power base. It didn't matter if you were in the party or not—it was the secret police had the power, and Stalin controlled the police. So there was a three-tiered system. Khrushchev's big reform was to dismantle the secret police, and return the power to the Communist party. So it was back to two tiers."

"How are we like that?" Shrike said, peering closely at the tenements surrounding us, looking into an open window where a woman washed clothes.

"You can see it as well as I! The first power system on Mars was the individual rule of the corporations here. The Committee was convened first to be no more than an information pool for the corporations and the Soviets. But the Russians and Americans decided to use the Committee to get control of the planet away from the corporations."

"That would be like Lenin's use of the party?" Shrike said, his voice mocking me with faked interest.

"Right."

"It's not a very close analogy, is it."

"Close enough. And the third step was when the Committee took over all planetary policy—took over the legislative, executive, and judicial powers. At that point Chairman Sarionovich—Kremlin-trained, remember—set up his own five-year plans, overstressing the Martian economy and of course the people, to prove to the two superpowers that we could make them money if he was given a free hand. And they gave him a free hand, and he increased the size and power of the police enormously to accomplish his goals. And so we got the Unrest."

"And now?" Shrike asked, humoring me. "Are we like Brezhnev, Andropov, Chernenko, Kerens?"

"Brezhnev was nongovernment. Confusion and corruption, even when he was healthy. And Andropov and Chernenko were still in the push and pull with the Americans. I'd say you're most like Kerens."

Shrike contemplated me with a big O of mockery rounding his lips. "Why, Hjalmar! What a compliment! That's the nicest thing you've said to me in months, are you sure you spoke correctly?"

"Ach," I said. "Quit being an ass and listen."

"I know. I'm not taking your history lesson seriously. But to tell the truth I find the analogy stretched. Don't you find historical analogies a bit . . . artificial? And you're distracting me from my walk."

"So you look around when you walk in this district! I should think you would turn away, to keep your conscience clean."

"My righteous professor," Shrike said with a wide grin. "My holy professor who shuns all the privileges of his class, and devotes every moment of his life to ending social injustice—"

"Shut up—"

"Who can't imagine any other way of working for change than moaning and groaning from the top of his ivory tower, and digging about in the dirt." By the width of his grin I saw I had angered him, and that surprised me.

"So I've hit a sore spot," I said.

"No! You've hit unfairly, as usual. You bitch at me every time we meet, as if it's impossible for me to be in pursuit of anything but personal power. And then you take advantage of my work every day of your life. So un*grate*ful." He grinned again. "Perhaps I am tired of you, Hjalmar. Perhaps I am tired of working for your good and being nagged about it too. Perhaps you should not have bothered me this evening at all."

But even in the dusk he could see the fear on my face, and after a moment's scrutiny he laughed. "Come back to my place, Hjalmar, and teach me some more ancient history. And leave the righteousness in the canal. You're doing no better than any of the rest of us."

And later that night, in bed, I woke from a doze and said, "Can you get rid of Satarwal for me? He's dangerous, I think."

"How so?" He was half asleep.

"He hates me. It's gone beyond obstructing my efforts, he wants to destroy them—he'll do anything. He's plotting with Petrini against me."

"We'll see. Maybe I've put him out there to keep you on your toes, eh, Hjalmar? To keep you sharp?" And he fell asleep.

*Olympus Mons—the tallest volcano in the solar system; its peak is 27 kilometers above the datum, and its volume is one hundred times that of the largest terran volcano, Mauna Loa.*

One day I ordered my team over the crater rim and into the rift once called Spear Canyon, to do a survey. Bill Strickland gave me an aggrieved look, as if because he had once mentioned the canyon I was obliged to acknowledge him every time the matter came up. Irritably I sent him packing, to complete the gathering of equipment; for this Hana gave me a piercing glare.

New Houston was set in a "splosh crater," meaning the ejecta shield is made of lobes of what was fluidized material directly after the impact. The shield is thus an even surface, except for a narrow rift created by two lobes of fluid being split by some prominence that was later buried by the falling ballistic ejecta of the rim. This rift or canyon broadens to split the shield's low outer rampart, so it opens up directly onto the surrounding plain. Altogether it seemed to me a promising avenue of escape for any party trying to slip away from the crater unobtrusively.

I led my team down the outside of the rim, switchbacking from ledge to ledge down the broken slope. The drop was about one in two, but the use of ledges as ramps made it an easy walk, down pitted rock sheets that lapped over each other like insulating tiles. Behind me the others remarked at the cold; it was a windy day, and most of them wore masks and goggles. But I enjoyed the chill of the harsh wind on me (Dr. Laird would be angry). The sky was the color of old paper; it made a fine dome to hike under.

We explored the length of the canyon, through the break in the rampart and onto the boulder-covered plain. In several places we found remnants of a road that had been cut into the south slope of the canyon. Landslides covered the majority of this road, but near the upper end of the canyon a good stretch of it was clear. The entire team stood on this trace and looked back up at the rim. "It must have switchbacked to the top," Bill said.

"Or stopped in this little cirque," I suggested, "where an escalator could take them up to the dome."

"Possibly," said Bill with a shrug.

"I wonder why they cut the road into the slope when the landslide danger was so great," Hana said.

"Mass wasting is a hundred times faster now," I said irritably. "They built for the erosion of their time."

Bill and Xhosa took off down the course of the road with metal detectors and seismic probes, intent on mapping what they could.

The others dug away at the edges of the slides, and searched the bottom of the canyon, where intermittent ice creeks alternated with slides that had filled the canyon and pushed up the other side. We would have stayed until dark, but the wind was rising. Plumes of sand spindrifted off the rim above us, turning the sun a dull copper and obscuring its troop of mirrors entirely. "We'd better get back," I shouted. "We can continue when the weather improves." For the weather satellite photos had shown a cyclonic system approaching.

So we hiked back over the rim, across the city and over the escalator to camp, swathed in masks and goggles for the final descent down a slope made invisible by the flow of wind-driven sand. The next day the storm broke in earnest, and we were trapped in camp for ten days while thick sandhail pummeled the tents and drifted against their windward sides. For my group it was a long wait, particularly since none of the old maps showed a road in Spear Canyon, implying that it had been built in the city's last days. When the storm broke we were ordered by Satarwal to help dig the camp out of the mud, and that took three more days.

On the afternoon of the third day Hana and Xhosa and I went up to the crater rim to look at the dome foundation above Spear Canyon, and check for signs of an escalator. The foundation was battered in this area, and Hana was giving one of her munitions lectures when something caught my eye. I stared down Spear Canyon, which snaked away from its head about half a kilometer down from the rim. There in the clear post-storm light, had something blinked? Some light had winked at me. I moved my head about experimentally, and there it was again: *blink*. Reflected sunlight, as yellow as fire. On the south slope. "Have either of you got a pair of binoculars?" I said, interrupting Hana.

"There's one in my tool box," Hana said. "What is it?"

"Something down there." I took the binoculars from their case. "Do you see a mirror down there, reflecting light at us? Here, stand where I was standing. On the road, about halfway down what we can see." I looked through the binoculars and focused them, fingers slipping in my haste.

"No light," Xhosa said.

"No, but the sun's moved, and it was small. Look there. There's a new slide, just above the road." Magnified twenty times, the slide was clearly a fresh one, dark brown and sharp-edged at the top and sides. "You should be able to see it even without the glasses, it's dark—"

"About halfway down," Hana said. "I think I see the slide, anyway."

The newly exposed face had the shimmery holographic look of things seen through binoculars. Something floated through the superimposed rings of vision, and I veered back to it. Near the upcanyon edge of the slide *something*—a regular shape, rust-colored, just darker than the smectite clay . . . something smooth, rounded, with a shiny patch in it, like glass. I moved from side to side, and the patch flared gold.

"By God." I cleared my throat. "I think it's—a hut or something. Take a look." I gave the glasses to Xhosa. Hana was shading her eyes, staring at it. "I definitely see the slide."

"I see it," Xhosa said. "Close to the upper end of the slide?"

"Yes."

"That's about where the road would be," he said, and handed the glasses to Hana. He and I looked at each other.

"Let's get down there," I said.

"I'll radio for help," Xhosa said, hurrying to the tool box. "It won't take long for them to catch up."

"I see it!" Hana said. "It looks like a field car to me."

When Xhosa was done radioing for reinforcements we hopped down the ledges of the rim slope like we were in a race. When we got to the head of the rift we jogged down the road. Halfway there we had to slow down and catch our breath. I turned up the oxygen supply from my suit and instructed the others to do the same. We hurried again, and after a short scramble came to the wet, rime-crusted rubble at the bottom of the new slide. A stiff climb up the canyon's side brought us as close to the object I had spotted as we could get without stepping on the new slide.

"It is a car," Hana said.

"Looks like burn marks on the front end there, see?" Xhosa pointed.

That stopped us for a moment; the implication was clear, and I saw foreboding mix with the anticipation on the others' faces. We had all found too many bodies.

I stepped onto the broken clay to test the stability of the slide. The clay was soft, and it seemed possible I might start another slide by walking on it. The car was only five or six meters from the slide's edge, and I wanted badly to reach it before anyone else arrived. Carefully I tamped a footprint down until it was ankle deep; stepped onto it, and tamped down the next one.

"Maybe you should wait," Hana said.

"We'll still have to do this."

"But it would be safer if you were roped to us."

"It seems solid enough."

And so it was. I continued very slowly, and was only a meter or two from the car when a large group came bounding down the canyon, all talking at once. "We scanned this section with a metal detector," Bill said peevishly. "I wonder how we missed this."

"Did you bring any rope?" I called.

"We brought everything," Petrini said. "Have you found buried treasure?"

"Maybe so," Hana said sharply.

"An old field car, slightly burned," I said. "Throw me one end of a rope, please." Now that a rope was available I felt exposed. Bill threw an end to me, and I tied it around my chest, just under my arms. Upcanyon McNeil and two students were hurrying to reach us. I stepped the final distance to the car, checked beneath a rear wheel to see what kind of ground it rested on, and found it was on the edge of the buried road. I hiked back over the slide, finding it solider than it felt before the rope's arrival, and took a holo camera from McNeil. Then I retraced my steps.

The door of the car still had its plastic window intact; it was this that had reflected the sunlight and drawn my eye. I cleared the window of a film of dirt, and peered inside. An empty interior; it looked like a little cave in the canyonside. The windshield was crazed but still intact. The opposite door's window was gone, and dirt spilled through it onto the floor of the car.

"Any bodies?" Petrini asked. Always the first question at New Houston.

"No bodies." It was an eight-passenger car, and the last two seats held boxes. I tried the door; it gave and opened with a loud creak. I reached in and put the holo camera on its stand, set for six holos. When the six beeps had sounded I took the camera out, and carefully tested the floor of the car with my foot. "Don't disturb anything!" McNeil said.

"Oh, McNeil!" several voices cried in unison. The car was firm as bedrock, and I stepped in to look at the boxes in the back.

"They're full of papers," I said, but no one heard me. I could hear my pulse hammering in my ears. Folders, notebooks, plastic sheaves, computer disks, folded maps, blueprints. I picked up a box and carried it outside, hefted it and walked on my prints one more time.

"There's going to be a time when you'll want it all in the position you found it, that's all I'm saying," McNeil muttered. But he looked in the box as curiously as the rest of us when I set it down. And when I returned with the next one he was on his knees with Petrini, poring over the contents.

As I picked up the last box, I noticed a notebook on the floor of the car, nearly buried by the spill of dirt from the broken window. It was a little plastic-covered spiral bound thing, and I almost missed it. I pulled it free, knocked some dirt from it, and carried it across the slide clamped in between glove and box. When I put the box down I kept the notebook in my hand, and showed it to the others. "This was free on the floor."

"Here's a news poster signed at the bottom by an Andrew Jones of the Washington-Lenin Alliance," Hana said from her crouch over one of the boxes. She showed it to Petrini, who read it swiftly, eyebrows lifted.

I was shivering; from the cold, from my excitement, I couldn't tell. I put the notebook in one of the boxes. "Let's get all this back to camp," I said. "I'm running low on oxygen." I looked at the group of clay-smeared people around me, and I couldn't help smiling. "There's a lot of work here."

* * *

*Lava Channels*

Plans for the city's defense; tapes and xeroxes of communications with the Washington-Lenin Alliance in other cities, and in space; lists of people, casualties, weapons, supplies; partial accounts of the revolution in New Houston and the Nirgal Vallis, and around Mars; memos from the Johnson still stations; and maps, including one of the east or lower end of Valles Marineris.

McNeil organized and catalogued as the little boxes were emptied, and he handed each piece or bundle of paper to an eagerly waiting scientist. Almost everyone in the expedition was in the main commons, helping to figure out what we had. Two Xerox machines were working full time to copy everything, several computer consoles were in action, and a cassette player suddenly spoke in voices obscured by radio crackle. The excitement in the air was as palpable as the smell of the copiers. Satarwal was there too, grimly working to appear unconcerned. Few people met his eye, or addressed a comment to him.

As for me—I felt as if I were dreaming. Kalinin and McNeil clapped me on the shoulders, and Kalinin said, "This is it right here, Nederland. You've got your proof."

Hana heard this and looked downcast. I didn't understand this; but then, reflecting on it, I thought I did. I followed her to the coffee machine in the hall.

"He's wrong, you know. We'll need every bit of supporting physical evidence that we can find." So that her taggarts would still mean something, you see.

And the way she smiled at me I knew I had guessed what troubled her. She had felt what I would have felt in her place; and I had figured it out and done something about it to help. I don't know if I am less able than other people to understand my fellow humans, but I suspect it is so. It happened so seldom like this, to see someone's face and know what they felt! Elation bloomed in me like a flower, and impulsively I shook Hana's hand. Even the sight of Petrini and Satarwal conferring down the hall could do nothing to dampen my mood. I returned to the main commons and wandered, looking over shoulders and congratulating students right and left for their good work, causing a growing ripple of smiles and laughter. I shook hands with McNeil, who was still cataloguing. Behind him the Kleserts were leaning over a table, absorbed in one of the notebooks. "It's like reading Scott's journal," Claudia said.

Satarwal came back into the room, and I approached him. "This material implies a cover-up by the Aimes Commission, you know," I said in a friendly way. "Aimes and many of the witnesses are still in government service. Questions are going to have to be asked." And the answers will make heads roll! I wanted to add. Satarwal gave me a cold look, and Petrini joined him.

Petrini, looking over at Satarwal to be sure he had it right, said, "We feel that even though the rioters here in New Houston obviously fancied themselves part of a larger thing, it is still a question whether any planet-wide revolution was planned. Especially given the great bulk of evidence to the contrary in the Aimes Report."

But it only made me laugh, at the time. I was too happy for such nonsense to disturb me. "You people will try to explain away anything. But how much longer can you carry it off?"

So I ignored them and went back to it. Bill Strickland was repacking one of the boxes of Xeroxes under McNeil's direction. He had a worried look on his face, and he said to me, "We should re-scan the whole south slope of Spear Canyon. There may be other things we missed."

"You do that." I saw by his elbow the little plastic notebook that had lain free on the floor of the car. Curiously I picked it up and tucked it under my arm; I had forgotten about it, and now I wanted to have a look at it. McNeil asked me where the boxes of duplicates should be sent, and that took a while. "Hiroko Nakayama and Anya Lebedyan will really enjoy these." Then there were more questions concerning the car from Kalinin, and a quick meal, eaten on our feet; then Hana wanted me to look at one of the city maps found in the first box, which showed that the Leaky Tap tavern had been one of the neighborhood defense centers. With these and other matters a few hours passed, and it was not until everyone but McNeil and I had gone to bed that I got a chance to sit down with the notebook and look at it. "You've had this copied?" I asked McNeil.

"Several times."

So I opened the dirty blue cover. The first page was blank; the second filled with careful, pointy handwriting.

*The first indication I had of the mutiny came as we approached the inner limit of the first asteroid belt. Of course I didn't know what it meant at the time; it was no more than a locked door.*

I followed the crabbed lines of script rapidly. "Emma Weil," I said, looking up at McNeil. "Have I heard that name before?"

"Hellas?" he said, without looking up. "I think she helped design the first city over the reservoir. I repaired the plumbing there once—it was good work for that time. I think she disappeared in the Unrest."

"Well, I've found her again. It says here she was on a mining ship."

"So how did she end up here?"

"I don't know yet."

McNeil came over to my table. "Where's a duplicate of that?"

I laughed. "Did I hear that from McNeil?" I went back to reading. McNeil found a duplicate of the journal, and joined me.

So a Mars Starship Association had started their own private revolution, using the larger one on Mars to cover their theft of three miners, their construction of a *starship*. . . . "That Soviet fleet," I said in wonder, and McNeil was far enough along to nod his agreement. "Have you ever heard of this Mars Starship Association?"

McNeil shook his head. "I just heard of it two pages ago." He looked up. "This is really something!"

"I know." And once I got to the point where Weil agreed to help the mutineers construct their jury-rigged starship, curiosity got the better of me, and I began skimming the pages to discover what happened next. Evading the police—readying the starship—departing for deep space—each incident set me reading faster, until Emma Weil returned to a Mars in the throes of revolution. At that point I slowed, and read with care. I cannot well describe my emotions as I made my way through the last part of her journal; each sentence seemed to answer some question I had, so that I was galvanized repeatedly by shocks of confirmation or surprise. It was as if her voice spoke to me in direct revelation, as if I had stumbled on the greatest samizdat account of them all. I was completely unprepared for the end of the account; on one page she was detailing their plans for the escape from the city, and the next page was blank. The notebook was only two-thirds full. I closed it slowly, thinking hard.

"Looks like they didn't make it," McNeil said. He had skimmed even faster than I. "Those burn marks—the car must have been hit."

"True." I stood to walk around. "But there weren't any bodies in the car. Maybe the car was hit, and in their hurry they left all this."

"Maybe."

"Where's that map of the chaotic terrain east of Marineris?"

"Second box, top. But it's such a small scale map, it couldn't have been used to lead them to anything. The marks may just be water stations."

"Same problem for them, though." I found the map and opened it. Topographic map in faint brown lines, marking the unmistakable forms of the eastern end of Valles Marineris, and the patches of chaotic terrain farther east; and in this wordless forest of closely set lines were four small red dots, three in the southern border of one of the sinks of chaos, and the fourth in its center. Without print I could not immediately name the sink, but a quick check with a planetary map was enough to recognize it; the red dots were in the Aureum Chaos, a deep sink of what was still untouched wilderness. "Maybe this was a general map, and they took the local ones with them."

"Maybe."

I folded the map and placed it in the notebook. "A starship! Can you believe it?"

"No. No wonder she thought they were crazy."

"Yes." But I liked the spirit of the group, their resistance to the Committee. "I wonder how they did."

"Weil was a good designer. If they had the fuel, and the supplies, they might have gone a long way. But who knows how far they would have to go. What did they think they would find? Another Earth?"

"Or another Mars. They were desperate people." Their hatred of the Committee—I knew the feeling, but I had never acted on it. All my work only helped the Committee. What had prodded them to action? What kept me from it? "Is there a spare copy of the journal?"

"Over on the far table."

I walked over and picked up a copy, took it to our mail slots, shoved it savagely into Satarwal's tray, where it wedged firmly. "I don't think he's gotten a chance to see this yet."

McNeil smiled. "The prize of the dig. Martian history won't be the same."

"Yes." I was warm all through, and I knew I was flushed dirt red and grinning like a clown, but I didn't care. I clutched Emma Weil's journal to my stomach and waggled my other hand speechlessly. It felt so strange to have what I wanted. An empty camp commons, tables covered with boxes and papers, lights faintly pulsing, coffeemaker faintly buzzing, a single colleague hunched wearily over a chair in the midnight calm: such a familiar scene in my life, and yet now utterly transformed by the words pressed against me. Now I was the victor in a strewn battlefield, the dreamer standing in his dream realized. "I almost . . . I almost lost hope." McNeil cocked his head at me, showing he was listening with the relaxed economy of a tired man. "But I didn't! And—" I felt the grin grow across my face again. "I'm going to go to bed and read this thing properly."

And so I did. That was the second reading. And how many times since then have I lain down at night to be with Emma Weil, and read her mind, and feel her anger and hope, and wonder fearfully at the blank pages, with their unwritten message concerning her survival and whereabouts, I would not care to guess. A hundred

times, perhaps, perhaps more. I lived with that notebook, and
Emma Weil became part of my mind, so that I often wondered
(fearfully) what she would have made of me, and a day never passed
when I didn't think of her. But I never read her again as I did on
that first night, when I trembled uncontrollably in my bed at the
shock of it, and each successive phrase was like a window into another person's mind—like a new world.

Within the week dozens of reporters joined us, and the students
guided them down Spear Canyon to look at the field car, which
had been completely excavated and pulled out of landslide danger.
The car appeared on all the Martian holo stations. I observed this
activity with great interest; Public Information and Publications
Review were letting all of these reports on the air, and I wasn't sure
what that meant. Satarwal's bosses in Planetary Survey had not released any statements concerning the find, and until they did we
wouldn't learn how they planned to deal with it. I answered reporters' questions over and over: "Some of this evidence contradicts the Aimes Report, yes. No, I can't explain it. Speculate? You
can do that as well as I. Probably better." Soon the reporters were
off to Burroughs, to question Aimes himself; but Aimes refused
comment. And the Committee and all its subcommittees stayed
silent. Still, since they had allowed the dig to take place, they surely
had plans to deal with a discovery like this. I waited to see what
they were.

Satarwal threw his copy of Emma's journal back on my desk.
"Bad luck for her, to fall in with such fools."

I smiled. "One might say the same of you." I tried to hide my
sense of triumph over him, but it may be I failed. "You see, there
was a Washington-Lenin Alliance fighting you."

He grimaced. "No matter what they called themselves, they
were still murderers."

Then a few days later he was recalled to Burroughs. He had all
of his policemen pack up, and they left together, in the cars of the
last group of reporters. What the reporters made of the opportunity I never discovered. I did not go out to see them off.

A few days after that, word arrived that Petrini and I had been made codirectors of the dig. No mention of Satarwal. With this announcement came news of a press conference to be held in the state office in Burroughs. We gathered to watch it on the holo in the main commons. Petrini shook my hand. "Now we are codirectors, as we should have been from the start."

"And with so much left to do," I said; but he took me seriously.

The Committee's spokesman was Shrike. I moved to the back of the commons to watch him, feeling uncomfortable under the eyes of the others in the room.

Shrike was as languid and charming as always with the press, and they loved it. He looked down at the podium, composing his features to an official seriousness: a lean, silver-haired man in a very expensive gray suit; small silver rings on each little finger and in each earlobe; sharp nose, thick eyebrows, dark blue eyes. He read a statement first. "The recent finds in the excavation of New Houston are an exciting and moving addition to our knowledge of one of the most troubled times in Martian history. Those months of 2248 called the Unrest were a time of great suffering and heroism, and this new account of the brave defense of a beleaguered city is inspiring to all of us who love Mars. The men and women who fought for New Houston were struggling for the rights and privileges that we now take for granted, and it is partly because of their sacrifices that we enjoy the free and open lives that we now live. We commend the fine archaeologists of the Planetary Survey and the University of Mars for their historic discovery."

And he looked directly into the cameras, knowing that I would be watching—so that I could feel the shock of his mocking smile, and know it was meant for me.

First newswoman: "Mr. Selkirk, don't these discoveries, particularly the proof of the existence of the Washington-Lenin Alliance, contradict the conclusions of the Aimes Commission Report on the Unrest?"

"Not at all," Shrike said cheerfully. "If you will read the Aimes Report again"—he stopped to allow the laugh he had drawn to extend as far as possible, smiling a little—"you will see that it concludes that there was a well-organized revolt against the legal authority on Mars, led by the Soviet mining fleet. The Commission never found the name of this organization, but the new discoveries in New Houston do substantiate what the Commission found. Eminent historians such as Hiroko Nakayama and Hjalmar Nederland have been working for years to identify the secret organizers of the Unrest, and in fact it was Nederland who discovered the so-called 'escape car' outside New Houston. In the same way other historians have been exploring the connections between the Unrest and the reforms made in Martian government in the century following the Unrest."

And the reporters nodded faithfully and whispered their approval into their wrist recorders, for the general populace, still in the mines and dormitories, to hear.

So they would explain it all away.

I left the room feeling sick. They would admit what they had to, and twist everything else to fit their new story, which would constantly change, constantly protect them. I tasted defeat like copper coating my tongue. Every thing I stabbed them with they would accommodate with elastic facts, until the thing was absorbed and dissolved.

But I had expected it. I was prepared for something of the sort; I had already made plans to keep stabbing away. Still, it had been a shock to hear Shrike lie like that. My old heart fluttered and my stomach clenched, and though I wanted to leave the main tent I had to sit down for a while first. Even though I had known perfectly well they would do something like this.

The computer link-up to Alexandria told me a little about Emma Weil. She was born in the Galle Crater camp on the rim of the Argyre basin, in 2168. Her parents divorced and she lived with her father. She studied mathematics on the campus in Burroughs, led the ecologic engineers designing the Hellas basin complex, broke records in four middle-distance runs. When the Committee took over the mining fleets in 2213 she was shifted from Royal Dutch to the center for development of life-support systems, then shifted again to active duty on the miners. The records for the asteroid mining projects were incomplete, because of damage to offices and archives in the Unrest; I found no account of *Rust Eagle*, or of Emma after 2248. And there was no comment on her disappearance.

For Oleg Davydov, I could find only a listing in the Birth Registry (born on Deimos in 2159) and an appointment as a rocketry and guidance cadet in the Soviet mining fleet. After that, nothing: no appointments, no trial, no command of *Hidalgo*. No mention of *Hidalgo*, either.

And I could find nothing whatsoever concerning the Mars Starship Association. Not a single word about it.

Clearly the censors had been at work. But the documentation of Martian history was damaged and disorganized for good by the Unrest. Pockets of information exist in odd places, and it is seldom the censors can catch everything. It would take a more extensive, on-site search than I could make from New Houston, but I thought that if I had some time in Alexandria, I might be able to ferret out more. I had done it before.

I gave up on that aspect of things and switched back to Emma. I had a picture of her sent out, one taken at the beginning of her mining service. She had an oval face, a serious mouth, brown hair and eyes, fine cheekbones and jaw; I liked her look. I stared at that photo for many a night, and read her journal, *I hated the Mars Development Committee as much as I hated anything. I hated their lies; that they were taking over power to make a better life on an alien planet etc. etc. Everyone knew that was a lie. But we kept our mouths shut; talk too much and you might get relocated in Texas. Or on Amor. The members of the MSA had compensated with a stupid plan, but they resisted! And me? I didn't even have the guts to tell my friends how I felt. I had thought cowardice was the norm, and that made it okay,* and so I sat in my plush university apartment writing papers about events three hundred years past, pretending I was the fiercest anti-Committee man on the planet, while I lapped up every sop they threw me, and fawned for the favors of a Committee member. What kind of resistance was that? What had I ever done but gesture and shout, before rulers who tolerated me and smiled behind their hands to hear one of the professors at it again. Oh Emma! I wanted to be like her, I wanted to be able to act.

Nakayama and Lebedyan and several others rose up in protest against the Committee's claim that what we had found in New Houston could be squared with the Aimes Report. Criticisms were flying in from every direction, and I only needed to stand aside and help orchestrate it, and keep records. Parts of Emma's journal were released by the university to the newspapers, and the whole thing was published soon after; it became a bit of a best-seller. It seemed there was a public intrigued by this news from their own forgotten pasts, at least for a week or two. Anya Lebedyan gave me a call to congratulate me and ask some questions, and without hesitation she began the conversation in Russian; I felt a thrill to speak in the language of the samizdat. I found I spoke Mars's underground language as fluently as I read it, though I could not remember the long-ago life in which I had learned it.

Out on the rim on a cloudy day: chocolate thunderheads scudded north, and thick bolts of lightning alternated with shafts of buttery sunlight. Then the clouds flattened out and covered everything like a rumpled blanket, and it was evening all afternoon. Below me my team worked in the dead city. Strolling the rim ridge I examined its texture as if I could see the world beneath the rock. Samuel Barber's "Adagio for Strings" floated through my mind. Down at the physical plant Hana and Bill discussed something intently. They paid more attention to each other than to their work. I hiked down the rock ledges to Spear Canyon, descended the canyon to the field car. Climbed in and sat down.

Here Emma Weil had once sat, perhaps in the very seat I was occupying. It had been night; their lights would have been off as they inched down the road with the canyon dropping away to their left. Police artillery hammering at the city. Hearts hammering inside spacesuits that are no shield against shrapnel—or bullet or heat beam. The electric motors are silent, and no helicopters fly in the primal atmosphere; but somewhere, on the rim perhaps, heat-seeking automatic artillery has turned in its bed, aimed and fired, and some cars explode, others are damaged and halt, still others, perhaps, turn off their motors and coast down the canyon, rolling to freedom.

Some of them undoubtedly were killed. But there had been no bodies in this car. If the police had removed the bodies, they would have taken the papers as well. The same was true of the rebels. Since we found the papers, no bodies had been removed. Thus the explosion that stopped the car had not killed the occupants. Or so one line of reasoning could lead one to conclude. And it appealed to me, oh yes, it appealed to me. Sitting there on the crackly frozen plastic seat I tried to *feel* what had happened to her; and in my vision she lived. There was no sense of death in that car. Perhaps she had only lived long enough to crawl out of the car, so that her body lay in the soil of her beloved planet just meters from me. But no. The metal detectors would have indicated her suit. No, she had escaped. Escaped to the hills. Not dead, not my Emma.

I took out the small photo of her that I carried in my suit pocket, and smoothed it over my thigh. They had been headed for refuges in the chaos, where they very well might have hidden, from that day to this. Emma still alive, working with her biogeo-cenosis on the planet she loved.

And it occurred to me that I might find her.

*Impact crater—with a diameter of 2,000 kilometers, Hellas Basin is the largest impact crater on Mars.*

Then came the discovery on Pluto. It was Strickland who brought word out to us in the city. We were digging out a defensive center that had been bombed flat, and I was down with Xhosa attaching crane cables to a beam we had cleared. "Dr. Nederland! Hana! There's news in from Burroughs," and *crunch* he jumped over the rubble and into the cellar with us. We stared at him, surprised, and he drew up like a policeman at attention.

"What is it," I said.

Hana looked into the cellar and Bill turned to her. I thought that in his agitation there was a certain pleasure. "They've found a monument on Pluto. The Outer Satellites Council sent the first manned expedition out last year, and they've just arrived and found some sort of monument. Rectangular beams of ice set on their ends, in a big circle. Apparently it looks very old—"

"But that's crazy!" Hana said.

"I know! Why do you think I ran over here shouting and all?" Bill sat on the ground, dialed up his oxygen flow.

"It is crazy," Xhosa said. "Somebody must have . . ."

"Come back to the tents and see," Bill said. "They sent pictures."

So we dropped our work as if it were nothing, and followed him back to camp. The main tent was already filled with people, and the clamor of voices assaulted us as we entered; it had never been so loud in there. I barged through the crowd and wedged into the group surrounding the largest table. Several photos were being passed from hand to hand; abruptly I reached out and snatched one as it was held across the table. "Hey!" my victim yelled, but I turned my back on her and plunged out of the crowd, into the dining room.

It was a small photo and it looked as though it had been taken in black and white. Black sky, a gray regolith plain marked by the low superimposed rings of ancient craters, and in the middle distance, a ring of tall upright white blocks, some slender, others thick and massive. They were lit by searchlights set off to one side, and five or six of the columns' faces were brilliantly white, as if they were mirrors catching the light. Human figures in bulky whitish suits were a quarter or a fifth of the height of the columns; they stood on the outside of the circle, heads craned back as they looked up at the closest block to them. The ring appeared to be about two hundred meters in diameter, maybe half again more. I couldn't be sure. A little stone circle (white stone?) on Pluto.

I must have stood hunched over that photo for half an hour. I don't know what I thought in that time; I was a blank. The photo seemed out of a dream. It was just the sort of thing I would dream. And I am always stunned to blankness in my dreams. Yet here my colleagues milled about the next room chattering, announcing the real.

Petrini banged on the table. "Please, people. I have more news. Listen here. Pretty clearly the group that recently arrived there was not the first to visit Pluto, as they thought they were. It must have been quite a shock! Anyway, they've sent back some information with these photos. The object is located at the geographical north pole. The towers in the ring are made of water ice. There are sixty-six of them, and one has fallen over and shattered. Another has an inscription on it."

This brought complete silence.

"Jefferson at the university library in Alexandria has identified the inscription as Sanskrit. I know, I know! Don't ask *me* to explain it. I suppose someone has been up to games out there. The inscription is a couple of verbs and a series of slashmarks. The verbs both mean roughly 'to push farther away.' The slashes make a simple arithmetical progression, two then two, then four then eight."

"Twenty-two forty-eight," I said. "The year of the Unrest." And immediately a certain passage in Emma Weil's journal came to mind. She had visited Davydov's cabin, found him sleeping, found plans on his desk. . . .

Petrinin shrugged. "If you assume the slashes are a date in our calendar. But with this I don't think it's safe to assume anything."

I scarcely heard him. "Where are the expedition's transmissions coming to?"

"Burroughs. The university's space center."

"I'm going to go there and send up some questions, and monitor everything they send down."

"But why?"

"I'll be back as soon as I can." I excused myself and left. Some curious looks were given me, but I didn't care. Let them think what they liked.

. . . *They were diagrams, several versions of the same thing . . . all circular, or near it . . . a circle slightly flattened on one side. Around this faint circumference were little rectangles, set at different angles, blackened by pencil. . . .* "Something to leave a mark on the world, something to show we were here at all—"

Perhaps, I thought, perhaps this discovery on Pluto, which had given me such a shock, and made me so uneasy, might be turned to advantage after all. Perhaps it was not the disaster it had felt to me down in that cellar.

\* \* \*

*Ejecta*

The Planetary Survey refused me permission to leave New Houston, so I called Shrike. "You need help," he observed.

"Yes."

"Did you see my press conference?"

"Yes. Did you write the speech yourself?"

"No."

"I didn't think so. Do you know how many lies there were in it? Or do you care?"

"Were there *lies* in it?"

"You don't care. You'd read anything you were given, wouldn't you. That's the fate of the new man on the Committee. It's disgusting."

"I thought you were calling for a favor?"

". . . I am."

"I'll think about it. But I'm disappointed you didn't like my performance."

"A performance is just what it was." I couldn't contain myself. "But it won't wash, you know. Lebedyan and the rest are already poking holes in what you said, and in all the other statements made by the Survey on the find. You can't pretend there wasn't a false history, Shrike. There are too many contradictions. What we've found here plain contradicts what Shay said about the assault on New Houston. Check it out in the Aimes Report."

"I'll do that, Hjalmar," he said with a smile.

"You'd better! Aside from the gall of it, which is disgusting, it makes you look foolish to get sent out there to spout obvious lies. It weakens your position because as the spokesman *you* get associated with the lies, and the clumsiness behind them. It's bad for you. And you aren't going to be able to lie your way out of this one. You'd better tell your bosses that, and start figuring out something else."

"Thanks for the statecraft lesson, Hjalmar," he said, mocking me.

"I'll trade it for a trip to Burroughs," I said roughly. "I want to find out more about that thing on Pluto."

"Fascinating, isn't it? It's the talk of Burroughs. What is it, do you think?"

"More trouble for you." But I saw his upper lip lift a touch, and I let off. "But good for Mars, my Shrike; you can bet on that."

"Hmph." And he made me sweat and plead for a while. But I said the right things, and he agreed to help.

Riding the train to Burroughs, forehead pressed to the window glass: copper clouds shredded under a dark brown sky. Sometimes I feel like those clouds, torn east and scattered in the gales of Time. I knew that with this trip another life of mine was ending. Around me in the train car voices discussed the marvel of the day, the mysterious monument on Pluto. Did it mean the Atlanteans had actually lived? And developed space flight too? In my mind's voice, so much more mellifluous than my own, I groaned and lectured the speakers severely. No crackpot theories, please! This is difficult enough as it is! But of course crackpot theories would spring up around this discovery like a ring of daughter mushrooms around one of those spore-exploding kinds. No avoiding it. Out on the rock-stubbled expanse of Sinus Sabaeus someone had cleared an area and lined up the collected rocks to spell REPENT. I stared at the message through the faint reflection of my head: tufted black hair, close-set eyes, grim little mouth. How could Shrike stand me.

I knew that my distress at this Pluto discovery was personal; it disrupted my habits. I had been in a situation I could predict, in a little society I could understand. I worked hard to create such nests of habit, as everybody does, for without habit life would be too abrasive and too long to live. And for a decade or two I would have been peacefully at work in the heart of the most important excavation in Martian history. The dig itself would have been Martian history. Now this Pluto monument had arrived like a meteor through the roof, knocking everything apart and thrusting me into the new. Now I wandered in new terrain, in the bare interregnum between successive exfoliations of life, completely exposed to the danger of the new.

Now the historical community and the fickle world would forget New Houston in favor of this more exotic discovery—*unless* I could show that Emma's journal held the key to the new find. Show that the starship she had refused to join had left the monument as marker and proof of their transplutonian passage; show that it was a monument to the Unrest. I would need more than the brief paragraph in her journal to stem the flood of crackpot theories. It would take an entire case, and the plan for that was clear: a search for the Mars Starship Association in the archives at Alexandria.

Another mystery to solve. I should have been pleased at the thought, but still I felt only the sharp distress of exposure, and something other than that which verged on fear, and which I did not recognize. Perhaps we undertake the solution of mysteries as a sort of training, so that we can attempt with some hope of success the deciphering of our selves.

In Burroughs I went to my apartment on campus to store my bags. Kitchen in mahogany and black-green ceramic; living room dominated by a bookcase that extended from floor to ceiling around two walls; a thick silver-gray carpet leading down a skylighted hall to a tiled bathroom the size of the living room, almost; and a bedroom filled by a square bed on a dais. The stupid splendor of the bachelor professor. I couldn't believe I had had it furnished myself. Who was that Nederland, anyway? No wonder I always wanted to be out on a dig.

I crossed the big campus yard, muttered, "Tear it all out, leave bare chambers of wood and plaster, books piled up, mattress in the corner." The yard lay above the city center and I paused near the statue of the Princess to look out at it. My year in New Houston had warped my sense of scale, and the skyscrapers by the river, the bridge of the water district, the broad boulevards like spokes of a bent wheel, radiating out to the higher residential areas on the slopes of Isidis Planitia, all of it seemed fantastically large to me, gigantic beyond the ability of city planners to conceive. An entire basin made into a river valley, a city of four million under the open sky: what would the citizens of New Houston have thought? What would *we* have thought of it, three hundred years before? . . . The past was a simpler place (I know that's wrong). Our minds are formed in our youth, and stay the same no matter how long we live. "Come on, fossil," I told myself. The Princess looked down on me compassionately. "Stone man, go see this circle of ice men." Students glanced at me, walked on unconcerned.

In the department office everything was the same, of course. Lucinda and Corey greeted me and gave me my mail. I have often thought of the department as family: secretaries as aunts and uncles, colleagues as fierce siblings, students as children. How much closer to me were these people than my biological family. Children, grandchildren, great-grandchildren, great-great, etc.—I don't know how far it extends—I had seen none of them in decades. Most of them were in the asteroids, or farther out, where the Outer Satellites Council lets anarchy reign. Blood, when you get right down to it, is not much thicker than water. But here in the familiar offices Lucinda asked how the dig was coming, how Hana and Bill were progressing, what Xhosa's latest complaint was— and what did I think of this remarkable thing on Pluto? "Alien radio receiver," I said, and they laughed. That's family for you.

My mail was junk, except for a long handwritten letter from my third wife. She was struggling with a funk, and this letter was part of her therapy. It had taken her a month to compose it, and it read like the diary of a zombie. "I took a walk by the canal. The ice was thick and starred by rocks thrown by little boys." Poor Maggie. I put the letter away to finish another time. She had written boring letters even when she wasn't in a funk.

Over in the space center's big projection room Stallworth, Lewis, Nguyen, and some others I didn't know were ready and waiting for me. "Roll it," Nguyen called to the technician.

Black room. Then over the floor appeared the dark ringed plain I had seen in the little photo. A star-thick night sky appeared against the domed ceiling; the sun was two or three times brighter than Sirius, and lay low on the horizon.

"Icehenge at its closest is fifty meters from the geographical north pole," Nguyen said.

"Icehenge?"

"That's what they're calling it."

"A henge is a circular earthen mound," I objected.

"The analogy is with Stonehenge," Nguyen said cheerfully. "Besides, the liths have been set on the rim of a subdued crater, so that they're a meter or two above the plain. So you can call the rim your henge."

"Ridiculous."

"So where is it?" Stallworth said. I had worked with him before on dating methods, his specialty.

"This holo was made by Arthur Grosjean, the chief planetologist on the *Persephone*. He gives us the same walking approach that they had. Note the jiggling horizon. It'll appear in front of us. It's summer in Pluto's northern hemisphere, so the megalith is in constant sunlight."

"Shouldn't that be megahydor?" I asked caustically.

"You know what I mean. Quiet, here it comes."

But Stallworth said, "This cratering must have spanned billions of years. How did a planet so far away from everything else get so heavily cratered?"

"There's no agreement on that," Lewis said. "One theory is that Pluto was a moon of one of the gas giants, and that after it took the usual heavy bombardment it was cast out to the edge of the system by a near collision."

"With what?" Stallworth said.

"I don't know. Ask Velikovsky." Lewis laughed. "Mountjove claims the cratering is fifteen billion years old, and that Pluto is a captive planet from a very early solar system."

The horizon was suddenly cracked by a dozen white points, like stars growing to spires of white light. We shut up. The cart that had carried the holo camera jiggled over a submerged crater wall. Soon the entire ring of towers was over the horizon and in our sight. As it came toward us my heart began to flutter painfully. The cart moved between two towers and into the center of the ring. The regolith surface was undisturbed; shouldn't the construction of the monument have chewed up the area with tracks?

The average towers were ten to fifteen meters tall, two or three meters wide, and one or two thick; some were much bigger. Three of the liths were triangular in cross-section rather than rectangular. One of the big squarish ones had broken off near its base and fallen in toward the center, shattering into scores of sharp-edged white blocks. The holo camera rolled toward this ruin, and when it stopped I walked over to that side of the chamber and stood waist deep in the mirage of an ice boulder.

The others chattered to each other about Saturn's water ice and the stone circles of Neolithic Britain, etc., but I shut my ears to them and looked at the thing. I fell into the illusion of vast space that the holo created, and tried to get a sense of the place.

"The north pole is beyond the sequence of very large liths," Nguyen said.

"Be quiet for a while and let us look," I said.

I walked around and looked at it. Someone had had a good sense of form. It was a human construct, I felt sure; it had the look of mind marking cosmos, like the paintings on a cave wall. Sixty-six liths. Distance between them, ten meters or so. Something brushed the edge of memory and I walked away from it, over to where the others were reading the inscription lith. Deeply cut curved calligraphy, and under that the sixteen slashes.

Was it Stonehenge I was reminded of? No—I had a postcard picture of that in my mind, a little domesticated thing in a protective dome, looking like a piece of sculpture by Rinaldi. And the lintels gave it a different shape. No, it was something else—a moor—the sea like pewter—

Another tendril of an image was drowned in the present. What the senses tell us can overwhelm all else, and that is good, but sometimes I could wish otherwise. Or was it relief I felt? Confused, I stepped away from the others. Looking around at the ice beams poking out of that stark landscape I was struck by the strangeness of it, and I sank to the floor, slipping through the gravel as if I didn't exist, as if I were the holo and the ground were real. The sense of the room left me entirely and for a moment I was on Pluto, on an almost transparent Pluto where you could sit unsuited, and breathe cool air, and stare at a megalith more silent and enigmatic than any pointing at Earth's sky. Awe—so rare, so longed for—so much like its cousin terror, when it does flood the mind. And it was the edge of deep fear that brought the elusive memory crashing out of *presque vu* into consciousness: the moor by the sea, a thumbnail crescent of moon, Madeleine's round face full of pity. I scrambled to my feet, frightened and excited. My trip to Earth—images from it were strung like algae in filaments, one led me to the next immediately. My nerves jangled and my blood spurted through me, and Pluto and Mars alike vanished.

I was holding my temples in my hand when the lights came up, and I am afraid my colleagues saw me in that pose and thought me mad. I barely noticed; I made some excuse to Nguyen and Stallworth, and stumbled out of the center into the surprising light of a clear afternoon.

*Lemniscate islands—in the outflow channels these knobs of rock harder than their surroundings were scoured into their characteristic shape by the catastrophic floods that carved the channels.*

I remember I spent the trip to Earth in the centrifuge, working out in terran gravity to prepare myself for landfall. My third wife Maggie had just left me; she hadn't wanted me to make the trip. I didn't want the marriage to end. We had children, my habits were firm. Nothing would have tempted me to break them but a voyage to Earth. The Committee hated anyone going, but I got the chance and I left, feeling utterly depressed, a whole life shattered behind me. Again I was in an interregnum, stripped of habits, painfully alive.

Quickly I took new habits, grew a new exfoliation. The voyage itself was a life, and I remember it all of a piece. I worked out every day until my body no longer felt like a backpack weighing me down; it was still heavy, but I could carry it. Every day I worked on those machines until I was too tired to think.

There was a woman there doing the same work, though her

motives were less negative. She worked to make her lungs pump like bellows, her skin pop sweat at every pore. She attacked the machines with brio, and laughed at my grimness. Have you tried this machine? she would ask. That one? I would shake my head and try them. She only talked about workouts, and I liked that. Her name was Madeleine. She was about my age—one hundred or so. Of her appearance I recall only a mass of thick dark blond hair, tied back in the centrifuge, let free in the commons, where it drew my eye always. And she was strong.

But it didn't occur to me that I was falling in love. How could I be? I was tired, sick of love, too drained ever to feel it again. How many times could it happen, after all? Wasn't love another finite power of ours, that would run out like water from an aquifer? And Madeleine was so distanced (but I liked that). So we talked for hours as we worked out. She taught me to jump rope. We traded our stories. She had helped to organize the tour, and had been to Earth twice before. And every day we worked until we collapsed, in the "air soup" of Earth. Perhaps that soup does something to the brain. Because I could feel it happening again, no matter what I commanded myself to think. It's *frightening* how helplessly people are themselves! We think, "I understand myself, I will change, I will take control, I will protect myself," and then in any kind of stress we behave with exactly the same character we were born with, the character beneath the "I." So I fell in love helplessly, as if catching a disease.

And Madeline liked me. I pumped weights until I could be pleased with my body, and I avoided looking in the centrifuge mirrors, where my red cheeks and stiff black hair would have mocked me. Too bad you can't work out on your face. (Vanity is slow to die; even past two hundred, when our faces resemble turtles', we value them as great maps of experience, histories of emotional lives. And at this time I was only a hundred, and looked very young.)

The memory exists in small linked cells, like diatoms of algae in a filament; next diatom: stepping out of a shuttle onto a desert floor, our group like a croud of Columbuses. Despite my workouts I felt heavy, and the blazing sun stunned me. It seemed the sky burned. And the blue—that color doesn't exist on Mars, but I felt that there was a part of my brain that was made to recognize sky blue.

Brief images of our tour: Madeleine led me up trails from Mac-chu Pichu; we laughed at the solemn statues of Easter Island; a tour guide deferred to my knowledge of some site or other. Though I felt a dreamlike recognition for Earth's ruins from my years of study, I still clumped around as wide-eyed and rubber-necked as the rest of our group. We looked like asteroid miners in Burroughs, I am sure.

Bigger diatom: at Angkor Wat one evening, Madeleine and I crawled over the crumbling temples under smeary twinkling stars. Standing on a vine-covered roof in the twilit jungle I saw a look I knew on her face. Just as I embraced her to kiss her a bug the size of my fist buzzed between our faces. We leapt back—"My God!"—stumbled on vines, laughed. "What was *that?*"

"I don't know," Madeleine said, "but it sure was ugly!"

"You're not kidding! A dragonfly?"

"You've got me." We looked about warily. "Hope there aren't more."

"Me too."

"Sure glad there aren't any big bugs like that on Mars."

"Me too. Pretty scary bug, all right."

And we laughed. That was the embrace. A few minutes later she said, "But we can't do it out here. We might get attacked by *bugs!*" And we went back to her room at the hotel.

And in Persepolis, one sharp image: as I strode over the hectares of strewn marble like Tamburlaine, euphoric with the raw impact of the past, she said to me, "You make it new."

But in Florence we joined another group, from the university in Hellas, and their guide and Madeleine were old friends. Wasn't that how it happened? They took off together into the city. Why not? Jealousy, what foolishness. Perhaps I am less able than most people to control my emotions. Florence reminded me of Bur-roughs, with the yellowing stone and the river running down the crease in the hills, and all the bridges. I walked the narrow streets with a marble pedestal in my stomach that almost bowed me over. The fierce sun beat on me in pulses and burned my neck, and I could hardly breathe in the thick wet air. Madeleine and her friend appeared in an alley, searching for local ice cream. I got sick of all the beggars and sat in my room at the hotel listening to the cutting melancholy of the "Souvenir of Florence." I forgot the Etruscans, the Renaissance; all I cared for was the feeling in that sextet. You can make unhappiness into an aesthetic experience, and everyone tries to, so there must be something to it; but I don't think it does much good. It only means you will remember it better, because of the coding in objective correlatives. It doesn't make you less unhappy.

Well, it was stupid of me. I admit that.

Last diatom, the largest—the one remembered in the holo chamber: we visited the Orkney Islands north of Britain, to see the passage graves and the stone rings of Stenness and Brodgar. The islands were abandoned, and a rime of frost covered the ground in the mornings, as it was early winter. I insisted that Madeleine take a dawn walk with me, over the heath to Stenness ring. The land we crossed looked almost Martian. I told her that I loved her, she said I didn't know her well enough to say such a thing. As if knowledge had anything to do with love. "You know what I mean," I said.

"I think I do. But you know Onega, the guide for the Hellas group?"

I nodded.

"I love him, Hjalmar. I have for years. Please don't be angry! I've enjoyed our trip," etc. Then she left, claiming duties at the hotel.

I walked among the standing stones of Stenness, overlooking the lochs of Harray and Stenness to east and west. The narrow irregular gray stones spiked up at the swiftly moving, stippled clouds. Off across the loch the ring of Brodgar, tiny in the distance, stood in a patch of sun. A world of slates. Slate people: old tales said these stones were farmers caught dancing in a pagan rite. I leaned my forehead against the pitted, lichen-covered side of one, and felt myself shake. So often this had happened and I had resolved never to extend myself again—the aquifer was drained, the land above collapsing!—and here just the slightest show of friendship and I had done it again. Not the slightest bit of control over myself. There was something wrong with me, I knew it. I *felt* it.

What I wanted then was a marriage like the Greek ideal, two strong trees grown round each other in a double helix, each stronger for the help of the other, and intertwined for good. Some people found such marriages even in our age, and I wanted one. I was just beginning to understand that my life was a series of discrete lives, and that I could not count on any family or friend to stay with me through more than one life. So that I would never really come to *know* anybody. Unless I could find that partner, you see, that Greek marriage.

But I couldn't. And leaning against that rough stone it seemed to me that there were two kinds of people: the attractive sociable people, who drew to each other and had their serious relations together; and the rest of us, the plain or ugly or maladroit, who had to make do with one another no matter how much we loved beauty and charm. And realizing this warped the maladroit even more, so that our relations among ourselves were filled with resentment and frustration and anger and pity, which doomed them to failure. As in my three marriages, and in all the other liaisons in which I had tried so hard and failed so miserably.

In the midst of this fit of bitter self-pity I caught sight of a dozen or so of our party, hiking in my direction and pointing across the loch at the stones of Brodgar. One great ring viewed from another, across a band of metallic water: it was an eerie, wonderful sight. The group was like a pantomime of excitement, and though I did not feel it, I understood. On all of Earth I had not seen a place more beautiful (that is, more like Mars). So the cheerful alien tourists approached, happy on familiar ground, and when they saw me some waved. They entered the ring. One of the women was telling them about the megalithic yard, and the astronomical significance of the stones' placement. She was a withdrawn, shy woman who had scarcely said a word during the rest of the tour, but the stone rings appeared to be her subject. "They could calculate the midsummer and midwinter sunrises, and they could even predict eclipses."

"Wrong," I told them. "Your information is as dated as the idea of ley lines. These rings had some simple sun alignments, but they were by no means scientific observatories. To think so is to impose our way of thinking onto the prehistoric mind, and so to distort the past. And the megalithic yard, by the way, is no more than a freak of statistical interpretation."

The woman looked down, turned away. The others glanced at her awkwardly; her reign as expert was done. But I saw they also thought me an ass, and I knew I had been rude at best. Immediately I wanted to apologize to the poor woman, to explain my ill humor, but I couldn't see how without bringing up my own affairs. Besides, she had been spouting nonsense; what was I supposed to have said? A tall, brown-haired woman broke the uncomfortable pause with a hearty, "Well, shall we see Brodgar and the Comet Stone?" And they trooped off around the shore of the loch, surrounding the expert, pointedly not inviting me along. The tall woman stared back at me.

I was left walking about the frosted hummocks of dead gray-green grass, feeling worse than before. I didn't want to stay there, but there seemed no reason to leave, and nowhere to go. I wrapped my arms around a lichen-chewed standing stone and watched the gray clouds blow over, leaving a white sky that turned pale blue at dusk. At my feet were little flowers, specks of color scattered over the rock and heather, violet, yellow, pink, red, white. I began to feel very odd indeed, and I banged my forehead against the stone rhythmically, thump thump thump.

My hands were as blue as the sky. A thin crescent moon hung over the distant loaf hill across the loch to the west. A cutting breeze wafted off the ruffled dark silver water, and I was cold. Four thousand years before, humans had put up these stones to mark the strangeness of the place, and of their lives in it; I knew four thousand times what they knew, but the world was no less strange and harsh for that. With the sun down the standing stones, the island, the loch, the little ring on the land beyond, the bone-bare hills in the distance, they all gleamed under the rich dark blue sky, and I was frightened by their starkness. A world stripped bare.

Near dark I roused myself and walked stiffly back to the stone hotel near the passage grave of Maes Howe. I sat before the fireplace and held my hands over the flames for a good part of the night; but I could not get the chill from them.

*  *  *

*Jökulhlaps—these glacial bursts occur in Iceland, where underground reservoirs heated by volcanic action melt through glacial caps in catastrophic floods.*

Now I begin to see that I have underestimated the memory. Events keep piling into it beyond its natural capacity, and it becomes packed tight. The chambers of the hippocampus and amygdala are overwhelmed. What remains of the distant past is jammed under the weight of subsequence, so that recollection is stressed, then disabled. But the memories remain. To be able to recall them takes a particular form of intelligence; so that when I curse my poor memory, I am really lamenting my stupidity.

The other form of remembrance, the epiphanic recollection, is not really recollection at all. Under the right pressure the past bursts into consciousness, as a string of images we have created— so we see not the past, but a part of ourselves, a sweet fragment to make us ache with the poignancy of time lost, and the beauty of connection with it.

In the interregnum, in the naked moment between lives, we are most vulnerable to experience.

On the Earth events have a sheer physical weight of significance.

When we leave our natural span, and venture into the centuries, we are like climbers on Olympus Mons, hiking up out of the atmosphere. We must carry our air with us.

I don't know what I am.

*Valles Marineris—just south of the equator are several enormous interconnected canyons, extending some four thousand kilometers from the Tharsis bulge east to low-lying areas of chaotic terrain.*

The Subcommittee for Planetary Affairs and the University Faculty Board and the Planetary Survey all denied me permission to visit the libraries at Alexandria—I suspected Satarwal was behind the refusals, exerting influence in Burroughs—and so I went to Shrike for help again, and got it. I knew it was bad to pile up too many debts to Shrike, but there was no other way to get the work done.

On the long train ride west I sat in a window seat in a nearly empty car. From the car ahead came the sound of a child playing, and I went up to have a look; it was a ten-year-old, flying plastic airplanes to his parents; and at the other end of the car was a crowd of spectators, watching curiously. The child ignored them as he retrieved his planes from under their hungry stares. I felt bad for him and returned to my seat. Outside, the train slid along the southern rims of Eos and then Coprates Chasma. Coprates, so simple and huge, gave me the feeling we were flying; the canyon floor was kilometers below us, and off to the north the other wall of the canyon made an abrupt horizon, as if Mars itself was rolling toward us in a fantastic tidal wave. It was like traveling in an optical illusion, and I could only watch it for moments at a time before it made me dizzy. The weather cooperated in this assault on my senses. High clouds topped a dusty sky, and the sunset was one of those extravaganzas of color too garish for art; but Nature knows no aesthetic restraint, and purples, pinks, and pale clear greens stained the tall dome of the sky, which altered imperceptibly from raspberry to blackberry above it all. Finally the sun fell, and in the mirror dusk the train crawled up the gentle slope of the bulge, appearing a filament of algae in the big barren world. I switched on my little overhead light and read for a bit—stared through my faint reflection at the canyon—read some more—looked out again.

I had purchased a book in the train's store called *Secrets of Icehenge Revealed*, by a Theophilus Jones. The introduction began, "Let us look at the case reasonably," which made me laugh outright. I flipped ahead. "The academic scientists have also ignored all signs indicating Icehenge's extreme age, so that they may explain it as an artifact of modern civilization. They find these explanations preferable to the one most clearly indicated by the facts—for all that we find points to the existence of a prehistoric space technology; evidence of it lies scattered over the Earth from Stonehenge to Easter Island. Icehenge was built by that antediluvean culture, whose language was Sanskrit, and whose spaceship designs can be found on Mayan temple walls. Over the years the ice liths have become pitted with age (see photos), and one has even been struck by a meteorite, an event that almost defies probability, and indicates the passing of eons."

Atlantis as home of this prehistoric high technology—Sanskrit as mathematical code, as well as the first language—Tibet as refuge of this ancient wisdom—the lost continent of Mu—the Nazca Plains "spaceport"—the "Great Pyramid" on Ios: this book had them all. I read it with a peculiar mixture of satisfaction and anger. On the one hand I found its utter stupidity reassuring; the primacy of my explanation was not threatened by this pap. On the other hand, my long letter pointing out the connection between the megalith and the Davydov expedition, as revealed in Emma's journal, had been published in *Marscience* without comment; while there were ten copies of this ragged collection of exotica in the train's bookrack.

I put the book down and looked out the window again. Now the mirror suns were setting, repeating the true sunset in muted tones of mauve and olive and dusky turquoise. When the mirrors blinked out over the bulge the shadowed sky darkened instantly, and the great black chasm lay obscured until Deimos (Dread) shot over the western horizon like a flare. The retrograde moon. . . . I leaned my head against the window, depression falling across me like the long shadows across the canyon floor.

I have always feared that one of these depressions will not end, that it will shift my biochemistry and help drive me into a funk. I know many people who have fallen into funks for years, or stayed in one until they died. The malady is fairly common among people my age. The purpose of life eludes them, and though they continue to exist their chemical balance shifts, and they lapse into trancelike indifference to the world, for ten, twenty, thirty years. Rip Van Winkle's disease, a comedian called it. Reduced Affectual

Function, say the medicos, but it is more than that. And once or twice I have felt the depression, the complete lassitude and indifference, that I imagine leads one into the empty world of a funk. This is one reason I pursue my projects so fiercely, I know—out of dread. We cannot live in a world without meaning! And yet so often that just is the sort of world it looks as though we've been placed in. When I pass people in funks being helped down the street, or sitting in doorways like zombies, I can barely look at them, afraid that they will convince me with their eyes that they are right. And their lives: they can be trained to minimal functioning, and left to wander like beggars—or they are kept in special asylums, full of kindergarten stimulation—or they are helped by a friend or relative or therapist—or they die.

Or, if they catch themselves sliding down the long slope soon enough, they move to Alexandria.

For Alexandria is a city of the senses, and one can live a full life there with the senses alone; this despite the libraries and the archives. I understood this anew as I debarked from the train and walked out of the station into the broad central boulevard—and part of me was relieved. The city is at the western end of Noctis Labyrinthus, and because it is nearly at the top of Tharsis (eleven kilometers above the datum), it is still tented. So the greenhouse air is warm, and pungent with smells. And the public buildings in the heart of town each are fronted with a different stone, so that the eye is surprised at every turn. As I walked across town toward the campus I passed a skyscraper of purple marble, another of rose quartz, both anchoring parts of the dome tent and blending into the color of the sky; the blocks of archival buildings alternated between serpentine, chalcedony and jaspar; the police station was a square tower of obsidian reflecting the buildings around it; and in the big central park were bathhouses of coral and olivine, turquoise and jade and chert. I cut through the park looking only at the Martian juniper and Hokkaido pine, and walked onto campus feeling virtuous. My rooms in the visiting scholars' apartment would be ready, but I hesitated, already feeling the spell of the city. Perhaps it would be all right to go to a bathhouse; perhaps it was just what I needed. From a dusk-dark kiosk shone a white handprint. This city looked nothing like the Egyptian sink of the old novelist, but in every way that mattered it was the same place—such is the power of naming. I shook off the attraction of the bathhouse, and took an escalator to the roof patio of the scholars' apartment. Off to the west the three great volcanoes appeared over the horizon like peaks of another planet entirely, their upper halves in full sun though I stood in murk. Ascraeus Mons, the one farthest north, had snow on its middle slopes. I felt as though my heart had expanded to fill my chest, and I recognized the emotion: Alexandria. . . .

It was a marvelous Idea they had had, to bring together all of the material of Martian history in a single spot, and create a Planetary Archives, and add to it a collection of libraries and galleries and conservatories and a campus of the university. (Chairman Sarionovich, trying to be Alexander the Great.) Alexandria, the Capital of Memory: but it could not be said that the idea had been realized with any success. A hothouse tented city full of money, on the route from Burroughs to Olympus Mons, from Arcadia to Argyre, Alexandria had drawn a whole other city into itself, and now co-existing with the city of libraries was the city of banks and brothels, bazaars and bathhouses, dorms and slum tenements.

In the archives there were failures caused chiefly by the Unrest itself. The rebels had destroyed all the records they could in the final days of the revolt, to hamper the ferreting of them; so data of all kinds for the years before 2248 were patchy. Another problem, almost as serious, was that each regime of archivists had used a different filing system, using different programs; one had to become a historian of programming to work through the records.

I set to work in the archival labyrinth in a fever of energy, as if struggling against a spell. I spent days typing before a screen, for most of the records were on disks: files of the Soviet mining fleet (fragmentary); minutes of the Mars Corporations Co-op for the Outer Satellites (trivial); records for all the people mentioned in Emma's journal. These last were the most interesting, for they confirmed that all those named in Emma's account had disappeared in the Unrest; and for most, there was no explanation nor any definite last locations. This was common in the annals of the Unrest, but still, it was something.

When I got sick of staring at screens I walked across a park to the Physical Records annex. Here were all the remaining documents. Some of them were originals for what I had found on disk, others had never been recorded. At first it was a relief to deal with the actuality of paper. I am happier with things than with facts, I know this. But in a few weeks the big rooms lined with file cabinets and shelves, filled with the excrement of bureaucracy, were more frustrating and depressing than the computer screens. In these rooms I could see the extent of my task, and I could finger the results of endless hours of wasted labor. And I could see the disorganization and the gaps, not merely as bad results on a screen, but as whole drawers and cabinets and *rooms* of botched filing, uncatalogued documents—unknown material. Eventually I was forced back to the computers, and I shuttled between them like that, driven by frustration.

In neither building could I find any mention of a Mars Starship Association. Three months after I came to Alexandria I hadn't found a thing. And there was still no response to my letter in *Marscience*.

> Emma searched;
> We research.

The city pulled at me. The smooth face of a young man, in a bathhouse door. On a sidewalk cafe table, lying in coffee stains face down: the Martian translation of Cavafy's poems. How well the old poet's work fit this namesake city. I saw the collected edition everywhere—on trolley seats, on the leafstrewn paths of the parks, in libraries misshelved under *Astronomy* or *Polynesia*; and from the back of every dog-eared copy, Cavafy's sad weird bespectacled gaze, which said: the scholar melts in Alexandria. I tried to ignore it. Same with the white handprint, glowing out of every dark alley. Mornings and afternoons I spent in the archives; evenings I ate in the plaza cafes, watching the poor who lived in great crowds around the big public buildings, eking a living from those inside. Nights I stayed in my apartment, blank as a computer screen turned off.

One night I glanced at my kitchen calendar and understood that I had lived a week without knowing it. If the thalamus breaks down, we are incapable of laying down new memories. Fearfully I dressed and took a late trolley downtown. I stood on the curb of the broad sidewalk before the skyscraper containing Shrike's apartment. Up there were his big rooms with all their windows, above the dome. I wanted to go into the foyer and ring his bell, I wanted him to be home, to ask me up. I went into the foyer and stood before the console. *Alexander Selkirk, 8008.* But he wouldn't want me calling him from the building, would he? If he were in town, he would have someone else with him. He wouldn't care what shape I was in; he wouldn't want to know I needed him. The idea would make him very polite—as unlike Shrike as it was possible to be. I couldn't stand the thought of it.

Under the curious eye of a policeman I left the building and walked around the corner into the nearest bathhouse. I paid my fee, shed my clothes and stuffed them into a locker, walked out into the tight network of red hallways, to one of the steamrooms. Sat in the hot water and tried to calm myself and feel sensually. In the dim red light bodies moved languorously, skin wet and gleaming, ruddy and smooth. Muscle definition of male backs. Smooth curves of female legs. Breasts and cocks, wet hair, parted lips. I took one of the hoses snaking about the bottom of the bath, ran the cold stream over my body. Across the room two lithe bodies tangled, slid together in a slow rhythm. They sloshed off, seeking one of the niches in the hallway corners. Another pair coupled in the corner of the steaming pool; blind eyes stared through me. I ran the cold spurt from the hose over my cock, felt nothing. Leaving the bath I wandered the halls, looking into niches. In one a woman straddled a man, slid up and down on him; she looked up and saw me, smiled, leaned forward to cover him; I felt a faint stir in my pelvis.

In a distant niche beyond the last bath Emma sat crosslegged, alone. She gestured to me—she crooked a finger at me. I knelt beside her in the niche, heart pounding. Up close I saw she only looked like Emma, but I banished the thought and kissed her. Our hands explored each other, I slid into her and we copulated right there where passers-by would trip over my feet. When we were spent she rolled me to one side, got to her knees; she put a finger to my lips, kissed my forehead, left.

So I added a new component to my life. Every night I visited bathhouses. Sometimes I met my Emma-partner, and we made love with ever-increasing facility. Most nights our paths didn't cross, and I merely soaked and watched, or found another partner. But what happened with her was different. We never said a word; that was what created the passion, we knew. Days now passed when I read Emma's journal and thought only of her, and on some nights I walked from bathhouse to bathhouse, searching for her. Once in front of the Physical Annex, we crossed paths; neither of us acknowledged the other by more than a meeting of the eye. But that night, in the bathhouse where we had met, we almost fused in our mute passion. We understood.

And I felt I was coming to life: when actually I was only coming to Alexandria.

We lead our lives as if perpetually waking from a long coma. What really happened to me in my first lives, to lead me to Alexandria? Some midnights on the streets, with all the poor, I would stop and ask myself that. How had I gotten to this strange state? What had my life been like? I knew I had been a child, a student, a driver for the Planetary Survey—but what had *happened*, what had it been *like?* "I only know it got me here, and here I am."

During the long days in the Archives I chatted with the people who worked there, solicited their help and their opinions, and told them about my task and my theory concerning the Pluto megalith and the Unrest. I am a very social person, you see; I need to talk to people every day, perhaps more than I have ever gotten a chance to. One day over an after-lunch Turkish coffee I asked an archivist I had just met, Vadja Sandor, if he knew of any records for the mining subcommittee that had been labelled confidential, and hidden in the data banks by a secret code. "Especially records for the years between the Committee takeover and the Unrest."

Sandor was a respected historian of that period; it was said he had sixty papers waiting for the approval of Publications Review. "I know of such records," he said in his musical Russian. "But they're still classified, and I don't have access. My requests for the entry codes have been denied."

I got out my notebook. "Tell me which ones they are. I'll make my own requests." And I sent off the forms that very day, wondering if I would have to ask Shrike for help again. If I could bring myself to it.

But I didn't have to. Perhaps Shrike helped without being asked. The codes were sent to me with letters from the police, loyalty oaths, etc. I threw them out and hurried to the Archives to type in the codes.

One of the many confidential files for that period was the Subcommittee on Mining's records on missing asteroid mining ships.

Five asteroid miners had been lost in the years 2150 to 2248. Wreckage of the first had been found, but not of the last four. And the last three had been commanded by Oleg Davydov, Olga Borg, and Eric Swann.

I called Sandor over to my console to take a look. He saw the list and nodded. "Yes, I've heard of those before. The Committee declassified a general report on mining history forty years ago that mentioned these."

"You didn't tell me about them?"

"But you knew they disappeared. No one denies it. Besides, I figured you had seen that stuff—it's right there in the public record."

"Damn it! I went back to the primary sources, and never looked in that report! You knew I was looking for something like this—"

He looked nonplussed, and I tried to calm down. I said, "The Committee must have been worried by these disappearances."

"Probably. But the report I read claimed that such disappearances weren't a complete mystery. If an explosion destroyed a miner and propelled a wreck out of the planetary plane, there would be little chance of finding it."

"But three of the five disappearances came in the five years before the Unrest! And now we've found the New Houston material, and the Pluto monument."

"Yes." Sandor smiled. "You've got something here, you should write it up."

"I need more."

"Maybe so, but that shouldn't keep you from writing this up and getting it out there. You might get some help."

So I wrote it up: a full article outlining the revisionist account of the Unrest, detailing what I knew of the MSA. I proposed that the Unrest included the mutiny and starship construction revealed in Emma's journal, and that the starship crew had built the Pluto monument to mark its departure from the solar system. I sent the article to *Marscience*, and they published it. My explanation of the monument was now out there competing with the Atlantean theory, the alien theory, the natural coincidence theory, and all the rest. No one seemed very impressed. Letters were sent to *Marscience* complaining about the sparseness of my evidence compared to the largeness of my conclusions; and then there was silence. It was like dropping a rock through the ice of a canal. I began to understand that there was jealousy among my colleagues. They thought that I was being given preferential access to classified sites and records—and I couldn't very well deny it—so naturally they disliked my work and snubbed it.

Discouragement in the mirror dusk of a sidewalk cafe: drinking a thimble of coffee I watched the poor go home, each face a map of trouble. Rust-coated policemen on every corner to watch with me. Someone had left a red-backed copy of *Justine* on the dirty tabletop next to mine. I paged through it. Strange jumble of thoughts and images: I liked the helpless lack of structure. "I simply make these few notes to record a block of my life which has fallen into the sea." Or: "I began to describe to myself in words this whole quarter of Alexandria for I knew that soon it would be forgotten and revisited only by those whose memories had been appropriated by the fevered city. . . ."

I was interrupted in my bemused reading by a young man and a pregnant woman, standing before my table. "Are you Professor Nederland?" asked the woman.

"Yes, I am."

"We've seen you on the news."

I lifted my eyebrows. Fame: a curious sensation, to be known by strangers. Maybe there really was something happening out there, with the news of the excavation and the thing on Pluto.

"Yes?" I said.

"I'm your granddaughter, Mary Shannon. Hester's daughter?"

"Oh, yes." I recalled Maggie mentioning her. I hadn't heard from Hester herself in more years than this young woman had lived. And here she was pregnant; they must have had influence somewhere.

"And this is my husband, Herbert."

"Hello." I stood and extended a hand toward the man. Mary lifted his arm and he took my hand, looking past me. I realized he was in a funk, and felt a stab of fear. "Pleased to meet you," I said, and napkinned my mouth.

"Pleased to meet you," he said. Mary darted a glance at him, smiled at me apologetically.

"And you're soon to be a great-grandfather again," she said. "As I guess you noticed."

"Yes. Congratulations." How could she have gotten permission to get pregnant when he was in a funk? I wondered if my name had been invoked in the permission proceedings. "It will be my ninth, if I'm not mistaken."

"No, Hester told me that Stephanie had another one two years ago."

"Oh? I hadn't heard."

"Oh. Well. . . . We're about to move to Phobos. So when I saw you I thought we should say hello."

"I'm glad you did. Phobos is an exciting place, I've heard."

"We've been ordered to move there, actually. But Herb works on sunsailers, so it will be good for him."

I felt a pang for this brave woman, exiled to Phobos with two such responsibilities. "I'm glad."

Family. A whole genealogical chart extending away in both directions—especially, for an old man like me, downward. A whole clan of descendants. Most of mine were on the Outer Satellites. I never saw the point of keeping in touch with so many strangers, who proved over and over again that nothing of you lasts beyond yourself. My granddaughter shuffled her feet, glanced at her husband anxiously. What would she be, sixty? Hard to say. She looked like a large child.

"We should let you eat," she said. "I just wanted to say hello. And that we enjoy hearing about you on the news."

"Good, good. Good to see you. Good luck on Phobos. Nice to meet you, ah, Herb. Take care, yes. Say hello to Hester. Bye bye."

I sat down again on the uncomfortable metal chair, picked up the book automatically. "I suppose events are simply a sort of annotation of our feelings—" I shut the book. Down the boulevard the white streetlights came on all at once. In the plaza fountain's basin water, squiggles of light *S*'ed over the glassy black surface. Couples walked around its edge. Some threw tokens in, the rest watched. It reminded me of Earth, somehow.

Those memories of my voyage to Earth that had burst into me in Burroughs, what did they mean? Was that really what happened? Suddenly I doubted it. Could we ever hold on to enough of the present to represent it accurately when it was gone? We try. We rehearse our pasts to ourselves in images and repeat them through the years until the images are all we have. Which means we have nothing. We are stuck in the knife-edged present, it extends everywhere—except during the hallucinatory moment of involuntary memory, when images impact like the real. I felt on the verge of such a moment, the pressure welled up at the bottom of my mind: something evoked by this granddaughter, descendant of a wife I scarcely remembered—something—something—

But it never came. A blocked epiphany. And suddenly I did not believe in my voyage to Earth. I remembered the night in Burroughs, after seeing the monument—but now it meant nothing to me. A hallucination. And how much of my written account of it was made up? I no longer believed any of it. Opening my notebook, I jotted a couplet to describe the process—in alexandrines, of course—

> The memory's the bone; imagination, flesh;
> The animating spirit?—is a forlorn wish.

Emma the only refuge, Emma the only anchor. How many nights I read her, and was re-oriented to the real.

The codes sent to me unlocked other classified information, and eventually I found a long list of files never programmed, which sent me running over to the Physical Annex. The reference was to Davydov, and the file collection was in a room I had familiarized myself with. I began searching the cabinets that stood in rows in the room. One bottom drawer was jammed with folders and pages; it looked like someone had ransacked it, or dropped the drawer and then replaced the contents in a hurry. Near the back I found the folder: *Davydov—Confidential.* Inside it was a sheaf of papers.

Soviet fleet papers. Expedition to the Jovian moons in 2182–8. Record of an assault on a superior officer. Permissions for a leave on Earth.

Then in 2211 he was brought before a court-martial, but he was found innocent. Written under *Charge* was *sedition—see Space Security, Valenski.* Nothing more.

The next document was a fifteen-page application for a lobbying association and club to be called the Mars Starship Association. "Ah ha!" I shouted. The application was dated 2208. At that time any meeting of over ten people had to be approved by the police, so the questions were detailed. Davydov was named copresident of the club along with Borg. All potential members were identified. Many I had seen in Emma's journal. Under *Purpose of Association* was typed, "To advocate the use of a certain percentage of mining profits for the construction of a long-range ship and the financing of a transplutonian expedition."

So I had found it. Independent confirmation of the Mars Starship Association, right there in a cabinet drawer open to anyone's inspection, in a cabinet I had casually glanced through several months before. That was archival cataloguing for you. I called Sandor to the room and got him to witness the find, and we had it copied. "You're building quite a case," he said.

I wrote it up, *Chronicle of Martian History* published it. No comment.

Oh, I suppose there was some comment, I got calls from Nakayama and Lebedyan and some others. But the theory popular that week was that Pluto was an erratic caught by the sun, and that the megalith was ancient, perhaps fifteen billion years old—nearly as old as the universe itself. Naturally this created a stir and there were calls for a new expedition to Pluto to investigate the megalith and test this theory.

Over a year's labor and all I had found were scraps. I thought they were important scraps, but few people agreed. Meaningless work. And me so deep in the rhythms of Alexandria that I could scarcely see out of them, to know they were habits I had recently sheathed myself in. Each night I visited the bathhouses, and cared not who I saw, who I joined for company. I no longer searched for the woman who looked like Emma; I still found her occasionally, and we still coupled, but it was tempered by familiarity. Even the strangest liaisons lose their mystery.

And relationships grow whether we want them to or not. Once I recognized the woman in a restaurant—we were both leaving. It was peculiar to see her with clothes on. She smiled and indicated I should follow; I accompanied her to what I assumed were her rooms, and inside we stripped each other violently—a new touch to our liaison—and made love in our customary silence.

Later, when I had dressed, we sat on the bed and looked out the window at an alley wall. She said, "And what are you running from?"

I felt my stomach drop. "My work." A pause. "And you?"
"The same."

We laughed. It was more intimate than anything we had shared thus far; sex can be as solipsistic as suicide. To laugh together was not *Alexandrian.* "Does it work for you?" she sputtered. I shook my head, still giggling. "Me neither," she said, and set us off again. After that we talked. She too worked in research, in one of the libraries. I told her she looked like Emma Weil, and she shrugged. Later, when we met in bathhouses, she merely smiled and continued on her way. Once we tried it again. But it was over.

Sometimes I get so tired. Day follows day follows day in an endless round, each day filled with habits constructed to patch over the emptiness at the heart of things. I exist and so I have to occupy my time. But there is no more to it than that. Apprehensions of this truth make it hard even to keep to the day to day. I feel like a stagehand moving all the props of the play by myself—holding the backdrops steady, placing the costumes on their hooks, conducting the pit band, cueing the players, rushing to and fro—and at the same time I am expending all this backstage effort I am supposed to pretend to believe that the production is real life. It's impossible.

I never felt this exhaustion more than in my last months in Alexandria. I kept to my habits out of the strength of habituation, and fear, but I was lost. I didn't know what next to search for in the archives, and grubbed in them randomly. I stopped paying attention to my dress; grew a beard to avoid shaving; paid no attention to my food, and ate semi-consciously on the schedule of habit; lived in an apartment piled with worn clothes and refuse; and if it weren't for the habit of the bathhouses, I doubt I would even have stayed clean. I was far enough into a funk that I didn't recognize it, and that is dangerously far.

I have always feared insanity. It seems to me the most horrifying of illnesses, and the Achilles heel of modern medicine. And I feel that I might be particularly susceptible to it. I am anxious and easily frightened, so that terror might overwhelm me. And I have little understanding of why other people act as they do, so that I

am often isolated to a nearly unbearable degree. —And I bear all
the physical marks of the potential schizophrenic: over-large head,
low ears, tufty electric hair, poor meeting of the bone ridges at the
intersection of eyebrows and nose. These are all signs, used by
doctors.

One day I found myself sitting outside the great jade library,
stroking one of the chert lions that flanked the steps, almost too
tired to move my hand. I couldn't remember how I had gotten
there, or where I had been, or what I had been doing, for . . . I
didn't know how long. And then I knew I was lost.

It was Shrike who pulled me out. One look at my face: "Jesus
Christ, man, you've fallen in a funk!" Right there at my front door.
"You of all people! I thought you were too full of bile. Here it's all
coming your way at once and you're falling in a funk. I don't understand you, Hjalmar, I truly don't." He looked past me at my
apartment with distaste. "Come on up to my place and clean up.
Where have you *been?*"

"I don't know."

He looked at me oddly. "You've been working too hard," he
said in a tone I'd never heard from him, and took me by the arm.

He led me across the city to his apartment, muttering all the
way. "Should have known something like this had happened, it's
been so long since you last pestered me. What's the matter, lost
your nerve? Got yourself on the big stage and found it a scary
place?"

"I don't know what you're talking about."

He took me by the shoulders and shook me. "*Wake up.*" Into
his bathroom, clothes yanked off, shower first boiling then freezing, and back and forth like that. "What's this," I moaned, "you got
a degree in physical therapy?" He laughed crazily. I felt his hands
like the hot water, his barbs like the cold. He pulled me out, forced
me to swallow some pills, slapped me, pushed me into the wall.
"Enough of this," I said. "I should think you'd get enough of pushing people around in your daytime work."

He shouted his laughter. "You prig! How you bore me with
your self-righteousness! What are you but a self-serving academic

bourgeois *ass*, after all, living fat off the very system you denounce. An *archaeologist!* Archaeology, what dull nonsense! Why pursue it at all? What could be less re-vo-LU-tionary?"

"Well, no," I said slowly, struggling. "That's not exactly right. It's a search for reality, you see. The presence of history in our moment. In those objects we can see truths of our nature. Expressed in the way we lived during the eons of prehistory. Which formed our brains and our desires and our goals and our satisfactions and our raptures—"

"What crap! What do you mean? We're not cavemen anymore, fool—"

"No! No. We also see the few millennia of change that transformed us from that stable cycle to our current misery on Mars."

"How you hate Mars. Why don't you go back to Earth if you hate Mars so much."

I wiped wet hair off my forehead. "Because I'm a Martian!" I burst out. I shook a fist at him: "I lived too long on Mars before I ever went to Earth, and so I grew the last part of my brain—the part grown by living—into the brain of a Martian. So when I went to Earth it was foreign to me, it fired synapses in the parts of my brain that never grew, and every waking moment was a dream. And I saw everything in a double focus of real and dream, Martian and ancient Earth mammal—so that I had to come back here to see clearly."

"So there you have it! Here—"

"Here I *do* see clearly, you Shrike, and what I see disturbs me! We could be making a utopia of Mars, the planet insists we create a new society with every bloody icy dawn—in fact we *need* to create such a society for our sanity's sake, because now we're all going to live a thousand years and *we* are going to have to live in the system we make, for year after year beyond our ability to imagine! *That's* what we've forgotten, Shrike. It used to be that people could say to themselves, why should I sacrifice my life for social change, it will take years and I'll not see the benefits of it, let this time be peaceful at least and the next generation can worry about it. That was one of the biggest forces against change, the selfishness of the individual who only wanted peace. But now people are dragging it out day to day on Mars forgetting that not their children but *they* are going to have to live in the future they build. Why I think they must forget it to keep from revolting that very moment in the streets! I see it on every face in every street of every city, all of them working desperately to make profits for people we never see. And we elite desperate at our collaboration in it—or at least I am—I *hate* my position and I want to strike out and I barely hold it in, I hop in the gutters to hold it in and I must *do* something—"

"*Please*, Hjalmar." Now he was in the kitchen, cutting vegetables on the wooden counter for the wok. "Look at it less idealistically. How can any person change anything singlehandedly?" Big knife: *chop chop chop chop chop.* "Aren't you taking on too much? Have you ever considered how well entrenched the system is?" *Chop chop chop chop chop.* He waved the knife at me like a baton, big shrug, sigh of resignation: "Marx never guessed how technology would fix wood-and-steam capitalism into concrete for the ages. We're just tiny organic components of a solar-system-wide machine, Hjalmar. How can you fight it?"

"Show where we came from. Show we were once an organism."

"But we're Martians. It was never an organism here. Things as they are have been destroyed, remember? We were always a machine. You can't show it here."

"*Show*, then, that once all the Martians revolted together, and broke spontaneously toward utopia. And show they almost succeeded, show they had a real, workable plan. Show how they were crushed, with the idea of indicating what they did wrong, so that implicit everywhere in the exposure is the idea of doing it right—of *doing it again*, with maps of things to be avoided. We are twenty million millennials on this planet, Shrike, condemned to live out every day of our lives. What mere *form* can hold us?"

"Pretty abstract."

"Okay—I'll be more concrete—why should we spend our lives making profits for Terrans? Why shouldn't we—why can't we—throw off Earth's colonial rule?"

"Perhaps we c—"

"And so *archaeology*, you see Shrike? It's the best way I can figure out to do it! I mean for me to do something to *start* it, or work in that *direction*, at *least*—"

"All right, Hjalmar. All right. Calm down. Ha! I knew you wouldn't fall into a funk. You were just on the big slide. But listen here. You're talking to a member of the Mars Development Committee, the newest and brightest. That means something. Things are changing. There's more ways to work at this than your own, and more people than you working at it. Keep that in mind! You're so wrought up these days, and I think it comes from this feeling that you're doing it all yourself—that no one else on Mars thinks!" He threw cabbage in the heated oiled wok, and it sizzled madly.

". . . That's because it's not working," I admitted, and felt myself drain again. "I brought the past back, and it doesn't matter. Your bosses are just slotting it into the machine. It isn't going to make any difference."

"You don't know that yet. Listen to this, wild man—you're going to be appointed head of the Planetary Survey."

I thought I had heard him wrong in the crackle of vegetables. "What's this?"

"Satarwal's out. You'll be given the authority to open up any site you want for a dig. And to convene an inquiry into the Aimes Report."

I must have looked like a cretin, I was so shocked; Shrike looked up from stirring and laughed like a maniac. "Go get some clothes on for dinner. And dry off first."

"But why?"

"So you won't get your food wet!"

"No, damn it, *why?* Why the appointment?"

"Haven't you been paying any attention to the effect your work has had?"

"Of course! It hasn't had any effect at all! I've barely found anything."

"Well. People say you are very conservative in interpreting your data. Which is all to the good as far as the rest of the Committee is concerned. You've got a reputation for responsible science. And though there hasn't been a big public reaction to your findings, you can hardly expect it, since none of them have appeared in the news. But the scientific community has been impressed, I'm told. It stands to reason—after all, what other explanation of Icehenge even makes sense? I ask you!"

"Don't ask me! I've often wondered that myself."

"Well there you have it. We've been contacted by Nakayama and Anya Lebedyan and other advisors to the Survey, who have pointed out the implications of your work for—for Mars. Here, eat. And the Committee has decided to make the appointment, so you can do the job properly."

"Ah," I said. Now I began to understand. "You're going to make me into a good party man, eh?"

Shrike grinned. "You were always a good party man, Hjalmar. You just didn't know it."

I dropped my fork in my plate, went to the bathroom, dried off and dressed. A great fear was filling me; I saw their plan, I saw what they were hoping to do with me. I returned to the living room.

"I'll show there was a revolution! A civil war!"

Shrike nodded. "I believe you. And you will show that Icehenge was constructed by Martians."

"By Martian rebels! Fighting the Committee!"

He nodded, smiling one of his private smiles, one that said, It won't matter. All those years the Committee had lied, they had crushed not only the revolution but the memory of it, and now so much time had passed that they could smile and say yes, that's what happened—it's true—we killed a fifth of the population, almost a million people—and then we buried it all. Now they've dug it up in New Houston, but so what? We're still here; everybody's happy; no one remembers it; nobody cares.

They were counting on our amnesia. They could co-opt any act, no matter how brutal, into their history; as long as it was old enough, it wouldn't affect them at all. It was as easy as co-opting a malcontent professor: give him an important-sounding job in the system, where he became part of the machine; let him taste a little power, let him censor himself to taste a little more—

"I'll be different!" I shouted at Shrike. "I won't fold up and do what you say to crawl higher! I'll use what you've given me against you, I swear. You'll regret giving me this chance."

Shrike nodded, eyes downcast, the little smirk still in place. It said, That's what they all say, at first.

"I have to get out of here," I said, suddenly terrified.

"This city is bad for you." He looked annoyed. "Why don't you eat?"

I crossed the room in search of my coat. "Didn't I bring a coat?"

"No! Damn it, Hjalmar, will you be reasonable? Sit down and eat this meal I've cooked for you!"

I was shivering. "I'm going to borrow one of your coats." I took one from the closet. "I've got to get out of here." I put on the coat and went to the door.

"Jesus Christ. Hjalmar! Wait a second—you'll take the appointment?"

"Yes," I said. "Yes, damn you."

I hurried down the wide boulevards in a frenzy. The big public buildings loomed over me like colorful Committee flags. Of course they gave me the codes to find what they wanted me to find. Of course their censors let me publish the results. All this happened with their permission, supervision, planning. Their power over me was as tangible and massive as the great stone libraries that I scuttled between. Furiously I packed a single travel bag and left my apartment. Down the boulevards to the giant olivine train station. I had to escape before they destroyed me. Faces I passed were slack and incurious, almost dead. Bathhouse doors gaped like wet mouths, the colored stone towers pulsed and wavered in the glow of the streetlights, bending until they almost met in the sky over me. In the train station I found that a sleeper to Burroughs was about to depart; it would make a stop at Coprates, where I could rent a car and return to New Houston. I had to get to New Houston, I would be safe there. I got on the train and huddled in a corner window seat, hugging my bag, shivering violently until with a gentle bump the train slid out of the station and into the night. After a time my body calmed; but my mind spun, I could not sleep.

Nothing I could do would bring them down.

\* \* \*

*Kolpos Crater—this small crater (Bt, 8 km. diameter) in the western section of Hellas Planitia is the lowest point on the Martian surface, four kilometers below the datum.*

Back in New Houston I found no changes. A reconstruction: "Twenty-sixth century archaeological dig, Mars." When they were done the place would be studded with plaques and roped off: the war trophy as historical landmark. McNeil showed me around the city. He was still going at it with a toothbrush, so it looked no different than it had a year before.

Petrini hurried up with a realistic smile of welcome. "Congratulations on your new appointment," he said. "We just heard about it today. It's quite an honor! I hope you'll remember your old friends when you're up there in Burroughs."

"I'll remember a lot of things."

Hana and Bill and Heidi and Xhosa were all at the physical plant, and they greeted me and showed me around the cleaned-up walls. The whole plant was ready for the plaques. "Well, it's something," I said. "I had hoped you would get more done." Later Bill and Hana took me up to the rim to see the work they had done on the dome explosions. It wasn't bad work, though one of them would have been enough for it.

"We're going to get married," Bill said.

"Yes?" I tried to hide my surprise. "I didn't know people did that anymore. Congratulations."

"We figured you would be back soon," said Hana, "so we delayed it a bit hoping you could make it. It'll be in the camp here on Saturday."

"Thanks for waiting," I said. "Tell me, have you gotten this work published?"

They gave each other a look.

"I know I'm supposed to be keeping tabs on your work, but I've been busy in Alexandria and I thought you might have gone ahead with it."

"We've got it ready for your review," Hana said slowly. "We had thought you would be co-author—"

"Oh no, no, dispense with that. Your paper. I wasn't even here while you did it." They looked odd, and Bill glanced at Hana. I said, "Ha—a little wedding present, so to speak." Only then did it occur to me that they might want my name on the paper, to get it attention. "Again, congratulations. I'll make a point to be there."

Marriage. What idealism. On Saturday afternoon we all gathered in the main tent, which was decorated with stained screens and strings of flowers. It was a fine day, the air still and clear, the sky a deep violet.

The ceremony was short. The Kleserts were matron of honor and best man; Xhosa, who was a Unitarian minister, performed the service. Bill and Hana exchanged the usual impossible vows, and the party began. Several cases of the finest Utopian champagne had been shipped in, and I did my share in downing them, going at it with a will. After seven glasses I moved to a corner to make room for dancing. Our whole community was there, nearly sixty people, and most danced to the complex crossed rhythms of Eve Morris tunes. I looked through their gyrations to the crater rim above our tent. How many weddings had taken place in New Houston? Had any of them miraculously survived? Not likely— but perhaps—out there in the chaos—

Petrini came and stood by me, glass in hand. "It must be nice to see your students get along so well."

"Is that what you call it?"

He laughed. "Something like that."

I saw he was a bit drunk himself. Alcohol is a strange drug. "We've got a lot of work to do at the Survey," I said, and downed my glass. "We'll be starting digs at all the proscribed sites, and farming out grants to the university where we have to. I might be able to send some money your way, if you want to start investigating what *really* happened in the revolution." I nodded seriously. "Maybe you could look into those green natives, eh?"

He was still struggling to form a response when Hana came and asked me to dance. She had tactfully chosen one of the slower numbers, and once on the floor we were able to circle sedately among the other couples, in a roar of music and voices. "You look beautiful," I said. She was wearing a white skirt and a blue blouse. I leaned to kiss her on the cheek and lost my step, kissing her too hard.

"Thank you."

"But I don't understand this marriage," I complained. "It's an archaic ceremony, it makes no sense in this day and age. I'd have thought you'd know better. You're twice as smart as Bill—"

She pulled away from me, and I saw the pained expression on her face and realized what I had done. Desperately I pulled her back into the dance and said, "Oh wait, Hana, please excuse me, that was a stupid thing to say, I'm very sorry. I'm—I'm upset. I've had too much champagne." She nodded once, looking down. "It's just that you're the best of them, Hana. The only one who never went along with Satarwal and his lies. And I worry about you. They can take anything you do and turn it bad, you know. Your victories are sucked in and used just as efficiently as your defeats. Everything can be used. You have to watch out. Don't let them suck you in, Hana—you're too good for that, too young, too smart."

"No, Dr. Nederland. I won't. But thanks for the warning—"

"Only right! That's part of my job, being your teacher. You're the best of them, and I've got to teach you what I've learned." I tried to give her another kiss and she held herself rigidly for it. Of course. Drunk advisor, coming on at the wedding reception itself. Disgusting. I saw that and stepped back, appalled. Hana stopped dancing and gave me a brief pitying look. To my relief McNeil cut in—he couldn't dance either, and had to take advantage of the slow song. I walked dizzily to the drinks table.

I drained a few more glasses and went outside. My mood plummeted and I pulled my hood off; the cold brought me to my senses, but I still felt black. I stared up at the bronze sun and its squadron of mirrors. When I ran away from Alexandria I had hoped I would escape this feeling; New Houston had seemed my home, my real life, my real work. But things were the same no matter where I went; here my work was just as useless, my life just as empty. No

matter where I ran it would be the same. I recalled the end of
Cavafy's poem "The City"—

> "Ah! don't you see
> Since your mind is the prison
> You'll live behind bars
> Everywhere now—over all of Mars?"

Sometimes I get so tired.

*The chaos—collapsed terrain characterized by jumbled arrays of short,
block-filled valleys and ridges.*

We left New Houston in six big expedition cars and two little
field cars, headed north to the Aureum Chaos, the dotted area of
the map found in Emma's escape car. Hana and Bill and Xhosa and
Heidi rode with me in the lead car, along with a surveyor named
Evelyn from the Survey office in Coprates, who navigated for us.
We drove over the plain in the gentle morning light of mirror
dawn: the four bright chips of the leading mirrors cast a clear light,
the sky was white gold, the plain amber, cut with shadows from
every pebble and boulder. Over the radio we heard the chattering
in the other cars, but in ours it was tranquil. We passed a steel
strut, protruding from the plain like a bone of Ozymandias; Evelyn identified it as the remains of a long gone pipeline, and she followed a line of these struts north.

Late that afternoon we came on a road. In the cratered terrain
roads are easy to construct; drive a car pulling a V-shaped snow-
plow, and a lane is cleared of loose ejecta, which form rows of piled
rock to each side of the road. "This one will take us most of the
way," Evelyn said. I looked back and saw the other cars following;
tall plumes of dust wafted away from our caravan to the east. We
drove between craters so old the rims were mere rounded bumps,
and occasionally the road led right over one. From these low
prominences we saw that the pocked rocky plain extended uni-
formly to a flat horizon eight or ten kilometers away.

On the road we made good time. We camped by it, and early the next day we left the road and turned east, to skirt the southern edge of Eos Chasma, and the whole bottom end of the Marineris system. Late in the day we came to the rim of Aureum. The plain dropped away in uneven segments, and to the north for as far as we could see was broken land, land that had collapsed from below. Because the Aureum was a sink, slumping two kilometers and more below the surrounding plains, we could see for many kilometers to the north—perhaps forty—and all of it was hacked and tumbled, like the no-man's-land of some giants' war. My heart sank as I gazed out at it; how could I possibly find the rebels' refuge in such topographic insanity?

But the map from Emma's car gave me courage. And as Evelyn directed us down a broad ramp into the edgelands of the chaos, I saw that each short valley was relatively flat-floored, though sometimes the pass from one valley to the next was pinched and steep. But crossing the terrain did not appear impossible.

The other cars followed us down: green metal bodies with clear bubble tops and big wheels at each corner. When the dusk created by shadows turned to real twilight, we stopped in a narrow defile and set the tents. Evelyn said we were on a road again, one that led to an old water station. Still I retired to my cot and unfolded Emma's map. The reality of Aureum made me anxious; I wanted the reassurance of a representation, with its inevitable ordering. Around the southern edge of Aureum were three water stations, set where they best exploited what was left of the ancient aquifer underneath them. All of them had once been little self-sufficient settlements, pumping water upcanyon to the arid highlands of Tharsis. One of the water stations had probably been used as a departure point for the hidden refuge, for building anything very big in the chaos would have required a few trips in and out at least. The station Evelyn was leading us to was the one closest to the red dot at the center of the map.

We reached the water station late the following day. It consisted of two plastic greenhouses, collapsed under sand, and five little block-houses made of brick. They had had a clever system: the old Johnson stills mixed soil and warm water, to free the oxygen in the soil; to the mud created in this procedure they added a fixative, and made "adobe" blocks with which the compound was built. The whole settlement was set on one of the mesalike blocks that protruded everywhere in the chaos.

We drove up a narrow ramp and got out of the cars to investigate. Another ruin of the Unrest. The brick buildings still looked ordinary enough to make broken windows a surprise. All the doors were open. The interiors were thick with dust and sand. I decided one building could be disturbed, and we entered it. In its kitchen were cupboards full of pots and pans, drawers full of dishware and utensils. No food. It was odd. Back outside I crossed the little yard created by the circle of buildings, and found Xhosa already testing the old pump. The generator still worked. Soon we would see whether the thawing, filtering, and pumping mechanisms underground also remained functional.

We set tents in the yard, and in the next couple of days while the others investigated the site, I hiked into the maze of valleys and blocks to the north. At first I found nothing. With the growing atmosphere tire tracks that before the transformation would have lasted a million years now would be buried. I explored in a fan pattern, checking avenues to the west and north, returning to the station to re-orient myself, trying again farther east. I left green marker balls to show where I had been, and came back upon them more than once.

But I found no sign of a road until the fourth day, when I tried a long sloping canyon that started two valleys east of the one leading to the station, and split the terrain to the northeast. I had stopped to inspect some Tibetan figwort growing between two rocks. I had seen a lot of lichen and alpine moss, but the figwort drew my attention. These sinks held a lot of air and water, to support such life. When I looked up from the cushion-shaped plant I saw that the little canyon floor was lined by two parallel depressions, like ruts almost filled in. I took out my little whisk broom and dusted away a few centimeters of fine sand, revealing a clear tire track. Our cars left tracks very like it. I followed the two ruts down the canyon and over a pass into a V-shaped valley that wound between ridges for as far as I could see; then, running short of light, I returned to the station.

That night I failed completely to hide my agitation. I forked my food as if stabbing ants. When the meal was finished I said, "I'm going to take one of the field cars for a few days and explore to the north."

Xhosa and Bill looked at each other. Hana frowned.

"It's possible some of the occupants of this place went north when it was abandoned. It's a bit of a long shot, and I don't want to disturb the main work here, but I'd like to follow some tracks I've found. I won't be long."

"It would be safer to go in a group," Xhosa suggested. "We can spare the people."

"I'm going to do it alone." And I began to feel how power could corrupt. It made things so easy. On the other hand, even though I had the authority, they had the force to be able to disobey, and stop me. Authority must be backed by force to be true authority. So I added, "Don't worry. I drove field cars for the Survey for more years than you all have lived."

Bill said, "We only have so much air."

"Get the Johnson still going again, then," I said roughly, with a wave of dismissal. "I won't take much."

"Easy to get lost out there," Xhosa said. "Safer if I came along."

"I'll be all right."

Speechlessly Hana was asking me a question. I said again, to her, "I'll be all right. I want to take a look up there, just for myself."

She nodded reluctantly. Xhosa looked worried; Bill frowned as if weighing his permission. Annoyed, I said, "Help me get a car ready."

Xhosa helped me fill a compartment of the car with green marker balls. "Set a lot of these," he said. "We'll listen for you on the radio."

It was the mirror dawn, and in the dimness I could not read his face. Plumes of frost fell from our breath. Hana and Bill emerged from a tent, and Hana approached me. "You shouldn't do this," she

said. "It isn't safe. We should stop him from going—" This to
Xhosa.

"You'll do what I say," I cried; and then, embarrassed at my
outburst, I had to make the rest of my preparations mumbling and
avoiding Hana's gaze. I climbed into the little field car without ac-
knowledging their farewells, feeling foolish, and drove down the
ramp.

Maneuvering the car over the two low ridges to my canyon was
easy enough, and then I followed the faint road. My car's wheels
almost fit the tracks. Turning off my radio I felt my spirit blossom
inside me, inspiring an exultant shout. I was off in search of Emma
and the rebels! I swore that if I found them I would join them and
never go back.

The tracks were easy to follow, and it took less than an hour to
retrace all my previous day's hike. Beyond the point where I had
turned back the V-shaped valley stretched for four or five kilometers, and the faint parallel ruts continued right down its middle. A
little creekbed, born since the tracks were made, ran between them
and sometimes over them; sometimes the bed was filled with jade
ice, mostly it was dry. But the ruts were visible until I came on a
box canyon ending the valley. There the ruts disappeared. I put the
car in reverse and retreated, and at the first pass over the side ridge
of the valley, I saw the two ruts again, cutting deeply over the pass.
I cursed my inattention, but mildly, since it had caused no harm,
and left a green marker at the turn before driving on.

Over the pass were scalloped ridges like dunes, offering no obvious way north; slowly I followed the tracks over this broken land,
and then they dropped into an area of massive blocks divided by
narrow canyons or defiles that offered a path through the blocks,
sometimes. Apparently the first long canyon and the valley after it
had been features of border terrain, and now I was in the chaos
proper. I could seldom see more than a kilometer in any direction,
and often less than that. It was as if I drove through the rubble-
filled streets of a city of jasper or chert, which had been struck to
shambles by a cataclysmic earthquake. At less than my walking
pace I drove over faint traces of tire track, and it seemed that the

only reason I kept finding it was that it was the only route through the maze. But in every kilometer's progress there were three or four choices to be made, and at each fork I stopped, looked at the two or three possibilities, and concluded I had lost the trail; then a line of rocks, or a smooth depression, or two parallel lines in the distance made by shifts in the soil that could not be perceived when near to them, would become evident, and with a hum of the car's electric motor I was off again. At each fork or crossroads I guided the robot arm out and stabbed a green marker ball into the hard sand. Looking back I could almost always see one.

As I proceeded north the height of the giant blocks diminished—or the defiles between them rose—and a few kilometers farther on the canyons ascended to the height of the blocks. I drove over a fractured plain, a sort of crazed plateau surrounded by jagged hills not much higher than it. It was the inversion of the maze: low ridges crossed each other everywhere on this plateau, dividing it into frozen ponds and drifts of sand. Passage over this ground was difficult, and the tracks skirted it to the west, leading me to another plateau, one split by fissures or crevasses so that to continue north the track had to wind in big S's. Here I ran into difficulty. The land was exposed to the wind, and in the fissures and etch pits were frozen ponds, surrounded by icy Syrtis grass, cushions of sandwort and rock jasmine, stiff leaf sedge, and boulders dotted with lichen of several colors. In this weird Arctic meadow the tracks were impossible to trace. I drove back to the last point I had been sure of seeing them—on one of the eskerlike ridges dividing the depressed plain—but once there, my own car's tracks marred the landscape ahead, and I saw no others. No other direction seemed feasible; to veer right was to return to the ridged plain, to turn left was to drop back into the maze that the old tracks had worked out of. It seemed most likely that the road had crossed the crevassed plateau I had driven onto, and that in the last century the tracks had been destroyed by erosion and deposition.

So I was on my own. But I was loath to believe that. I got out of the car and ranged forward on foot, inspecting each route between fissures for sign of the road. Nothing. The rough jumble of peaks to the north might protect a canyon section of the road enough for it to reappear—or so I hoped—and in the last hour of daylight I drove north across the plateau, zigging and zagging to avoid fissures. When blocks began to dot the plateau like immense erratics on a dusky morraine, I slowed the car and kept close watch. I saw only a pebbly broken plain, which became canyon mouths as the blocks became more frequent and continuous. I drove up one anxiously; then for no reason I looked up at the left wall of the new canyon, and there, dug into the rock like three cracks, was an arrow, like so:  ➤  . I laughed aloud. "Thank you very much," I said. "I was wondering about that." I drove on, but immediately I saw that the shadows of late afternoon would obscure any sign of the trail. I backed out of the canyon onto the plain to have a view for the evening, and stopped for camp beside one of the frozen ponds. The evening mirrors were pinpricks in a burgundy sky. I heated some beef soup, dipped crackers in it. After eating I sipped a cup of brandy, and located my position on the map. The fissured plain was clearly marked, an island in rougher terrain. The red dot was still a good distance to the north. The sky darkened to blackberry, the mirrors winked out over a horizon like a row of black teeth. The stars glowed yellow, making the clear dome of the car a planisphere. Sleep was difficult. Late in the night I jerked awake and knew I had been speaking with Emma, in a long conversation, a crucial one. What can you offer, she said. I tried to remember it; the starlit chaos, a vast jumble of black and gray, disoriented me, and even Emma's last words fled. The whole dream forgotten. And so much of our waking lives are lost in the same way. I felt a pang of grief for the way we live, for all that we go through, and can never return to.

When the mirror dawn came I ate some cereal, and at true dawn I started the car and hummed up the arrow canyon, determined to find the road again. The canyon led to another stone maze, with forks at every turn that might have been paths through to the north; but there were no signs of passage to show me the way. I drove back to the arrow and considered what to do. Studying the map, it seemed to me that I could navigate my own way to the red dot. It was about sixty or seventy kilometers away, and the terrain in between did not appear markedly different from that I had already crossed. It was midmorning already, and I didn't have an endless supply of air; in fact, my choice was to press on without the road, or turn back.

So I resolved to press on without the tracks. The rest of that morning I made good time north. The tumbled-down stone city I entered seemed to have split into hexagonal "city blocks": a dog-leg of thirty degrees right, followed by the same to the left, brought me time after time to Y-shaped canyon intersections where I could make the same choice again. Then a long broad fault allowed me to drive directly north for several kilometers, pausing only to maneuver over slides. My spirits rose, and with them my hopes (and a bit of fear): perhaps I would reach the region of the red dot that very day.

But I had forgotten that maps do not contain very much of reality. In the Aureum Chaos it would have been more accurate to leave a blank, with the legend "This is chaos—terra incognita—no map can show it and be faithful to its nature." For I drove into a narrow valley where the map indicated I could continue northward and downward to the center of the chaos, the bottom of that huge bowl—

And the valley ended in an escarpment. Not a very tall one, but tall enough—ten or twelve meters—and it extended east and west for as far as the eye could see. The whole land took a step down, in a sheer drop. A cliff!

Angrily I pulled out the map. In the appropriate area was a contour line—in fact two of them, drawn together, in a dark line that I had taken for an index contour. Disgusted, I tossed the map to the floor. Contour line or no, the escarpment was there; I could drive no farther.

For nearly an hour I sat there and thought. Then I packed some food into the survival cart, filled its water tank, filled my field suit with its maximum load of oxygen: a hundred hours, on minimum flow. In the drawers of the cart I put map, bivouac tent, lamp, etc., and then I shoved the cart out of the car's lock. The rush of cold air filled my lungs, but it was warmer than I had expected; there was more air down in this sink than I was used to.

The car's trunk contained a rope ladder and a big square flag of lime-green nylon. I used the ladder to lower the cart down the cliff. Rocks served to hold down the corners of the green flag, and I dropped the unsecured end over the side. Then I climbed down the rope ladder's metal rungs. The flag stood out against the cliffside clearly enough, and I tied its two bottom corners down with line so it couldn't be blown back over the top by a north wind. Satisfied, I took another look at the map, put it in my thigh pocket, and set off hiking, pulling the little cart behind me.

Now there was no chute too narrow, no pass too steep. I hiked almost directly north. According to the map the red dot was about fifteen kilometers away, so I would have to hurry. But I had started late in the day, and soon the sun fell, and I had to use the mirror dusk to pull the bivouac tent from the cart and inflate it. That done, I climbed through the little lock and pulled the cart in after me. I fixed and ate a meal rapidly, as if I were going to be able to hike again when I was finished.

It was a cloudy night. Through scudding breaks the stars twinkled, and Deimos flew eastward like an omen. I could not sleep; hours passed; I was surprised to wake and find that I had been drowsing in the mirror dawn. I slipped out of the tent and the shock of frigid air burst my senses awake. Soon after the tent was back in the cart the sun rose, and I started hiking again.

Hours passed, and there was nothing for me in the world but that maze of canyons and the map. It is a form of grace to become nothing but a task; one can believe in meanings because they are all that exist. At each fork in the system of giant fissures I got out the map and made a choice. The sun overhead warmed the air, and ice on the clumps of Syrtis grass turned to drops of water, sparking like prisms in the light. Icicles hanging off rocks dripped, and the surfaces of the ice ponds got slick and smooth. Junipers and needle grass filled cracks, and sprays of saxifrage and gentian surprised me with their color. Sometimes it was hard to match the terrain to the map, which was too small-scaled for my purpose. Estimating heights and distances in the dense amber air was difficult; at times I had a prospect of fifty meters, other times I could see all the way across the chaos; what appeared to be mountains in the distance often proved to be blocks just over the next ridge, and vice versa. Each correspondence I made between my location and a point on the map was more of a guess than the last—but once, in the afternoon, I climbed a tall rock and had a look around, and the view corresponded perfectly to a point on the map five or six kilometers southwest of the dot. Full of confidence I hiked on.

The general slope of the terrain tilted up against me, and hauling the cart up stone terraces got to be hard work. The dawn mirrors had set and the sun was about to, when I sat in a narrow pass to rest. I had just caught my breath when I saw a trail duck, right there before me in the sand. Four flat rocks laid on top of each other. "Yes!" I exclaimed. I knelt to inspect it. A human construct. I hooted loudly, and leaving the cart I ranged down both sides of the pass looking for another duck. I found nothing. "Which way?" I said, suddenly free to speak. "No one makes only one duck— where's the next?" In both directions I saw nothing but a rumpled carpet of rock, a shambles of brown and black and red. "Odd. Order leaps to the eye, I should be able to see two ducks, one before, one behind." But perhaps the others had fallen, or been buried. Or maybe I was supposed to continue in the same direction, and when the route changed direction another duck would appear. "Yes. Carry on, a sign will appear."

I was tired. By the time I returned to the cart the sun was down, and it was the most I could do to get the tent up and wiggle inside before dark. Once again I made soup, sipped brandy, pored over the map and charted a course for the next day, lay back in my bag, looked up at low dark clouds. Failed to sleep, except in fits and starts near dawn. Dreamed, and forgot the dreams on waking.

Next morning I was stiff, and it took a while to break camp. Before leaving I made a reconnaissance of the area, and over a steep ridge to the east of my pass I found another duck. Sand had drifted around it until it looked like a mound of dust filled with pebbles, but there it was. Lichen growing on the sides of it. I crunched back over the ridge to the cart. The new duck indicated a different course than the one I had charted the night before, but at one-to-one-million scale, the map wasn't going to give me much help once I got into the immediate area of the red dot, and the duck might be part of a trail leading straight to it. So I hauled the cart over the ridge, and very nearly twisted an ankle. "That will never do." The tendinitis in my knee was flaring up, but I ignored it. At the second duck I left the cart and searched for a third. I found it over another ridge; it was a fairly big duck, though it had fallen on its side and looked like a talus spill if you didn't look closely. It was unfortunate the terrain was so rough. But it made sense. The rebels would have put their refuge in the most inaccessible location they could find. Still, it took me nearly an hour to recover from the crossing of that ridge. I turned up my oxygen supply a bit, and searched again.

The next duck led me up a narrow, shallow chute, one that gave me a way to climb a broad tilted face that was like the side of a mountain. Thankful that I was done with ridge crossings, I hauled the cart up the chute twenty steps at a time, pausing after each twenty to catch my breath and strength. Out on the slope it was very hot, at least on the side of me facing the sun. I was surprised to find it was after noon. The sweat on my brow tasted good. When I moved my hand I saw it blur through space a bit. Wondering vaguely when the next duck would appear, I started climbing again.

I was near the top of that pitch, and feeling that the chaos must have turned on its side, when I saw the figure climbing ahead of me. My heart pulsed violently, its thump banged in my ears. "Hey!" I called weakly, and gathered myself for a shout. "Hello! Hellooo!"

The figure kept climbing. It wore a helmeted suit, and was bent nearly double in the steep last section of the chute. It was fast; I would have to hurry to catch up. I turned up my oxygen flow again, and started after this mysterious climbing partner. It disappeared over the top of the chute, and when I topped out myself I was surprised to see it hiking across a plateau that seemed relatively level after the wall we had just ascended.

So the rebels had placed their refuge in a knot of steep hills at the center of the chaos, giving them a view of the whole bowl. Admirable. Sweat got in my eyes and stung them badly; the whole world wavered through my tears. My breath came in such harsh gasps I could hardly talk. "Don't hike so fast! Hey up there! Stop."

The plateau suddenly folded up and then dropped away. The edge of the fold led up to the right, and on the plateau's side it was a broad ridge, easy to climb. But broken layers of rock lay on the ridge like shingles, and pulling the cart up each step was hard. My body felt like the skin was everywhere aflame, and I sloshed in my own sweat. Above me on the ridge the figure was standing upright, looking back at me. It waved a hand, gesturing for me to follow. "Yes! Yes," I said, and gasped, "only, go slow, er." But it didn't, and I had to continue to hurry, losing ground on it all the time. Not far above it was a knob of rock, and above that sky, meaning soon it would top this ridge and head off in another direction. Fearfully I yanked the cart sideways and braked the wheels with stones, then left it and hurried up the ridge by myself. I was glad I had; even alone I could barely walk up the ridge to the top knob, and once there I had to crawl on my hands and knees over the knob, which was not very tall.

Once over the knob I found myself standing on a small saddle that led to an even higher peak. I could see for kilometers, all across a world that curved slightly upward as it moved away from me. We were on a knobby saddlebacked hill, at the bottom of the huge bowl of Aureum. The figure was standing in the saddle, looking at me. Its helmet faceplate reflected the low blood-red sun. I waved a hand over my head several times. The faceplate tilted up and the sun's reflection disappeared; then the glass came down and turned red again. I stumbled off the lower knob, made my way onto the saddle. All my strength was gone. I could barely walk. Mercifully my companion stayed put. Soon I stood before it. It watched me without moving. I spread my hands. "I'm here."

No movement. Then it lifted a hand, laconic in gesture, and pointed at its ear.

"You don't need full helmets anymore," I said. "There's air enough to breathe now, air enough to talk in. You can't talk to me with that on."

No reply. I lifted my hands and mimed unlatching the helmet, but that got no response either. I took a step forward, it took a step back. I raised my arms and displayed the palms of my gloves; what could I, played out, do to it? Perhaps my companion understood this expression. In any case it allowed me to approach. I came at it from the side, so that the reflected sunlight slid away, and I saw that it was Emma.

She looked almost like the photos: brown eyes, down-swooping mouth, a strand or two of dark hair. All my breath left me. "So you did survive," I whispered. "Oh, Emma. It's me. I mean, my name is Hjalmar Nederland. I found you. I came here looking for you. I found your journal. I want to join you out here. I'm not going back, not ever. There's nothing for me back there—" a wave at the world. "Nothing, I say. I've left it for good."

She nodded once, very slightly, and turned and walked along the saddle's spine looking once over her shoulder to see if I was following. I kept at her heels, stumbling because I would not look away from her. I could not see enough of her—Emma Weil! There she stood! I could scarcely contain my amazement, my joy. Even when walking she was fast; I had to work to keep up with her runner's walk, but now I was strong, I could do it.

By the time we closed on the higher peak of the saddleback the sun had set, and we stood in the half light of the evening quartet. Now her faceplate was glass only, and her slim face was clearly visible. I indicated again that she should remove her helmet; she shook her head. She looked older, I was glad to see; she looked a woman my age, in her fourth century of life, skin lined with experience, eyes suffused with wisdom. She led me by the hand up the last slope to the summit, and I saw that under the final nest of peak boulders was a band of empty air. That is, there was a chamber without walls that she led me into. Its floor was flagged with smooth stone, and a circle of fluted columns twice our height was all that stood on this floor; and these pillars held up an equally smooth roof, on which the serrated boulders of the summit knot rested.

Emma smiled at my obvious astonishment, and led me between two pillars into the center of the . . . pavilion. The light of the dusk mirrors flooded the chamber, and the shadows of the pillars banded it. All the chaos lay below us, striped with light and shadow in a fantastic tumble of rock.

"What is this place?" I asked. "Is this your lookout, invisible from above? Is this a temple, and your refuge nearby?"

She nodded.

I walked to the edge of the room to the north, opposite where we had entered. Another broad ridge led down into shadows. I sat on the edge of the flagging, feeling very tired, very happy. Emma came and stood beside me, a hand resting on my hood. "I see now why you stay out here," I said. "It's not fear of the Committee. It's this place. Here you have Mars the way we always should have had it. A Greek temple from which to contemplate the land, a slowly wrought sculpture that the planet controls. And the life— lichen and moss, stonecrop and Syrtis grass, primrose and rock jasmine—isn't it lovely, struggling there around the edges of the ponds? All the meadows in this desolation. And soon it will be treeline down here—Martian juniper, have you seen it? Oh, Emma—what a world we have! What a world!"

She took my arm, pulled me up, led me several steps down the north ridge. When I began to wonder at her purpose she pointed down, at the ground between us. Under the glowing indigo sky I could barely make them out at first, but then I saw what she pointed at, and I thought that she must have heard what I had been saying. They were alpine flowers, tucked between the plated angular rocks: gentian and saxifrage, primrose and Tibetan rhubarb, little points of light color in the gloom.

I looked up, and she was gone. Then I caught a glimpse of her down the ridge, descending swiftly. Crying at her to stop I hurried after. I stumbled, lost ground. "Emma, don't leave. Don't leave."

It was dark. I no longer saw her. Perhaps she had been running out of air. I tried to hike back up the broad ridge, and couldn't. I would never be able to make it back to the cart. Slowly I pulled the thick woven cup of the facemask over my nose, and slid the hood's goggles down over it. I turned up the heat dial on my suit's forearm console, and climbed until I couldn't take another step. Then I lay down. I didn't know if I could survive the night or not.

So I lay in the lee of a boulder, thinking, she must have run low on air. Or, this is a test, a way to weed out the weak ones. She'll come back and get me in the morning. And I fell into unconsciousness.

Several times in the night cold stabbed deep enough to wake me, but I only shifted and slept again. At last the cold conquered even my exhaustion, and I sat up stiffly, flexed fingers and arms to generate warmth. I could not tell the time. Already the night seemed to have lasted years. And all I could do was wait.

Dawn in the chaos. Archimedes the first mirror sun cracked the distant horizon, and the world shifted from black to gray; then two mirror suns appeared, and another, and the diamond pattern of morning mirrors was complete. In the mirror dawn the chaos was gray, capped by a pearl sky. It was very cold. I had a bad sore throat, a pulsing headache.

The sun rose an hour later, and its brilliant yellow light rolled over the land like a gel. I got up and climbed the ridge, very slowly; but it seemed it led me to a different peak. No pavilion under a dolmen greeted me when I topped the ridge, though it was a broadly saddled hill. I crossed the saddle and inspected the other knob, thinking I might have confused them in the twilight. But it too was an ordinary hilltop; and down the ridge that led away to the south was my cart.

I hiked down to it and drank a liter of water, then ate a bit. Curiously I reascended the hill and climbed all over the two peaks, looking for signs. It seemed possible that the pillars could have descended into the hilltop, bringing the peak boulders back down to their proper roost. But I could find no sign of a break under them. I found quite a few footprints, though, and despite Emma's odd disappearance the night before, I was still reasonably sure that her refuge was nearby. Perhaps a search in the canyons around the hill. . . .

I checked the gauges in my forearm console, and stopped short. Came to. My oxygen supply was low, I only had twenty-five hours minimum flow left! I couldn't believe it. I had used a lot to survive the night, but how could I have let it get this low and never checked?

But if I found the refuge, it wouldn't matter.

I stood there, undecided, on the saddle, between the two peaks. Both of them solid rock. But the pillars could have been retractable, the refuge nearby, Emma low on air, testing my resolve, my desire. . . .

I shook my head. I was afraid to risk it. I backed away from the taller north peak, unwilling to turn from it. The refuge could have been right under it, a fortress under the mountain!

I tore myself away, hiked down to my cart, started the tedious process of lowering it down the long south ridge.

Quickly I found that the long day's hike and the night's exposure had sapped me of all strength. The cart kept trying to plunge away from me down the long chute, and when I managed to ease it to the bottom of that gruelling slope, pulling it farther was nearly too much for me. The hike became nothing but a brute struggle to haul that cart through the rock jungle.

The great sun and its flock of goslings flared overhead, until it seemed the sky burned. All the world, stone and sky, blazed in shades of red, and every pebble and boulder in my path pulsed with my heart, as if I walked in my body, across a plain broken like retina or tongue. The man as planet. Ponds glared white and I kneeled, consumed by thirst, to suck down the skim of water over the ice. Around one pond tufts of Syrtis grass broke from their ice sheaths and stood like green miracles in the talus. I dragged myself from stunned contemplation of them and hiked on, wandering in the chaos with the great poem of winter rolling deliriously in my head.

Lost in one of the canyon mazes, overwhelmed by exhaustion and headache, I checked my oxygen gauge and wondered if my folly had led me to death. The thought was like a spur to every cell in me, and I drank more water, checked the cart's radio compass. I even got out the map and tried to consult it, but ended up tossing it aside and laughing weakly. A map of chaos! What an idea!

Something in the planet broke, and a lump bulged up under Tharsis. This stressed the land around it, and the biggest fracture was the giant canyon system of Valles Marineris. Deep underground, water ran downhill through the gardened regolith, and it pooled underneath the lower end of the canyons in great aquifers. Tharsis kept upwelling and the pressure on the aquifers continued, as well as the fracturing in the crust, and eventually the aquifers burst onto the surface in massive outflows. Great outflow channels were scoured in the land downhill, to the north and east; and the land over the aquifers collapsed into chaos.

And so I came here. This is the only map we have. Death is the mother of beauty, the old poets said; but I think they lied to console themselves in the face of their premature end. I felt the weight of death on me that day, and all that expanse of stone and the blaze of suns in the chrysoprase sky were reduced to nothingness. Only the landscape of the next few steps meant anything. I felt each breath in my raw throat as the work of a plant, turning rock into root. I felt my burned nose, throat and lungs taking the world in with a constant and insatiable thirst. If that drinking of air ever stopped, I would die: I could feel the cold rasp of that truth in me. To die was to become *so sick* that the body broke down and stopped, utterly and irreparably. It was such a radical dysfunction that I had never been able to properly imagine it. But now I could feel in my body how it would happen. And then beauty was the last thing in the world that might have occurred to me.

And danger did not sharpen my senses, either. The chaos was blurred, my limbs were wood; tears leaked from my eyes and hurt my chapped cheeks, I moaned wordlessly, I dragged myself and the cart on with only a last patching together of the will. Up a small scarp, by lifting the front of the cart and putting the wheels on the higher ground. Backtracking to avoid a long fissure. Righting the cart. Pulling one wheel over a four-centimeter pebble. And so that whole long day passed, in work like that, in the dreadful confused blur of a nightmare.

In the fanned horizontal beams of sunset I sat on a rock. I had intended to heat some soup, and eat my remaining candy, but I was too tired to move. I sat there and watched the light of my last sunset drain off the land. When the sun disappeared I felt the sobs in me that I was too tired to make. Above the horizon the diamond pattern of mirror suns cast a streetlight glow over the dark land.

And there in the plum sky, so high that it was still lit by the sun, was a bird, I could see its broad wings catching the westerlies, dipping and flapping once or twice as it pursued the sun. Canyon hawk, or Arctic eagle. Or more likely a garok, a big Tibetan crow. A Martian bird. Manipulation of their gene stock made it possible for them to live. That bird is an idea, I thought. I felt my thirst, and stirred to get water from the cart. I needed to clean my suit of wastes, dump the flask in the cart for recycling. The idea floated over the chaos, observing it with hungry care. It must have been blown east by the wind. "Should be over the canyons with the foxes and moles. Nothing here but mouse hares and snow finches, living in the same holes together." Winds filled my chest, I breathed in and out unevenly, the soaring bird wavered in my sight and then held firm. Flight is a miracle, you know; it was bold to think of it. "You are an idea, Nederland. And you had better eat some soup, or the planet will forget you."

I ate soup, crackers, candy, beef sticks. Drank a lot of water. I got out the cart's little spyglass and turned it south. Through the glass I saw a low line of cliff, still catching mirror sunlight. My escarpment. And perhaps a green point on it, there to my left. I drank more water, feeling my rehydration. I had only six hours of oxygen left. I packed the pockets of my suit with food, water bottle, telescope. Then, leaving the cart behind (a find for some future archaeologist to ponder), I hiked south through the mirror dusk.

The bird still soared over me; I got a good look at its beak, and decided it was a garok. No disappearing vision this, but a real bird. I remembered then something I had once read, that it was not uncommon for solo climbers at high altitude to hallucinate a companion climber, ahead or behind on the pitch. Unhappily I banished the thought. I didn't want to think about what had happened to me.

When the last mirror sun disappeared the temperature plummeted. Night-time temperatures on Mars: forty degrees below zero. But there was no wind, my facemask and goggles were in place, and my suit's heater and my exertions kept me warm. It was an odd sensation—the suit radiated heat all over my skin, while breathing turned my insides to ice.

For an hour or two I advanced cautiously, resolutely, checking my landmarks and watching every step. After that exhaustion and dehydration made me clumsy, and inexorably the cold expanded from my lungs through my body. Every breath tortured my sore throat. I was thirsty, and my water was ice; I was tired, and my bed was rock. In the night's dark the floor of the chaos was a field of fanglike seracs, hanging overhead as if I ascended a stone glacier. My head and throat roared, I thought I might go blind with the ache of it. And I could not sit down and rest for fear of dying. A few steps, a standing rest; a few steps, a standing rest—and on forever.

Then I ran out of oxygen. My pulse tripped crazily, I was sure I was dying. What a stupid idea, I raged, to hike out here alone! What were you thinking? My body pumped air that was like dry ice in and out of me; my throat even lost its pain, or went beyond it. Here was the test: Could Martian air alone keep a man alive at night? Waves of faintness nauseated me and I saw the dim shadow world in pumping red, then in greens, and I leaned against a rock wall, all my powers focused on holding to consciousness. Breathing dry ice. Carbon dioxide, argon, inert gases, a fat dollop of oxygen—all at three hundred and ninety millibars, maybe four-fifty in Aureum—was it enough?

Apparently it was. For the moment. Enough to move? I tested it, and found I could walk. But now the cold was more penetrating than ever. I couldn't think, and I could barely walk, but I was afraid to sit. So I staggered on, slowly freezing to death, and killing my brain with lack of oxygen. Hours passed, and I carried on. The oxygen deprivation induced a mild euphoria in me; not a euphoria of spirits, exactly, but rather a sort of physical lightness. I stepped, stood, swayed, all with the distinct impression that if I did not keep my balance I might float away.

And then dawn came. Archimedes burst over the horizon without warning, taking me completely by surprise. I had forgotten daytime. Chapped lips broke to blood in a deathly grin. "The sun . . . is an idea."

And it showed me I had somehow kept hiking south. The escarpment was no more than two kilometers before me, and hiking toward it I saw off to my left the green flag. "Dead reckoning, all right." My headache was gone, and I felt free to sit for a moment and rest. I nearly failed to stand again, but when I managed it I floated along fairly well, feeling quite relaxed. Just after sunrise proper I made it to the bottom of the cliff, where I considered the problem of the rope ladder. There was no way around it; I was going to have to climb the thing. I took three quick steps up and hung my arms over a rung until I caught my breath. Then I added two rungs, and hung against the scarp again; and did it again, and repeated the maneuver until every muscle screamed, and my lungs pumped fast as a bird's. Getting over the edge was a technical problem that stopped me cold; but the idea of surviving the whole night and then falling at the last bend was too distasteful, and I lunged up and onto flat land. On hands and knees, without looking up, I followed the ladder to the car. Then through the lock—hard work—and into the inexpressibly warm air of the car. From my knees I switched on the car's systems, and collapsed onto the couch. I looked out at the great sink of Aureum, flooded by the lemon light of a new day, and falling asleep I shook my fist at the scene. "I went as far as I could for you, Emma Weil!"

And so I had. I slept without stirring until late that day, when intense thirst roused me. I found I was almost too stiff to move: I had pulled a muscle behind my left knee, tendinitis locked my right, and my arms and armpits were bruised and sore from the ascent of the ladder.

I stripped off my suit, shuddering at the sour smell; tossed it in the laundry drawer, and went to the toilet to clean up. I stared at myself in the mirror, appalled. My beard was like a stubbed field, and sweat covered this field like a white frost. My cheeks and nose were cracked and whitish. "They'll have to regrow that skin. Dr. Laird will be angry." Beady eyes were sunken deep, the skin under them was black. So I would look on the last day of my life. So my corpse would appear. I splashed water onto my face and felt the sting voluptuously: water of life, sting of living.

I went back to the driver's seat and looked out the window. Dusk in the chaos, brown-black shadows under a banded sky. The violent purples of the world's end. But it was just another day. Every day was a stroke on the calendar: live a thousand years, it was still true. I had lived my life as if I were immortal, but now I knew differently. Extend as far as I could, there would still come the day of the dysfunction, the radical breakdown, the end. And the face in the toilet mirror believed it.

So I had lived my life on false premises. All those complaints about the pain of existence—what a fool I had been to ape the ennui of the immortal, ignoring the flesh metronome ticking inside, marking each of a finite number of moments we could never return to. I had behaved as if I were a god, and hiked alone into the chaos careless of my own life; and in the cold night learned better, the hard way.

And as the light leaked out of the sky, and black clouds loomed out of the north over the land like immense dark beings, I felt that all my springs of action were wrong. I groaned, shuffled to the heating ring and the cabinet below it. Making each move like a wooden man I rehydrated a packet of beef stroganoff, and stirred it in a frypan. I got out the brandy and drank from the bottle. At the smell of the beef my stomach growled. All those times when Shrike had pricked me with his scorn; each time he had been right. I took another swig of the brandy. "You're an ass, Nederland. An idiot, a fool. You've lived your life like a mouse hare in its hole, while all the while red Mars spun through the ether like a top. A hare pawing over stones, wanting to feel the same way over and over, alive only when the shrike seized you and impaled you on his thorn bush." Another swallow of brandy, burning its way down, swimming in the brain. I poured the stroganoff onto a plate and sat before it at the tiny table. Only the heating ring illuminated the compartment; I turned on a lamp, and faint reflections of the interior appeared in the windows, obscuring the cloudy sky outside. I ate for a while; then the fork halted over the plate, and I stared out at the night. "You must change your life."

The next day I followed my route back, driving with a ruthless skill that returned to me from my life in the Survey. That had been a good time, those years of driving over the planet; I remembered that in my hands, in the act of driving itself, and it gave me something to ponder during the trip from marker to marker. It was still early afternoon when I drove up the ramp onto the mesa, and into the cold water station's yard. The whole crew tumbled out of the buildings and gathered around the car to greet me. As I eased my way awkwardly out of the lock, and looked at all their round-eyed faces, full of curiosity and dismay, I knew what it was to be a prophet returning from the wilderness, I felt that my stubble should have been a beard flowing to my knees, that I should have carried tablets or the like. Xhosa's face was split into a big grin; Hana tried to help me walk, and I brushed her off irritably, limped across the yard and into the biggest tent, followed by the whole congregation. "What happened to you?" Bill asked in a horrified tone.

I told them a little, leaving most of it out. When I got to the escarpment and my decision to hike, Hana sucked air through her teeth as if I were still in danger. And when I mentioned my night in the open without oxygen, Xhosa whistled. "I'm not sure that's ever been done before," he said.

That intrigued me, and later I looked into it. I found that a group of four climbers in the Kasei Vallis had lost their cart in a crevasse (easy to do!) and been forced to bivouac a night in suits, without oxygen, at two kilometers above the datum. Two of them died, but the other two were rescued the next day. So I was not the first human to spend a night free on the surface of Mars; but close enough.

When I was done with my story, Bill said, "There's been a radio message for you. They want you to return to Burroughs as quickly as possible. Apparently you're to head an expedition to Pluto, to dedicate Icehenge."

"Dedicate Icehenge?"

"To the memory of those killed in the Unrest. The Committee is sponsoring the expedition, and Mr. Selkirk is organizing it. He hopes they can leave soon, he wanted to tell you—he would like to have the expedition reach Pluto in time to coordinate the dedication with the three hundred and fiftieth anniversary of the convening of the Committee."

I couldn't help laughing. Pierce me, Shrike! Prick me to life! Of course my companions stared at me as if I were mad. Yes, I could see them thinking it: he wandered in the chaos and suffered oxygen deprivation, and it's killed so many brain cells that he's over the rim at last. That's the trouble with a reputation for eccentricity; after you've got it, even the most ordinary behavior looks odd, just because it's yours.

So after I had my skin tended to, and rested a couple of days, I took a car and a couple of students I barely knew, and started back, taking a detour so I could visit New Houston one more time. Selkirk's expedition would wait for me.

### The Aquifer

In New Houston I limped up and walked around the rim, to look down into the town of my birth, now a ruin. And then I went down to the abandoned field car, and sat in it. Through the starred windshield the sun shone brightly.

Here sat Emma Weil. Here in New Houston lived Emma Weil, for a few embattled weeks, anyway—weeks when I too had lived here. I rubbed the seat's arms with a gloved finger. Soon I would be off to Pluto, to "dedicate" the monument left behind by Oleg Davydov and his band of voyagers—to dedicate it to the Mars Development Committee, the very force that had driven Davydov's group to its desperate act.

And yet Davydov and Emma and the Mars Starship Association *would be remembered*; this megalith would be theirs, now, forever. The Committee flexed back where it had to like a judo wrestler, hoping to pull me off balance and spin me away; but if I kept the pressure on in the right way, I might topple it. This time their plan might be foiled. The Mars Starship Association had resisted, Emma Weil had resisted, I had resisted, and I would keep resisting; and perhaps one day we would make Mars free.

What does it mean to love the past? Each day disappears into nothingness, and we must live every moment of our lives in the present. The present is the whole of reality. But human beings are more than real. We plunge through the years like giants, as the poet said, and not one of us can be understood except as creatures continuously exfoliating. When memory fails to contain us we must love the past more than ever, to hold it to us—or else the present becomes a meaningless blaze of color and sound, in which no two humans, great elongate beings, will be able to do more than touch at their very lips, their spatial selves—no one will ever truly understand another. To love the past is to become fully human.

I clutched the armrests of that old car seat as hard as I could, and heard them crackle. Here a human being I understood had once sat. Whether she had died here or escaped, I would never know. My pilgrimage to find her had failed, and all I had met out there in the broken land was myself; or ghosts. But then the realization came to me that it didn't matter. It didn't matter. Immediately I was filled, as with water or air, with an overwhelming sense of peace. Whether Emma lived or died that night in Spear Canyon, she had lived, she had resisted—one great woman loved Mars and struggled for it, committed the whole continuum of her self to the idea that we could live here as free human beings. And I knew that it was so. So that whether she escaped from the car or died right there in the very seat I sat in, she lived on in my heart, in my mind and my life. And that was enough.

Our lives are plants, creating leaves and flowers that fall away and are lost forever. I suppose that writing this account on these leaves will make little difference; words are gossamer in a basalt world. Still I am glad I did it. Soon we will descend to the ninth planet, and in this interregnum I feel completely cast loose, on the edge of a new world, a new life; stripped of all habits, opinions and expectations, I tremble like a blade of grass in the open air. The old life swirls in my mind like rock jasmine blooms down a canyon stream, and I wonder what will live on into my new existence, for even my unsheathing feels like a dream to me now, fragmentary, delirious, unreal. Still, spun into gossamer these parts of a world may remain within my ken: what we feel most, we remember best. The weak link is.

# III

◆

# EDMOND DOYA

## 2610 A.D.

"Ill did those mightie men to trust thee with their stories,
   That hast forgot their names, who rear'd thee for their glorie:
For all their wondrous cost, thou that hast serv'd them so,
What tis to trust to Tombes, by thee we easely know."

—*Michael Drayton*, "Poly-Olbion"

**Sometimes I dreamed** about Icehenge, and walked in awe across the old crater bed, among those tall white towers. Quite often in the dreams I had become a crew member of the *Persephone*, on that first expedition to Pluto in 2547. I landed with the rest of them on a plain of crater-pocked, shattered black basalt, down near the old mechanical probes. And I was there, in the bridge with Commodore Ehrung and the rest of her officers, when the call came in from Dr. Cereson, who was out in an LV locating the magnetic poles. His voice was high, it cracked with excitement that sounded like fear, and radio hiss sputtered in his pauses:

"I'm landing at the geographical pole—you'd better send a party up here fast . . . there's a . . . a *structure* up here. . . ."

Then I would dream I was in the LV that sped north to the pole, crowded in with Ehrung and the other officers, sharing in the tense silence. Underneath us the surface of Pluto flashed by, black and obscure, ringed by crater upon crater. I remember thinking in the dreams that the constant radio hiss was the sound of the planet. Then—just like in the films the *Persephone* brought back, you could say I dreamed myself into the films—we could see forward to the dark horizon. Low in the sky hung the crescent of Charon, Pluto's moon, and below it—white dots. A cluster of white towers. "Let's go down," said Ehrung quietly. A circle of white beams, standing on their ends, pointing up at the thick blanket of stars.

Then we were all outside, in suits, stumbling toward the structure. The sun was a bright dot just above the towers, casting a clear pale light over the plain. Shadows of the towers stretched over the ground we crossed; members of the group stepped into the shadow of a beam, disappeared, reappeared in the next slot of sunlight. The regolith we walked over was a dusty black gravel. Everyone left big footprints.

We walked between two of the beams—they dwarfed us—and were in the huge irregular circle that the beams made. It looked as if there were a hundred of them, each a different size. "Ice," said a voice on the intercom. "They look like ice." No one replied.

And here the dreams would always become confused. Everything happened out of order, or more or less at once; voices chattered in the earphones, and my vision bumped and jiggled, just as the film from that first hand-held camera had done. They found poor Seth Cereson, who had pressed himself against one of the largest beams, faceplate directly on the ice, in a shadow so that he was barely visible. He was in shock as they led him back to the LVs, and kept repeating in a small voice that there was something moving inside the beam. That frightened everyone a bit. Several people walked over and inspected a fallen beam, which had shattered into hundreds of pieces when it hit the ground. Others looked at the edges of the three triangular towers, which were nearly transparent. From a vantage point on top of one of the beams I looked down and saw the tiny silver figures scurrying from beam to beam, standing in the center of the circle looking about, clambering onto the fallen one. . . .

Then there was a shout that cut through the other voices. "Look here! Look here!"

"Quietly, quietly," said Ehrung. "Who's speaking?"

"Over here." One of the figures waved his arms and pointed at the beam before him. Ehrung walked swiftly toward him, and the rest of us followed. We grouped behind her and stared up at the tower of ice. In the smooth, slightly translucent white surface there were marks engraved:

अभ्युद्द अभ्युसद्

♦♦  ♦♦  ♦♦♦♦  ♦♦♦♦♦♦♦♦

For a long time Ehrung stood and stared at them, and the crew behind her stared too. And in the dream, I knew that they were two Sanskrit words, carved in the Narangi alphabet: *abhyud*, and *aby-ut-sad*. And I knew what they meant:

> to move, to push farther out;
> to cause to set out towards.

Another time, caught in that half sleep just before waking, when you know you want to get up but something keeps you from it, I dreamed I was on another expedition to Icehenge, a later one determined to clear up once and for all the controversy surrounding its origins. And then I woke up. Usually it is one of the few moments of grace in our lives, to wake up apprehensive or depressed about something, and then realize that the something was part of a dream, and nothing to worry about. But not this time. The dream was true. The year was 2610, and we were on our way to Pluto.

There were seventy-nine people on board *Snowflake*: twenty-four crew, sixteen reporters, and thirty-nine scientists and technicians. The expedition was being sponsored by the Waystation Institute for Higher Learning, but essentially it was my doing. I groaned at the thought and rolled out of bed.

My refrigerator was empty, so after I splashed water on my face, I went out into the corridor. It had rough wood walls, set at slightly irregular angles; the floor was a lumpy moss that did surprisingly well underfoot.

As I passed by Jones's chamber the door opened and Jones walked out. "Doya!" he said, looking down at me. "You're out! I've missed you in the lounge."

"Yes," I said, "I've been working too much, I'm ready for a party."

"I understand Dr. Brinston wants to talk to you," he said, brushing down his tangled auburn hair with his fingers. "You going to breakfast?"

I nodded and we started down the corridor together. "Why does Brinston want to talk to me?"

"He wants to organize a series of colloquia on Icehenge, one given by each of us."

"Oh, man. And he wants me to join it?" Brinston was the chief archaeologist, and as such probably the most important member of our expedition, even though Dr. Lhotse of the Institute was our nominal leader. It was a fact Brinston was all too aware of. He was a pain in the ass—a gregarious Terran (if that isn't being redundant), and an overbearing academic hack. Although not truly a hack—he did good work.

We turned a corner, onto the main passageway to the dining commons. Jones was grinning at me. "Apparently he believes that it would be essential to have your participation in the series, you know, given your historical importance and all."

"Give me a break."

In the white hallway just outside the commons there was a large blue bulletin screen in one of the walls. We stopped before it. There was a console under it for typing messages onto the board. The new question, put up just recently, was the big one, the one that was sending us out here: "Who put up Icehenge?" in bold orange letters.

But the answers, naturally, were jokes. In red script near the center of the board, was "GOD." In yellow type, "Remnants of a Crystallized Ice Meteorite." In a corner, in long green letters: "Nederland." Under that someone had typed, "No, Some Other Alien." I laughed at that. There were several more solutions (I liked especially "Pluto Is a Message Planet From Another Galaxy"), most of which had first been put forth in the year after the discovery, before Nederland published the results of his work on Mars.

Jones stepped up to the console. "Here's my new one," he said. "Let's see, yellow Gothic should be right: 'Icehenge put there by prehistoric civilization' "—this was Jones's basic contention, that humans were of extraterrestrial origin, and had had a space technology in their earliest days—" 'But the inscription carved on it by the Davydov starship.' "

"Jones," I scolded him. "You're at it again. How many of these solutions have you put up?"

"No more than half," he said, and seeing my expression of dismay he cackled. He made me laugh too, but we straightened up and put on serious frowns before we entered the dining commons.

Inside, Bachan Nimit and his micrometeorite people were seated at a table together, eating with Dr. Brinston. I cringed when I saw him, and went to the kitchen.

Jones and I sat at a table on the other side of the room and began to eat. Jones, system-famous heretic scholar of evolution and prehistory, had nothing but a pile of apples on his plate. He adhered to the dietary laws of his home, the asteroid Icarus, which decreed that nothing eaten should be the result of the death of any living system. Jones's particular affinity was for apples, and he finished them off rapidly.

I was nearly done with my omelet when Brinston approached our table. "Mr. Doya, it's good to see you out of your cabin!" he said loudly. "You shouldn't be such a hermit!"

Now I left my cabin pretty regularly to party, but when I did I was careful to avoid Brinston. Here I was reminded why. "I'm working," I said.

"Oh, I see." He smiled. "I hope that won't keep you from joining our little lecture series."

"Your what?"

"We're organizing a series of talks, and hope everyone will give one." The micrometeor crew had turned to watch us.

"Everyone?"

"Well—everyone who represents a different aspect of the problem."

"What's the point?"

"What?"

"What's the point?" I repeated. "Everyone on board this ship already knows what everyone else has written and said about Icehenge."

"But in a colloquium we could discuss these opinions."

The academic mind. "In a colloquium there would be nothing but a lot of arguing and bitching and rehashing the same old points. We've wrangled for years without anyone changing his mind, and now we're going to Pluto to look at Icehenge and find out who really put it there. Why stage a reiteration of what we've already said?"

Brinston was flushing red. "We hoped there would be new things to be said."

I shrugged. "Maybe so. Look, just go ahead and have your talks without me."

Brinston paused. "That wouldn't be so bad," he said reflectively, "if Nederland were here. But now the two principal theorists will be missing."

I felt my distaste for him turn to dislike. He knew of the relationship between Nederland and me, and this was a jab. "Yes, well, Nederland's been there before." He had, too, and it was too bad he hadn't made better use of the visit. They had done nothing but dedicate a plaque commemorating the expedition of asteroid miners that he had discovered; at the time, his explanation was so widely believed that the megalith hadn't even been excavated.

"Even so, you'd think he'd want to be along on the expedition that will either confirm or contradict his theory." His voice grew louder as he sensed my discomfort. "Tell me, Mr. Doya, what did Professor Nederland say was his reason for not joining us?"

I stared at him for a long time. "He was afraid there would be too many colloquia," I said, and stood up. "Now excuse me while I return to my work." I went to the kitchen and got some supplies, and walked back to my room, feeling that I had made an enemy, but not caring much.

\* \* \*

Yes, Hjalmar Nederland, the famous historian of Icehenge, was my great-grandfather. It was a fact I remember always knowing, though my father never encouraged my pleasure in knowing it. (Father wasn't his grandchild; my mother was.)

I had read all of Nederland's books—the works on Icehenge, the five-volume Martian history, the earlier books on terran archaeology—by the time I was ten. At that time Father and I lived on Ganymede. Father had gotten lucky and was crewing on a sun-sailer entered in the InandOut, a race that takes the sailers into the top layer of Jupiter's atmosphere.

Usually he wasn't that lucky. Sunsailing was for the rich, and they didn't need crews often. So most of the time Father was a laborer: street sweeper, carrier at construction sites, whatever was on the list at the laborer's guild. As I understood later, he was poor, and shiftless, and played the edges to get by. Maybe I've modelled my life on his.

He was a small man, my father, short and spare-framed; he dressed in worker's clothes, and had a droopy moustache, and grinned a lot. People were always surprised to see him with a kid— he didn't look important enough. But when he lived on Mars, and then Phobos, he had been part of a foursome. The other man was a well-known sculptor, with a lot of pull in artistic circles. And my mom, being Nederland's granddaughter, had connections with the University of Mars. Between them they managed to get that rare thing (especially on Mars), the permission to have a child. Then when the foursome broke up, Father was the only one interested in taking care of me; he had grown up with me, in a sense, in that my presence as an infant was what brought him out of a funk. So he told me. Into his custody I went (I was six, and had never set foot on Mars), and we took off for Jupiter.

After that Father never discussed my mother, or the other members of the foursome, or my famous great-grandfather (when he could keep me from bringing up the topic), or even Mars. He was, among other things, a sensitive man—a poet who wrote poems for himself, and never paid a fee to put them in the general file. He loved landscapes and skyscapes, and after we moved to

Ganymede we spent a lot of time hiking in suits over Ganymede's stark hills, to watch Jupiter or one of the other moons rise, or to watch a sunrise, still the brightest dawn of them all. We were a comfortable pair. Ours was a quiet pastime, and the source of most of Father's poetry. The poems of his that exerted the most pull on me, however, were those about Mars. Like this one:

> In the Lazuli Canyon, boating.
> Sheet ice over shadowed stream,
> Crackling under our bow.
> Stream grows wide, bends out into sunlight:
> A million turns following the old vallis.
> Plumes of frost at every breath.
> Endless rise of the red canyon,
> Mountains and canyons, no end to them.
> Black webs in rust sandstone:
> Wind-carved boulders hang over us.
> There, on the wet red beach:
> Dull green Syrtis grass. Green.
> In the canyon my heart is pure—
> Why ever leave?
> The western sky deep violet,
> In it two stars, white and indigo:
> Venus, and the Earth.

Even though Father disliked Nederland (they had met, I gathered, only once) he still indulged my fascination with Icehenge. For some reason I loved that megalith; it was the greatest story I knew. On my eleventh birthday Father took me down to the local post office (at this time we were on bright Europa, and took long hikes together across its snowy plains). After a whispered conference with one of the attendants, we went into a holo room. He wouldn't tell me what we were going to see, and I was frightened, thinking it might be my mother.

The room holo came on; and we were in darkness. Stars overhead. Suddenly a very bright one flared, defining a horizon, and pale light flooded over what now appeared as a dark, rocky plain.

Then I saw it off in the distance: the megalith. The sun (I recognized it now, the bright star that had risen) had only struck the top of the liths, and they gleamed white. Below the sunlight they were square black cutouts, blocking stars. The line quickly dropped (the holo was speeded up) and it stood revealed, tall and white. Because of the model of it that I owned at the time, it seemed immense.

"Oh, *Dad.*"

"Come on, let's go look at it."

"Bring it here, you mean."

He laughed. "Where's your imagination, kid?" He dialed it over—I went straight through a lith—and we were standing at its center, near the plaque commemorating the Davydov Expedition. We circled slowly, necks craned back to look up. We inspected the broken column and its scattered pieces, then looked closely at the brief inscription.

"It's a wonder they didn't all sign their names," said Father.

Then the whole scene disappeared and we were standing in the bare holo room. Father caught my forlorn expression, and laughed. "You'll see it again before you're through. Come on, let's go get some ice cream."

Soon after that, when I was just fourteen, he got a chance to go to Terra. Friends of his were buying and taking a small boat all the way back, and they needed one more crew member. Or perhaps they didn't absolutely need one, but they wanted him to come.

At that time we had just moved back to Ganymede, and I had a job at the atmosphere station. We had lived there nearly a year, off and on, and I didn't want to move again. I had written a book describing the deep space adventures of the Davydov expedition, and with the money I was saving I planned to publish it. (For a fee anyone can put their work in the data banks, and have it listed in the general catalogue; whether anyone will ever read it is another matter, but I had hopes, at the time, that one of the book clubs would buy the rights to list it in their index.)

"See, Dad, you've lived on Terra and Mars, so you want to go back there so you can be outside and all. Me, I don't care about that stuff. I'd rather stay here."

Father stared at me carefully, suspicious of such a sentiment, as well he might be—for as I understood much later, my disinclination to go to Terra stemmed mainly from the fact that Hjalmar Nederland had said in an interview (and implied in many articles) that he didn't like it.

"You've never been there," my father said, "else you might not say that. And it's something you should see, take my word for it. The chance doesn't come that often."

"I know, Dad. But the chance has come for you, not me."

He scowled at me. In a world with so few children, everyone is treated as an adult; and my father had always treated me as an equal, to a degree that would be difficult to describe. Now he didn't know what to say to me. "There's room for you too."

"But only if you make it. Look, you'll be back out here sailing in a couple of years. And I'll get down there someday. Meanwhile I want to stay here. I got a job and friends."

"Okay," he said, and looked away. "You're your own man, you do what you want."

I felt bad then, but not nearly so much as I did later, when I remembered the scene and understood what I had done. Father was tired, he was going through a hard time, he needed his friends. He was about seventy then, and he had nothing to show for his efforts, and he was tired. In the old days he'd have been near the end, and I suppose he felt that way—he hadn't yet gotten that second wind that comes when you realize that, far from being over, the story has just begun. But that second wind didn't come from me, or with my help. And yet that, it seems to me, is what sons are for.

So he left for Terra, and I was on my own. About two years later I got a letter from him. He was in Micronesia, on an island in the Pacific Ocean somewhere. He had met some Marquesan sailors. There were fleets of the old Micronesian sailing ships, called *wa'a kaulua*, crisscrossing the Pacific, carrying passengers and even freight. Father had decided to apprentice himself to one of the navigators from the Carolines, one of those who navigate as they did in the ancient times, without radio or sextant, or compass, or even maps.

And that's what he has been doing, from that day to this: forty-five years. Forty-five years of learning to gauge how fast the ship is moving by watching coconuts pass by; memorizing the distances between islands; reading the stars, and the weather; lying at the bottom of the ship during cloudy nights, and feeling the pattern of the swells to determine the ship's direction. . . . I think back to the hand to mouth times of our brief partnership, and I see that he has, perhaps, found what he wants to do. Occasionally I get a note from Fiji, Samoa, Oahu. Once I got one from Easter Island, with a picture of one of the statues included. The note said, "And this one's not a fake!"

That's the only clue I've gotten that he knows what I'm doing.

So I stayed on Ganymede and lived in dormitories, and worked at the atmosphere station. My way of life had been learned in the years with my father; it was all I knew, and I kept to the pattern. Dorm mates were my family, and that was never a problem. After my name came up on the hitchhiker's list I moved out to Titan, and while waiting for a job with the weather company I joined the laborer's guild, and swept streets, and pushed wheelbarrows, and unloaded spaceships. I liked the work, and quickly became quite strong.

I got a room in a boarding house that had advertised at the guild, and found that most of my housemates were also laborers. It was a congenial crowd: the meals were rowdy affairs, and the parties sometimes lasted through the night—our landlady loved them. One of the older boarders, a woman named Angela, liked to argue philosophy—to "discuss ideas," as she called it. On cold nights she would call a few of us on the intercom and invite us down to the kitchen, where she would brew endless pots of tea, and badger me and three or four other regulars with questions and provocations. "Don't you think it is well established that all of the assassinated American presidents were killed by the Rosicrucians?" she would demand, and then tell us how John Wilkes Booth had escaped the burning barn to live on, take on another identity, and shoot both Garfield and McKinley. . . .

"And Kennedy too?" John Ashley asked. "Are you sure this isn't Ahasuerus the Assassin you're discussing here?" John was a Rosicrucian, you see, and was naturally incensed.

"Ahasuerus?" Angela inquired.

"The Wandering Jew."

"Did you know that originally he wasn't a Jew at all?" George asked. "His name was Cartaphilus, and he was Pontius Pilate's janitor."

"Wait a second," I said. "Let's get back to the point. Booth was identified by his dental records, so the body they found in the barn was definitely his. Dental records are pretty conclusive. So your whole idea falls apart right at the start, Angela."

She would contest it every time, and we would move on to the nature of evidence, and then the nature of reality, while pot after pot of tea was brewed and consumed. I would argue Aristotle against Plato, Hume against Berkeley, Peirce against the metaphysicals, Allenton against Dolpa, and the warm kitchen echoed with our fierce talk. Many was the time when I vanquished the rest with my mishmash of empiricism, pragmatism, logical positivism, and essentialist humanism—or I thought I did, until late in the night when I went up to my tiny bookwalled room on the fourth floor, and lay on my bed and stared at the books and wondered what it was all about. Could it really be true that all we knew was what our senses told us?

Once John Ashley brought down to our kitchen group a volume called *Sixty-six Crystals on the Ninth Planet*, by a Theophilus Jones. After he had explained it to us, I couldn't have been more scathing. I was familiar with Jones's earlier works, and this new argument did nothing to bolster his case. "Don't you see how illogical he's being there? He has to contradict the whole picture of human history, the work of hundreds of scientists using thousands of pieces of evidence, just to establish the *possibility* that a prehistoric highly advanced civilization existed. Which by no means would prove that they flew out to *Pluto* of all places to set up a temple. I mean, why would they do that?"

"Yes, but look at all he says about how *old* Icehenge is."

"No no no, none of those are serious dating methods. Calculating the chances of a lith getting hit by a meteorite? Why, it doesn't matter *what* the chances are. The fact is it could have been hit by a meteorite the day after they completed the thing, and damn the probabilities. It doesn't prove anything. That megalith was put there by Martians about three hundred years ago, by the Davydov expedition. They are the only ones who had the means to get out to Pluto so long ago. Read Nederland, he's got the whole case worked up beautifully. He even found mention of the plans for the thing, in the Weil journal. With that kind of evidence you don't need this far-fetched stuff. It's nonsense, John."

And John would argue right back that it wasn't, and Angela and George and the others would usually support him. "How can you be so sure, Edmond? How can you be *sure?*"

"By looking at the evidence we've got. It stands to reason."

Not that I was always so positive in my feelings toward my great-grandfather. Once I was walking home after a hard day of loading pipe. I had had some beers after work with the rest of the loading gang, and I was feeling low. Passing a holo sales shop I noticed a panel discussion in the window holo and stopped to watch, recognizing one of the doll-like figures to be Nederland. Curiously I contemplated him. He was discussing something or other—on the street it was hard to hear the store's speaker—with a group of well-dressed professor types, who looked much like him; he was authoritative, impeccably groomed, and on his tiny face was an expert's frown—he was getting ready to correct the speaker.

I remembered that once I had badgered my father: "Why don't you like Great-grandpa, Dad? Why? He's famous!" It took a lot of that to get Father even to admit he disliked Nederland, much less explain it. Finally he had said, "Well, I only met him once, but he was rude to your mother. She said it was because we had bothered him, but I still thought he could have been polite. She was his own granddaughter, and he acted like she was some beggar dunning for change. I didn't like that."

I left the holo shop window and continued home thinking

about it, and when I came to my shabby old boarding house, and looked at its stained walls and etched windows, and remembered the sight of Nederland on that expensive Martian stage in his fine clothes, I felt a little bitter.

But most of the time I was pleased to have such a historian for an ancestor; I was fascinated by his work, and made myself an expert in it. One wall of my book-lined room was covered with shelves of books by Nederland, or about Nederland, or about Oleg Davydov and Emma Weil, and the Mars Starship Association, and the Martian Civil War, and the rest of early Martian history. I became a scholar of that whole era, and my first publications were letters of comment in *Chronicle of Martian History* and *Shards*, correcting errors in articles on the period. The publication of these letters in such prestigious journals convinced me that I was a gypsy scholar, a laborer intellectual, the equal of any university man. And I studied harder than ever, quite pleased with myself—a dabbler in a field where I had not had a single moment's contact with the primary sources of data: one of Nederland's many followers in the widespread revision of Martian history.

So years passed, and Icehenge, and Nederland's explanation for it, the astonishing story of the Davydov mutiny, remained a central part of my life. The turning point in my history—the end of my innocence, so to speak—came on New Year's Eve, when the year 2589 became 2590. By that time I was working for the Titan Weather Company. Early in the evening I was on the job, helping to create a lightning storm that crackled and boomed over the raucous new town of Simonides. Just after the big blast at midnight—two huge balls of St. Elmo's fire, colliding just above the dome—we were let off, and we hit town ready for a good time. The whole crew, all sixteen of us, went first to our regular bar, Jacque's. Jacque was dressed up as the Old Year, and his pet chimpanzee was in diapers and ribbons, representing the New. I drank several beers and allowed a variety of capsules to be popped under my nose, and soon like most of the people there I was very drunk. My boss, Mark Starr, was rolling on the floor, wrestling the chimp. It looked like he was losing. An impromptu chorus was bellowing out an old standard, "I Met Her in a Phobos Restaurant," and inspired by the mentioning of my native satellite, I started singing a complicated harmony part. Apparently I was the only one who perceived its beauties. There were shouts of protest, and the woman seated next to me objected by pushing me off the bench. As I recovered my footing she stood up, and I shoved her into the table behind us. People there were upset by her arrival and began pounding on her. Feeling magnanimous, I grabbed her arm and pulled her away. The moment she was clear of them she punched me hard in the shoulder, and swung again angrily. I parried the blow with a forearm and jabbed her on the sternum, but she had a longer reach and was much angrier, and I had to retreat quickly, warding off her blows. Despite a couple of good jabs I saw that I was outmatched, and I slipped through the throng at the bar and escaped out the door and into the street.

I sat down at the curb and relaxed. I felt good. There were lots of people on the street, many of them quite drunk. One of them failed to notice me, and tripped over my legs. "Hey!" he shouted, kneeling before me and grabbing my collar. "What d'you mean tripping me like that?" He was a big barrel-chested man, with thin arms that nevertheless were very strong; he shook me a little and it seemed to me his biceps looked like wire under the skin. He had long tangled hair, a small head, and he reeked of whiskey.

"Sorry," I said, and tried to knock his hands away from my collar. I failed. "I was just sitting here when you ran over me."

"Sure!" he shouted, and shook me again. Then he let go of me, and his eyes rolled a little; he crumpled back onto his butt, took stock of his situation dizzily, and slid himself over so that he was seated in the trash in the gutter, out of people's way. I shifted away from him a foot or two, and he waved at me to stop. He took a vial from his shirt pocket, opened it with awkward care, waved it under his nose.

"You shouldn't use that stuff," I advised him.

"And why not?"

"It'll give you high blood pressure."

He peered up at me with bloodshot eyes. "High blood pressure is better than no blood pressure at all."

"There is that."

"So you'd better try some of this, hadn't you."

I didn't know if he was serious or not, but I decided not to test it. "I guess I'd better."

Slowly he levered himself up onto the curb next to me. Seated he looked like a spider. "You got to have blood pressure, that's my motto," he said.

"I see."

He waved the vial under my nose, and immediately I felt the rush of the flyer. He left it there until I almost fainted with euphoria and lack of oxygen. "Man," he said, "on New Year's Eve everybody just goes *crazy.*"

"Gosh I w-wonder why," I managed to say.

Then Mark and Ivinny and several more of the weather crew crashed out of Jacque's. "Come on, Edmond, the chimp has got hold of a fire extinguisher and any minute it'll be blasting us."

I stood up, much too quickly, and when the colored lights went away I motioned to my new companion. He started to stand, we helped him the rest of the way. He stood a score of centimeters taller than the rest of us. We trailed my group of friends, talking continuously and barely listening to each other, we were so high. Then a forty-person free-for-all swirled out of a side street and caught us up in it; Simonides was filled with Caroline Holmes's shipworkers, and it was nearing dawn, and from the roar bouncing down on us from the dome it appeared that there were brawls going on all over town. My new companion's arms were only thin in relation to his giant torso, and with their length and power he was able to clear an area around him. I stayed close on his heels, and was hit on the side of the head by his elbow. When I regained consciousness a few seconds later he was dragging me by the heels after Mark and the rest. "What are you doing attacking me from behind, eh?" he shouted. "Don't you know that's dangerous?"

"Uh." A vial shoved up one of my nostrils and I was clear-headed again. I staggered free of my companion and followed him and the weather crew through the clogged streets.

At dawn we were on the east edge of town, sitting on the wide concrete strip just inside the dome. There were seven or eight of the weather crew left, laughing and drinking from a tall white bottle. My new friend arranged pieces of gravel into patterns on the concrete. On the horizon a white point appeared, and lengthened into a knife-edge line dividing the night: the rings. Saturn would soon be rising.

My friend had grown a little melancholy. "Sports," he scoffed in reply to a comment I had made on the night's brawling. "Sports, it's always the same story. The wise old man or men against the young turk or turks, and the young turk, if he's worth his salt which he is by definition, always seems to win it, every time. Even in chess. You heard of that guy Goodman. Guy studies chess religiously for a mere twenty-five years, comes out at age thirty-five and wins three hundred and sixty tournament games in a row, trounces five-hundred-and-fifteen-year-old Gunnar Knorrson twelve-four-two, Knorrson who held the system championship for a hundred and sixty-some years! It's damn depressing."

"You play chess."

"Yeah. And I'm five hundred and fifteen years old."

"Wow, that's old. You're not Knorrson?"

"No, just old."

"I'll say."

"Yes, I've seen a lot of these New Year's Eves. I can't say I remember very many of them. . . ."

"Long time."

"Yeah. Besides I doubt I'll even remember this one tomorrow, so you can see how they might slip away."

"You must have seen a lot of changes."

"Oh yeah. Not as many, though, these last couple of centuries. It appears to me things don't change as fast as they used to. Not as fast as in the twentieth, twenty-first, twenty-second, you know. Inertia, I guess."

"Slower turnover in the population, you mean."

"Yeah, that's right. Everyone takes their time. I suppose it's a commonly observed phenomenon."

"Is it?"

"I don't know. But damn it, why doesn't the wise old man beat the young turk? Why don't you keep getting better? Where does your creativity go?"

"Same place as memory," I said.

"I guess. Well, what the hell. Winning ain't essential. I'm doing fine without it. I wouldn't have it over." He shook his head. "Wouldn't do like those Phoenixes. You heard of them? Folks banded together way back when in a secret society, and now they're knocking themselves off on their five-hundredth birthdays?"

I nodded. "The Phoenix Club."

"Phoenixes. Can you believe such stupidity? I never will understand those folks. Never understand those daredevils, either. Seems like the more you have to lose the bigger thrill you get from risking your life for no reason. Those damn fools dueling with sharp blades, trying to stand on Jupiter, having picnics on some iceberg in the rings—get themselves killed!"

"You really think people have more to lose by dying now than they did when they lived their three score and ten?"

"Sure."

"I don't."

He shoved me onto my side, roughly. "You're just a kid, you don't know anything. You don't know how strange it's going to get." Angrily he swept his pattern of gravel aside. "There's only a couple hundred people in the whole system older than me. And they're dying off fast. One of these days I'll go too. My body'll toss off all this medical manipulation and *stop*"—he snapped his fingers—"just like that. They still don't know why. And God damn it, I'm not used to the idea. Do you understand what it feels like to live this long? No, you don't. There's no way you do. I tell you, I wouldn't mind having another six hundred years. I try talking my body into the idea all the time. And I'm *damn* glad I didn't go at seventy or a hundred. What kind of a life is that? Man, I've done so many things. . . ." His eyes, aimed at the concrete we were sitting on, were focused for infinite distance.

"You done everything you wanted to?"

He shook his head, irritated with me.

"Me neither."

He laughed scornfully. "I should hope not."

I was still drunk; my head throbbed, and my whole life seemed to swirl before me, over the concrete outside the dome. "I'd like to see Icehenge."

He jerked around, stared at me with an odd look in his eye. He pulled tangled hair back to see me better. "You'd like to see *what?*"

"I'd like to stand at its center, and walk around and look at it. Icehenge, you know, the Davydov megalith, out there on Pluto."

"Ha!" he cried. Several sharp laughs exploded from him. "Ha! Ha! Ha!" He rolled to his knees, got to his feet. "Davydov, you say!"

"He headed the expedition that put the monument there."

In his agitation he circled me, and again sharp barks burst from him. He stood before me, leaned down to hold a tightly bunched fist before my face. "He—did—*not.*"

At last his anger penetrated the fog of my drunkenness. "What?" I said, sobering quickly. "What did you say?"

"What makes you think this Davydov had anything to do with it?"

"Um." I gathered my thoughts. "A historian named Nederland tracked down the story on marks, he found this journal—"

"Well he was wrong!"

I was taken aback. "I don't think so, I mean, he has it all well documented—"

"Idiot! He does not. What does he say—some asteroid miner put together a half-baked starship and take off, what's that got to do with Pluto? Think about that for a while." He stalked over to the dome, slapped it hard with an open palm.

I stood up and followed him, confused but instinctively curious. "But they were the only ones out there, see—process of elimination—"

"No!" He almost spoke—hesitated—turned on his heel and walked away from me. I followed him, and when he stopped I circled him. His hands were clenched tightly before him.

"What's wrong?" I said. "Why are you so sure Davydov's expedition didn't—"

And he swung around, grabbed me by the upper arm and yanked me toward him. "Because I know," he said, voice thick. "I know who put it there."

He let go of me, took a deep breath. At that moment Saturn broke over the horizon, and everyone on the dome strip started to cheer. All over Simonides voices and sirens and whistles and horns and bells marked the dawn of the new year with their ragged chorus. My companion tilted his head back and hooted harshly, then began to move through the crowd away from me.

"Wait!" I cried, and struggled after him. "Wait! Hey!" I caught up with him, grabbed his sleeve, pulled him around. "What do you mean? Who put it there? How do you know?"

"I *know*," he said fiercely. He stared at me. In all that cacophony we two were still, face to face, gazes locked. And something in his expression told me that he knew. He was telling the truth. This was the moment that made the difference; this was the moment that changed me. I learned then that in certain times, in certain places, we *connect* in such a way that deception is impossible. The intensity of the flesh jumps the gap from mind to mind. This man's bloodshot basilisk glare held me transfixed, and I knew that he knew.

Not that that satisfied me. "How?" I asked.

He must have read my lips. He pointed a gnarled forefinger at his own face. "I helped build it! Ha!" In all the noise it was hard to hear him, and he seemed in part to be talking only to himself, which made it even harder to hear him, but he said something like, "I helped build it, and now I'm the last one. She only"—the blast of a horn—"old men and women out there, and now they're all dead but me!" He said more, but the shouting crowd drowned his words.

"But who, why?" I shouted. "Wh—"

He cut me off with a jab in the sternum. "You find that. I give you that." He turned and shoved his way toward the streets again, leaving people angry enough to make it hard for me to follow. I slipped around groups and barged through others, however, desperate to catch him. I saw his wild tangle of hair beyond a small knot of people, and I crashed through them—"Wait!" I shouted. "Wait!"

He heard me, and turned and charged me, knocking me down with a hard shove. I scrambled up swiftly, and saw his head sticking above the crowd, but as I hurried after him my pace slowed: what was the use? If he didn't want to talk I couldn't force anything from him.

So I stopped chasing him, and stood there in smoggy dawn sunlight completely disoriented, as if this new year had brought with it a new world. Around me strangers stared, pointed me out to others. I realized that I was filthy, disheveled—not that that made me stand out particularly in that crowd, but I was suddenly conscious of myself as I had not been for several minutes, at least. I shook my head. "Happy New Year's!" I called out to my circle of observers—to my stranger with his strange news—and tried to re-trace my steps, to find what remained of the weather crew.

That man had known something about Icehenge, I was certain of it. And that certainly changed my life.

My food had run out, and my memory was exhausted, so I decided to get away from the keyboard and my memoirs for a day or two, and hang around in the commons. Maybe I would run into Jones, or I could seek him out. Some people aboard, I had heard, were affronted because Jones had been invited along (by me). Theophilus Jones was an outcast, he was one of those strange scientists who defied the basic tenets of his field and others'. But I found the huge red-haired man to be one of the most intelligent people on the *Snowflake*, and by far the most entertaining. And he was more inclined than the rest to talk about something other than Icehenge. Before I left for the commons I went to my library console to print up one of Jones's books. Should I read from *The Case for Prehistoric Technology* (Volume Five)? Sure. I typed out the code for it.

In the kitchen I got a large bowl of ice cream, and went to a table to eat and read. The commons was empty—perhaps this was the sleep shift? I wasn't sure.

I opened my crisp new book, pages still stiff around the ring binding, and began to read:

> . . . We must suspect alien presence in the unsolved problem of human origins, for science has significantly failed to discover the beginnings of human evolution, the point at which human beings and a terrestrial species might meet; and the recent finds in the Urals and in southern India, in which fossilized human skeletons one hundred million years old have been found, show that the scientific description of human evolution held up to this time was wrong. Alien interference, in the form of genetic engineering, crossbreeding, or most likely, colonization, is almost a certainty.
>
> So it is not impossible that a human civilization of high technology existed in prehistoric times—an earlier wave of history, now lost to us. That such a civilization would be lost to us is inevitable. Continents and seas have come and gone since it existed, and humanity itself must have come close to extinction more than once. If there had been a great and ageless city on the wide triangle of India, when it was a splinter of Gondwanaland inching north, what would we know of it now, crushed as it must have been in the collision between Asia and India, thrust deep beneath the Himalayas by the earth itself? Perhaps this is why Tibet is a place where humans have always possessed an ancient and intricate wisdom, and what we now know to be the oldest of written languages, Sanskrit. Perhaps some few of that ancient race survived the millennial thrust skyward; or perhaps there are caves the Tibetans have found, with deep fissures winding down through the mountain's basalt to chambers in that crushed city . . .

My ice cream bowl was empty, so I got up and went to the kitchen to refill it, shaking my head over the passage in Jones's book. When I returned, Jones himself was in the room, deep in conversation with Arthur Grosjean. They were at the long black-

board, and Grosjean was picking up a writing stick. He had been
the chief planetologist on the *Persephone* in 2547, and had co-
authored the only detailed description of the megalith. He was an
old man, nearly five hundred, short and frail. Now he was tying a
piece of string around the stick, listening to Jones's excited voice.
I sat down and watched them as I ate.

"First you draw a regular semicircle," said Grosjean. "That's
the south half. Then the north half—the half closest to the pole,
that is—is flattened." He drew a horizontal diameter, and a semicircle below it. "We figured out the construction that will flatten
the north half correctly. Divide the diameter into three parts. Use
the two dividing points *B* and *C* for centers of the two smaller
arcs, radius *BD* and *CE.*" He drew and lettered busily. "At their
meeting point, *F*, draw a perpendicular line through centerpoint *A*
to south point *G*. Draw *GBH*—and *GCI*—then the arc *HI*, from
center *G*. And *voilá!*"

"The construction," Jones said. He took the writing stick and
began making little rectangles around the circle.

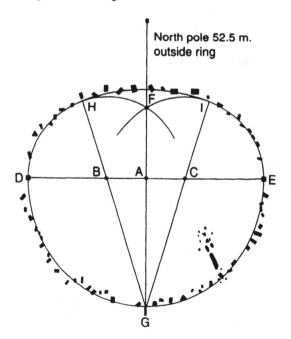

North pole 52.5 m.
outside ring

"All the sixty-six liths are within three meters of this construction," Grosjean said.

"And this is a prehistoric Celtic pattern, you say?" asked Jones.

"Yes, we discovered later that it was used in Britain in the second millennium B.C. But I don't see how that supports your theory, Mr. Jones. It would be just as easy for later builders of Icehenge to copy the Celts as it would be for the Celts to copy earlier builders of Icehenge—easier, if you ask me."

"Well, but you never can be sure," Jones said. "It looks awfully suspicious to me."

Then Brinston and Dr. Nimit walked in. Jones looked over and saw them. "So what does Dr. Brinston think of this?" he said to Grosjean. Brinston heard the question and looked over at them.

"Well," Grosjean said uncomfortably, "I'm afraid that he believes our measurements of the monument were inaccurate."

"What?"

Brinston left Nimit and approached the blackboard. "Examination of the holograms made of Icehenge show that the on-site measurements—which were not made by Dr. Grosjean, by the way—were off badly."

"They'd have to be pretty inaccurate," Jones said, turning back to the board, "to make this construction bad speculation."

"Well, they were," Brinston said easily. "Especially on the north side."

"To tell you the truth," Grosjean informed Jones, "I still believe the construction was the one used by the builders."

"I'm not sure that's a good attitude," Brinston said, his voice smooth with condescension. "I think the fewer preconceived notions we have before we actually see it, the better."

"I have seen it," Grosjean snapped.

"Yes," said Brinston, voice still cheerful, "but the problem isn't in your field."

Jones slammed down the writing stick. "You're a fool, Brinston!" There was a shocked silence. "Icehenge is not exclusively your problem because you are *the archaeologist*."

I stood up, jarred by the tableau: plump Brinston, still trying to look unconcerned; angry red-headed Jones towering over him;

frail grim Grosjean completing the triangular composition; and Nimit and I across the room, watching.

Jones's lip curled and Brinston stepped back, jaw suddenly tensed. "Come on, Arthur," said Jones. "Let's continue our conversation elsewhere." He stalked out of the room, and Grosjean followed.

I remembered Nederland saying to me, It will become a circus. Brinston approached us, his face still tense. He noticed Nimit and me staring, and looked embarrassed. "A touchy pair," he said.

"They're not touchy," I said. "You were harassing them, being a disruption."

"*I'm* a disruption!" he burst out. "You're the disruptive force on this ship, Doya, hiding in your cabin all the time as if you had nothing to do with us! Refusing to join our talks! Living on Waystation for twenty years like a bum has made you some sort of misanthropist."

"Not wanting to play with *you* doesn't make me a misanthropist," I said. "Besides, I'm working."

"Working," he sneered. "Your work is done." He walked into the kitchen, leaving Nimit and me to stare silently at each other.

Waystation—where I lived for fifteen years, not twenty—is the freight train, the passenger express, the permanent high-speed rocket of the Outer Satellites. It uses the sun and the gas giants as buoys, or gravity handles to swing around. It travels about the same distance as Saturn's orbit in a year—a fast rock. It began as an idea of Caroline Holmes, the shipping magnate who built most of the Jupiter colonies; and she profited from it most, as she did from all the rest of her ideas. Her company Jupiter Metals took a roughly cylindrical asteroid, twelve kilometers long and around five across. The inside was hollowed out, one end was honeycombed by the huge propulsion station, and off it went, careening around the sun, constantly shifting orbit to make its next rendezvous.

I boarded it on a shuttle from Titan, in 2594. My name had finally come up on the hitchhiker's list—the Outer Satellites Council provides free travel between the satellites, which otherwise would be too expensive for most individuals, and all you have to do is put your name on the list and wait for it to come to the top. I had waited four years.

Jumping on Waystation is like running in a relay race, and handing the baton to a runner five times faster than you—for getting a transfer craft up to Waystation's velocity would defeat the purpose of having Waystation at all. Our shuttle craft was moving at top speed, and we passengers were each in anti-G chambers (called the Jelly) within tiny transfer craft. As Waystation flashed by the transfer vessels were fired after it, at tremendous acceleration, and the transfer crews on Waystation then snagged them and they accelerated some more, while the crews reeled us in.

Even in the Jelly the sudden accelerations were a strain. At the moment we were snagged, the breath was knocked out of me and I blacked out for a second. While I was unconscious I had a brief vision, intense and clear. I could see only black, except for the middle distance, directly before me: there stood a block of ice, cut in the shape of a coffin. And frozen in this glittering bier was me, myself—eyes wide and staring back at me.

The vision passed, I came to, shook my head, blinked. Waystation people helped me out of the Jelly, and I joined the other passengers in a receiving room. Several of them looked distinctly ill.

A Waystation official greeted us, and without further ceremony we were escorted through the Port and into the city itself. It was crowded at that time—drop-offs to Jupiter were just about to be made, and there were a lot of merchants in town, moving goods. I found a job washing dishes first thing, and then went out to the front end of Waystation, rented a suit and took the elevator to the surface near the methane lake. I sat there for a long time. I was on Waystation, the next step outward.

For I was still chasing Icehenge, yes, I was. My dreams, my acceleration-induced visions, my studies, my physical movement, all centered around the idea of the megalith. And after the chance meeting with the stranger on Titan—after my most cherished story had been shattered—I returned to my studies with an obsessive purpose, fueled by a vague sense of betrayal: I was going to find out who put that damn thing there.

And I took my time about it, too. None of Nederland's hasty rushing about. In his need for precedence—his drive to be the one who *solved the mystery*—he had been reckless, he had jumped to too many conclusions, and taken too many facts for granted. I would not make the same mistake. With the memory of the stranger's bloodshot glare in mind, I hunted through the records of the Mars Development Committee, and the Outer Satellites Council, and the various mining companies that had plied the outer satellites, and the shipyards of the spaceship manufacturers, and the *Persephone* expedition, and so on: years and years of work. And slowly I began to see the pattern.

Some years after my move to Waystation I woke up one morning in the park, arms wrapped around a very young girl. The Sunlight had just come on and was still at half strength, giving its comforting illusion of morning. I stood up, went through a quick salute-to-the-sun exercise to alleviate the stiffness in my legs. The girl woke up. In the light she looked about fifteen or sixteen. She stretched like a cat. Her coat was wrinkled. She had joined me the previous night, waking me up to do so, because it was cold, and I had a blanket. It had felt good to sleep with someone, to spoon together for warmth, to feel human contact even through coats.

She got up and brushed off her pants. She looked at me and smiled.

"Hey," I said. "You want to go over to the Red Cafe and get some breakfast?"

"No," she said. "I have to go to work. Thanks for taking me in." She turned and walked off through the park. I watched her until a stand of walnut blocked my sight of her. Rare to see someone so young on Waystation.

I went and ate—said good morning to Dolores the cashier as she typed my money from me to them, but she just shrugged. I went out and strolled aimlessly up the curved streets. Sometimes the real world seems just like the inside of a holo, where nothing you say or do will have any effect on what is happening around you. I hate mornings like that.

For something to do I went down to the post office and checked my mail. And there, in my March 2606 issue of *Shards*, was *my own article*. My first published article, containing sixteen years' work. I hadn't expected it to appear for months yet. I whooped once and disturbed people in the booths next to mine. I read quickly through the introduction, working hard to comprehend that the words were still mine.

### Davydov and Icehenge: A Re-examination
by Edmond Doya

There are many reasons for supposing that the megalith on Pluto called "Icehenge" was constructed within the last one hundred and fifty years, by a group that has not yet been identified.

1) 2443, when the Ferrando Corporation's Ferrando-X spaceships were first made available to the public, is the earliest date at which ships capable of making the round trip from the outermost space ports to Pluto and back existed. Before that date, because Pluto was at its aphelion, and on the opposite side of the solar system from Jupiter and Saturn, and because of the limited capabilities of all existing spaceships before the Ferrando-Xs, Pluto was simply out of human reach. So a *working assumption* can be made that Icehenge was constructed after 2443.

2) The Davydov Theory, which is the only theory that pushes back this necessary time limit, asserts that the megalith was built by asteroid miners who were leaving the solar system in a modified pair of spaceships of the PR Deimos class. But a close examination of the evidence supporting this theory has revealed the following discrepancies:

a) The *only* data indicating the existence of the Mars Starship Association—the group of miners that supposedly built Icehenge—were found in two places: a file found in Cabinet 14A23546-6 in the Physical Records Annex in

Alexandria, Mars; and the journal of Emma Weil, found in
a buried field car during the excavation of New Houston,
Mars. While Mars Development Committee records do
mention the existence of Davydov and the others named in
this file and journal, they do not mention *anywhere else* the
Mars Starship Association. This fact becomes more disturbing with the introduction of new evidence concerning
these sole supports for the Davydov Theory:

b) Jorge Balder, professor of history at the University of
Mars, Hellas, searched the Physical Records Annex in
Alexandria in 2536, as part of his research on a related incident in early Martian history. His records show that he
searched Cabinet 14A23546 (all six drawers) at that time,
and he catalogued its contents. In his catalogue there is no
mention of the file found in 2548 by Professor Hjalmar
Nederland, on Oleg Davydov and the Mars Starship Association. The implication is that the file was placed in the
cabinet at a later date.

c) The records of the New Houston excavation show
that William Strickland and Xhosa Ti, working under Professor Nederland, did a seismic scan of precisely the area in
which the abandoned field car was found, two weeks before
it was discovered. Their scan showed no sign of such an object. During the intervening two weeks a storm kept all
workers out of the area, and the car was found because of a
landslide that could have easily been triggered by explosives.

The article went on to list exactly what was documented about
Davydov and the rest, and to show where information about them
and the MSA should have been located but wasn't. After that were
suggestions for further inquiry, including a physical examination
and dating, if possible, of the abandoned field car, Emma Weil's
notebook, and the file from Alexandria. My conclusion was tentative, as was only proper at that point, but still it was a shocker:
". . . Thus we are inclined to believe that these artifacts, and the
Davydov theory that depends upon them, have been manufac-

tured, apparently by the same agents who are responsible for the construction of Icehenge, and that they constitute a 'false explanation' for the megalith, linking it to the Martian Civil War when it apparently was erected at least two centuries later."

Yes, that would open their eyes all right! It threw the whole issue into question again. And *Shards* was one of the major journals, it was read system-wide. Nederland himself would read the article. Perhaps he was reading it at that very moment. Something in the notion was disturbing. I said to myself, The battle is on.

Quitting time at the restaurant. I went over to see Fist Matthews, one of the cooks. "Fist, can you lend me ten till payday?"

"Why do you want money, wild man? The way you eat here you ain't hungry."

"No, I need to pay off the post office before they'll let me see my mail."

"What's a dishwasher like you doing with mail? Never mess with it myself. Keep your friends where you can see them, that's what I say."

"Yeah, I do. It's my foes I want to hear from! Listen, I'll pay you back payday, that's the day after tomorrow."

"You can't wait till then? Oh all right, what's your number. . . ."

He went to the restaurant's register and made the exchange. "Okay, you got it. Remember payday."

"I will. Thanks, Fist."

"Don't mention it. Hey, me and the girls are going bodysurfing when we get off—want to come along?"

"I've got to check my mail first, but then I'll think about it."

I threw a few more dishes on the washer belt—grabbed a piece of lobster tail the size of my finger, tossed it in my mouth, fuel for the fire, waste not want not—until my replacement arrived, looking sleepy.

The streets of Waystation were as empty as they ever get. In the green square of the park, up above me on the other side of the cylinder, a group was playing cricket. I hurried past one of my sidewalk sleeping spots, stepping over prone figures. As I neared the post office I skipped. I hadn't been able to afford to see my mail for several days—it happened like that at the end of every month. Post office has mail freaks over a barrel, and they know it.

When I got there it was crowded, and I had to hunt for a console. More and more people were going to general delivery, it seemed, especially on Waystation where almost everyone was transient.

I sat down before one of the gray screens and began typing, paying off the post office and identifying myself, calling up my correspondence from the depths of the computer. I sat back to read.

Nothing! "Damn it!" I shouted, startling a young man in the booth next to me. Junk mail, nothing but junk. Why had no one written? "No one writes to Edmond," I muttered, in the singsong I had given the phrase over the years. There was an issue of *Archaeological Review*, and a notice that my subscription to *Marscience* had run out, for which I thanked God, and an inquiry from a local politician, asking if this was my current mail number.

I blanked the screen and left. Keep your friends where you can see them. Well, it was good advice. There were more people in the streets, on the trams, going to work, getting off work. I didn't know any of them. I knew almost all the locals on Waystation, and they were good people, but suddenly I missed my old friends from Titan. I wanted something . . . something I had thought the mail could give me; but that wasn't quite right either.

I hated mornings like this. I decided to take up Fist's invitation, and got on a tram going to the front of the town. At the last stop I got off and took the short elevator through the wall of the asteroid to the surface. Leaving the elevator I went to the big window overlooking Emerald Lake. We were somewhere near Uranus, so the lake was full. The changing room, however, was nearly empty. I went to the ticket window, and they took more of Fist's ten. The suit attendant helping me looked sleepy, so I checked my helmet seam in the mirror. The black, aquatic creature—like a cross between a frog and a seal—stared back at me out of its facemask, and I smiled. In the reflection the humorless fish grin appeared. The slugbroad head, webbed and finned handscoops, long finny feet, torso fins, and the cyclopslike facemask transformed me (appropriately, I thought) into an alien monster. I walked slowly into the lock, lifting my knees high to swing my feet forward.

The outer lock door opened, I felt the tiny rush of air, and I was outside, on my own. It felt the same, but I breathed quicker for a time, as always; I'd not spent very much time in the open recently. A ramp extended out into the lake, and I waddled to the end of it.

Around the lake, flat blue-gray plains rose up to the close horizon of an ancient worn-down crater wall. It looked like the surface of any asteroid. Waystation's existence—the hollowed interior, the buildings and people, the complicated spaceport, the huge propulsion station on the other end, the rock's extraordinary speed—all could seem the work of an excited fancy, here by this lake of liquid methane, trapped in an old crater.

Below me the stars were reflected, green as—yes, emeralds—in the glassy surface of the methane. I could see the bottom, three or four meters below. A series of ripples washed by, making the green stars dance for a moment.

Out on the lake the wave machine was a black wall, hard to distinguish in the pale sunlight. Its sudden shift toward me (which looked like a visual mistake caused by blinking) marked the creation of another tall green swell. The swells could hardly be seen until they crossed the submerged crater wall near the center of the lake; then they rose up, pitched out and fell, breaking in both directions around the submerged crater, throwing sheets of methane like mercury drops into space, where they floated slowly down.

I dove in. Under the surface I was effectively weightless, and swimming took little effort. Over the sound of my breath was the steady *krkrkrkrkrkrkrkrkrkrkrkrkr* of waves breaking, and every ten or fifteen seconds I heard the emphatic *ka-THUNKuh* of the wave machine. Ahead of me the green of the methane became murky, because of the turbulence over the submerged crater. I stuck my head above the surface to see, and all sound except that of my breathing instantly ceased.

A few other swimmers were out, and I guessed some of my fellow restaurant workers were among them. I swam around the break, out beyond the crater, where the swells first hit the shelf and started to rise to their full height, which today was nearly ten meters. Three of my friends were out there, Wendy, Laura, and Fist; I waved to them, then floated on my back and waited for them to take their turns. Rising and falling on those smooth swells I felt quite inhuman; all that I saw, felt, and heard—even the sound of my own breath—was strange, alien, too sublime for human sensibility.

Then I was alone at the point break. A swell approached and I backstroked away from it, toward the point where it would first break, adjusting my speed so I would be just outside that point when the wave picked me up.

The wave reached me and I felt its strong lift. I turned luxuriously onto my stomach, skimmed down the steepening face until I felt that the swell was pitching out over me. From my thighs up I was clear of the methane, skating on my handfins—I turned them left, and swerved across the wave, just ahead of the break, flying, flying. . . . I moved my feet to retard my speed a fraction, and the roof of the breaking wave moved ahead of me. It got dark. I was in the tube. My hands were below me, jammed into the methane to keep me from falling down the face. I was motionless yet flying, propelled through the blackness at tremendous speed by the liquid which rushed up past my left shoulder, arched over my head, and fell out beyond my right shoulder. Before me there was a huge tunnel, and at the end of this swirling obsidian tube a small ellipse of velvet black, packed with stars.

The opening got smaller, indicating that the wave was past the submerged crater, and receding. I dropped to gain speed, turned back up and shot through the hole, over the swell and back onto the smooth glassy surface, under the night.

Swimming slowly back to the point break, I watched another swimmer spin silently across the next rushing wall. She rose too high and was thrown over with the lip of the wave. If she hit the crater reef and broke the seal of her suit, she would freeze instantly—but she knew that, and would be careful to avoid being forced too deep.

I radioed the shore and had them pipe Gregorian chants into my headphones; and I swam, and rode waves, and hummed with the chants when I could catch my breath, and thought not at all. And later I switched over to the common band, and talked at great length with Fist and Wendy and Laura, as we analyzed every wave and every ride. I swam till there was too much sweat in my suit, and not enough oxygen.

Back on the tram into town, I felt good: free and self-sufficient, cosmopolitan, ready to work. It was time to attack the next facet of the Icehenge problem: the identity of its builder. My research had given me a good idea of who it might be, but the problem would be to prove it—or even to make a convincing case. And the next day I checked my mail again, and there was a long rambling letter from Mark Starr. PRINT, I typed, and out of the slot in the side of the console it appeared, blue ink on gray paper, just as always.

One day I went down to Waystation's News and Information Center in search of the latest Nederland press conference. The lobby of the center was nearly empty, and I went directly into a booth. The index I called up listed only Nederland's regularly scheduled lectures, and I had to search through the new entries to find the press conference I wanted. Finally I discovered it and typed the code to run it, then sat back in the center chair of the booth to watch.

The room darkened. There was a click and I was in a large conference room, fully lit, filled with the holo images of upper-class Martians: reporters, students, officials (as in any Martian holo there were a lot of these), and some scientists I recognized. And there was Nederland, moving down an aisle next to me, toward a podium at the front. I moved through people and chairs to the aisle, and stood in front of Nederland. He walked right through me. Smiling at my little joke, and at my quick moment of involuntary fright at the unfelt collision, I said, "You'll see me yet," and kicked about until I relocated my chair.

Nederland reached the podium and the irregular percussion of voices died. He was a small man, and only his head showed over the podium's top. Underneath his wild black hair was a look of triumph; his bright red cheeks were blazing with excitement. "You hopeless old romantic," I said. "You've got something up your sleeve; you can't fool me."

He cleared his throat, his usual sign that he was taking over. "I think my statement will answer most of the questions you have today, so why don't I start with that, and then we'll answer any questions you might have."

"Since when has it been any different?" I asked, but it was the only response. Nederland looked at his notes, looked up—his eyes crossed mine—and he extended a benedictory hand.

"The recent critics of the Davydov explanation claim that the Pluto monument is a modern hoax, and that in my work on the subject I have ignored the physical evidence. The absence of any disturbance in the regolith around the site, and our inability to find any signs of construction, are cited as facts which contradict or do not fit my explanation.

"I submit that it is the critics who are ignoring the physical evidence. If the Davydov expedition did not build Icehenge, why did Davydov himself study the megalithic cultures of Terra?"

"What?" I cried.

"What are we to make of his stated intention to leave some sort of mark on the world? Can we label it coincidence that Davydov's ship disappeared just three years before the date found on Icehenge? I think not. . . ."

He went on, outlining the same arguments he had been espousing for the last fifty years. "Come on," I groaned, "get down to it." He droned on, ignoring the fact that his critics had shown the whole Davydov story to be part of the hoax. "I know you've got something new up your sleeve, let's see it." Then he flipped over a notecard, and an involuntary smile creased his face. I sat forward.

"My critics," he said in his high voice, "are simply attacking in a purely destructive way. Aside from the vague claim that the monument is a modern hoax—perpetrated by whom, they cannot say—there is no theory to replace mine, and nothing to explain away the evidence found in the archives on Mars—"

"Oh, my God, exactly wrong!"

"—Which are constantly being re-ordered and refiled."

"Oh. You hope."

"The general claim of people like Doya, Satarwal, and Jordan, is that there is nothing at the site which will prove Icehenge's age. On the other hand, there is nothing there that shows the monument to be modern, either, which given the sophistication of dating methods there almost certainly would be, if it were indeed modern.

"In fact, there is now evidence conclusively proving that Icehenge *cannot* be modern." He stopped to let the statement sink in. "You are all aware that micrometers, the dusty debris of space, are continually falling on all the bodies of the solar system; and that when they fall on those bodies without an atmosphere, they leave small traces. Even the tiniest of fragments leave their mark. The fall of these micrometeors is regular, and is a constant throughout the system. Professor Mund Stallworth, of the university here, has received a grant from the Holmes Foundation, and he has done extensive work in this field. He has established rates of fall for different gravities, and thus a micrometeorite count can now be used as an accurate dating method. Professor Stallworth has made a detailed computer scan of the exposed faces of the liths, and of the surrounding grounds, which the builders swept clear; and the count as revealed in these holograms is such that he puts the date of the erection of Icehenge at a thousand years before present, plus or minus five hundred years. His paper on the subject will appear in the next issue of *Marscience*. In it he explains that it is impossible to be more precise given the short time spans involved, and the fact he worked with holograms only. This places the latest date of construction one hundred and fifty years or so before the date left on the Inscription Lith, but this may be explained by the fact that the smooth surfaces of the liths record a higher percentage of blemishes than other surfaces. In any case, it is impossible that so many micrometeorites could have fallen in the short amount of time postulated by those who think that Icehenge is part of a hoax.

"Thus there is nothing that factually disproves the Davydov theory—there are only the doubts and fanciful speculations of detractors, some of whom have clear political motivations. And there *is* something that factually disproves the notions that these detractors hold. I thank you for your attention."

Pandemonium broke loose among the previously attentive figures around me. Questions were shouted out, incomprehensible under the noise of cheers and applause. "Oh, shut up," I said to the image of the woman next to me, who was clapping. As questions became audible—some of them were good ones—order was re-established, but apparently the news service people had considered the question and answer period unimportant. With another click the scene disappeared, and I was again in the dark, silent holo room. Lights came on. I sat.

Had Nederland proved his theory at last? Was the stranger on Titan wrong after all? (and I as well?) "Hmm," I said. Apparently I was going to have to start looking into dating methods.

I woke up in the alley behind one of Waystation's main boulevards. I had been sleeping on my side, and my neck and hip were sore. I took off my coat and shook the dust off it. Pushed my fingers through my hair and made it all lie down flat, brushed my teeth with a fingernail, looked around for something to drink. Put my coat back on. Flapped my arms.

Around me prone figures were still slumbering. Waking up is the worst part of living on the streets of Waystation; they drop the temperatures down to ten degrees during the nights, to encourage travelers to take rooms. Helping out the hotel trade. A lot of people stay on the streets anyway, since most of them are transients. They aren't bothered in any way aside from the cold, so they save their money for things more important than a room for the night. We all have the necessary shelter, inside this rock.

Low on money again, but I needed something to eat. Onto the tram.

Down at the spaceport I spent my last ten in Waystation's cheapest restaurant. With the change I bought myself a bath, and sat in a corner of the public pool resting and thinking nothing.

When I was done I felt refreshed, but I was also broke. I went to my restaurant and hit Fist for another ten, then I walked around to the post office. Not much mail; but there at the end, to my great surprise, was a letter from a Professor Rotenberg, head of the Fine Arts Lecture Series at the Waystation Institute for Higher Learning (which, like many of the institutions on Waystation, had been founded by Caroline Holmes). Professor Rotenberg, who had enjoyed my "interesting revisionist articles" on Icehenge, wondered if I would consider accepting a semester's employment as lecturer and head of a seminar studying the Pluto megalithic monument literature—"My my *my*," I said, and typed out instructions to print the letter with my mouth hanging wide open.

I went out of my cabin for the first time in a while, to restock my supply of crackers and orange juice. The wood and moss hallways of *Snowflake* were quite empty; it seemed that people were staying in their rooms, or in the tiny lounges that the rooms opened onto. Dr. Lhotse had brought Brinston by for a peacemaking visit, and they had dropped in on Jones as well. Now we interacted, when necessary, with careful politeness; but mostly we were just settling in for the last wait. It would be a few more weeks until we reached Pluto. That wasn't long; everyone is patient, everyone is good at waiting in this world where everything proceeds so slowly.

Yesterday was my birthday. I was sixty-two years old. One tenth of my life done and gone, the endless childhood over. Those years feel like eternity in my head, and the thing is hardly begun. Hard to believe. I thought of the ancient stranger I had met on Titan, and wondered what it meant to live so unnaturally long, and then die anyway. What have we become?

When I am as old as that stranger, I will have forgotten these first sixty-two years and more. Or they will recede into depths of memory beyond the reach of recollection—the same as forgotten—recollection being a power inadequate to our new time scale. And how many other powers are like it?

Autobiography is now the necessary extension of memory. Five centuries from now I may live, but the *I* writing this will be nothing in his mind but a bare fact. I write this, then, for that stranger myself, so that he may know who he has been. I hope it will be enough. I am confident it will; my memory is strong.

My father sent me a birthday poem that arrived just last night. He's given me one every birthday now for fifty-four years; they're beginning to make quite a volume. I've encouraged him to put them and the rest of his poems into the general file, but he still refuses. Here is the latest:

> Looking for the green flash
> At sea, north of Hawaii.
> Still day, no clouds:
> On a dark blue plane,
> Under a limpid blue hemisphere.
> Our craft one mote in Terra's blue dance
> Of wind water and light.
> Sunset near.
> To the west the ocean midnight blue
> Broken by blued silver.
> The sun light orange,
> Slowing down,
> Flattening as it touches horizon:
> Earth is between us and sun by now,
> Only light bending through atmosphere
> Left to us: image of sun.
> Half down, don't look, too bright.
> Sky around sun white.
> Mere sliver left, look now:
> Bare paring turning back
> From orange to yellow,
> Yellow to yellow-green,
> Then just as it disappears,
> Bright green!

Walking back to my room with my food, saying his poem to myself in my mind, I realized that I miss him.

I met with the Institute seminar I was to teach about a month after I got the invitation from Professor Rotenberg. At my urging we decided to meet at the back table of a pub across the street from the Institute, and we moved there forthwith.

It quickly became clear that they had read the literature on the subject. What more could I tell them?

"Who put it there?" said a man named Andrew.

"Wait a minute, start at the beginning." That was Elaine, a good-looking hundredish woman on my left. "Give us your background, how you got into this."

I told them my story as briefly as possible, feeling sheepish as I described the random meeting that had triggered my whole search. ". . . So you see, essentially, I believe I met someone who had a hand in constructing Icehenge, which necessarily eliminates the Davydov party from consideration."

"You must have been astonished," Elaine said.

"For a while. Astonished, shocked—betrayed . . . but soon the idea that the monument was put there by someone other than Davydov obsessed me. It made the whole problem unsolved again, you see."

"Part of you welcomed it." That was April, a very attentive woman sitting across from me.

"Yeah."

"But what about Davydov?"

"What about Nederland?" asked April. She had a rather sharp and scornful way of speaking.

"I wasn't sure. It didn't seem possible that Nederland could be wrong—there were all those volumes, the whole edifice of his case. And I had believed it for so long. Everyone had. If he was wrong, what then of Davydov? Or Emma? Many times when I thought about it the certainty I had felt that night—that that stranger *knew* what had happened there—faded. But the memory . . . refused to change. He had known, and I *knew* that, I was sure of it. So the search was on."

"How did you start?"

"With a premise. Induction, same as Nederland. I started with the theory that Icehenge was not built until humans were capable of getting to Pluto, which struck me as very reasonable. And there were no spaceships that could have taken us there and back until 2443. So Icehenge was a relatively modern construct, made anonymous in the deliberate attempt to obscure its origins."

"A hoax," April said.

"Well, yes, in a way, although it's not the structure that's a hoax, I mean it is definitely there no matter who set it up—"

"The Davydov expedition, then."

"Right. Suddenly I had to wonder whether Davydov and Emma—whether any of them had existed at all."

"So you checked Nederland's early work." This from Sean, a very big, bearded man.

"I did. I found that both Davydov and Emma had actually existed—Emma held some Martian middle-distance running records for several years, and some records of their careers were extant. And they both disappeared with a lot of other people in the Martian Civil War. But the only things connecting them with Icehenge were a file in the Alexandrian archives that apparently was planted, and Emma Weil's journal, which was excavated outside New Houston. Now I got a chemist named Jordan interested in the case, and he has been investigating the aging of the field car that the journal was found in. You know metal oxidizes to an extent when buried in Martian soil, and the rate is measurable—and Jordan's analysis of the field car seems to indicate that it was *never* buried in smectite clay, but apparently was exposed to the atmosphere. That is very suspicious, of course. And an engineer named Satarwal has figured out a list of the equipment necessary to construct Icehenge, and by Weil's own account the asteroid miners didn't have all of that equipment. So the Davydov explanation has been falling apart from more than one angle in the past few years, and in fact this seminar is one sign of that collapse."

"So what did you do, then?" Sean asked.

"I made a list of qualities and attributes that the builder of Icehenge *had* to have had, thinking that I could then draw up a list of suspects. They had to have had a lot of money. They had to have help—my stranger for one, I guessed. They had to have a fairly big spaceship, and one that could be taken out of the usual flight control logbooks, which is a difficult task. And they had to have some specialized equipment, some of which was a little unusual. After I made this list I started making assumptions, about motivation and so forth, that were less certain, though they helped me a lot—"

"But you could make assumptions forever," April said. "What did you do?"

"Uh. I did research. I sat in front of a screen and punched out codes, read the results, found new indexes, punched out more codes. I looked through shipping records, equipment manufacturing records, sales records—I investigated various rich people. That sort of thing. It was boring work in some ways, but I enjoyed doing it. At first I thought of myself as working my way through a maze. Then that seemed the wrong image. In front of a library screen I could go anywhere. Because of the access-to-information laws I could look in every file and record that existed, except for the illegal secret ones—there are a lot of those—but if they had code call-ups, you know, were hidden somewhere in larger data banks—then I could probably get into those too. I bumped into file freaks and learned new codes, and learning them took me into data banks that taught me even more. Trying to visualize it, I could see myself as a tiny component in a single communications network, a multibank computer complex that spanned the solar system—a dish-shaped, invisible, seemingly telepathic web, a wave pattern that added one more complication to the quark dance swirling in the sun's gravity well. So I was not in a maze, I was above it, and I could see all of it at once—and its walls formed a pattern, had a meaning, if I could learn how to read it. . . ."

I stopped and looked around. Blank faces, neutral, tolerant nods. "You know what I mean?" I asked.

No answers. "Sort of," said Elaine. "But our time's up."

"Okay," I said. "More next time."

One night after a party in the restaurant's kitchen I wandered the streets, my mind in a ferment. The Sunlight was off and the other side of the cylinder was a web of streetlights and colored neon points. It was the day after payday, so I stopped at the News and

Information Center and waited until I could get a booth. When I got one I sat down and aimlessly called up indexes. Something was bothering me, but I didn't know exactly what it was; and now I only wanted to be distracted. Eventually I selected Recreation News, which played continuously.

The room darkened and then revealed a platform in space. The scene moved to one side and I could see we were on the extension of a small satellite, in a low orbit around an asteroid.

The lilting voice of one of the sports commentators spoke. "The ancient game of golf has undergone yet another transformation out here on Hebe," he said. We moved farther out onto the platform, and two golfers appeared at the edge of it, in thin hoursuits. "Yes, Philip John and Arafura Aloesi have added a new dimension to their golfing on and around Hebe. Let's hear them describe it for themselves. Arafura?"

"Well, Connie, we tee off from up here, that's about it in a nutshell. The pin is back down there near the horizon, see the light? It's two meters wide, we figured we deserved that much from up here. Mostly we play hole-in-one."

"What do you have to think about when you're hitting a shot from up here, Phil?"

"Well, Connie, we're in a Clarke orbit, so we don't have to worry about orbital velocity. It's a lot like every other drive, actually, except you're higher up than usual—"

"You have to watch out for hitting it too hard; gravity's not much around a small rock like this, if you drive with a one wood you're liable to put the ball in orbit, or out in space even—"

"Yeah, Connie, I generally use a three iron and shoot down at it, that works best. Sometimes we play where we have to put the ball through one orbit before it can hit the ground, but it's hard enough as it is, and—"

"All right, let's see you guys put one down there."

They swung and the balls disappeared.

"Now how do you see where it's hit, guys?"

"Well, Connie, we got this radar screen following them down to the horizon—see, mine's right on track—then the green has a hundred-meter diameter, and if we land on that it shows on this screen here. Here, they're about to hit—"

Nothing appeared on the green screen beside them. Phil and Arafura looked crestfallen.

"Well, guys, any future plans for this new twist?"

Phil brightened. "Well, I was thinking if we were to set up just off Io, we could use the Red Spot as the hole and shoot for that. No problem with gravity there—"

"Yes, that'd be one hell of a fairway. And that's all from Hebe for now, this is Connie McDowell—"

My time ran out and the room was dark, then bright with roomlight. Eventually the attendant came in and roused me. Again my mouth was hanging open: the astonishment of inspiration. I jumped up laughing. "That's it!" I said, "golf balls!" Still laughing wildly: "I got the old fool this time!" The attendant stared at me and shook his head.

Only a month later (I had written it in a week) a long letter of mine appeared in the Commentary section of *Shards*. Part of it said,

> There is no good evidence concerning the age of Ice-henge. This is because most dating methods that have been developed by archaeologists are applicable to substances or processes found only on Terra. Some of these have been adapted for use on Mars, but on planetary bodies without atmospheres, most of the processes that are measured simply do not occur.
>
> The ice of Icehenge, it has been determined, is about two billion years old. But when that ice was cut into beams and placed on Pluto has proven more difficult to determine. Two changes in the ice beams offer possible dating methods. First, a certain amount of the ice has sublimed spontaneously, but at seventy degrees Kelvin this process is extremely slow, and its effects at Icehenge are too small to measure. (This argues against any very great age for the megalith—those ages proposed by all of the "prehistoric"

theories—but is no help in determining the date of construction more precisely.)

An attempt has been made to measure the second
change occurring in the ice, which is the pitting that results
from the fall of micrometeorites. Professor Mund Stallworth, with the help of Professor Hjalmar Nederland and
the Holmes Foundation, has developed a micrometeorite
count method by which he claims to have dated the monument. This method is the equivalent of the terrestrial dating method of patination, and like patination it relies on an
intimate knowledge of local conditions if it is to achieve
any accuracy. Stallworth has assumed, and assumed only,
that micrometeor fall is a constant both temporally and
spatially. After making this assumption he has been fairly
rigorous, and has taken counts on artificial surfaces on
Luna and in the asteroids to establish a reliable short-term
time chart. According to his calculations, micrometeors
have fallen on Icehenge for a thousand years plus or minus
five hundred. This makes Icehenge at least a hundred and
fifty years older than the 2248 dating, but is considered
close enough by Nederland, who has used Stallworth's results to support his theory.

But the main problem with this dating (aside from the
fact that the method is based on an assumption) is that the
micrometeor fall on Icehenge could be part of the manufactured evidence. Micrometeorites are, for the most part,
carbon dust. A handful of carbon dust sprinkled from a few
hundred meters over the monument would create exactly
the same effect as a thousand years of natural micrometeor
fall. There would be no way of telling the difference.

Also, this is a precaution that would occur very quickly
to the builders of Icehenge if they were attempting to make
the monument appear older than it really is, for micrometeorites would be the only force acting on the structure
over the short term. Though a method for measuring this
action did not exist at the time of the monument's con-

struction (and still does not, in my opinion), the existence of micrometeor fall was known, and so the dating method could be both foreseen and dealt with, by an artificial fall. Given the elaborate nature of this hoax it is a possibility more likely than not. . . ."

At the next seminar meeting, in the same pub, after we had had a few drinks, Andrew waved a finger at me. "So give, Edmond," he said. "We want to know who put it there."

I put down my glass. I had never written this down; never said it to anybody. All their eyes were on me.

"Caroline Holmes," I said.

"What?"

"No!"

"What?"

"No, nooooo. . . ."

They quieted down. Sean said, "Why?"

"Start from the beginning," Elaine said.

I nodded. "It started with shipping records. You remember the list of criteria I gave you last time? Well, it seemed to me that access to a spaceship would be the best point on the list for narrowing down the group of potential suspects. The Outer Satellites Council licenses all spaceships, and keeps flight logs for all flights made. The same is true for Mars and Terra. So the flight to Pluto would have to be made, um, off the books, you know. So I started checking the records of all the spaceships capable of making the round trip to Pluto—"

"My God!" Sean said. "What a chore."

"Yes. But there are a finite number of those ships, and I had a lot of time. I wasn't in any hurry. And eventually I found that Caroline Holmes's shipyards had tucked away a couple of Ferrando-X spaceships for five years in the 2530s, for unspecified repairs. So I started investigating Holmes herself. She fulfills all the criteria: she's rich enough, she has the equipment, the spaceships, the employees that depend on her for everything and wouldn't be likely to talk. Her foundation financed the development of Stallworth's micrometeorite dating method, by giving him a grant. And there was something about her—she wasn't obviously secretive, I mean we all know something about her—but it was curious how little I could find out about her once I tried. Especially about her earlier years."

"I know a fair bit about her company," Sean said. "It domed Hyperion Crater on Ganymede, where I was born. Nearly half of the first Jovian colonies were her projects, as I understand it. But I don't know anything about her before that."

"Well," I said, "I never found any record of her birth. And no one knows how old she is. Her parents were Johannes Toquener and Jane Leaf. Leaf was the chairperson of Arco until she was killed in a docking accident on Phobos, in 2289. The next year Holmes named herself and moved to Ceres. With her inheritance she started a shipping, mining and exploration firm, and she got the patents on several recycling devices that were widely used in the Jovian colonies. Between 2290 and 2460, when the Outer Satellites Council was formed on Titan, she had become one of the major developers in the outer satellites. I know most of the general outline of her story—my question is, can any of you *explain* it?"

"Good business sense," Andrew said.

"She's completely ruthless," said April.

"She had good business sense," insisted Andrew. "She was a smart miner. She could find metal ores that were in short supply on Terra faster than her competitors. I worked in mining, I know. She was a legend. Like once they thought all the manganese ore was gone. They were dragging nodules off of Terra's ocean floors, and since heavy metals are less frequent the farther away from the sun you get, there wasn't much hope held for finding any more outside of Mars. But Holmes's Jupiter Metals supplied thousands of tons of the ore in the 2370s. It was like she was pulling the stuff out of her hat. That in itself made her a billionaire, and that was just part of it."

"And after that," I said, "she could just leave it up to gravity."

"*What?*"

"Acute students of finance will have observed that money, abstract concept though it is, behaves as if it had mass. Economic laws imitate physical laws. Everyone's collection of money is a planetary body, in other words, exerting influence on everyone else's. Thus the more money you have the stronger its gravity is, and the easier it is to attract more. Now most of us own mere asteroids of money. But some people own stars of money, and some of those stars, like Holmes's, reach their Chadresekhar Limit and turn into black holes. Now any money that comes close enough to Holmes is sucked in. There is an event horizon, of course, where this captured money appears to slow down, like Apollo in Zeno's Paradox, ever closer by smaller degrees to Holmes's Jupiter Metals—but in actuality those 'subsidiary corporations' have flashed invisibly to the nopoint of infinite mass which is Holmes's wealth."

Andrew and Elaine laughed; the rest stared at me. "Edmond, you're crazy tonight," Elaine said. "But we've run out of time again, and I have to get to work." She was a bartender.

"No, finish the story!"

"Next time," I said. "Okay—assignment, here. Next time come with some information about Caroline Holmes. We'll see what you find."

Elaine and April then left, and Andrew and Sean and I settled down for some serious drinking, some serious argument.

In those weeks when the seminar was running I had a bit more money than usual, even after I had paid Fist what I owed him. One night when I was walking the streets for entertainment, hanging out with the locals I knew, I decided to do some mental traveling instead. It was a pastime I had indulged fairly often when I first arrived on Waystation, and had a little nest egg of savings. I went to the nearest Recreation Center, and paid for three hours in one of the sensory deprivation tanks.

I stripped in the locker room and went down to one of the little chambers. The attendant slapped the drug band on my arm, and helped me into the warm bath. "Lie back and float." I did, and found it very near weightlessness. The attendant left, and shut the door; the lights went out. It was completely dark, completely silent, odorless, and in the body temperature water I could scarcely feel a thing. I was nothing, it seemed, but my mind. I rested.

The first hallucinations were auditory, as always. I heard faint music in the distance, which gave me the impression of being in a vast open space, and I thought, as I often had before, that if I could remember that music I would be a great composer. Then I heard whispers, from a group of voices around me. As I concentrated they became the choral babble you hear in audiences before a show begins.

Lights bobbed in my peripheral vision. "Hello?" I said aloud, and felt I was in a universe of salt taste. Talking to yourself again? I thought. No answer but the babbling. The lights circled and wove until they were in front of me, several meters away. When they bobbed up they flashed in my eyes like a security's flashlight. Then I noticed something in front of the lights, blocking them off. A short figure it was, perhaps human. "Hello?" I said apprehensively.

For a long time I floated, pulsing with my heart, and the voices around me said *gudda gudda gudda gudda.* . . .

The short figure approached me. It said, "I feel *(gudda gudda gudda)* that you are . . . *(gudda gudda)* . . . afraid."

"I'm not," I said, suddenly fearful. Talking to yourself again, I thought, this is silly. But the figure stood before me as real as a bedpost. The circling lights moved like fireflies into my peripheral vision, and bobbed up from time to time, illuminating the figure's face in quick flashes. A woman. Face thin, eyes and hair brown, a rich brown that I could see, in flashes, as clearly as the lights bobbing to the side, and the black all around.

The anima takes many forms, but I had met this one before. "Emma!" I said, and then, boldly: "I don't believe in you."

She laughed, a musical sound that blended in with the background babble, echoed, redoubled on itself, filled space.

"And I don't believe you," she said, in a contralto as musical as her laugh. "I'm here, aren't I?"

"Yes, but it isn't you. Who are you, exactly? Where are you now?"

"You always ask the same questions." She pointed an arm, blocking out the lights behind her. "Come along."

And then we were both moving, rushing through salt space together, with the voices keening in flight all around us. I felt her hand clasping my wrist, and for a time we conversed soundlessly of matters that were vital, though I couldn't have said exactly what they were, not aloud.

Then she pulled away from me, and floated over a pulsing black-red plain. I said, "It seems like I've been looking for you all my life, but you're never there. When I was a kid I read your journal and I thought you would be coming out soon. I thought you were hiding, and that any day now you would appear."

Her clear laugh sounded like a bell and below her the black-red mountains vibrated at the sound. "I was killed after I finished the journal, and left my body. No hiding."

"Ah," I said, filling with sadness, and then with dread; I was talking to a ghost, then. "I knew that, though. I shouldn't be afraid, I knew that, even when I was a kid."

"But you are afraid."

"I . . . maybe. Because it's not the same now, don't you see that? The journal . . . it isn't yours. Someone else is doing this, you aren't the woman I thought you were."

The choral babble rose up around us, the black-red mountains bobbed like a wheat field in the wind, and Emma moved away from me, slowly. The lights blinked behind her, under her arm, she was nothing but a silhouette; and the fear that had been tightly bound in my chest burst through me. "Don't leave, Emma," I whispered. "I'm alone, I don't know why I do the things I do. You could help me."

"Don't fret." Her voice was distant, the chorus grew behind it, roaring like the sound of a sea. "You can't be helped by what you don't believe, can you. Look to what you believe in. Look to what you believe in. Look. . . ." Her voice drowned in the babble, *gudda gudda gudda.* Off among the lights I saw her pass, a tiny silhouette. I tried to follow her and realized I was trapped—that somehow I had been frozen in my tracks. Suddenly I was terrified, the lights swirled and the babble roared and I was out there all alone, thrashing in place. . . . Some part of me remembered the release button in my left palm, and I squeezed it hard, again and again. I felt myself drop; they were draining the tank. They were letting me out. And there far across the blackness, a tiny black figure. . . .

Lights, bumps, the sounds of the attendant unstrapping me,

taking me out. I couldn't look at him. I checked the clock on the wall; two and a half hours had passed. The drugs were still at work, and in the dim red light of the chamber I stood unsteadily, watching the walls pulse in and out. The attendant observed me without much interest. I walked down to the locker room, got dressed, stepped out into the bright lights of Waystation. Silently I cursed myself. What kind of entertainment was that? The stands of walnut and maple waved their arms covered with turning leaves, yellow and red all intermixed, and all sparkling in the light. I cursed again and started to walk it off.

The next time the seminar met, they were ready to go.

Elaine began. "Caroline Holmes visited Terra only once, in 2344. She was part of an archaeological tour, and they visited Mexico, Peru, Easter Island, Angkor Wat, Iran, Egypt, Italy—and Stonehenge and some other British stone circles. She liked ruins."

"Tenuous stuff," said April decisively. Elaine looked annoyed.

"Yes, I know," Elaine replied. "But as we all know, the concerns of youth endure. Anyway, it was a fact that *I* thought was interesting."

"Aside from shipping and mining, what has she done with her money?" I asked.

"She started the Holmes Foundation," April said. "Which gives grants for scientific research of various kinds. In 2605 the Foundation gave a grant to Dr. Mund Stallworth of the University of Mars, who used it to develop the dating method that places the construction of Icehenge around Davydov's time."

"Or a little before," I added.

"Yes. He had had trouble getting the project funded up to that time."

"Is there anything to indicate that Holmes herself influenced the Foundation's decision?" asked Elaine.

"Not that I could find," April said defensively, "although it's well known she takes a great interest in the Foundation's work."

"Pretty tenuous," Elaine said, drawing the words out.

"Anything else?" I asked.

"Yes," Sean said, with a slight smile at me. "One of Holmes's companies built the settlement on Saturn Twenty-five, which was intended to be an artists' colony. Of course very few artists went to live there, and Holmes was ridiculed pretty harshly in the intellectual media for planning to remove artists from the society at large. She was called stupid and vulgar more than once, and it occurred to me that she might have taken offense, and decided to get back at them in a sense."

"Ah ha," I said. "Here we get into the curious ground of the mentality of the hoaxer. The motivation for such an act."

Andrew said, "Something similar to that might be Holmes's Museum of the Outer Satellites, on Elliot Titania. You know how much critical condemnation that received."

"This is pretty weak evidence," April said.

"I know," I replied. "But they are interesting indications. The question of motivation is a hard one. Olaf Ohman, a nineteenth-century hoaxer, once said, 'I should like to do something that would bother the brains of the learned.' I thought that these little incidents might show that Holmes had a similar feeling."

"But you're only guessing at her reaction! The scorn of intellectuals may have just made her laugh."

"Who laughs at scorn?" said Elaine.

"Someone who has done as much as she has," April said. "To someone who has had such a major hand in the development of the outer satellites, that museum and that artist colony must seem like the most minor of efforts, small failures in a giant success story. Why should she care what people say about them? She can look all over space beyond Mars and see her colonies, places she had built—and those are her cultural efforts."

"That's probably true," I admitted. "Although some people like that get proud, and then any little failure gets to be extremely irritating. But I have to admit that in all the research I've done on Holmes, I've never found a single solid, central motive for building Icehenge. If she did it—and I'm almost certain she did—then the reason remains a mystery. But the more I've thought about it, the less surprised I am by that. It seems to me that the reasons one might perpetrate such a hoax are not the sorts of things that can be discovered by examining the public records years and years later. Chances are much higher that they would be something very personal, very private." I sighed. "Meanwhile, we have these indications that you've found. And certainly something seems to have affected her, because in 2550 she put a large satellite into a polar orbit around Saturn, and has lived in seclusion there ever since. No more projects of any kind. It appears she has become a hermit."

"For the time being," April said.

"It would help if she had written an autobiography," said Andrew. "But there's not a thing by her in the files."

"That in itself struck me as odd," I said. "In this age of autobiography, who does not write one?"

"A hoaxer?" Sean suggested.

"Maybe she did write one," April said. "Maybe she just didn't publish it. Lots of people don't publish their autobiographies— Nederland never has, has he? And what about you?"

"All right," I said. "You're right. All the motivational stuff is weak. But when you add it to the concrete points, the qualities that the builder absolutely *had* to have, then she becomes almost the only person to fill the bill. She had an organization large enough to conceal the disappearance of a ship or two for a few years—something that no single ship owner could have done. And in fact two of her ships were mysteriously drydocked for five years. Her Foundation supported the research that helped to establish the Davydov theory, or to shore it up. And lastly, I got on the vidphone last week and called up her father, Johannes Toquener. He still lives on Mars, but the Institute here paid for the call. I asked him if he had ever written anything about his daughter, and if so whether I could read it. He said he hadn't written anything. Then I said I was doing an article on her and asked if he would give me some information about her youth. He said he'd rather not, and then, when I pressed him to at least tell me how old she was, he said she had been born in 2248. He was surprised to hear there was no birth certificate—he said it must have been destroyed in the civil war."

Sean whistled. "Same as the number on the Inscription Lith!"

"That's right. Icehenge has her birth year carved on it. And it could have been coincidence, but now there were too many of them. Now I was sure."

Later that evening, after we had taken a break for drinks, April said, "You sure do guess a lot."

I laughed. "Do you think so? I suppose I prefer to call it inductive reasoning. It's the method everyone uses, no matter what they claim. My methods are no different from Nederland's, or for that matter Theophilus Jones's!" They laughed. "These days Jones is claiming that the monument was an alien message device sailing through space, that speared Pluto by coincidence and stuck there. Seriously! And he has 'facts' to back up the premise. Everyone does. The difference comes in how careful you are with your premise, and then how rigorously you test it. And it helps not to have a big emotional investment in the premise. Nederland, for instance, really wanted very much for Icehenge to be built by the Davydov expedition, because it helped him in his political jockeying on Mars. And that meant he only saw the facts he wanted to see."

"You need to go out there," Andrew said. "All this searching through records can only accomplish so much. You need to go out there and tear up Icehenge and find some solid evidence of who put it there. A rigorous investigation, with trained archaeologists—"

"Which I'm not," I said.

"I know. You're a historian."

"A file freak," said April.

"You need to have people run as many different tests as they can think of," Andrew continued.

"That's right," I said. "That's precisely what we need."

But how to get such an expedition underway? The expense would be enormous. And no one would be in any hurry about it. In this world of long-lived people nobody hurried about anything. It all would happen, eventually; why rush? Especially into something so costly.

So I decided to spur the action, and publish an article that would finger Holmes without actually naming her. I sent a short letter to *Shards*, and they published it in their very next issue:

... With the evidence now available we can provisionally list several attributes of the agent who constructed Icehenge:

1) Access to at least one spaceship equal or superior in capabilities to the Ferrando-X, and possibly to one or two more of the same class.

2) The ability to remove this ship (or these ships) from the Outer Satellites Council flight control and monitoring system, and from all other space flight recording systems extant during the period of the megalith's construction. This removal would not have been simple by any means and the fact that it was accomplished implies the use of some large resource base, such as a fleet of spaceships, a large shipyard, an entire space flight corporation, or the like.

3) The ability to obtain the cooperation and subsequent silence of at least the twelve people necessary to operate a spaceship of the Ferrando-X class, and possibly many more.

4) Access to Cabinet 14A23546 in Room 319 of the Physical Records Annex in Alexandria, Mars, between the years 2536 and 2548.

5) Access to a Ford field car of the mid-Twenty-third century, and the means and ability to half bury it outside New Houston crater during the stormy two weeks beginning October 2547.

6) The ability to remove fairly large ice boulders from the rings of Saturn without being noticed; this would be easiest for an agent who is a constant presence around Saturn.

7) The tools and equipment with which to cut these ice boulders into the liths of the monument, and place them into position without leaving signs of construction, would have to be available to the builder—as they were not to

the Davydov expedition, even granting the latter's existence.

8) The wealth needed to accomplish all of the above.

Other attributes of the agent are implied by the appearance of the megalith:

1) A knowledge of the megalithic cultures of prehistoric Britain.

2) Some significant connection with the number 2248.

Two weeks after the publication of this short article I received a letter.

Mr. Edmond Doya                     18 September 2609
Box 510
Waystation

Dear Mr. Doya:

Please visit me for a talk about matters of mutual interest. I will provide your transportation from Waystation to Saturn and back. If it is convenient to you, Captain Pada of the *Io* can leave Waystation immediately; and if you can stay for a week or ten days (which I urge you to do) she can return you to Waystation by the New Year.
Sincerely,

*Caroline Holmes*
Saturn Artificial Satellite Four

Saturn looked like a striped basketball in the viewscreen of the *Io*. Five or six of its moons were visible as white crescents. Titan was immediately recognizable because of its size and its atmosphere-fuzzy crescent points; I watched it with the interest one has when seeing an old home.

Captain Pada, a quiet woman I had seldom seen on the voyage to Saturn, pointed above the planet. "See the moving white point? That's her satellite. We'll meet it just below the rings."

She said *her* with a special emphasis, I noticed. I said, "Does it have a name?"

"No. Just Sas Four."

Pada left the room. I stayed, and kept the screen locked on Saturn until the knife-edge of the rings began to broaden, and the whole vista became too large for me, in my distraction, to focus on. I found the coordinates for Holmes's satellite, and switched the screen to it.

We were closing on it fast. It was big: a torus spinning slowly, a wheel a kilometer across. A thin crescent on the sunward side was bright with reflected sunlight, and another half of the surface facing me was Saturn-lit, a dusky, burnished yellow. Handrails, locks, and small bays studded or indented the curving metal. There was a small, classically designed observatory sticking out of the hub on the side opposite the dock; its telescope appeared to be trained on Saturn. The spokes connecting hub and wheel looked thin as wire. At regular intervals in the torus itself there were windows, some of them half globes protruding into the vacuum. Many of the rooms behind the windows were lit, and I caught quick glimpses, as we circled it, of red and gold walls, rich brown furnishings, marble busts, a huge crystal chandelier. The total effect was that of a nineteenth-century fantasy, a bathysphere cast by some accident into the wrong time and medium.

The largest of the windows was almost dark—the room behind it was filled with dim, dusky blue light—and someone stood in this window, a black silhouette that appeared to be observing our approach.

Over the intercom Captain Pada called me to the transfer room. We were about to dock.

While crossing the ship I felt the bump of docking, and I stopped for a moment and tried to quell my excitement. Just an old woman, I thought, just a rich old lady. But the old epithets had little effect, and I was nervous as I floated into the transfer room.

The locks were already open. Captain Pada was there, and she shook my hand. "Nice having you aboard," she said, and waved me forward. I thought this formality a little odd; would the crew of the *Io* stay in their ship for the duration of my visit?

I passed through the docking sleeve and was in Holmes's world. A man dressed in red coat and pants, embroidered with gold, stood at attention before me. He nodded. "My name is Charles, Mr. Doya. Welcome to Sas Four. I'll show you your rooms and you can arrange your belongings. Caroline will receive you after that."

He took off with a neat leap and I hurried after him. We dropped down a hall with clear walls, in which terrestrial seashells were embedded; again I thought of the bathysphere. Another hall perpendicular to that one enabled us to walk, in light gravity, and I deduced we were in the torus itself. This hallway did indeed curve always upward, and after a short walk Charles opened the door to a room off the hall.

The room we entered was walled with reddish Persian rugs, and the ceiling and floors were a light wood. The floor was on several levels, with broad steps separating them.

"This is your room," said Charles. "That control panel over there will provide whatever furniture you need—wardrobe, bed, screens, desk, chairs. The robots will obey you." He indicated two boxes on wheels.

"Thank you."

Charles left, somewhat to my surprise. But I assumed he would return soon, and went to the control panel, which was behind a wall tapestry. I pushed *Bed*. A circular section of floor slid away and a circular bed rose. I traversed the room to it, flopped down, and waited for my things to arrive. And wondered what I would say to Holmes. My stay on her satellite was going to be conducted entirely on her terms, I was beginning to see; and that frightened me a little. Once again I pondered without success her purposes, her motivation in all this. Icehenge and the Davydov explanation were such an *elaborate* hoax. . . . It occurred to me that if I were correct, and Holmes had manufactured all the parts of the story that Nederland and the *Persephone* expedition had between them discovered—and everything that had happened recently reinforced my conviction that I *was* correct—then I was soon going to meet the author of Emma Weil's journal. I would be confronting the mind that had created that story that had so enthralled me as a boy—so in a sense I would be meeting Emma Weil. But what an odd way to think of it, given what I now knew! I shook my head, and muttered to myself something that I had said more than once in the seminar: "A hoax is a curious thing."

I sat on the bed and waited—lying down to nap more than once—for what seemed like hours. There was no way to measure the passage of time in the room; there were no buttons on the control panel labelled *clock*. Presumably I could call somebody on the intercom, but I didn't know whom. Eventually I got hungry, and that, combined with growing irritation, drove me into the hallways. I decided to find my way back to the docking bay; my hope, though there was not much to support it, was that Charles would be there. Or somebody.

I came to the hallway that led up to the hub, the one with the clear walls and the hundreds of seashells. As I pulled myself up it using a brass railing that extended from one wall, I could see a wavery dark image moving up the hall with me, which I thought to be my reflection. But when I stopped for a moment to inspect a huge nautilus, the form continued to move. Surprised, I caught up with it and pressed my face against the glass, but its thickness, and some ripples in it, reduced the image on the other side to a brown blob. The blob, however, had stopped across from me. Perhaps it was pressed to the glass also, trying to see me. It appeared to be wearing dark green—hair perhaps gray. It moved again, in the same direction, and I followed it up until the wall changed from glass to teak, and the figure disappeared.

Almost simultaneously with this disappearance there was a click, below me in my hallway. I looked down, on a head of gray hair, a woman wearing a dark green jumpsuit . . . a silver ring on her left ring finger tapped against the railing as she pulled herself up. Confused, I pressed my face to the last section of clear wall, looking for the figure I had been following.

The woman pulled up beside me, and I looked over at her. I am afraid my mouth was still hanging open a bit with my surprise at this strange "teleporting" that I seemed to have witnessed. Then again the woman—it was Caroline Holmes—looked just a trifle surprised herself. I don't look much like a scientist, I suppose—I let my hair do what it wants, and that plus my face got me called the Wild Man on Waystation—and so I had seen this look once or twice before, and recognized it.

But quickly it was gone. "Hello," she said, in a well modulated alto voice. She was tall, and her gray hair was tied back in a single knot and then let loose over her back. Under the jumpsuit she appeared thin. Her face was handsome in a severe sort of way: deeply lined and aged, slightly tanned, with the finest of silky hairs just visible on her cheeks and upper lip. The line of her jaw and nose were sharply defined, giving her an ascetic look. Her eyes were brown. It was a hard face, marked by centuries of—who knows what?—and seeing it made me swallow involuntarily, aware of what I was up against.

"It's good to meet you," she went on. "I've been reading your articles with interest."

First probe. "I'm glad," I said, and searched for more words, stupidly fumbling in a moment I had imagined many times. "Hello."

She said, "Why don't we go to one of the observation rooms and have some food sent there."

"Fine."

She let go of the railing, and drifted down the hallway to the main hall of the torus, where she led me. She had a long stride, one that revealed bare feet.

We left the hall and stepped down a broad spiral staircase into a large dim room, which was walled and ceilinged with wood. The floor was clear; it was one of the windows I had seen while approaching. To one side of it Saturn shone like a lamp globe. It was our only illumination. There were couches arranged in a small square near the middle of the room. Holmes sat on one, leaned forward, and looked down at the planet. She appeared to have forgotten me. I sat down on the couch opposite her, and looked down.

We were over one of the poles, looking at Saturn and its rings from a perspective none of its natural satellites ever had. The latitude bands marking the planet (half of it was dark, though slightly illuminated by light reflected from the rings) were light greens and yellows, with streaks of orange. Seen from above they were full semicircles; bright cream in the equatorial bands, yellow in the higher latitudes, dusky green at the pole.

Outside the planet were the rings, scores of them, all of them perfectly smooth and circular, as if drawn with a compass, except for three or four braided sets that were not so smooth. The entire sight reminded me of a dartboard: the pole was the bull's-eye, the rings the outermost circles; but it was impossible to imagine Saturn flat, because of its dark side and its shadow erasing the rings behind it; so that it seemed a dartboard with an odd hemispherical center.

This uncanny sight filled one whole side of our floor-window. Around it a few bright stars gleamed, and seven of Saturn's moons were visible, all of them perfectly aligned half moons. As we sat there like statues and watched, the scene shifted perceptibly. Saturn's shadow on the rings appeared to shorten, the moons were becoming crescents, the rings were tilting and becoming huge ellipses; and all slowly, very slowly, as in some inhuman, natural dance.

"Always the same but always different," I said.

After a long pause, she said, "The landscape of the mind." I became aware of the profound silence in which we were speaking. "There are more beautiful places on Terra, but none that are so sublime."

I know about your trip to Terra, I thought. And then I looked at her face and thought again. There were the centuries, written across it—and what could I say I really knew of her? She might have visited Terra a dozen times.

"Perhaps," I said, "that is because space itself has many attributes of sublimity: vastness, simplicity, mystery, that which causes terror. . . ."

"These exist only in the mind, you must remember that. But space provides much that reminds the mind of itself, yes."

I considered it. "Do you really think that if we did not exist, Saturn would not be sublime?"

I thought she wasn't going to answer. The silence stretched on, for a minute and more. Then: "Who would know it?"

"So it is the knowing," I said.

She nodded. "To know is sublime."

And I thought, that is true. I agree with that. But . . .

She sat back and looked across at me. "Would you like to eat?"

"Yes."

"Alaskan king crab?"

"That would be fine."

She turned and called out, "We'll have dinner in twenty minutes," to the empty room.

A small tray covered with crackers and blocks of cheese slid out of a new aperture in her couch. I blinked. A bottle of wine and two glasses were presented on individual glass trays. She poured wine and drank in silence. We leaned forward to look at the planet. In the odd illumination—dusky yellow light, from below—her eyesockets were in shadow, and appeared very deep; the lines in her face seemed chiseled by ages of suffering. To my relief the meal was brought in by Charles, and we leaned back to attend to it. Below us Saturn and its billion satellites still wheeled, a stately art deco lamp.

After the meal Charles took away our dishes and utensils. Holmes shifted on her couch and stared down at the planet with an intensity that completely discouraged interruption. Between watching Holmes and Saturn I was kept busy enough; but the longer the silence continued, the more disconcerted I became.

Holmes remained in her contemplation until the ringed ball was nearly out of our floor window, and the light in the room was a murky brown. Then she stood and said, "Good night," in a companionable tone, as if this were a routine we had established through years and years of dining together—and she walked out of the room. I stood, filled with confusion. What could I say? I looked down at the stars for quite some time, then I made my way without difficulty back to my room.

When I awoke the next morning I felt sure I had slept for an uncommonly long time. I showered in water as cold as I could stand, disturbed by dreams I couldn't remember.

Apparently I was being left to my own devices again. After a long wait on my bed, wondering if I should be annoyed as I felt, I went to the control panel and called every destination on the intercom. No replies. I couldn't even find out what time it was.

Remembering the previous night, I left my room and ventured into the hallway again. If I had never left my room, I wondered, would I ever have met Holmes?

Today she wasn't in the room we had dined in, or behind the seashell wall. I circled the satellite entirely, checking room after empty room, and becoming slightly disoriented, as the central hallway of the torus often disappeared into short mazes of multiplicity. Quite a few doors on every level were locked. The silence on board—actually a pervasive, soft, electric *whirrr*—began to bother me.

I took an elevator up one of the spokes to the observatory in the hub, and tried the door; to my surprise it opened. Inside I heard a voice. I entered the weightless room and found it a tall cylindrical chamber, with a domed ceiling. The telescope, a long shiny silver and white thing, extended from a vertical strip in the curved ceiling to the center of the chamber, where a crow's-nest arrangement with a leather and brass chair was welded to it.

Holmes stood behind that chair, leaning over it to look into the mask of the eyepiece. Every few seconds she called out a string of figures, her voice vibrant with intensity. Charles, seated at a console in the wall of the chamber (still in his red and gold), tapped at a keyboard and occasionally quoted a set of numbers back to Holmes. I pulled myself down the bannister of a short staircase into the room.

Holmes looked up, startled, and saw me. She nodded, said "Mr. Doya" in greeting, looked back into the eyepiece. She pulled away again and stared down at me; I was braced against a platform railing a meter or two below her. "So you think I built Icehenge, eh, Mr. Doya?"

And then she looked into the telescope again. I stared up at her, at a loss. She read off another string of figures, sounding as vitally interested as she had when I entered the room. Finally she called to Charles, "Lock it on the inside limit of ring forty-six, please," and turned on me again.

"I've been reading your articles," she said. "I've been a student of the Icehenge controversy for a long time."

"Have you," I managed to say.

"Yes, I have. I followed it from the beginning. In your last article in *Shards* I can see you are implicating me, and I want to know why."

I looked away from her, over at Charles, down at the end of the telescope. Adrenaline flushed through me, preparing me for flight, but not for conversation.

Finally I raised my eyes to meet hers, and decided not to say anything. A staredown developed; I could have laughed, but it was too serious.

"Who *are* you?" she said irritably.

I shrugged. "A dishwasher."

"And I am a suspect in your little investigation? You can admit that much?"

". . . You are a suspect, Ms. Holmes."

She smiled. And leaned over to stare into the damned telescope again. I crossed my arms over my chest, feeling completely confused.

"Have you lived on Waystation long?" she asked.

"Not long."

"And where did you come from?"

I tried to pull myself together and make a coherent story of my past—a difficult task under the best of circumstances—but my distraction must have been obvious.

Holmes cut me off. "Would you like to retire now, and continue this conversation later?"

Upon reflection I agreed that I would, and I left hastily, remembering as I returned to my room the calm smile she had given me when I told her she was a suspect. So strange! What did she want of me? I called up my bed and collapsed on it, and lay pondering her purposes, more than a little fearful. Much later one of the robots brought me a meal, and I picked at it. Afterwards, though I was sure I never would, I fell asleep.

*   *   *

"Tell me," demanded Holmes, "is it true that Hjalmar Nederland is your great-grandfather?" Her face loomed over me.

I didn't want to answer. "Yes."

"How odd," she said. Her hair was arranged on her head in a complex knot (like my mother used to have it). She was wearing earrings, three or four to an ear, and her eyebrows had been plucked to thin black arches. She was looking out a window, at the sun.

"Odd?" I said, though I did not want to say anything.

"Yes," she said, annoyance lacing her voice. "*Odd.* All this marvelous work that you've done. If your theory is accepted, then Nederland's theory—his lifework—will be destroyed."

Her glare was fierce, and I had to struggle to reply. "But even if his theory was wrong," I said, "his work was still necessary. It is always that way in science. His work is still good work."

Her face was close to mine. "Would Nederland agree?" she cried. She pointed a finger at me. "Or are you just lying to yourself, trying to hide what will really happen?"

"No!" I said, and weakly tried to strike back at her: "It's your fault, anyway!"

"So you say," she sneered. "But you know it's your fault. It's *your fault,*" she shouted, looming over me, her face inches from mine. "*You* are the one destroying him, him and Icehenge as well, *you—*"

A noise. I twisted around in my bed, looked down at my pillow, realized I was dreaming. My heart was hammering. I rubbed my eyes and looked up—

Holmes was standing over me, looking down at me with clinical interest (hair piled on top of her head)—

I jerked up into a sitting position, and she disappeared. Nobody there.

I tossed the bedsheets aside and leaped out of bed. I hurried to the door; it was locked on the inside, though I couldn't remember locking it. In fact I was sure I hadn't. The dark room reeked of sweat, it was filled with shadows. I ran to the control panel and switched on all the lights in the room. It blazed, white streaks everywhere on the polished wood. It was empty. I stood there for a long time, waiting for heartbeat and breathing to slow. I walked over and lifted the covers to search beneath the bed. Nothing there but a platform flush with the floor. The image I had seen over me, I thought, could have been a hologram. I began circling the room, inspecting the wood for apertures.

But the dream. Did she have a machine that created images within the mind, as a holograph created them without?

I didn't sleep again that night.

"Mr. Doya."

"What?" I had been drowsing.

"Mr. Doya." It was Holmes's voice, on the intercom.

"Yes?"

"The sun will rise over Saturn in thirty-five minutes, and I thought you might like to see it. It's quite spectacular."

"Thank you." I tried to figure out what she was up to. "I would."

"Fine. I'll be in the dome room, then. Charles will show you the way."

When Charles showed me in she was seated in the lotus position, staring out. The room was shoved out from the body of the satellite, so that the clear dome served as both floor and walls. Saturn was outside one wall, just clear of the surface of the torus. The planet was dark, but its polar cap glowed green, as though lit from within. To the sides the rings, thin now, shone like bright scimitars.

"Most of Saturn's mass is at its core," Holmes said without turning her head. "The upper atmosphere is very thin, enough so that the sun shines through it just before rising."

"Is that what that glow is," I said warily. The luminous green gained brilliance near the pole, and seemed even brighter contrasted with the dark side of the planet. Finally I could see the sun itself, a fiery green gem that flared to an intense white as it cleared Saturn. The green faded and became a crescent of reflected light: the sunward side of the planet. The rings broadened and separated into their multiple strands.

"Well," said Holmes. "Good morning."

"Good morning." I stared at her closely. She ordered breakfast innocently enough, and we ate in silence. When we were done she said,

"Tell me, am I your only suspect?"

I saw that she intended to have it out. I said shortly, "I think you put it there."

"Genoa Ferrando fits the qualifications as well as I. So does Alice Waite, and a couple of others as well. Why do you think it was me?"

In a burst of impulsive anger I decided to show her how thoroughly she was found out. I told her the tale of the long search, gave her all the pieces of the puzzle she had left behind, put them together for her. It took quite a while.

At the end of it she smiled—again that calm, enigmatic smile. "That isn't very much," she said, and swiftly got up and left the room.

I took a long, deep breath, and wondered what was going on. "What do you want?" I shouted after her. No reply. My head was spinning, my vision was a field of pointillist dots. Had my breakfast been drugged? Was I full of some sinister truth serum, thus to tell her everything I had? But hadn't I wanted to tell her? Oh, I was becoming confused, no doubt of it; confused and frightened. Yet I certainly did feel dizzy, and my vision was somehow altered. I tried to shrug off the thought, and failed. If she had drugged me—invaded my room—my dreams—what would she not do? Before me Saturn glowed, a huge crescent of swirled cream and green, wave patterns curling between every band of color. I watched for a long time, as the planet and its delicate minions continued to turn, in arcs and curves and ellipses of light, slow and inevitable and majestic, like the music Beethoven might have written had he ever seen the sea.

That night I couldn't sleep for dreaming.

In the morning I dozed, then awoke cold and sober. I made my way up to the observatory.

She was there, working again with Charles. "Pay attention to what you're doing," she snapped at him as I opened the door.

She watched me enter, smiled politely. "Mr. Doya," she said. She put her head down to the eyepiece, then pulled up; I am sure she never saw a thing. I was just below her. "Would you like to take a look?"

"Sure," I said.

"Do you want to see the rings first?"

"Sure."

She pushed buttons on a console beside her. The telescope and its containing strip in the ceiling shifted, and there was a low, vibrating *whirrr*; though I could barely sense it, clearly the entire chamber was revolving. Holmes leaned forward and looked into the eyepiece, pushed buttons with her eyes still to it.

"There." She pushed a final button and got up. I sat in the chair and looked in. The field was jammed with white boulders, irregular ice asteroids.

"My." Even as close as we were in the satellite, with the naked eye the rings appeared to be solid strands, scores of narrow solid white bands.

"Isn't it a nice view?"

"How big are they?"

"Most of them are like snowballs, but some are as large as a kilometer in diameter, or more. That's what creates the grooved effect."

"It's amazing what a thin plane they stay in," I said.

"Yes. It's a wonderful display of gravity at work. I find it fascinating—a force the workings of which we can describe and predict with minute accuracy, without understanding in the slightest."

"It seems to me you can say that about almost any natural force."

"Or about anything at all, I'm sure."

That caused me to shake my head, and she laughed. "Here, I'll shift the field to include this ring's outer edge. It's a good example of the rigor of gravity's laws."

She pushed buttons, and the field became a flurry of white, like a snowstorm, I imagined. When it cleared again there was white rubble there still closely packed together—and then, straight as a ruler, the boulders ceased and black starry space began. "My," I said.

"A couple of the kilometer-sized moonlets share an orbit here, and sweep the smaller pieces inside."

"And how thick is the plane?"

"Twenty-five kilometers or so."

One of the boulders, long and narrow like a beam, caught my eye. It occurred to me that she was showing me her quarry. . . . I decided to make the first lunge this time.

"You know," I said, "some physicists on Mars have determined that the columns of Icehenge came from here."

"Yes," she replied. "A ring of ice boulders made from ice taken from a ring of ice boulders. How nice."

I continued to look in the eyepiece, mimicking her behavior. "Some would say that that fact tends to support the idea that a resident of the Saturn area built Icehenge."

"So they might, but it's just circumstantial evidence. Hasn't Nederland shown how easily Davydov's expedition could have passed by here?" Her voice was unconcerned. "Your whole case against me is circumstantial."

"True. But you can make a very good case if there are enough circumstances."

"But you cannot *prove* your case, no matter how many circumstances."

I pulled my head back to look at her, and she was smiling. "And if you can't prove it," she said, "you can't publish it, since it would constitute defamation of character, slander, libel. . . . I am fascinated by the monument, I have told you that, and it is amusing that you believe I built it, but both I and Icehenge have enough troubles without a connection being made between us. If you make one I will see that you are destroyed."

Taken aback, I cleared my throat. "And if I find proof—"

"You will not find proof. There is none to be found. Be warned, Mr. Doya. I will not tolerate having my name associated with it."

"But—"

"There is no proof," she said, patiently but insistently. We hung there silently, and I could feel myself blushing. Was this why I was here, and all that preceded it a preparation, lending force to her warning? The thought angered me, her self-assurance angered me, everything she had done angered me; and as an angry idea came to me I spoke it.

"Since you are so sure of this, perhaps you would, um, help me close my investigation?" She stared. "The Waystation Institute for Higher Learning wants to sponsor another expedition to Pluto, to investigate the questions I and others have raised." I was making this up, and it was exciting. "Since you are so certain I will never find any proof that you did it, perhaps you'd be interested in funding this expedition, to lay all questions to rest? And as a favor in return for my visit?" I nearly smiled at that.

She saw it, and smiled in return. "You think I won't do it."

"I hope you will."

After a long pause she said, "I'll do it." And then, with a casual wave of her hand: "Now you must excuse me, I must return to my work."

After that conversation I seldom saw her. I wasn't invited to dinner that evening, and after a long wait I had one of the little square robots bring a meal. For the next three days I was on my own; Holmes sent not a single message. I began to think that supporting an expedition to Pluto disturbed her more than it had seemed when she agreed to it. Perhaps she was having second thoughts.

There is an old truism: every hoaxer secretly wants to be discovered, eventually, and so they sow the seeds of their own destruction. But I was never very sure about that truism; I didn't quite believe it. In any case, the two conflicting urges—to deceive, to be discovered—must create in every hoaxer's mind a terrible ambivalence. And it seemed to me then that Caroline Holmes basically wanted to keep deceiving, to stay secret; so that if for a moment the contrary urge had seized control and granted me my expedition, Holmes herself might soon regret it. But maybe not. I could not be sure; she was a mystery to me.

She continued with her binary behavior, however, which I felt I did understand: she either chatted pleasantly about other things, as if we had no central disagreement to discuss, or else she flipped over instantly into direct discussion of our problem. Once I met her in the clear-walled hallway, and she spent quite a bit of time telling me about some of the seashells in the glass; then in the midst of this dispassionate lecture, she said, "Are you aware of the political ramifications that the overthrow of Nederland's work might have on Mars?"

"I don't care. I'm not a political person."

The deep lines in her face twisted into a grimace. "How I hate people who say that! *Everyone* is a political person, don't you understand that? You would have to be autistic or a hermit to be truly apolitical! People who say that are merely saying they support the status quo, which is a profoundly political stance—"

"All right all right," I said, cutting her off. "Let me put it another way. Mars is a moribund bureaucratic police state, in the service of even more oppressive forces on Terra. I can't imagine why anyone in their right mind would live there, especially when they have the alternative of the outer satellites. I have little respect for Martians, therefore, and I don't care much about their problems. If by *ramifications* you mean the admissions that the Martian government made about their conduct in the civil war after Nederland published his discoveries at New Houston—ah ha—I see you do—then I don't agree that the exposure of the problems in Nederland's work will make any difference."

"Of course it will!"

"No it won't. The Martian government made their admissions, and opened up the evidence that proved conclusively they crushed a major revolution. They can't go back on that now. It doesn't matter whether what prompted them was the truth or a lie. In fact—if that's the effect you wanted to create with your Icehenge story"—and I stopped and stared at her closely, for it seemed to me that there might be a faint blush on her lined old cheeks—"then you got it. Nothing that happens now will change that."

"Hmph. You don't know Mars as well as you think you do." But I had set her to thinking, and since she wanted to think, why she just turned around and pulled herself down the hall away from me.

"That's because I'm not a political person," I muttered, feeling a grim satisfaction. Even a wild man dishwasher gets his points in once in a while.

One night I dreamed that Holmes and I were in a weightless, locked room: her hair waved around her nude shoulders like snakes, and she shrieked, *"Don't go on! Stop!"*

I woke up immediately, sitting up with twisted bedsheets clutched in my hands. After a while I laughed uneasily; Holmes was prevented from violating my dreams, because such interference frightened me so badly that I would wake up.

And as I thought about it, I realized that this idea of a dream holograph was nonsense. Nobody has a machine that can violate your dreams. The idea had come to me because, in the first days after my arrival, Holmes's behavior had definitely shaken me. And our interactions had been so charged that I dreamed about them at night, continuing our arguments; it was a simple case of day residue.

But I thought there was a very good chance that she *had* drugged me, that morning. I fell asleep again thinking about that, not quite so self-assured, so confident I was winning our bout, and safe. I wouldn't be truly safe until—well . . . I wasn't sure when.

The next day I was still thinking about a locked room. I wandered around the torus, looking methodically for any sections that were closed off. Many small rooms were locked, but there was one big section—an arc of the torus below the main hallway—that I couldn't enter. It took a lot of wandering around that area to make sure, and when I was, my curiosity grew.

That night my dreams were particularly violent; though Holmes never appeared in them, my mother did, and my father was in several, always leaving for Terra, asking me to come along. . . .

The following morning I decided to break into the closed arc. In a room down the hall from mine there was a console of the satellite's computer; I sat before it and went to work. It only took me half an hour of sifting through satellite layout diagrams to find the locking codes I wanted, there in the original blueprints of the thing. I scribbled down a few numbers and left the console.

I checked to make sure Holmes and Charles were in the observatory—they were—Holmes seemed truly obsessed by those rings—then I went to the inoperative elevator above the closed arc. On the console beside it I punched out the command codes I had written down. When I was done the elevator doors slid open. I walked in.

I was on the third of seven floors, the interior control panel told me. I pushed seven. The doors closed and I felt the beginning of the elevator's drop.

The elevator stopped, the doors opened and I walked out into another passageway. The floors were black tile, the walls and ceiling darkest wood. I walked up and down hallways. Aside from the walls and ceilings, nothing seemed to be different. Rooms I looked into were empty. (Where was Pada and her crew?) I had walked for some time (always staying aware of the location of my elevator), and was starting to feel disappointed, when I rounded yet another corner: there before me I saw a door that seemed to lead into the vacuum of black space; and in the center of that space was Icehenge.

It was small, and as I hurried toward it across a glass floor, I thought it was a holocube standing on a table. Then I saw that it was made instead of actual pieces of ice, standing in a big sphere of glass that rested on a white plastic cylinder.

The room itself was spherical, a tiny planetarium, with a clear bisecting floor. There were stars above and below, and the sun, just a few times brighter than Sirius, was just above floor level. It was Pluto's sky.

The ice liths of the model were nearly transparent, but aside from that it looked like a perfect representation, even down to the little fragments of the Fallen Lith. After a time I circled it slowly, and found an unmarked control console on the other side of the plastic stand.

There were small colored buttons in a row on the console. I pushed a yellow one, and a long narrow beam of yellow laser light appeared in the room. It just touched the top of one of the triangular liths, on the flattened side of the ring, and the top of the shortest lith, on the southeast side. . . . And aligned like this, the slender cylinder covered the sun and turned it yellow.

The other buttons produced laser beams of different colors, marking the sight lines that certain pairs of liths established. But these sight lines were not there for observers on the surface of Pluto, for they extended across lith tops in both directions into space. And the sight lines would be good for only a certain point in Pluto's orbit—in fact, for only a certain moment in Pluto's history. And one could only see them if an elaborate model such as this were constructed. . . . It was a private reference, to a single moment. I pushed the other buttons, wondering if there were some way I could figure out what moment that had been. Or would be. Violet was Sirius. Orange was the Pleiades. Green was, I guessed, Pluto's moon Charon. A blue beam extended straight up out of the tallest lith, and defined Kachab, Pluto's pole star. And red, stretching across the two remaining triangular liths, turned Barnard's Star—Davydov's destination—into a Mars-red ruby.

"Mr. Doya?" Holmes was on the intercom again.

"What?" In my dream my father had been telling me a story.

"Captain Pada can leave for Waystation today, if you like."

"Oh . . . all right." All of a sudden I was furious. Sending me off like that!

"Would you join me for breakfast?"

". . . Sure. In an hour."

She wasn't in the dining room—that is, the first room we had eaten in—when I got there, so after a short wait I called the robots in and had them bring me a meal that I ate alone. I looked out at Saturn. It was hard to chew the pastries, because I was grinding my teeth with anger.

When I was done with breakfast, an image of Holmes, seated in a chair, popped into being across from me.

"Excuse me for saying good-bye to you like this," she said. "You are in a holo field yourself, so we can converse—"

"The hell we can," I said. "What's the meaning of this? You come out here where I can see you in the flesh!"

"We will talk this way—"

"We will *not* talk this way—"

"Or not at all."

"That's what you think," I exclaimed, and ran from the room. Something about it just made me furious. I pulled my way up to the hub and barged into the observatory. Empty. Back in the torus's main hall I began to realize I was going to have a problem confronting her. The satellite was too big—I didn't even know where her quarters were. When a bulkhead-like partition dropped down and blocked off the hallway ahead of me, I knew I was beaten. I returned to the dining room. The image of Holmes still sat in the image of a chair, watching me as I entered.

"What's the meaning of this?" I burst out, and went over and stepped right into the image of her. "Don't you have the nerve to confront me in person?"

"Mr. Doya," she said icily. Over the intercom her voice rang a bit. "Quit being stupid. I prefer to speak to you this way."

I stepped back out of her semitransparent image, so that our faces were just a few centimeters apart. "Speak, then," I said. "Can you see me well enough? Am I looking directly at you? Can you hear me?"

"I hear you all too well. Let me speak. I want you to understand that my desire not to be associated with Icehenge is very serious."

"You shouldn't have built it, then."

"I didn't."

"You did," I said, and hoped my image's eyes met hers. "You built it and then built the false explanation that went with it—and all for naught! All for naught." I swung a hand through her head, then tried to control myself. "Why did you do it? With all that money, Ms. Holmes, why did you build nothing but a hoax? Why construct nothing but the story of a starship when you could have made it real? You could have done something great," I said, and my voice hurt in my throat. "And instead you've done nothing but make a fool of an old man on Mars."

"Not if the Davydov story holds true—"

"But it won't! It hasn't! And the sooner it falls the less foolish he appears." I turned and walked toward the door, too angry to look at her a moment longer.

"Mr. Doya!"

I stopped, half turned, enough to see she was standing. "Ice-henge . . . was not my idea."

"Then why is that model of it here in your home?"

A long pause. I walked back to see the image of her face more clearly. Again she smiled, that same mysterious half smile—and in a flash I understood that she had meant me to find it. Perhaps she saw that on my face, perhaps not; her smile shifted, changed character, was marred by trouble—and in one of those subtle shifts of musculature I seemed to recognize someone else in her, someone I had known, or seen—who *was* this woman, anyway? What in God's name did she want? Shocked, disoriented, I lost all sense that I could read her face; emotions were playing across it one after another, that was certain, but what they were I had no idea. I felt the abyss that lies between any two of us gaping under me, and I knew that the image of the face before me, great map of emotion though it was, masked an utter stranger, completely unknown to me; everything that I knew about Caroline Holmes was as nothing when weighed against this feeling.

I shuddered convulsively. "If you analyzed the ice in that model," I said carefully, "you would find it the same as the ice in the liths on Pluto. They are splinters of the same boulder."

She stared at me, her face still a mask. "You may think what you like, Mr. Doya," she said. "But you will never know." She and her chair disappeared.

Charles opened the door of the room. "The *Io* is ready," he said. "Your luggage is aboard."

I followed him to the docking bay, crossed into the *Io*. As I pulled myself to the bridge I felt the *clank* of our disengagement, and realized I was shaking.

The viewscreen in the lounge had an image of the satellite in it. Helplessly I hung before the great wheel and watched, shaking still. For a moment, seeing its windows and rails and the observatory, I thought again of a bathysphere. As we moved away I could see the domed floor, a clear glassine bubble; and inside it the tiny figure of Holmes paced around the dome's perimeter, upside-down as it seemed, watching us. Her purposes, I thought. Had she accomplished them?

I remembered a moment in the journal of Emma Weil. She too had stood before a window, and watched a spaceship depart, just as Holmes now watched me. And I felt like the ghost of Davydov—the ghost of a ghost—leaving behind me everything known, and venturing outward. Suddenly the satellite shrank with great speed, to a white dot over the ringed eldritch ball. And we were on our way.

There was a holo message transmitter on board the *Io*. After a month or so of waiting out the long reach back to Waystation, I went into the transmission room. I was nervous and I had to compose myself before I faced the empty row of chairs that indicated where the audience receiving the message would sit.

"Begin," I said. The red light in the center chair blinked on.

"Professor Nederland," I said. "This is Edmond Doya. Our previous interactions have all occurred in the periodicals, but now I want to communicate with you as directly as possible." I leaned against a table, kicked rhythmically at one of its legs. "The Waystation Institute for Higher Learning is mounting an expedition to Pluto, to make another investigation of Icehenge that will attempt to clear up the present mystery concerning its origins."

I cleared my throat. That last wouldn't go down too well with him. "I know you believe that there is no mystery concerning its origins. But—" I stopped again, tried to recollect what I was going to say. All of the sentences I had thought of during the previous month jammed together, demanding to be spoken first. I stood and paced back and forth, looking frequently to the red dot that represented my great-grandfather.

"But I think you must admit, having read my work, that there is at least the possibility of a hoax. Certainly the possibility. Yet in the present state of knowledge there is no way of telling who really built the monument, I truly believe that." So? "So . . . all of the

serious researchers and, and theorists, of Icehenge, will be invited
to join the expedition. As the senior and principal theorist your addition to the company would be valued by all."

Somehow that didn't sound right. I was being too stiff, too artificial; this was an invitation, I wanted to show how I felt. But it
was too complex. I just couldn't talk to a chair. Still, I had to try to
fix this, or I would have to tape the whole thing again.

"I know that many people have construed my work to be an attack on you. I assure you, Professor Nederland, that isn't true! I admire the work you did, it was a good investigation, and if someone
was deliberately misleading the investigation . . . there was no way
for you to know. And I don't agree that believing it a hoax de-
stroys the monument's aesthetic worth. Davydov or not, the megalith is still there. Human beings still constructed it. Emma's story
still exists, no matter who wrote it. . . ."

It was coming out wrong. I couldn't say it. I paced even more
rapidly. "Perhaps I am wrong, and Davydov did build Icehenge. If
so, then we should be able to prove that on this expedition. I hope
you agree to join us. I . . . bid you farewell. End transmission."

The red light blinked off.

The following day, at about the same time, the reply arrived. I sat
down in the chair with the red dot. The scene appeared, and I
blinked while my eyes accommodated the light.

He was sitting behind a Martian Planetary Survey desk, in one
of those big luxurious government offices. He looked just as he did
in the press conferences: black hair slicked down except in a couple of places, where it was flying out of control; pinched face,
chapped cheeks; expensive suit (the latest Martian style), pressed
and carefully adjusted. It was the official, pontificating image.

"Mr. Doya," he said, looking just to my right. I shifted. "We
haven't met before, even by means of this illusory medium, yet I
am aware that we are related—that I am your great-grandfather.
How do you do. I hope we meet in the flesh someday, for I can see
we have common interests as well as common blood." He smiled
for a moment, and adjusted a sheet of paper on the desk. "Let me
assure you, I understand that your arguments concern archaeology

and are not directed against my person." He moved the paper again, and began tapping it with a forefinger. The corner of his mouth tightened, as if he were about to perform an unpleasant task.

"I disagree with many of the things you said in your invitation. There isn't any evidence in your work sufficient to convince me that the Davydov explanation is not true. So I don't believe an on-site investigation made up of diverse theorists, each attempting to prove his own case, can become anything but a circus. For these reasons I decline your invitation, though I thank you for making it." He stopped, and appeared to consider what he had just said. He looked down at the paper again, then up, and this time he seemed to be looking directly into my eyes.

"When you say that Emma's story will still exist no matter who wrote it, you imply that it doesn't matter whether Emma's story is true or not. I say it does matter. I think in your heart you agree with that, and there is no reason for you to misrepresent the situation, as if to disguise its meaning. If your theory becomes accepted, I know what that will mean as well as you do."

He looked down again, made desultory taps with his fingers. "I cannot wish you good luck. End transmission."

Blackout. I sat there and thought of many things. I thought of Nederland charging around Mars so ferociously in the last century, breaking apart the whole history of the planet with his work; and then of the gray old bureaucrat, lying in press conferences to accomplish a cover-up of his own. And refusing to join an archaeological dig. I thought, he's changed, he's not the man who wrote the books you read when you were a child. I sat in the dark.

We were close, very close. Activity began on the *Snowflake*—like water thawing after a long winter, people began to move in the halls, to meander past each other, scuffing at moss and greeting shyly. . . . Jones and I escaped the expedition group and went down to the crew's lounge, where they were drinking and sniffing drugs. At the appearance of Jones and me they declared a party, and we all went at it with a will, turning the music up loud and bouncing up and down against the newly returned deceleration gee. There was a viewscreen in the lounge displaying the space we were headed toward—a black square sparkling with stars.

"So where is it?" said Jones to one of the crew. She pointed out Pluto, just ahead of Aries. It was about second magnitude, and there beside it was Charon, barely visible. Jones lifted his drink bulb to it, and cried, "You're right! There's Icehenge, I see it right there on top!"

Later, after we had danced to exhaustion (and a number of bruises, because deceleration gee wasn't all that strong), Jones and I hunkered over to one of the corner tables. I was pretty drunk, and ideas swirled dizzily in my head. "I've been writing a lot of this down, Jones. A sort of journal." He nodded and snapped a capsule under his nose. "Sometimes—sometimes it seems to me that what I'm writing is the sequel to Emma Weil's journal—which I'm certain was written by Caroline Holmes."

"Umph," Jones said.

"I'm *certain* of it," I said, interpreting his grunt of doubt accurately. "If you had seen Holmes like I saw her during my visit, you'd know what I meant. When I told her I had found the Icehenge model. . . ."

"Umph." But that one meant understanding. I had described my stay at Holmes's to Jones in great detail, and now with some big sniffs he nodded.

"And my story—my story tells of a voyage to Pluto, which is exactly what Emma said was going to happen. And this voyage is being paid for by Holmes! Sometimes, I tell you, that old woman looks very much in control of things out here . . . sometimes I wonder how much of it she may have planned, and what she has in store for us out there. . . ."

"Who knows?" said Jones. "There are so many influences on our lives that we don't control—you might as well not worry about another one that you may be making up. Right? Whatever happens on Pluto, I'm looking forward to it. I'm anxious to get there. We are close, you know." Dramatically he pointed at the screen. "I can see those ice towers! I can!"

*  *  *

And then we were there. We were there, circling the ninth planet. When the orbit was established Dr. Lhotse gave the orders and we rushed into the LVs, burst out of the bays of the *Snowflake* and fell in long arcs onto the cratered polar plain, settling with a gentle last bump like little crystals of the mother flake. I felt solid and substantial, heavier than I had in years and years. The dust thrown up by our landing cleared and off beyond the glare-white area under the spotlights I saw a horizon almost flat. The flattest horizon I had ever seen. "This is the biggest thing I ever stood on," I said aloud, though in the scramble for suits no one heard me. "I'm on a planet. First planet I ever stood on, and it's *Pluto.*" Something in the thought was odd and distressing, and by the time I shook it off all the suits had been claimed. "Hey!" I shouted. "Someone give me one of those—I'm the one who got you out here!" But they all ignored me or pretended not to hear me or counted on someone else to oblige me, and in three great noisy charges they crushed into the lock and were spewed onto the surface. I was left to fume and leap around the main room cursing and fizzling with a few others, until Arthur Grosjean (who had seen the megalith before, and, I think, was doing me a favor) returned early and gave me his suit. "Thanks, Arthur," I babbled, "I really appreciate it," and the static shocks jumped between us as he helped the suit onto me— and then I was into the lock, and through, and stumbling onto the surface. I started to run and immediately fell full-length into the gravel. It made me laugh, because I knew then that the rocks were real, that I was really there.

The dust we had thrown up in our landing served to hold a little of the light from our searchlights, and so there was a faint glow in the sky to show me where the megalith was, as well as a wide road of footprints. Some of them were no doubt footprints from the *Persephone's* people, perfectly sharp-edged after more than sixty years. I broke into a trot, keeping my eyes on the smooth horizon to the north, and damned if I didn't trip and fall again.

I got up and ran, kicked my own heel and fell. Sitting there on Pluto's gravelly, dusty surface, I looked north and saw the very tops of the liths, rising just behind a low hill. The sun was off to my right, a dazzling morning star just a few degrees over the horizon. On their eastern sides the liths were patches of gleaming white; to the west they were barely visible black shadows.

I was shivering, as if I could feel through my suit a touch of Pluto's cold, only seventy degrees above the absolute zero of total stillness. I got up and walked with a long slow stride, as if I were in a parade. Icehenge, Icehenge, Icehenge, Icehenge, Icehenge. Every step brought more of it over the horizon to me, until I topped the low mound and it was all there, the whole ring, silent and expansive on the plain before me.

The little human figures were standing in groups inside the giant circle, or bounding about from lith to lith, and to my surprise I appreciated their presence very much. I turned on my intercom and heard them all talking at once so that not one of them could have understood anything, and it made me laugh. They were so small—one of them stood by the Fallen Lith, and even he appeared insignificantly short. Exhilarated, I continued my march down the slope to it, humming *bum, bom, bum, bom, bum, bom.*

I passed between two liths. Looking down the curving row of columns I saw that they were much more irregularly placed than they had ever seemed in holograms. Just the act of transmitting and imaging them had somehow given their ensemble more order. Here, in reality, their placement seemed jumbled, the work of an alien intelligence. The ring was huge, monstrous; the area encircled by the white beams was a giant field! It took a while to walk to the center of it. There, in a circle trodden smooth by prints, was the plaque left there by Nederland's Martian expedition. I ignored the plaque and looked around. The ring was a rough circle—I couldn't perceive the flattened side to the "north," for the different dimensions of each lith, and the varying angles of placement, created an irregular display of white and black parallelograms that were hard to get in perspective. Most of the western liths gleamed in the sun, though some were darkened by the endless shadows cast by the liths to the east. The eastern liths themselves were black cutouts against the starry sky, except for a few that caught the reflected light from some more westerly lith, and gleamed dully.

To the north the Six Great Liths stood like a huge curving line of towers; yet the jagged arc of small liths near the fallen one seemed not much shorter, though the shortest ones were all there.

Groups of people approached me, and I shook hands with everyone before they headed back. We all chattered happily, saying nothing yet conveying just what we wanted to. Then they were all off over the low rise to the south, to the landing vehicles. The last figure approached; by his height and gait I already had identified him as Jones. "Hey, Theophilus," I said. "Here we are." He extended his arm and we shook hands. Through his faceplate I saw his bright eyes, and a wide grin. He drew me toward him and hugged me, and then, without a word, he turned and left.

I was alone at Icehenge.

I sat down and let the feeling saturate me. All my life I had wanted to be here, and now I was. A pebble held between gloved fingers resisted all the pressure I could put on it. Yes, I was really here. No hologram this. I could hardly believe it.

The ring was roughly contiguous with a very old, subdued crater, so that some of the liths stood on low knobs or prominences of the almost-buried rim. It made for a very beautiful effect: each lith appeared to be "placed" with the utmost of care, in the spot perfectly appropriate for it. This impression co-existed with the obvious irregularity of the ring, in that liths were bunched together in groups of four or five or six, placed markedly out of line, placed so that their broad smooth faces pointed at every direction of the compass. . . . And the combination, I thought, was wonderful.

I stood and walked over to the Inscription Lith. The words and the 2-2-4-8 slashes were deeply incised in the surface, and as the sunlight slanted across the ice the words were easy to read. I imagined the megalith's discoverer Seth Cereson, staring up at that alien-looking script. To move, to push farther out; to cause to set out towards. It was a good motto. My father's remark came back to me: It's a wonder they didn't all sign their names. So true, I thought. If the Davydov expedition had built the monument, why hadn't they said so? It only made sense if they identified themselves, it seemed to me. Wasn't this message an obvious attempt to be enigmatic, so that its goal was a clear ambiguity?

Continuing around the circumference of the ring, I touched my glove lightly to the sharp edge of one of the triangular liths, then walked into the field of broken ice boulders that was the Fallen Lith. Here every crack and splinter of ice looked absolutely fresh, in places as sharp as chipped obsidian. Ice at seventy degrees Kelvin is terrifically hard and brittle, and whatever hit it—meteor, construction tool, we would no doubt find out in the next few weeks—had shattered it into scores of cracked pieces, which had fallen to the inside of the ring. Looking through a clearish pane of ice (sort of like Holmes's wall of wavy glass), I thought that the cracking looked very recent. It was true that ice sublimed very slowly at this low temperature, but it did sublime; yet I could see nothing but those fine obsidian edges. I wondered what the scientists would make of it.

Then I continued my circumference hike, skipping in places, and using the arc of liths as a slalom course in others, just as I would have done if I had truly been at the megalith back on my eleventh birthday. From every vantage point I saw a different Icehenge, as the play of sunlight and deep shadow shifted; when I noticed this each step brought me a new megalith, and jubilantly I circled the ring again and again, until I was too exhausted to skip, and had to sit on a waist-high block of the Fallen Lith. I was here.

Over the next week or two the various teams established their pattern of investigation. Those working on the ice spent a good deal of their time in the landing vehicles' laboratories. Dr. Hood and his team worked to determine what kind of cutting tool had shaped the liths. Bachan Nimit and his people from Ganymede were following a new line of inquiry that I thought held promise; they were looking at pieces of the Fallen Lith in hopes of finding out if as many micrometeors had hit the hidden underside of the fragments as had hit the exposed surfaces.

But the most visible, and it seemed the most energetic, team was Brinston's excavation group. Brinston was showing himself to be extremely competent and well organized, to no one's surprise. The day after we arrived he had his people out laying down the gridwork, and quickly they were making the preliminary line digs. He spent long hours at the site, moving from trench to trench, inspecting what was revealed, consulting and giving instructions. In conversations he was confident. "The substructure of the megalith will explain it," he said. At the same time he warned us against expecting any immediate information: "Digging is slow work—even with as simple a situation as this, one has to be very careful not to tear up the evidence one is looking for, which in this case is something as delicate as the marks of a previous excavation and fill, in regolith no less. . . ." He would talk on endlessly about the various aspects of his task, and I would leave him nearly as convinced as he that he would solve the mystery.

The teams established a common working period that they called "day," and during this time the site swarmed with busy figures. Outside these times the landscape emptied.

I had no specific work to do, I was uncomfortably aware of that. The investigation I had stimulated was being made, by professionals competent to the task. There was nothing left for me but to witness what they found. So I quickly took to visiting the monument in the off hours. Those few who stayed, or returned to visit, soon became still, contemplative figures, and we didn't bother each other.

At those times, wandering among the massive blocks in a vast silence, the abandoned equipment and all the trenches and mounds gave it the look of a work in progress, a work of giants left unfinished for unknown reasons . . . leaving the skeleton or framework of something larger. I sat at the center point of the ring for hours, and learned the various aspects it presented at different times of the Plutonian day. It was spring in the northern hemisphere— coldest, longest spring under the sun—and the sun stayed just over the horizon all the time. It took nearly a week for Pluto to spin around, for the sun to circle our horizon; and even at that slow speed I could see the movement of light and shadow, if I watched long enough, creating a different Icehenge at every moment, just as when I had run around it that first day; only this time I was still, and it was the planet that moved.

Near the center of the ring was the memorial plaque left by Nederland's expedition. A block of brecciated rock had been hauled into the old crater, and its top had been cut flat and covered by a platinum plaque.

> This Marker Has Been Placed Here
> To Honor the Members of the
> MARS STARSHIP ASSOCIATION
> Who Built This Monument Soon After the Year
> 2248 A.D.
> To Commemorate the Martian Revolution of 2248
> And To Mark Their Departure From the Solar System.
> *There Will Never Come An End to the Good That They*
> *Have Done.*

Staring at this oddity I tried to sort it all out in my mind. Apparently those three asteroid miners *had* disappeared in the years before the Martian revolution; it was a fact documented in a variety of times and places. So the three ships had disappeared, yes. But almost anything might have happened to them. And since the documents—some of them—concerning their disappearance had been released in the early 2500s, Holmes could have found out about them, and decided then to explain her monument as an artifact left by those miners . . . thus creating an attractive tale of successful resistance against the Martian oligarchy and its police state, and recovering a victory from the unmitigated defeat of the failed revolt. This gave the hoaxer a motive beyond that of mere mystification . . . and it was the kind of story people liked to believe.

And so the file on Davydov in Alexandria, and the buried field car, miraculously unburied at New Houston. The file, simply enough, had not been in the cabinet in Alexandria just a few years before Nederland searched there. He could claim for as long as he liked that records were always being shifted around the archives, but the truth was that such shifts were also documented, and that this cabinet had not been tampered with, officially. The file, in short, was a plant. Part of the hoax.

That implied very strongly that the New Houston field car was also part of the hoax, planted there for the archaeologists to find. Their initial survey of Spear Canyon had found no metal bodies on that buried road; and after the storm that had trapped the archaeologists in their tents, tracks had been found in the snow to the north that no one was ever able to explain. So it looked as though the car had been placed there during the storm. But there was still a storm of controversy raging over that point, back on Mars. The journal of Emma Weil—part of the hoax!—had been dated to the mid-twenty-third century, the time of the revolution—or so it was claimed. Others contested that, and still others attacked the authenticity of the car itself, of the weathering of its surface, of the secondary documents found in it, of the likelihood of the slide that had revealed it. . . . From every angle conceivable the field car and the entire Davydov theory was challenged, and found lacking, and poor Nederland ran around mars like the Dutch boy, poking his fingers in the holes of a dike that was about to collapse entirely. The Davydov expedition was a fiction. There never had been any Mars Starship Association. It was all a giant hoax.

Bitterly I kicked the plaque. It was set solidly. I picked up a double handful of regolith, dumped it on the marker. Several handfuls made a good pile; it looked like a cairn of pebbles, set on a big flat boulder. "Stupid romantic story," I muttered. "Preying on what we want to believe. . . ." Why had she done it?

My only regular companion during these off hours' meditations was Jones. It was natural that he should prefer these times, for only then did the monument fully regain its solitary power, its shadowed majesty. But I thought, also, that he felt self-conscious doing his work before the others.

For work he was doing, laboriously and painstakingly, with a surveying distance gun. He was measuring the megalith. When I switched to the common band on the intercom, I heard him muttering numbers to himself, and humming snatches of music. He had arranged to have music piped in to him from the landing vehicles while he worked; usually when I switched to that band one of Brahms's symphonies was playing.

Occasionally he enlisted my aid. He would stand at a lith and aim his gun at me while I held a small mirror before a lith; then I walked to the next lith, and repeated the operation. I laughed at the tiny figure across the central crater.

"Sixty-six times sixty-six, that's a lot of measurements," I said. "Just what do you think you're doing?"

"Numbers," he replied. "Whoever built this was very very careful about numbers. I want to see if I can find the lith by looking very carefully at the numbers that are made by the monument."

"*The* lith?"

"The patterns are singling out a particular lith, I feel."

"Ah."

"Therefore I must try to find the unit of measurement they used when building. Note that it was not metrical or foot and inch. Long ago a man named Alexander Thom discovered that all of the stone megaliths in northern Europe used the same unit, which he called the megalithic yard. It was about seventy-four centimeters." He stopped what he was doing, and I saw the tiny red dot of his gun wander over the liths to my left. "Now, no one but me has ever noticed that this megalithic yard from northern Europe is almost exactly the same length as the ancient Tibetan unit—"

"And the Egyptian unit used at the Pyramids, undoubtedly, but isn't that because they're the standard elbow to finger units of early civilizations?"

"Maybe, maybe. But since the flattened ring construction here is one of the common patterns for British henges, I thought I'd check to see."

"How is it coming along?"

"I don't know yet."

I laughed. "You could find out in seconds on the *Snowflake's* computer."

"Yeah?"

"I'm glad you're here with us, Jones, I really am."

He chuckled. "You like having someone here crazier than you. But just wait. The numerology of Icehenge was always a rich field, even before these new measurements I'm taking. Did you know that if you begin at the Fallen Lith and count counterclockwise by prime numbers, the width of each lith increases by one point two three four times? Or that the heights of each foursome of consecutive liths add up to either ninety-five point four, or one hundred and one meters? Or that each length divided by width ends with a prime number—"

"Who says all this?"

"*I* do. You must not have read my book, *Mathematics and Metaphysics at Icehenge.*"

"I missed that one, I guess."

"One of my best. See how much you don't know?"

In this manner several weeks quickly passed. Brinston's face took on a slightly anxious expression, though he was finding out some interesting things. It appeared that for every lith a large cylindrical posthole had been dug—the ice beam had been positioned on the floor of the hole, which was invariably bedrock, and the hole was then filled. The only other fact they had discovered was that there were no individual postholes for the Six Great Liths. Perhaps because they were so near each other, a single big hole, still cylindrical, had been dug for all of them. Brinston's team had marked out the circumference of this cylinder, and it encompassed nine liths. "But I don't know what it means," he confessed irritably.

The day Brinston presented this information, Jones and I walked out to the site. Jones was excited, but he wouldn't tell me why.

It was after the working hours, and we were the only ones out there. We walked through the circle of towers and on to the pole, to watch the henge from there. Dr. Grosjean had had a short metal pole placed at the axis of rotation to help his first survey of the site, and it stood there still, a little less than shoulder high. We sat on either side of it. The sun was on the other side of the megalith, and the liths were more obscure than ever—faint reverse shadows, dim areas of lightness against the pervading black. The gravel underneath me felt cold.

"Now we're spinning like a top," said Jones. "Feel it?" I laughed easily, yet as we sat there I could suddenly visualize Pluto as a tiny twirling ball, a handful of ice toothpicks stuck in its top, two antlike creatures seated on the axis of rotation.

I moved and the sun disappeared behind a lith. I felt the ancient fear—eclipse, sun death.

After a long silence Jones took his distance gun from his suit's thigh pocket and turned it on. He pointed it at the henge. On lith number three, the tallest one, a red spot appeared; brighter than the sun. Jones moved the spot in a small circle on the lith.

"That one," he said. "There's something special about lith three."

"Aside from it being the tallest?"

"Yes." He jumped up and took off rapidly toward it. "Come on!"

I hurried after him. As we approached it, he said, "I told you I would find something in those measurements. Though it wasn't exactly what I had expected."

We stopped before it, standing just outside the arc of the Six Great Liths. Number three was massive, endlessly tall, big as a Martian skyscraper. On this side it was in total darkness, or rather, was illuminated only by starlight, which was barely adequate for our vision; the circle of shadows reared up into eerie obscurity. We stared up into it.

"If you take the centerpoint of the lith," Jones said, "at ground level, and measure from there. Then every center of every lith in the henge is an exact multiple of the megalithic yard away."

"You're kidding."

"No, seriously. It doesn't work for any other lith, either."

I looked up at his faceplate, but it was too dark—from a meter or two away I could barely see him. "You used the computers."

"Yes."

"Jones, you amaze me."

"What's more, number three is right near the center of that big excavation that Brinston and his folks found. That's interesting.

For the longest time I've thought that it was the triangular liths that our attention was being drawn to. Now I'm pretty sure it's this one—that it's the center of the henge."

"But why?"

"I don't know."

"You don't know!"

"No! Perhaps to satisfy an alien geometry, perhaps to provide a key to a code—it could be anything. My brilliant investigation has gone only so far."

"Ho, ho." We circled the lith slowly, looking for some remarkable sign, some new attribute. There were none evident. A rectangular slab of ice—

A thought, slipping at the edges of consciousness. I stopped and tried to retrace my thinking. Stars, nothing . . . I shifted my head through the position it had been in when I had the thought, tried all the other remembering tricks I knew. I looked up at the top of the lith, and stepped back, and as I did so a bright star appeared, defining the top of the lith. Was that Kachab, brightest star in Ursa Minor? I found the other stars of the constellation—it was. Pluto's Pole Star.

I remembered. "Inside it," I said, and heard Jones's surprised breath. "That's it! There's something inside it."

Jones faced me. "Do you really think so?"

"I'm certain of it."

"How?"

"Holmes told me. Or rather, Holmes gave it away." I reminded him of the model with the laser sight lines, in the spherical planetarium: "And there was one beam of blue light pointing straight out of the tallest lith. It must have been this one. And it was the only laser beam coming directly out of a lith."

"That could be what it means, I suppose. But how do we find out?"

"Listen," I said. I pressed my faceplate against the surface of the lith and rapped hard on the ice. A certain vibration . . . I hurried to the adjacent lith and did the same. Vibrations again, but I couldn't tell if they were different.

"Hmm," I said.

"I hope you wouldn't melt holes in it—"

"No, no." The certainty of my guess, which had felt so much like an act of memory, didn't fade. I switched my intercom to a landing vehicle band. "Could you get me Dr. Lhotse, please?" The crew member called him up.

"Dr. Lhotse? This is Doya. Listen, could you run an easy test to find out if one of the liths had any hollow spaces in it?"

"Or spaces occupied by something other than ice?" Jones was on the band as well.

Lhotse considered it for a moment—it sounded as if he had been asleep—and then supposed that some mass tests, or sonar and x-ray and such, could determine it.

"That's excellent," I said. "Could you bring out the necessary gear and people? . . . Yes, now; Jones and I have found the key lith and we suspect there is a hollow in it." Jones laughed aloud. I could imagine Lhotse's thoughts—the two strange ones had finally gone over the rim. . . .

"Is this serious?" Lhotse asked. Jones laughed.

"Oh, yes," I said. "Quite serious."

Lhotse agreed to do it and hung up. Jones said. "You'd better be right, or we may have to walk home."

"There'll be something," I said, feeling an apprehension that verged, curiously enough, on exhilaration.

"I hope so. It's a long walk."

There was a hollow column in the center of the lith, running from top to bottom.

"I'll be damned," said Lhotse. Jones and the sonar people were whooping. Searchlights flashed off the ice as from the surface of a mirror. Circles and ellipses of white bobbed around the ground and caught dancing figures, flashed in my eyes. The surrounding scene was blacker, more obscure. My heart pounded the inside of my chest like a living child.

"There must be an entrance at the top!"

There was an extension ladder that could be roped to the liths, on the other side of the site. Lhotse ordered the people he had brought with him to set it up, and he called back to the LVs. "You'd better get out here," he told Brinston and Hood and the rest. "Jones and Doya found a hollow lith."

Jones and I grinned at each other. While they were moving the ladder across the dark old crater bed, Jones told Lhotse the story of our search. I could see Lhotse shaking his head. Then the ladder was moored against the lith and secured. Huge lamps, their beams invisible in the vacuum, made Lith number three a blazing white tower, and it cast a faint illumination over the rest of the henge, bringing the beams into ghostly presence. Lhotse climbed the ladder and set the next section in place. It just reached the top. I followed him up, and Jones clambered at my heels.

Lhotse kneeled on the top, roped himself to the ladder securely. I looked down; the painfully bright lamps seemed far below. Lhotse's quiet voice in my ear: "There are cracks." He looked up at me as my head rose over the edge, and I could see that his face was flushed red, and dripping with sweat. I myself felt chills, as if we were in a wind.

"There's a block of ice here plugging the shaft. It's flush with the surface, I don't know how we'll get it out." He ordered another ladder sent up. There were a lot of people talking on the common bands, though I couldn't see many of them. I tied myself to the ladder and climbed onto the top of the lith. Jones followed me up. It was a big flat rectangle, but I worried that it might be slippery.

Eventually we secured a pulley above the lith, on two ladder extensions, and then sank heated curved rods into the plug. The line was rigged and when those on the ground pulled, the trap door—a square block about three meters by three by two, cut like a wedge so it would fit into the top snugly—rose up easily. The blocks of ice were too cold to stick to each other. Jones and Lhotse and I, standing on the ladders, stuck our heads over the black hole and looked down. The shaft was cylindrical, and a little smaller than the plug cut. With a powerful light we could distinguish an end or turning in the shaft, far below.

"Bring up some more rope," ordered Lhotse. "Something we can use for belay swings, and some of those expanding trench rods. If we used crampons we'd kick the lith down before we cut even a scratch in this stuff." The block was lowered, the ropes brought up, and we were tied into torso slings, and given lamps. Lhotse climbed in and said, "Let me down slowly." I followed him in, breathing rapidly. Jones hung above me like a spider.

The walls of the shaft were slick-looking under our bright lights. We inspected the ice as we pushed off and descended, pushed off and descended.

Lhotse looked up. "You probably should wait till I get to the bottom." The people at the top of the ladder heard him and Jones and I slowed. Lhotse dropped away swiftly.

The descent lasted a long time. Our lamps made the ice around us gleam, but above and below us it was black. The ice changed to dark, smoothly cut rock. We were underground.

Finally we hit a gravelly floor. Lhotse was waiting, crouched in the end of a tunnel that—I struggled to keep oriented—extended away from the ring, therefore northward. It descended at a slight slope. Ahead lay pitch blackness.

"Send another person down to this point for a radio relay," said Lhotse, and then, holding his lamp ahead of him, he hurried down the tunnel.

Jones and I stayed close behind him. We walked for a long time, down the bottom of a cylindrical tunnel. Except for the fact that the walls were rock—solid basalt, the tunnel had been bored through it—it might have been a sewer pipe. I was shivering uncontrollably, colder than ever. Jones kept stumbling over me, ducking his head at imaginary low points.

Lhotse stopped. Looking past him I could see a blue glow. I rounded him and ran.

Suddenly the tunnel opened up, and I was in a chamber, a blue chamber. A cobalt blue chamber! It was an ovoid, like the inside of a chicken's egg, about ten meters high and seven across. As Lhotse's lamp swung unnoticed in his hand, streaks and points of red light gleamed from within the surface of the blue walls. It was like a blue glass, or a ceramic glaze. I reached out and ran a gloved hand over it; it was a glassy but lumpy surface. The points and lines of dark red came from chips under the surface. . . . Lhotse raised his lamp to head level and rotated slowly, looking up at the curved ceiling of the chamber. His voice barely stimulated the intercom. "What is this. . . ."

I shook my head, sat down and leaned back against the blue wall, overwhelmed.

"Who put this here?" Lhotse asked.

"Not Davydov," I said. "There's no way they could have put this under here."

"Nor Holmes neither," suggested Jones.

Lhotse waved his lamp, and red points sparked. "Let's discuss it later."

So we stood, and sat, in silence, and watched the blue walls coruscate with red. The constantly shifting patterns created the illusion of extended space, the room seemed to grow larger even as we watched. . . . I felt fear, fear of Holmes, fear that I had been in her power. Who was she, to have created this? Could she have?

Questions, doubts, thought receded, and the three of us remained mesmerized by light.

After a time white flashes from the tunnel, and voices on the intercom, snapped us awake. Our air was low. Several others were coming down the tunnel, crowding into the chamber, and we moved out so they could see and marvel freely.

Jones, through his faceplate, looked stunned. His mouth was open. As we trudged slowly back up the sloping tunnel, he was shaking his head, and I could hear his deep voice, muttering, ". . . Strange blue glass under lith . . . star chamber, red light . . . a space . . . underground."

Then they hauled us up the long narrow shaft of the hollow lith. I stood on the rim at the top, and looked up, up to the great blanket of stars.

It gave the scientists a lot more to work on.

They soon reported that the chamber was directly under the pole—that is, the pole passed directly through the chamber. The walls were covered by a ceramic glaze, fired onto the bedrock.

Dr. Hood and his team soon discovered traces of the drill bits used to bore out the tunnel in the bedrock—tiny smears of metal, of an alloy exactly like that used for the bits of a boring machine designed to cut tunnels through asteroids. The machine had been first produced in 2514 . . . by Caroline Holmes's Jupiter Metals.

And Brinston was ecstatic. "Ceramic!" he cried. "Ceramic! When they fired that glass up to melting temperature, they started up a clock. They put a date on it as clear as those marks on the Inscription Lith—with no chance of lying, either."

It turned out that thermoluminescence measurement was a method that had been used to date terrestrial pottery for centuries. Samples of the ceramic are heated to firing temperatures, and the amount of light released by them is a measure of the total dose of radiation to which the ceramic has been exposed since the last previous heating. The technique can determine age—even over short periods of time—with an accuracy of plus or minus ten percent.

After a week Brinston triumphantly released the results of the tests. The Blue Chamber was eighty years old. "We've got her!" Brinston cried. "It was Holmes! Doya, you were right. I don't know why she did it, or how she did all of it, but I know she did it."

The reporters had a field day. Icehenge was once again a nine-day wonder. This time the scoop was that it was a modern hoax. Speculation was endless, but Holmes was named most often, by more people than she could ever sue—or destroy. They called this the Holmes explanation—or Doya's Theory.

I sat around the site.

One day I heard that Nederland had been interviewed on the holonews. Several hours later I went down to the holo room and ran the scene through. I couldn't help it.

It wasn't at the usual Planetary Survey press conference room. As the scene appeared, Nederland was leaving a building, and a group of reporters circled him, trapped him against the side of the building.

"Professor Nederland, what do you think of the new developments on Pluto?"

"They're very interesting." He looked resigned to the questioning.

"Do you still support the Davydov theory?"

His jaw muscles tightened. "I do." The wind ruffled his hair, left tufts of it poking out.

"What about—But what about—What about the fact that a twenty-sixth century drill bit was used to bury the Blue Egg?"

"I think there may be some other explanation for those deposits . . . for instance—"

"What about the thermoluminescence dating?"

"The ceramic measured was buried too deep for the method to work," he snapped.

"What about the alleged inauthenticity of the Weil journal?"

"I don't believe that," he said. "Emma's journal is genuine—"

"What's your proof? What's your proof?"

Nederland looked down at his feet, shook his head. He looked up, and there were deep lines around his mouth. "I must go home now," he said, and then repeated it in such a low voice the microphones barely caught it: "I must go home now. . . ." Then, in his full voice, "I'll answer all these questions later." He turned and made his way through them, head down, and twisted to avoid a reporter's grasp, and as he did so I saw his lowered face, and it looked haggard, exhausted, and I slammed the holo off and made my way blindly to the door, struck it with my hand, "Damn it," I said, "damn it, why aren't you dead!"

The day before we were to leave, a bulletin came in from Waystation. A group there at the Institute—led by my old student April—had presented a new solution. They agreed that it was a modern construct, but contended that it was put up by Commodore Ehrung and her crew, right after they arrived on Pluto, and just before they "discovered" it. The group had a whole case worked up, showing how both Davydov *and* Holmes were red herrings, planted by Ehrung's people. . . .

"That's absurd!" I cried, and laughed harshly. "There's a dozen reasons why that can't be true, including everything that Brinston just found!" Nevertheless I was furious, and though I laughed again to hide it as I left the room, the people there stared at me as if I had kicked the holo projector.

*　*　*

Later I walked out to the site. The henge was gleaming in the washed-out clarity of Pluto's day. It looked unchanged by all our new discoveries; it was just the same, obscure and strange, a sight to make me shiver.

Jones was out there. He had taken to spending almost all of his time at the site; I had even chanced upon him lying between two pieces of the Fallen Lith, fast asleep. For days he hadn't spoken to anyone, not even—or especially not—to me. Brahms coursed through his intercom all the time, nothing else.

This time—our last hours on Pluto—he sat near the little boulder at the center. I walked up to him, sat down beside him. Nederland's memorial plate lay buried under my stack of pebbles; I couldn't bear to look at it. The sight of the Six Great Liths (one shackled with ladders) left me numb.

We sat in silence for a long, long time. Eventually I switched to a private band and nudged him to do the same.

"Did you hear about the new theory from Waystation?"

He shook his head. I told him about it.

Again he shook his head. "That isn't right. I've gotten to know Arthur Grosjean pretty well, and he would never be a party to something like that. It won't wash."

"No. . . . That won't keep people from believing it, though."

"No. But I've heard a better one than that."

"You have?"

He nodded. "Say the Mars Starship Association really existed. Davydov, Weil, the whole group. They hijacked those asteroid miners, got a starship built, sent Emma and the rest back to Mars. Emma escaped from the police, hid in the chaos for a certain number of years. Then she decided she wanted back into the world. She concocted a new identity—maybe she got her father to take a new identity, too, to give her story a back-up. She went out to the Jovian system, made her fortune in mining and life-support systems. Then she got curious to see if Davydov's ship had left a monument on Pluto, as he had hoped they would, and she went out to look. But the starship people were in a hurry, and worried about the Martian police—they couldn't take the time, and there wasn't anything there, on Pluto. So Emma decided to build it for them. Then how could she show the world who it was really for, without revealing herself? She took the journal she had written so many years before, planted it outside New Houston. Planted Davydov's records in the archives. She slipped the truth back into the world, just as if it were a lie—because she herself was the lie, you see?"

"So Caroline Holmes is. . . ."

"Or Emma Weil is Caroline Holmes, yes."

I shook my head. "They don't look anything alike."

"Looks can be changed. Looks, fingerprints, voice prints, retinal prints—they all can be changed. And the last pictures of Emma were taken before she was eighty. People change. If you saw pictures of me at eighty you wouldn't believe it."

"But it won't work. Holmes has been well documented all her life, almost. You can't make up a whole past like that, not a really public one."

"I'm not so sure. We live a long, long time. What happened two, three, four hundred years ago—it isn't easy to be sure about that."

"I don't know, Jones. An awful lot survives." I shook my head, tired of it all. "You're just adding an unnecessary complication. No, Caroline Holmes did it. *Something* happened to her . . . I just don't know what it was." Still, Jones's idea: "But I can see why you would like the idea. Who gave it to you, now?"

"Why, you did!" he said, leaning back to peer down at me with mock surprise. "Isn't that what you were telling me just before planetfall, when we got drunk with the crew?"

"No! For God's sake, Jones. You just made that whole thing up."

"No, no, you told me about it. You may have been too drunk to remember it."

"The hell I was. I know what I've said about Icehenge, and that's for sure. You made that up."

"Well, whatever. But I bet it's true."

"Uhn. What's that, your fifteenth theory of the origins of Icehenge?"

"Well, I don't know. Let me count—"

"Enough, Jones! Please. Enough."

I sat there, utterly discouraged. The memorial boulder before us mocked me; I stood, kicked it with a toe.

"Hey! Watch out, there."

I swung at my stack of pebbles and knocked them flying out over the dust. Hands trembling I removed the remaining stones, dropping them randomly. When the plaque was clear I ran my fingers between the letters until all the dust was gone. I looked around at the scattering of pebbles. "Here," I said. "Help me with these." Wordlessly he stood, and slowly, carefully, we gathered up all the pebbles and made a small pyramid out of them, a cairn set beside the plaque's boulder. When we were done we stood before it, two men looking down at a pile of stones.

"Jones," I said, in a conversational tone, though my voice was quavering, I didn't know why, "Jones, what do you think really happened here?"

He chuckled. "You won't give up, will you. . . . I'm like the rest of us, I suppose, in that I think much as I thought before. I think . . . that more has occurred at this place than we can understand."

"And you're content with that?"

He shrugged. "Yes."

I was shivering, my voice hardly worked. "I just don't know why I did all this!"

After a while: "It's done." He put his arm around my shoulder. "Come on, Edmond, let's go back. You're tired." He pulled me around gently. "Let's go back."

When we got to the low hill between the site and the landing vehicles, we turned and looked at it. Tall white towers against the night. . . .

"What will you do?" Jones asked.

I shook my head. "I don't know. I've never thought of it. Maybe—I'll go back to Terra. See my father. I don't know! . . . I don't know anything."

Jones's bass chuckle rumbled in the vacuum's silence. "That's probably as it should be." He put his arm around my shoulders, steered me around again. We began walking toward the landing vehicles, going back to the others, going back. Jones shook his head, spoke in a sort of singsong: "We dream, we wake on a cold hillside, we pursue the dream again. In the beginning was the dream, and the work of disenchantment never ends."

Made in the USA
San Bernardino, CA
12 January 2016